# Sugaree Rising

A Novel

By J. Douglas Allen-Taylor

FREEDOM VOICES

SAN FRANCISCO

Sugaree Rising ©2012 by Jesse Allen Taylor.

Published by:
Freedom Voices
P.O. Box 423115
San Francisco, CA 94142
www.freedomvoices.org

FIRST EDITION

Cover design by Fonta Allen
Map of Yelesaw Neck ©2012 Stephen McLaughlin.

Summary: "The story of a young African-American woman coming of age in the Depression years in an African-spirit-based community in the South Carolina Lowcountry while her community is threatened with being flooded out by a rural electrification project."

ISBN 978-0-915117-21-5


Library of Congress Cataloging-in-Publication Data

Allen-Taylor, J. Douglas.
  Sugaree rising : a novel / by J. Douglas Allen-Taylor. – 1st ed.
    p. cm.
ISBN 978-0-915117-21-5 (alk. paper)
1. Gullahs–Fiction. 2. Depressions–1929–South Carolina–Fiction.
3. African American families–South Carolina–Fiction. 4. African
Americans–Religious life–Fiction. 5.  South Carolina–History–
Fiction. 6. Sea Islands–Fiction. 7. Historical fiction. 8.
Bildungsromans.  I. Title.
  PS3601.L4387S84 2012
  813'.6–dc23
                                                    2012036943

*For Ronnie, who had to leave early, and so we missed the best part.*

# Table Of Contents

Illustrations

# How The Yay'saws Came To Yelesaw

*(Summer Of 1933 Or '34, The Girl Not Exactly Remembering Which)*

Once in a mystic time of the deepsummer night, the full moon grew so heavy that it could not hold its own weight, but sank down low, like a dream, into the soft bed of the ink-black sky, and with a gentle push of its warmbreath wind, drew up a blanket of banked clouds to cover its milkwhite undercovers. On such a night, the country girl sat with her long legs stretched out across the top plank of the porch steps, looking up at the old man sitting in the porch swing above her, and asked him, "Grandpa, you ever reckon us'n might one time just up and left Yelesaw?"

The old man answered her, abruptly, without pausing to give it a thought.

"You can leave any time you got a mind for go," he said, not looking her way, stopping his quiet blowing on his mouth-harp only long enough to get the words out. "Walk you'self down to the cable-crossing, stir up Lem Washington out he bed, and get him for ferry-you on acros't. Ain't nobody's stopping you." He sent a thick glob of tobacco-spit over the porch railing as an exclamation point, and then ran off a few harmonichord notes for a coda. How the old man could harp-blow and 'bacca-chew all both at the same time was a feat of accomplishment that never failed to amaze the girl when she watched him do it. She wondered how his mouth knew how to manage it, and how he kept from swallowing and choking on his chaw in the process. But he never did.

"I ain't mean just me," she answered him.

"What you mean, then?" the old man said. "Speak you' mind, girl, and don't walk-round the whole yard and field a'fore you does."

"I mean all'a us'n. And lefting for good, not just for 'wisit."

"*Us'n?*" The old man abruptly stopped both his swinging and mouth-harp playing, the porch swing letting known its protest with a loud squawk from its chain hangings. The old man turned his one good eye towards the girl, frowned as he looked her up and down, then asked her, "What this 'us'n' you talking about? Us'n meaning us'n the Manigault or us'n meaning us'n the Yay'saw?"

"The Yay'saw us'n."

The old man braced his bare feet on the porchboards and took off swinging again. He had walked home from the fields that evening boot-shodded, as always, and, as always, he had kicked the boots off carelessly into a corner of the porch as soon as he had mounted the stairs. Now one of the yard dogs was lying curled around the boots, comfortably asleep with the master's scent in its nose. Neither the old man's father nor his mother had ever laced a shoe over the arches of their feet a single day of their lives, but the old man himself liked his brogans for the fields, though before work and after, he saw no use for them except as doorstops and dog pacifiers. But now he was not thinking of shoes, but of the impertinence of the girl on the porch steps below him.

"How you figure you got to be us'n with we Yay'saw?" he asked her in mid-swing.

"Grandpa...!" The girl drew out his name with as much of a hint of exasperation as she dared. "Don't tease."

"I ain't teasing," the old man said. "I don't tease no childrens. I ain't got time for no teasing. Truth to tell, I ain't even know how you figure I you' grand'pap." While he continued his lazy swinging he considered her for a moment, both eyes blinking slow and deliberate, like an owl might do, both the black-brown good eye and the milky-blue cloudy-up one, while she squirmed, uncomfortably, on the porch step, pulling her legs in and then stretching them out again, several times. She was getting a little dizzy trying to keep eye contact with him while he swung back and forth above her, but she dared not look away while he was talking to her, as that *would* be disrespectful. "Who you' pap is?" he asked her, after a time.

"You know who my pap is, Grandpa," the girl said, careful not to say it in a sassy kind of way. "Him Benjamin Kinlaw."

"Kinlaw? Kinlaw?" The old man sucked on the name with a sour look on his face, as if he *had* accidently swallowed a bit of his chewing tobacco. He shook his head with finality. "Kinlaw ain't no Yay'saw name." He tapped the edge of the mouth-harp on the porch railing several times to get the spit out, gave the instrument a brief inspection to see if all the moisture was gone, then jerked his head back and in the same motion, sent another stream of black tobacco-juice over the railing and out across the sandy yard. "What part of Yelesaw this-here Mister Ben Kinlaw, him come from?"

"My pa ain't from no Yelesaw," the girl answered, although she knew full well that the old man knew this, too. "Him from cross'oba-the-river."

The old man snorted.

"Well hell iffen you and me is blood kin, then," he said. "I sure ain't no kin to no oba'deys." The old man chewed noisily on that thought for a moment, poking around with two fingers in his pockets for a refreshener for his chaw.

"Grandpa—" the girl said, as he searched.

"Grandpa, what?! You as aggravating as that mama 'a you'rn. Neither one of you got the sense to give a field-hand a hour of peace."

The girl waited a respectful moment, and then continued with her point.

"Grandpa, you still ain't answer me."    .

"Answer you, what?"

"Answer me if you think the Yay'saw, us might ever left Yelesaw."

The old man snorted.

"Shuck, you *must* be a oba'dey child, you ain't know the answer to that. The Yay'saw ain't never leaving Yelesaw because Yelesaw is the best place to be. You know how the Yay'saws get over-here to this side of the river?"

"Ain't the whitefolk brung'd us in the slavery-times?"

"Some folks done says that, some folks ain't. I suppose I better be done tell you the truth of it. I wouldn't want nobody's for know I let a child ignorant as you hang'round my porch step every night. Plus, you ain't fixing to give me no peace tonight 'lessen I do, is you?"

"Nossir."

"No, I reckon you ain't."

The old man planted his feet on the porchboards again and reached down under the porch swing to retrieve the brown jug he kept there. He spit the shapeless wad of chewed tobacco out of his mouth into his palm and flung the wad over the porch railing. Then he pulled out the jug's cork stopper with his teeth, dropped it into his open hand and, in one practiced motion, swung the jug up to his mouth by the index finger of his other hand that he'd crooked in the handle, leaned his head far back, and took a long swallow. When he was finished, he stoppered the jug up again, found the tobacco-plug—at last—in one of his pockets, pulled it out, and bit off a fresh wad.

While the old man was making his preparations, the girl wrapped her long arms around her legs and settled the side of her face on her knees. She had heard the Yelesaw story before, of course, many times, but she loved the telling of it, almost as much as she loved the mock tug-of-war that led to the tell of it. When they were both ready, and the jug was back under his feet and out of the way and the new tobacco-chew was well on the way to being mashed down into comfortable pliability in his mouth, the old man knotted his fingers together across his stomach, pushed back in the porch swing, and began.

"Back in the back'away days," he said, "the Oba'Nigger, the Yay'saw, and the Buckra, all three been living in the old home back on the other side 'cross the saltwater, but they wasn't fixing for stay there.

*They were all preparing to go to their new homes on this side of the water, and each one of them was pretty anxious, because they didn't know exactly where they were going to be staying when they got over to the new land, and each one wanted his home to be the best one. They were sitting at the fish-pond one afternoon studying on the subject, each one going on and on describing the house and plot he was going to live in, going round and round, one after the other, each one making his place grander and finer than the last, until they had themselves living like kings in palaces and holding acres of farmland rolling with crop and thick with fat stock.*

*They talked so loud and long that they woke up a possum who was up in the tree above them. He listened to them for a while, and when he got tired of hearing all their boasting, he called down to them, "All that big talking y'all a'doing down there, ain't a one of y'all knows what you' home 'cross that saltwater fixing to be. But if y'all really wants for pick out you' place before you gets over there, I can tell you how."*

So the Yay'saw and the Buckra and the Oba'Nigger all gathered around the foot of the tree and begged the possum to please let them know how they could pick out their new houses before they went across the water, and because he wanted them to shut their talk and let him go back to sleep, he told them.

"Y'all must go down to the Crossroads just at midnight," Cousin Possum said. "That when old Gwa-Gwa, him come out he' hole. And when you catch that Gwa-Gwa twixt him and that hole, you grab him by him ear and don't turn him go, and 'mand him for grant you whatever place over the saltwater you asks him, 'less you hold him there all night 'til the sun come up. And the Gwa-Gwa got for grant you, 'cause you knows him can't stand for let the sun look on he backside, 'cause that make him stuck in this world forever, and he be done lose all he power."

Now this satisfied the Oba'Nigger and the Buckra, and they made their plans to go home right away so they could get some sleep before going down to the Crossroads that night, and all the time they were thinking about the fine homes and property they were going to get for themselves over on the other side, and already making plans for how they were going to live over there. But the Yay'saw, he thought about it a minute, and was sort of troubled in his mind. And he asked the possum, "What were to happen iffen alla'we up and picks the same house and plot? How we settle on which one'a we be fixing to get it?" And the Oba'Nigger and the Buckra, they both wished they'd thought of that, too, because the Yay'saw had a point.

So Cousin Possum told them, "The one what gets to the Gwa-Gwa the first, him get the first pick, and the ones what come after, thems gets the hind-parts." And right away, the Buckra and the Oba'Nigger started thinking about a way they could get out early and beat the other ones down to the Crossroads that night. And the possum could see the plotting and planning in their eyes, and so he said, "But y'all mind and 'member, the Gwa-Gwa, him don't come out 'til midnight on the chiming, and iffen y'all come to the Crossroad too early, y'all be done spook him, and him won't come out not a'tall, and y'all won't get nothing but a long walk for you' troubles."

So with that on their minds, they all walked back to their cabins to get some sleep before midnight. And while they were walking, they decided that they assemble in front of their places at a half hour to midnight, and they would take off running down to the Crossroads together, and whoever got there first would catch the Gwa-Gwa first, and get the first choice of house and land over across the saltwater. They all agreed to that, but all the time, the Buckra was figuring that *wouldn't work, because he knew both the Yay'saw and the Oba'Nigger were way faster than he was, and he had no chance to get down to the Crossroads ahead of them. So while the Yay'saw and the Oba'Nigger went straight inside their cabins and got in their beds, the Buckra found some chores that needed doing first around his yard. As soon as he figured that the other two were asleep, he went into the woods and found a thick vine and cut off four long pieces, and then he went back and tied one piece each around the door-latches of the Yay'saw and the Oba'Nigger, front and back. And when he was sure he had all their doors secured so that they couldn't get out, no matter how they tried, the Buckra went over to his own cabin to get himself some sleep.*

*When eleven-thirty came that night, all three of them awoke and jumped up out of their beds and put on their pants. But while the Buckra ran right out and took off down the path to the Crossroads, the Yay'saw and the Oba'Nigger found that they couldn't get out of their cabins. Hard as they pulled and pounded, neither their front doors nor their back doors would budge, and they were stuck inside.*

*The Buckra got down to the Crossroads right at midnight, and hardly had time to hide in the bushes before here came the Gwa-Gwa out of his hole in the ground, whistling and swinging his conjure-stick and stepping over to the Crossroads to do his work. But before he could get there, the Bucka jumped up out of the bushes and grabbed the Gwa-Gwa by the ear, and wouldn't turn him loose. And the Buckra told the Gwa-Gwa, "I gots you and you can't get'way, and now you must take me 'cross-over the saltwater and lay my claim to the house and plot I wants over there, or I'll make you stay out here 'til the sun come up."*

*So the Gwa-Gwa agreed, and took the Buckra down into his hole, and led him through the tunnel under the saltwater, until they came out on the other side, and there the Gwa-Gwa gave the Buckra his pick of the new land. And the Buckra took the best planting land he could find, flat, with good soil, and shady trees alongside a lake and a river of clean water. And there the Buckra said he would build his home and farm. And the Gwa-Gwa left the Buckra contented on his land, and came back through the tunnel under the saltwater, and popped out of his hole on the other side.*

*Now, the Buckra hadn't done as good a job at tying up the Oba'Nigger's doors as he had the Yay'saw's, mostly because he was more worried about the Yay'saw getting free than he was the Oba'Nigger, because the Yay'saw was the faster and the stronger and the cleverer of the two. So by the time the Gwa-Gwa got back from his trip through the tunnel under the saltwater, the Oba'Nigger had broken free and gotten out of his house, and had run down to the Crossroads just in time to catch the Gwa-Gwa coming out of his hole. And the Oba'Nigger grabbed the Gwa-Gwa by his hair and shook him, and told him, "Take me back underneath the water and let me lay out my land, or I'll shake you like the dog shake the barn rat 'til the hair come offen you' head."*

*So the Gwa-Gwa took the Oba'Nigger back down the hole and through the tunnel underneath the saltwater. But when they got on the other side, and it came for the Oba'Nigger to pick the spot for his plot and home, he found that there wasn't anything good left that the Buckra hadn't already picked. The Buckra had taken all the best land for himself. All that was left was stump-land and rock-land and bottom-land where only the weeds and thistle-bushes would grow. And the Oba'Nigger wandered around looking for something good he could find, and when he couldn't find anything that suited, he settled for the best of the poorest land that was left, and that's where he laid out his plot, and that's where the Gwa-Gwa left him.*

*When the Gwa-Gwa came back out of his hole on the other side of the saltwater for the third time, here came the Yay'saw to the Crossroads, finally. The Buckra had tied his doors the tightest, with a triple knot, so tight that the Yay'saw couldn't break it, and he had to wriggle up the chimney to get out of his house, and when he got to the Crossroads, he was even blacker than usual from the chimney-soot and dripping sweat, and it took him a while to catch his breath, he'd been running as fast as he ever had in his life. And the Yay'saw looked so pitiful standing there bent-over that the Gwa-Gwa felt sorry for him, and didn't even wait for the Yay'saw to try to catch him, but when the Yay'saw got his breath back, the Gwa-Gwa told him to come on down the hole, and he'd take him over to the other side.*

*When they got there, what a pitiful sight for the Yay'saw. The Buckra had the best land and the Oba'Nigger had the hindmost, so that it seemed like there wasn't anything left to take at all. The Yay'saw walked around all the rest of the night and through the next day, but every place he came to had a sign on it, either "This Place Belong To The Buckra" or "This Place Belong To The Oba'Nigger," and "Everybody's Else, Y'all Stays Off."*

*Finally the Yay'saw came down to the edge of the Swamp, which nobody wanted, only the alligators and the snakes and the cuta's, and the only thing growing were palmetto bush and scratchweed patches. And the Yay'saw was so tired and discouraged and hungry, he sat down with his feet in the swampwater and picked the seeds off of the scratchweed and chewed on them, because there wasn't anything else around to eat. The seed was so brittle and hard, it hurt his teeth to chew it, and when he had swallowed as much as he could stand, it made a hard knot in his stomach. And he couldn't eat any more, so he decided to toss the rest of the seed in the water. But while he was sitting there tossing it, seed by seed, and trying to think of what he would do next, he pricked one of the seeds with his fingernail, and it broke open in his hand. Inside the brown husk was a little white grain, and that gave the Yay'saw an idea. He got some clean water out of a creek that was running into the Swamp and put it in a hollow in a rock he found, and made a fire under it, and broke open all the scratchweed seeds he had left and put them in the water and boiled them, and when it was done he ate them, and they were soft and sweet, and it was the tastiest meal he'd ever had. But that only made him hungrier, because it wasn't hardly a handful to eat, and there weren't any more scratchweed bushes around or seeds to pick, so he laid down and went to sleep, and hoped he would forget the growling of his stomach, and the fact that he still had to find himself a place for his house and farm.*

*The Yay'saw slept there on the edge of the Swamp for a long time, and when he woke up, what a strange and different sight he saw. All of the seedgrains he'd tossed in the water had risen up and sprouted rows and rows of scratchweed plants, and the seedgrains were growing out of them like crazy. And the Yay'saw said, "Oh, sugar, that sure look nice to me." But he had broken off one of the seedgrains and was sucking on it when he said it, and so instead of the word coming out "nice" it came out "rice," and that's what people have called it ever since.*

*Now while the Yay'saw was down in the Swamp finding out about what rice could do, the Buckra and the Oba'Nigger had been busy, too. Because the land the Oba'Nigger had gotten was so poor, he'd had to hire himself out to the Buckra to work the Buckra's land, and when the crop came in, he had to hire himself out again to carry the Buckra's crop for him to sell at the market in town. The road to the market led down by the Swamp, and by-and-by, while the Yay'saw was standing there looking at all those rice plants growing out in the swampwater, the Buckra and the Oba'Nigger came walking by. And both of them laughed at the Yay'saw, because both of them—even the Oba'Nigger— thought they'd got the better of the deal over on this side of the saltwater. And the Oba'Nigger told the Yay'saw, "iffen you still looking for land, I might have a dry patch or two you can squat on, iffen you ain't mind digging out the rock for me all'around." But the Yay'saw told him, "No, Cousin, y'all got me beat and I reckon I'm too tired to move, from all this walking and hunting-up I've been doing, and I reckon I'll just stay here with my feets in the swampwater and end my days." But all the time he was smiling to himself, because he'd found out that rice was the best crop to sow, and the best place to sow it was right down there in the*

*Swamp, and that's right where he had landed.*

"And that swamp-edge land, that-there been Yelesaw, and that how the Yay'saw done gets here, and that where we been, every since."

Here the old man stopped talking and closed his eyes and took to rocking back and forth in the porch swing again, pushing against the porchboards with his bare feet, making the chains give out the sharp squeaks of the melody, while the boards marked the tempo with groans. Warming to the music, the old man took his mouth-harp out of his front pants pocket where he had deposited it, put it to his lips, and began blowing out a quiet tune in accompaniment. Over across the dark of the yard in the patch of grass around the bottle-tree, the crickets took up the melody with their leg-fiddles, and at the foot of the porch, the fireflies danced about in the night air to its measure. The girl closed her eyes and leaned back against the porch railing and listened, thought for a moment, and then spoke up.

"Grandpa," she said, "ain't you done tell me one time how the Affika'folk, they knowed about rice-planting back over the water, and that-why they was took and brought over here?"

The old man sniffed in a measure of air and grunted.

"That were a different story," he told her. "You got for keep you' story straight, elsewise you'll never get the point of 'em."

"Yessir."

In the silence that followed, both of them took to their own thoughts, until the old man asked her, "Why-for you ask'ded me that?"

"Ask'ded you about the Affika-folk? I'm sorry. I ain't mean for disrespect."

"No, goose! Ask'ded me about the Yay'saw lefting Yelesaw. What done draw something like that up outten you' head?"

"Oh." The girl hunched her shoulders and held out her palms in front of her and gave him a puzzled look. "I ain't know, Grandpa. It just come to me, is all."

"It just come to you, is it...?" The old man's voice trailed off. It was not really a question to her, and she did not know how to answer it, so she didn't. He did not press the point and so she leaned back against the porch frame again, her feet stirring at the loose sand under the steps, letting her body relax to the massage of the warm wind blowing through the hair that grew thick along her bare legs and arms, enjoying the moment and the quiet of the night. The old man turned and sent a stream from his fresh tobacco-chew out into the yard, the black drops arcing in the air and then dropping with a soft pattering sound, making a broad and odd pattern across the white sand. He studied the placing of the drops for a moment to see if he could catch its meaning, but they disappeared into the ground before they revealed themselves, and he gave a silent sigh and turned away. The two of them sat there like that in the dark of the evening for a while, each in their own thoughts, and the girl did not notice that every so often, the old man turned and stared at her, thoughtfully, out of his one good eye, trying to catch the meaning of her, as well.

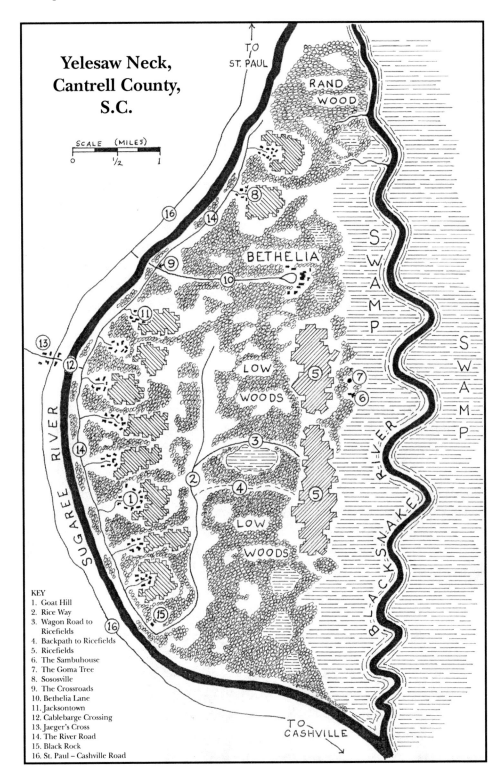

Yelesaw Neck,
Cantrell County,
S.C.

SCALE   (MILES)

0        ½        1

TO
ST. PAUL

RAND
WOOD

S
W
A
M
P

S
W
A
M
P

BETHELIA

LOW
WOODS

LOW
WOODS

SUGAREE   RIVER

BLACK-SNAKE   RIVER

TO
CASHVILLE

KEY
1. Goat Hill
2. Rice Way
3. Wagon Road to
   Ricefields
4. Backpath to Ricefields
5. Ricefields
6. The Sambuhouse
7. The Goma Tree
8. Sososville
9. The Crossroads
10. Bethelia Lane
11. Jacksontown
12. Cablebarge Crossing
13. Jaeger's Cross
14. The River Road
15. Black Rock
16. St. Paul – Cashville Road

# 1

## The News From Cross'Oba-The-River

### *(Fall, 1935)*

She heard it as she was walking the narrow footpath through the cattail field, a sharp "*hep! hep! hep!*" and the drumming of hooves like someone was running a horse out on the road beyond in something of a powerful hurry. It had to be a horse, because a mule could never be made to run that fast. Yally'Bay Kinlaw stopped in her tracks, a full dinner-basket balanced easy on the top of her head, and craned her long neck upwards to try to get a better look.

She had shot up over the summer without notice, like a sapling planted at the back-end of the yard that nobody had bothered to check on for a while, because its fruit wasn't expected quite yet. You could tell at 15 that the youngest Kinlaw child was going to be tall—tall even in a family full of big folk—with limbs suddenly pushed out so skinny and long that Cu'n Boo and her brother, Dink, had taken to calling her Nansi-leg because, as they said, her gangly arms and legs looked so much like a spider's. She was tall enough that standing on her toe tips, she could see over the waving cattails grown head-high with the summer's heat to the line of trees beyond, but, unfortunately for her, not tall enough to be able to see the sandy Rice Way that was the boundary between the cat'field and the woods, or who it was that was driving their horse so hard out along it.

It was most likely the Jackson boys, she figured, Lam and his younger brother Dokie, staging a drop-hat race with some of their kinfolk out along the Way. The Jacksons were one of the few families at Yelesaw to keep horses rather than mules. But while the older Jackson men often paced their horses out on the River Road where there was plenty of room to run, the younger ones like Lam and Dokie were fool enough to do it down here, on the narrow Rice Way—where they were subject to pitch themselves into trees or bushes or creeks or ponds, or gallop down anyone walking or riding in their path. It was a welcome piece of excitement in the middle of a routine day of house and yard work. Steadying the dinner-basket on top of her head with one hand, Yally lifted her skirts with the other and hurried out to the Way so she wouldn't miss the sight.

It was a sight that came powerfully close to not missing her.

She came out of the cat'field path and onto the road almost directly in front of the onrushing horse. It was Lam Jackson riding, bareback on a blacktail mare, leaned low over withers and neck, knees high, shouting and flank-whipping with his hat for all he was worth. It was only his good horsemanship that kept him from riding Yally over. Before she had time to react he was already snatching back and out on the reins, breaking the horse away from the girl with a sharp dig of his knee. The mare reared its head and lifted its forelegs high into the air as if it were going to take off and fly, its hind hooves digging and sliding through the sand, sending a spray that showered over Yally in a hard patter, covering dress and skin and headscarf and all, and she only closed her eyes just quick enough to keep it from blinding her. Not letting go of the dinner-basket, she jumped backwards into the cattails and out of the way. Then, as the mare seemed ready and sure to rise so high that it would tumble over backwards, Lam Jackson snapped the reins back down again, and just that quick the horse dropped its forefeet to the ground in obeyance, and catching its balance, danced around in a furious circle several times, first in one direction and then in the other, slowing, finally, to a nervous canter, bucking its hind legs every now and again in protest, flipping its head back and forth all the while so that it could keep at least one wild, rolling eye on the basket-headed creature now off the road and out of its path, but still a threat to possibly pounce again. It took the mare a moment to realize that it was only a girl, and not something out of wood or swamp that feasted on horses, but that did not seem to mollify it.

"Dammit, dammit, *dammit!*" Lam Jackson shouted down at Yally with a fierce look that was meant to intimidate her. She had too many brothers and close boy-cousins to be thus intimidated and Lam Jackson was up and down on the Hill with her brothers enough to be like a cousin himself, and besides that, he looked so ridiculous trying to keep his seat atop the mare, which was still twisting around in the road like a county fairgrounds merry-go-round creature, that she broke into a giggle at the sight, which made her swallow some of the sand that the horse had thrown into her mouth. She bent over and tried to cough it out, the continuing giggling interfering. Lam Jackson missed the giggling and only caught the discomfort, and the fierce look on his face softened. "I'm sorry, Yally'Bay," he said, finally pulling the whirlygigging mare to a transitory halt. "I ain't mean for curse you like that, but you liken to scare the nothing outten me, jumping out from the bushes like that." He leaned down as if he were going to help brush some of the sand from her face and headscarf, but the mare drew the line at that, stepping back a few skittish paces, and refusing to come any closer. "You alright?" Lam Jackson asked Yally, from a distance.

She spit the last of the sand out of her mouth and straightened back up. Through it all, without even thinking about it, she had not lost a grip on the basket parked on her head. There were many things that would set Mama off, and one of them was the scattering of the men's dinner, regardless of cause. Now she set the basket down behind her in a cattail patch—out of reach of the mare's hooves in case the horse had a mind to to try to stomp it dead—and pulled her headscarf off, snapping it to get out any stray sand, and then moving her fingers through the thick naps of her hair to catch the rest. Then she took a quick survey of herself.

"I'll do," she said. She now had time to give a look up and down the Rice Way. It was empty of anyone else, as far as she could see. "Who you was racing with?" she asked him. "You sure done lefted them in the dust."

He frowned as his look of concern for her wellbeing went away, and he raised back up on the mare with an air of importance growing over him, as if horseracing on the Rice Way was something that only little boys or people with no pressing business did, and he was neither of those. "I ain't racing with nobody's," he told her with a huff in his voice. "I ain't got time for no racing. I got news for fetch." He wiped at the sweat on his head with the brim of his hat, smearing both with brown road dust. He pointed with his hat over across the cattail field, back towards Goat Hill. "Who out to y'all house, right now?"

Yally's interest had raised at the word "news." A Jackson boys horserace on the Rice Way was always exciting, but a new report from Yelesaw news-carriers could be better, depending.

"What news you fetching?" she asked him.

He clucked his tongue in annoyance.

"You' Mama at you' house or ain't?" he said. "I were fixing for stop there first, but I ain't iffen ain't nobody's there."

"Mama and Eshy there, all two, I reckon," Yally said as she retied the scarf over her hair. 'Least they was when I left. You really ain't fixing to tell me, Lam'jackson?"

He hesitated at the look of supplication on her face and almost melted, but then he stiffened and gave his head a shake. "Iffen I stop for talk with every crow on the branch, I'll never get the word out to nobody," he said. "I got for go. I done told you I got news for fetch. Big news." Jamming his hat deep down back on his head again, he bent over to tighten the bit in the mare's teeth, which had loosened up with all his recent reins-pulling. The mare stamped its hooves apprehensively. Yally folded her arms over her breasts and watched the preparations. She had started to tell him that she wasn't no crow on nobody's branch but then decided against it, figuring that might offend him more than it would encourage him to talk. Instead she tried to guess what his big news might be. "It about Joday Prioleau' baby?" she asked him." The Prioleau girl was two weeks overdue, and had sent over just that morning for Aunt Orry to come and induce a delivery.

Lam Jackson turned the mare back up the Rice Way in the direction he'd been going, but the horse was still balking, tossing its head, snickering, doing a little sideways dance in the sand instead of gathering itself for another bolt down the road, getting this strange encounter out of its system. "You just ask you' folks," Lam said as he pulled at the rope-reins to get control.

"Ask my folks, what? The baby done come'd?"

"I ain't know nothing about that girl' baby." As the mare increased the pace of its prancing, turning from one side to the other, Lam Jackson had to look back over first one shoulder, then the other, to keep Yally in view as he talked. Yally was getting dizzy trying to follow all the movement. "Ask them 'bout the news I'm fetching, what you think?" Lam Jackson went on. "I done already told'ded them all about it, down there at the fields. Anyways, I got for get. Mornin'!"

And then he was gone. He had dug his knees into the horse's flanks and snapped the reins hard on its haunches, and grateful to be going again, the mare took off in a leap. Yally watched its hooves churning up the sand behind as it galloped away, young man and mare growing smaller down the road, until they made the far bend and disappeared from her view, the sound of the run-drumming gradually fading into the late-morning creature-chatter of field and wood. Along the line of trees far down the Rice Way, past the curve where she could no longer see, a flock of birds scattered up into the air, startled by the horse and rider, the only sign left of their passing.

"Well, alright, then boy, and 'morning' back at you," she called after him as she stooped down to take up Mama's dinner-basket. Setting it back on her head, she stepped out on the Rice Way, and continued on her errand down to the fields.

IT WAS THE last of the warm-out days of the fall season. By next week, a cooling in the air was due—she could feel it coming—and there might be need at the house to make the morning fire for warming-up instead of just breakfast-cooking, and she and Eshy would be getting the quilts out of the back shed for the beds and pallets and the heavier clothes for everybody. She feared the cold and hated the summer to pass. But today she could walk and feel the heat on the back of her neck and her bare legs, and the sweat-trickles running from under her arms and down the insides of her thighs. She loved that feeling, ticklish as it was.

She had broken out into a stride that was long and quick and easy, now that she was out of the cat'tail path and back onto flat ground again. She was a country girl and therefore by definition a good walker, and though she had left in plenty of time, she held a pace that ate up the sand and packed dirt in front of her. She was not in any particular hurry. She was just following what the road told her to do.

If some stranger had been sitting, hidden in the woods nearby, and had the sense to keep quiet while they watched her pass, they would have seen the very image of an orisha stride by, so assured and content within itself and its growing young beauty and rising African womanhood that it had no need to be concerned with the lack of self-acknowledgement or even self-awareness of those qualities by the girl herself—the orisha Oshun, almost certainly, the spirit of rivers and all sweet water—Oshun, the rain to Shango's lightning—the proud and seductive Oshun, walking as she had in the days when Olodumare first made the world, with a flowing, An'gullahn ease to herself, head high and level, arms swinging in loose rhythm from her wide shoulders, doe-fluid hips rotating seemingly unconnected to the strong straightness of her back. What had long been gangle was now sliding natural into grace. For herself, Yally Kinlaw saw none of that. She had long ago accepted herself as the skinnybiddy in the family. Her brothers and Eshy and even Papa, now and again, had long ago set that in her mind, in the jokey, boisterous way that was the Kinlaws. Yally accepted it and it did not bother her. Each had a place in the Kinlaw family that was set and solid, and being the po'bones of the litter was hers. She kept her mind busy with other things.

Today her mind was on the birds, and while she was away with them, high up and flying far, her feet were like a good plow mule that carried her down the familiar way without her having to lead or even think about it. She could walk down to the ricefields blindfolded, if she cared to, or in the deep of a moonless night without a lamp or torch and never stumble on a root, she had walked this way so many times in her life.

AFTER HER FAILURE to get him to give up any details, she dismissed any more thoughts about Lam Jackson's news. The Jacksons were the great information-carriers and gossip-spreaders at Yelesaw, begun by the family men in the first years of the spreading out after the fall of the old plantation, when the Yay'saws were lonely for the lost closeness that had come from the side-by-side living in slave quarters cabins and the working in one vast field, and the Jackson horses—which they had taken out of the ruins of Old Bethelia—were the best means of closing the lonely miles of fields and woods they Yelesaw people had put between themselves. The Pony Éxpress, folks began to call them, but without the normal standard of priority levels to their mail system. The Jacksons had no sense of perspective of the proper hierarchy of things in the world, no *siftiness* about themselves, as some of the older women put it, drawing on a kitchen fixing table analogy. The Jacksons didn't seem to know how to *sift* things into their proper place, the older women explained, and so were unable to grade between the largeness or smallness, importance or triviality, of the information they fetched. They just loved the act of fetching it. If it had indeed been information about the birth of Joday Prioleau's baby Lam Jackson had been carrying, Yally knew he would have gotten just as worked up in the telling of the shape of the baby's nose and head as he would have about whether the baby had come out alive or dead. Every bit of news was the same to the men of the Yelesaw's Pony Éxpress, each bit of equal importance, their only concern that they were the first one carrying it. There was no need for Yally to try to speculate, therefore, on what Lam Jackson's news might be, once she found she could not convince him to tell her. It could be anything, and the best thing to do—the only thing, actually—was to wait until she could hear what the men down at the ricefields could tell her.

THE MAIN WAGONROAD that cut off from the Rice Way eventually led down to the fields in a wide sweep through open marshlands that avoided the bogs and most of the wet spots, but that was by far the longer and duller passage, and so long before she came to it, Yally had turned onto her own little backpath and passed down into the Low Woods.

The lower boundary of the Rice Way broke off far different from the side that Yally had just come from through the cattail field, as if they were two straight slices of bread from different bakings—cornbread and lightbread—set down on the table next to each other with the butter knife in between. The ground in the Low Woods was dark and semi-muddy rather than the light and sandy of the upper side—thin, sticky, suckpatch mud from which a slight, dank smell of sweetrot rose—the grass spread out in between in thick, spiked patches, wilder and slightly dangerous, threatening with thorned edges to grab at bare legs, interspersed with palmetto groves that grew heavier and more numerous the further down you went. Scattered throughout were the beginnings of silent oil-black pools, small and isolated at first, but slowly connecting, merging, and growing larger even as they multiplied. At first the woods were made up mostly of oak and pine and wide-leaf catalpa and ash, but they began gradually to change to swamp willow and scale-barked water tupelo and cypress, some of the trees with thickroots rising from the pooled waters themselves, the limbs spreading out above her—heavy with trailing gray-green moss like bearded old men—thick enough to begin to filter out the sunlight, so that the way gradually became dimmer, and cooler, and she had to steady the dinner-basket on her head with one hand and duck down slightly, now and again, to keep a low-hanging limb from reaching down to knock the basket off. The low ceiling of trees served to magnify the woods-sounds down on this side as well, the fussy chatter of flocks of birds hidden in the groves, the call-and-response of peepers on the edge of the ponds, the plop of kutas slipping into the waters from their sunning places on the rocks as she passed. Fat, black mosquitoes replaced the nitties and yellowflies of the open fields on the other side of the road, and clouds of them began to follow her and sing their tinny greetings in her ears. She slipped her headscarf off from under the basket with her free hand and swatted at them with it, as if that would do any good. They scattered for a moment, reformed like disciplined armies, and came after her again, relentless.

The ground on which the path wound its way began to drop in gentle, terraced slopes, so that while it seemed as if she was always walking level, when she looked back, after a time, she could see that she was down far below the lip of the road. The path at times would have been difficult to find if she did not know it so well, overwhelmed and overrun as it was in places by the lush and quick-growing grass, and she knew that if she strayed off it and bore to the right, skirting that side of the ricefields, and walked far enough, she would eventually drop down into the Swamp itself. She had never been all the way into the Swamp, had only been close enough with Papa, once or twice, for him to point out its beginnings, the lily ponds and wide lagoons, dim-green and dark-moist, deep down beyond the last of the hard-ground thickets. Even Papa had never been in the Swamp himself, she didn't think, though he loved hunting and fishing, and it was supposed to be especially good down there, the best on Yelesaw Neck. But Papa made it plain that the swamp-edge was a boundary not to be crossed. None of Yally's brothers or close-cousins had been down in there, neitherways, probably or, if they had, only for a step or two, and not far enough to get out of sight of the Low Woods, not because their parents forbade it, but for fear of being lost. You didn't want to get lost, not down there in the Swamp.

But she knew the path well, both by her head and by her feet, and even distracted, there was never any danger of her wandering off.

SOMETHING WAS NAGGING AT HER, and it was not just the mosquitos.

The Low Woods ended at last, opening up into a marshy palmetto plain, and just at the edge between the two, she found a patch of horsemint amidst the grass in a little rising spot beside the pathway. She set the dinner-basket down and stopped to gather some of the leaves and crushed them between her palms, rubbing the sweet-mint oil residue on her arms and legs and over her face and neck to help keep the mosquitos away. It was there that the thing began disturbing her—whatever it was—and she strayed for a moment while she tried to figure at it. Whatever it was danced away and could not be caught, and so she picked the basket back up and walked out onto the plain. At its far edge she could see the sandy ridge that marked the barrier beyond which were the Manigault ricefields. Back on flat ground, she picked up her pace again, which had slowed during her time in the woods. She tried to concentrate on the soon-coming end to her walk and the delivery of Mama's dinner to the men in the fields, and the laughing and teasing and conversation she knew was to come, but something still seemed off-kilter, so vexingly out-of-sorts that she stopped in her tracks after only a short distance to try to fish it out.

With no trees to block it now the sun could concentrate all of its weight and thought upon her, and she lifted the basket a bit and slipped off her headscarf again to wipe the sweat-trails from around her eyes. By the time she got the scarf back on, the water was running down all across her forehead as if from the spout of a primed pump. She blinked back the salt-sting but did not bother to try to stop it any more. Instead she stood silent, her neck craned, listening to the high-humming of thicket bugs and chorused bellowing of frogs squatted down in their waterpools— the last they'd be heard from until next spring, she knew—and the lonely calls of the marshbirds back and forth over the open field, and then the sharp, hard beating of wing against downy side as a partridge flock, skittish and startled by something's presence, took sudden flight from where they had been hiding in the shrubs only a few yards away. The sounds of the partridge flock died away as they distanced themselves up the plain, and in the silence that followed, she now—of a sudden—realized what had been bothering her. There was no singing coming from the men working the ricefields on the other side of the sand-ridge. And never in her life could she remember walking the palmetto field except to the sound of those work-songs. It was something she always looked forward to.

The memory of Lam Jackson's hurriation out on the Rice Way suddenly came back to her, and she had a quick flash of insight, a pit of worry opening up in her insides, revealing what the news he had been fetching might have been. Until now, she had thought that it was about a happening over in the settlements. But now she wondered if, instead, it had been something from out of the fields, maybe even the Manigault ricefields. Certainly, the Manigault ricefields.

It was no idle worry. It was the time of the fall burnoff, which also meant the time for timber cutting and dike repairs, so bad news from the fields could mean anything from a serious mule kicking to a tree-saw accident to a snakebite to a suck-down-into-sinkhole. There were too many dangers in the ricefields to even speculate on. Papa and Grandpa and her brothers were all out there, and close-cousins and all the other Manigault men as well. Which one it could have been who might have been accidented on, she did not want to guess. Maybe more than one, like the year the rice-canal bank had collapsed on the Butlers in a hard rainstorm, smothering three of them to death. But clearly, now that she put her mind to it, it struck her that there must have been some sort of an accident down in the ricefields, so serious that it had sent Lam Jackson at the gallop to bring the news to the Hill. She could feel that something bad had happened, and feelings of hers like that too often turned out to be true.

Pulling the dinner-basket off of her head and gripping it against her side with two hands, she took off at a quickened pace across the palmetto plain. The marshy ground sucked at her bare feet and ankles, trying to slow her down, but that made her trot all the faster, picking up speed as she went. She passed through the plain in a blur of gathering anxiety. By time she had sprinted up to the top of the ridge, the sand kicking back behind her in her wake, her chest was heaving with the effort and she had to stand for a moment both to get her breath and to figure out the meaning of what she was seeing in the ricefields beyond.

The mudded, sunken flats stretched out between the ridge and the far scrubline as they always did this time of the year, at the end of harvest, criss-crossed like an intricate quiltlining with the dikes and canals and gated sluiceways that were the veins and arteries of the ricefields. With the last of the rice crop long in the sheds back home, the canals were dry now. The fields themselves were no longer the lush, emerald green of late summer but were smudge-black, covered with burnt stubble, and a rank layer of gray-green smoke from the burnoff hovered over them.

None of the men were tending the smouldering fires, however. Instead, they were all over at the far end of the field where the main water-canal ran out from the ricefields and down towards the Swamp. All of them were there, as far as Yally could see, which meant the ones who should have been out on the canal lines had come back in to join the ones working on the field-burning. None of the men were working, as they should have been until dinner had actually arrived. Instead they were gathered in a small knot around the two elders of the family, Grandpa Budi and his brother, Tibo, some standing, some sitting straddled on fallen trees, axes and shovels and long-handled hoes now only props to lean against, as they engaged in what appeared to Yally to be the most serious of talks.

There had clearly been no disaster, at least, not that she could see.

She watched the men down below as their heads were either nodding slowly or shaking in some sort of disagreement, some of them clearly getting in a word now and then, but mostly they seemed to be listening to Grandpa Budi, who was sitting on a tree stump in the center, talking, every now and again waving his big hands in a flat, wide gesture that seemed to be taking in not only the ricefields but the Swamp and the marshwoods surrounding.

He also had eyesight good enough—even if he only had only one good eye—to see a talling-up girl standing on the ridge across the field, and so, as soon as Yally saw him look up in her direction, she came down off the ridge, waving one hand in the air, giving out the dinner call. They turned to the sound of her voice and then, with a last word from Papa'Budi, the conversation broke up, and the men laid down their tools where they stood and started up across the burned-off fields to meet her, and to get their dinner, some calling back at her and gesturing for her to hurry forward with the food, as if nothing at all unusual had been happening down there, at all.

THE MEN WERE LONG USED to hiding their business from their children and even, sometimes, from the women of the settlements as well, or passing their concerns and troubles off with a shrug as part of life's necessary burdens, and so by the time they had reached Yally in the middle of the fields, they were all smiles and jokes and eagerness to see what she'd brought in the basket, with no trace at all of the seriousness that had hung over them only a moment before.

As always, Mama had sent down a big pot of rice-and-peas in the wagon with the men in the morning, and it had been slow-cooking over an open fire alongside them as they worked, timed just right to be ready for the dinner meal, so that all Yally had to fetch with her in the basket was the sidemeat and cornbread. As she passed them out she searched out her father, looking into his face for some sign or other as he stood in front of her with his usual wooden bowl in his hand, questioning him with widened eyes. He only gave her his usual quick grin and a thank'y nod in return, ribbing her a little for probably having stopped to eat her own meal in the woods during her walk and therefore being late with the men's dinner (which she hadn't done and hadn't been), and that told her nothing.

When they'd gotten their portions, the men wandered off in small knots to sit or squat and talk among themselves while they ate. She wanted to join them, especially the group with her grandfather and grand-uncle, because she knew the news, if any, was surely still being discussed, but since it seemed clear they were keeping their deliberations from her, and she could hardly sit anywhere close by without them noticing, she had to seek out another way to find out. She spied Dink and Cu'n Boo lounging under a small grove of trees, together as always, of course. She gathered up her basket and the dinner leavings and after stopping to give one of the two family mules, Bay-say, a half-an-apple she had brought in her dress pocket for just that purpose, she went over to join her brother and cousin.

They had finished eating already, gulped their meal down as if they were under-the-back-porch hounds, the forks and empty tin plates in a small pile next to the tree. Boo was lying on his back on the ground, his hands behind his head, slouch hat covering his face, as if, just that quick, he had gone to sleep, which he could easily do, regardless of the time or location. Dinky sat beside him, carving at a keeshee stick-man, back bent over so that his face was only a few inches from the figure, tongue out, mouth set, eyes focused and intent, but his big hands with the loose, easy grip on both stick and knife of a long-practiced artist.

Yally sat down next to them, leaning her back against one of the trees. She waited for a moment, taking a long look to see if Boo was really sleeping, decided that he wasn't, but knowing that this would make him all the harder to rouse. "Can't wake somebody's what ain't sleep," she repeated to herself one of the old folks' sayings. She turned to Dinky, watching him as he carved in silence. She decided against trying to pull the news out of him outright, since unlike Boo, that was more likely to make Dinky withhold it, just for the tease. Instead, she asked him how his wife, Sister 'Eet was doing.

"Big and fussy, how you th-think?" Dinky said, not looking up from his stick-carving. He had a stutter on t's and s's that he only had nominal control over until he got excited over something, and then his tongue would lock up on him and refuse to let anything come out of his mouth at all. "All the s-s-sweetness done gone'd out that 'uman. Her does lose it everytime she big-up with a new child. Iffen her keep that sourness about her, I'm'a send her back t-to she mama 'til that baby drop."

"Well, tell her I'm fixing to come over tomorrow morning, after chore. Aunt Orry making up a remedy for her. That should help she feel something better."

Dinky grunted. "Iffen it don't, I'm'a ask Aunt Orry for a go-for-s-sleep remedy for me so's I can get me some rest my own self. I ain't had a good night of sleep for onto two month t-time now. That what I got this-here keeshee for."

Yally didn't much like keeshee-talk, so she turned her attention to Cu'n Boo, nudging his leg with her big toe. "Sit up and talk with me, boy," she said.

Boo did not move, but, instead, a loud, artificial snore came from under his hat.

"You know you ain't 'sleep," she said. "Mou'ght-well sit up and tell me." She dug the heel of her foot into his thigh, hard, and he groaned from under his hat and slid his body away from her.

"I *would* been 'sleep, iffen you'd let me," he said, lifting his hat from over his face and giving her the most pitiful look of suffering resignation he could manage.

"Then tell me."

"Tell you what?"

"Tell me what y'all mens been talking over when I come down to the field. I seen Lam'jackson out on the Rice Way, and him say him had word for get out. What word y'all give him for fetch?"

Cu'n Boo snorted. "Whatever word that old fool carry off with him, him done fetch here with him. Ain't nobody's tell that boy nothing. Ain't nobody's *can* tell that boy nothing. He dumb as goat crossed with mule." He clamped his hat back over his face and dug his shoulders deeper into the dirt beneath the tree to find a softer spot for them.

"Well, what word him bring?" she said to Cu'n Boo's hat. When neither Boo nor the hat answered, she turned back to Dink, who was still busy with his carving, eyes squinting now, making a delicate cut under the stick-man's head to create a chin. "What Lam'jackson tell y'all?" she asked her brother.

"Old Éx-press ain't t-tell you he own self?" Dink asked back. "I thought him been all fire'-up for holler it out to all'a Yelesaw, the way him been acting."

"Him ain't had time. Him told me for ask y'all."

Dink pulled a sliver of wood from the keeshee-figure with his thumb and finger, brushed it off on his pants, then held the figure up in front of him, turning it around once or twice while Yally fidgeted in place. He put the edge of his knife back to the figure, pulled it back, then set it at a more proper spot to carve. "That boy ain't said nothing but s-something 'bout a big flood fixing to come, is all," he said, finally.

"That were him news?"

It certainly didn't seem like something to make that much of a fuss over. The Yay'saw lived out their lives in the bosom of the water'loa, in bog-filled bottomlands between two rivers and a swamp amidst myriad rivers and creeks and lakes and pools, with two full rainy seasons a year and sudden, swift cloudbursts or heavy thunderstorms or all day downpours the rest of the time, and where the normal irrigation of the family's main crop was complete inundation of the fields several times between planting and harvest. In Yally's lifetime alone she had twice seen the Sugaree overflow its banks, though never as far up as the road, and more times than she could count, the Bigyard transformed into a low pond. Everybody had a favorite flood story, and most more than one. In such an environment, serious flood-talk was no joking matter. On the other hand, the idea of a flood in the abstract was no great cause for concern. Water had to be more imminent-threatening than that to shake a Yay'saw. And like any country girl, Yally could track the weather—as well as the time of day or the current phase of the moon, for that matter—through a complex interaction between all of her senses and the world surrounding. She gave a glance at the cloudless fall sky, but that was not even needed. No coming-up rain was in the air, nor had there been more than a few falling droplets in several weeks, not nearly enough to raise up the level in the well behind the house, certainly not enough to raise up a flood.

Dink had not bothered to answer her "that were him news" question, so she pressed on.

"How Lam'jackson figure on a flood without no rain?" she asked him.

"Don't need no rain. Him believe the whitefolk can do it, without," came the answer from under Cu'n Boo's hat.

"A Jackson'll believe anything a whitefolk t-tell 'em," Dink added.

"What the whitefolk got to do with Lam'jackson' flood?" Yally broke in, but the two cousins ignored her. Instead, a deep chuckle came from under Cu'n Boo's hat. The hat came off as Boo turned over on his side and raised up a little, leaning on one elbow with his cheek resting in his hand, waving the other hand at Dinky.

"You 'members the time old Coot bought that feedcorn from that buckra up to the fair, the buckra say it would pregnant a hog?" he asked. "Coot give it to him old brood sow, say it gonna make her start up littering again. Only thing come outten she belly the next six month been a belching gas."

"The whole Jackson family done fool," Dink said. "Lam. Dokie. The papa. The cousin. And that mama, her the worst of all, and her ain't even Jackson born. What the whole lot of them got in they head, you couldn't feed a sparrow for supper."

"'Cepting for horses," Boo added.

"Yeah, that's true. 'Cepting for horses. They knows they horses. And one or two of them can banjo something special. And fiddle. Them Jackson boys can make a fiddle cry a wet tear."

"But that ain't on the Jackson side. That on they' mama side."

They could have chattered on between themselves like that for hours—or until Grandpa Budi called them back to work—as had been their way since they had first learned to talk, but Yally leaned over and brought her elbow down, hard, into Boo's stomach, making him double up and let all the air out of himself with a great oomf.

"What the whitefolk got to do with Lam'jackson' flood?" she asked Dink, pressing her elbow into his stomach while he tried to fend her off.

"Hurry up and tell the girl before her hit we again," Boo said between laughs and struggling. "I'm'a lose my dinner."

"Before her hit *you* again, what you mean," Dink said. He held up the stick-man. "Her ain't fixing for hit no me. I got me the keeshee."

Gradually, by alternating cajoling and begging and threats of more elbow punches, Yally dragged the whole story out of them. Lam Jackson's daddy, Bonk, had heard it across the river at Jaeger's Store that morning, and when he got back over on the cable-barge, he had gone out with his two sons, Lam and Dokie, to spread the news. The whitefolks were making plans to put a dam across the Sugaree River somewhere just above Cashville, the closest town to Yelesaw Neck. The dam—if what Bonk Jackson had heard could be believed—would leave a deep lake in the bottomlands basin from Cashville all the way north to the county seat at St. Paul and between the town of Sandy Station to the west and the Swamp to the east—the rivers and creeks, hundreds of homes, thousands of farmland acres, a wide collection of villages including the little junction of Jaeger's Cross just over the Sugaree from Yelesaw, the bulk of the Swamp, as well as Yelesaw itself. Until now, the only dams she had ever known were the little blockages of sticks and mud she and other Yelesaw children put over the creeks sometimes to make a small barrier pool to fish or swim in, but this one—if Bonk Jackson could be believed, of course—would flood out or touch its waters on practically every place she had ever been in during her entire life. The enormity of it was too much for Yally to take in.

"Why the whitefolk want for flood-up all'a that?" she asked, in bewilderment.

"Who know, maybe for make it easier for catch fish," Dink said, sucking his teeth.

"You think Bro'Bonk really heard something like that?"

Boo shrugged. "Might've. Might've not. Could be Old Pop Jaeger's corn liquor talking. Don't hardly matter, neither way. Papa'Budi say that flood-talk come up every ten-twenty year or so, since he been sisa-size, and nothing ever come of it."

"Grandpa don't believe it none?"

"Papa' Budi say the Jackson been raising a crop of new fool every year, all'a way back before the Big House burned, and the ones coming up now ain't no different," Boo answered, settling back down under his hat for one last bit of sleep before the call back to work. "Him say you listen at Jackson talk, they be done get you' wagon bog down in the first turn in the road, for sure. That what him say."

OTHERS ON YELESAW NECK were not so dismissive.

By the time Yally had gotten back to the Bigyard at Goat Hill, Lam Jackson and his blacktail mare had already come and gone, off to the other settlements down the River Road. Meantime the word had fanned out from Lam and his father and his brother, Dokie—before them, behind, and on all sides—like a crowflock spreading out across the pale-autumn sky. There was a great coming and going all up and down Yelesaw Neck all the rest of the afternoon, what with the walking from house to house to make certain everyone had gotten the news, and gotten it right, and then the going back again to determine if might maybe something fresh had been heard since the last visit, and then someone new showing up from out of the fields or the hunt-woods or fish-creek or up from their garden who hadn't yet heard anything at all, so that they had to double back and start the process all over again. Between all the dissemination and confirmation and re-evaluation going on, the flooding of the river was the main dish in every kitchen on every supper table on Yelesaw Neck by nightfall, with little appetite for anything else.

In every kitchen and at every supper table on the Neck except Mama Kinlaw's, of course. There, no talk about the whitefolks' flood was allowed. Not in Mama's kitchen. Not in Mama's yard. Not in the vicitinity of Mama's house or, most especially, not in Mama's presence.

It was a house like almost every house on Goat Hill: one large bigroom where all the common living was done, including the cooking and the eating; a stone fireplace to the front and an iron cookstove to the back; the main room decorated in every available space with jars and cans of bright flowers from Mama's flower gardens; one bedroom to one side where Papa and Mama slept, the only covering over the entrance a white sheet-curtain hung from the sill in the summer, a colored quilt in the winter; two more smaller bedrooms to the other side, one for the boys and the other for the girls; a privy and a food storage shed just out back away from the porch, but still considered part of the house. In this house, Bo and Ula Kinlaw had brought eight children into the world: Lusi and Yito and Dink, all married and moved out now, Eshy and Mookie and Yally, still at home, one boy child—Owo—who had never seen the light of his first day, plus a girl baby—Pakky—who had not lived to see her first birthday, both of whom were buried out in the family graveplot at Goat Hill. Papa had built the house with his own two hands and the help of the other men on the Hill and on the first day they had moved in, he had put his old boyhood shotgun up above the inside of the front door. But it was Mama's house, with Mama's spirit and Mama's rules, and this night it was her rule that there be no conversation about the news Bonk Jackson and his boys had brought back from cross'oba-the-river.

They ate their evening supper in a deliberate and artificial calm. Papa and Mama passed back and forth the kind of uninteresting talk that grown folks did when they knew that children were around and listening but didn't mind them hearing;

Papa about where the best hunting and fishing might be found as
soon as the work in the ricefields was done; Mama about the
patching needed on the back of the house roof and the side of the
storage shed so that the fall weather wouldn't take hold, and
reminding Papa of the promise he had made last spring to take
out that stump so there would be room to expand the potato bank,
all added to other needed chores around the house and yard that
came to her mind that would put any hunting or fishing far down
deep on the list of things to do. Of the news of the lake-flooding,
nothing was said.

Yally fretted over how to bring it up. There was no use trying to
to get Mookie to raise the subject. Yally's next-oldest brother was
eating his supper with his usual thoughtful seriousness, thick brows
furrowed down over his heavy-lidded eyes, seemingly deep in study
over things apparent to no-one else, speaking when spoken to in a
way that assured that, yes, he had been listening to everything that
was being said, but with his mind in another world all at the same
time.

*A natural two-head boy we got living in this house with we,* Yally
thought, not for the first time. *One head in this world, t'other in the
next.* He was Mama's heart, and the only one of the children who
could ignore Mama's dictums with impunity. But while Mookie
might up and ask about the watercoming at any time, it would be a
time of his own choosing, and not by any goading Yally could
conjure.

Meanwhile Eshy—who was always game to try anything once,
and twice or more, if she thought she could get by with it—had
already gotten her marching orders from Mama, without any
confusion to them, as she had told Yally that afternoon. Eshy and
Mama had been in the back yard doing the wash when Lam
Jackson had galloped into the yard like a pack of niggerdogs was
chasing him, starting in immediate on his great news, going on
and on about the river-damming and the watercoming, so
excitable and fast that at first Eshy had no idea what he was saying.
Mama had stopped him with a hard stare and a fist propped on
one hip.

"I ain't 'member slepting with you last night, Brother Jackson,"
she told him, and before he could stop and correct himself, she
added, tartly, "I ain't know what pass for manners over to
Jacksontown, but here on the Hill, we general' starts off with a
greeting when we see's folks first-off in the day."

Lam Jackson had stammered an apology and a belated

greeting, but before he could finish, Mama had broken in again, saying, "—and menfolk takes they hats off when speaking with 'uman-kind on *this* hill, 'lessen they thinking they ain't speaking with no lady—" causing Lam to jerk off his hat and crumple it tight to his chest and apologize some more. By that time, Mama had counseled Lam Jackson on talking to grown folk while on horseback, so he had gotten off his horse and now, thoroughly mollified, he went back over his news, slow and understandable this time. Mama listened politely without comment and when he was finished, she asked him how his mother and father were doing, and his grandmother and several aunts and uncles, as well, and other assorted Jackson family folk, and then into the Sheffield clan, his mother's people, and while she was getting the information about their well-being, she sent Eshy back into the house to fetch a jar of okra-and-tomatoes because she knew Grandma Sheffield was partial to them. She then thanked Lam Jackson for his news and sent him on his way with the vegetable jar tucked down deep into his overalls pocket. After Lam had gone— somewhat disappointed that his news had not caused a greater reaction at the Kinlaw house and hoping he would have better luck across the rest of Goat Hill—Eshy had asked her mother if she thought the Jacksons were right, and the water was coming for-true. Without missing a beat, as Eshy later told it, Mama had given her daughter back a withering stare and answered, "The water coming when you go out to the pump and fetch it in that bucket like I done already tol'ded you for do." And Eshy, who liked to say about herself that Bo and Ula Kinlaw's fourth child might have been fool but weren't no fool, got the message and went for the water, and did not press the point.

"Why you reckon Mama ain't want for talk about the flooding?" Yally had asked her sister.

Eshy had shrugged.

"Who know?" she had said. "You know Mama. Maybe she thinking the whitefolk done learned root and fixing to hoodoo it up."

And that, of course, had settled the question. Mama had a well-known aversion to all things root-work and hoodoo, regardless of whether whitefolks were involved in it or not. It was the Kinlaw household's deepest and oldest taboo.

Now at the supper table, with Mookie and Eshy no help, and no reason to believe she'd be successful in broaching the subject herself, Yally figured that she would have to get Papa away from the house—certainly away from Mama—to get his opinion about the flood-news and whether it should be taken seriously.

She did not have to wait that long.

Towards the end of supper, after he had searched his plate over and could find nothing else interesting in it, Papa pushed himself a little bit away from the table, found his pipe in his shirt pocket, sucked on it a bit to clear out any blockage, and while he was tamping down a fill of tobacco into the bowl with his index finger, asked Mama if she thought she might need anything from over to Jaeger's Store right soon.

"Might," Mama answered, without looking up from her plate. "When you fixing for go?"

"Tomorrow early, I reckon."

Mama had been sopping up the last of her chicken gravy with a piece of cornbread, but now she paused and looked up at Papa. "Y'all done finish with them canal that quick?" she asked. "I thought all that bottom end got tore'd up in that last bad rain."

"It did. But it don't look like we got hardly the board-lumber we fixing to need for patch it all."

"Mens." Mama said the word as she would about a barely-tolerated burden, sucking her teeth as she did. "Y'all been over that river ten time, or more, since the summer, and ain't think to get no lumber when you gone. Must be something cross-over to that Jaeger's y'all crave that y'all ain't getting over here, you got for keep making trip over there."

Papa gave a noncommital shrug, wisely deciding not to speak to Mama's last accusation, which he knew had no seriousness to it.

"Thought we had enough, but them bank tore-down more than it look, to the first. And the rest'a the work down there going faster than we thought. Papa'Budi say, iffen it go tomorrow morning like it done today, he won't work much past noon. Which-in-while, look like we's getting a little low on patch-tar, too. Might have enough for the canal, but iffen you want me for patch all the rooftop, too, we'ga need some more."

"*Everybody's* done low on patch-tar?" Mama said. "You can't borry none from nobody's else?" Her brows had begun to furrow together in a slight frown as it began to dawn over her what might be the real purpose of the trip across to Jaeger's.

"Well, you know you can't just stop at no Yelesaw house and ask for something and get it and go. I reckon I could 'quire around, but 'time I ride all over the Neck doing all that asking, and sit for coffee and hear all t'other talk what folk got for talk

about, and have to come back from down the road when they call
me back 'cause they forgot the most important thing they had for
tell me, well, after all that riding and talking and talking and
riding, it be done flooded-up all inside the house and barn and we
and the mule all be sleeping in boat." When Mama stiffened and
her head jerked up at the word "flood," full-alert now, he added, as
if as an afterthought, "Flooding from the winter rain, what I mean
for say. Iffen I don't patch-up them roof with some tar, like you
want me to. Not flooding from nothing else. What I mean.
Anyways," he went on as he began to fish around in his pockets for
his matches, "since we's got around to talking about *flooding*—" he
drew the word out while deliberately refusing to look across at
Mama, who was glaring at him to beat Cuffy's goat—"whiles I'm
over to Jaeger's, I suppose I could ask and see if old Bonk really
heard any news over there, or no."

He found his matches finally and, still ignoring Mama's fierce
look, pulled one out, struck it effortlessly with the nail of his
thumb, and sucked the fire down into his pipe. Mama watched his
actions through narrowed eyes, sorting out her options. If she
chastised her husband for bringing up the subject of the flooding,
he would almost certainly ask her why it couldn't be talked
about—knowing well how Bo Kinlaw's mind worked—and then
the subject would be out full-out around the table, and no putting
it back in the pot. And if she got up from the table in protest and
left the room, that would be the signal for a talk on why she had
left, and that would be the opening for the rest of the family to
talk about the whitefolks' flooding. Blocked on two sides, she cut
her losses and stayed at the table, lowering her eyes and chewing
on her sop-bread in silence, glowering, but keeping her thoughts
to herself. When Papa reminded her that she hadn't told him if
she wanted anything from across-the-river, she gave him back only
a noncommittal grunt, and said nothing more.

THEY WERE STILL talking about the Jacksons' news in the
ricefields and all over Goat Hill the next day, but after the initial
excitement, concerns began to level off. All of the older
Manigaults had been hearing talk of river-damming or creek-
diversion or canal-digging or some other sort of whitefolks'
watercoming most of their lives, none of which had ended with any
more water than you could drink out of a tin cup. This one
sounded no different than the rest. And after all, it was reckoned,
it *was* Bonk Jackson who had originally heard the news and sent it

out, and who knows what it was that old Éxpress had actually heard, and gotten tangled and tumble-up in the river-crossing coming back over and the hard horse-riding afterwards.

Yally spent the day listening to the course the talk took as it crisscrossed the Bigyard, carried by the various family members running errands or visiting back and forth or stopping on their way to and from the fields. By midmorning, skepticism began to catch up with deep concern, finally overcoming it sometime just after dinner, and by late afternoon, the water-talk was running neck and neck with stories about other messages the Jackson clan had famously gotten wrong, going all the way back to the family's days as horse hands back at old Bethelia.

Yally knew that opinion on the Hill could just as swiftly switch back again to deep worry by the receipt of more news on the subject, or even on a whim, but she was comforted by something Cu'n Boo passed on about a story Grandpa Budi had told the men out on the field the day before. It was about a time—Grandpa and Grandma had just jumped broom, Boo believed Grandpa had said—when the whitefolks said they were planning to dig a diversion spillway from the Sugaree out to the sinklands towards Sandy Station to the west, to try to keep the periodic Sugaree floodwaters from inundating Cashville downriver.

"Papa'Budi say the talk got so bad, a nigger from over to Sandy Station built a boat in he yard, waiting for the water to come," Cu'n Boo had said. "Sit on he porch every evening with two or three fishpoles, waiting. Finally stopped putting out crop or fixing things up, him figure there ain't no use iffen they going underwater. The boat stay there in that yard so long, Papa'Budi say the chicken take to sleeping in it, 'til the nigger' wife up and turn it to a roost. Ain't no spillway never got itself builded, ain't no flooding never get out to Sandy Station, and eventual, the county take that nigger' land for taxes, and him had for move him family into St. Paul and take work out to the pulp mill."

"Papa'Budi don't think ain't fixing to be no flooding?" Yally had asked her cousin.

Boo had pursed his mouth and shook his head. "No, him say all that dam-up-the-river talk ain't nothing but a old whitefolk' trick, trying to bumbooloo peoples offen they land. Him say the only water coming is the tear in them niggers' eyes what take up and break camp, when they find they done been t'ief outten sickle-n'-sand."

PAPA STAYED AWAY ALL DAY across the river at Jaeger's, and Yally hung around the house for as long as she could stand it, waiting for him with a growing restlessness and concern.

After dinner she wandered across the sprawling sandy yard that connected all of the houses on Goat Hill, still keeping an eye out on the wagonpath on the far side that led in from the River Road and the cable-crossing, looking for Bay-say's mottled muzzle to appear pulling Papa in the wagon. She walked up on a collection of her girl-cousins doing a clapchant circle-dance under a chinaberry tree, and they called for her to join in. She stepped in for a moment, but her mind was not in it, and she mis-jumped more times than was her usual practice, and so soon walked away. She followed sounds of laughter and shouting further down the Bigyard and found some of the older boys and younger men holding wrestle-matches down near a stock pen, many of them perched up on the top of the pen railings, sweating, grinning, legs dangling, most with their shirts off, enjoying the late fall warmth and their half-day reprieve from the fields. Boo and Mookie were there joining in the wrestling, as well as her oldest brother, Yee. Dink was off to one side, lounging against the pen rail, watching, but not taking part. No-one ever wanted to wrestle with Dinky. He was narrow-built, like the Kinlaws, but had the big hands of the Manigaults, enormous hands, hands the size of a spread-out palmetto frond, that you never wanted to grip you, the fingers so powerful that more than once, Yally had seen him put his palm down on a small watermelon, wrap his fingers around it, and lift it straight up, without slip or strain, and seemingly with no effort at all. Once Dink had his fingers around you in a wrestle-match, it was all over, and so he rarely got the chance to wrestle on the Hill.

Yally went over to stand next to Dink, and instantly regretted it. He was still working on his keeshee-man. He stopped carving on it as she walked up, regarded it for a moment, and then held it up and pushed it towards her face, the figure's hollowed eyes staring directly into hers. She winced and ducked her head and put up her open palm up to ward it off. "Don't do that," she said, turning her face away.

"S-something s-scary, inna?" Dink asked. He put the stick-man up against the fencepost and began gouging the point of his knife into one of its eyes to make it larger. "I'm making it for Eet," he said. "She say a hag been coming 'round the house every night, t-tryin' for ride the baby. I be done finished it 'fore the evening. I got me two white pebble, I'm'a paste in the socket-hole, here, when I'm done. Then I'm'a stick it on the bedroom sill and put a candle next to it, so's that old hag be done see he shiny eye and won't come in the house."

"Well, I ain't need no scaring," Yally said from behind her hand. "I ain't no hag."

Satisfied with the result he'd gotten, Dink shrugged. "Iffen you ain't no hag, ain't nothing for you be scare-over, then," he said, and went back to his carving.

There was a flaw in her brother's logic, of course, but before Yally could figure it Boo was coming over from the wrestling crowd, mud-streaked and sweating, pulling his shirt back on. The two cousins were inseparable and had been that way since they'd been sand-babies and had squalled—Dink—or sulked—Boo— when they were forced to be out of each other's presence. Whatever they did—working, hunting, swimming, or courting— they did together. Cu'n Boo became so frequent a presence around the Kinlaw household while the two were growing up that he had a regular place at the supper table, and many was the evening when Uncle Ya or Aunt Too had to send for him to remind him he had his own home and was wanted at it, just so they wouldn't forget how he looked. Papa sometimes called Dink and Boo Crow and Crow'brother, but seemed to switch the two names between them randomly. When Yally asked him about the names one time, he explained that it came from a rope-jump song he used to hear his sisters and girl-cousins sing back at the Kinlaw home across the river:

> *Here come Crow*
> *Here come he brother*
> *Don't see one*
> *Without which t'other*

And then there was the night, part of the Kinlaw family legend now, when Mama, distracted over something or other, had ordered the nephew, Boo, off to bed while sending her own child, Dinky, "home" to his "own parents." Cu'n Boo, of course, had been delighted and gone immediately to the bedroom, but Dink had stood before Mama, puzzled-up, until Mama had realized her error and told him that he had brought the confusion on his own self for not growing tall as a proper Manigault man ought. When Papa, from the table, had inserted that actually Dinky was not a Manigault man at all but a Kinlaw, Mama had just propped her fists on her hips and turned away with her head raised in triumph as if, in fact, that had been her point all along.

The old folks had all thought that Dink and Cu'n Boo would grow out of their inseparability and at least abate it, somewhat, upon reaching manhood. They did not. Instead, they had courted and then married two sisters, Ita and Kiya Washington, and now lived in cabins side-by-side, midway between their parents' houses. Eshy always maintained that after their wives went to sleep at night, the two cousins would slip out their respective back doors and into their common barn so they could lay under the same cover in the mule-hay until dawn, they could not stand being out of each other's company overnight.

Now Boo, coming up from the wrestle-match, pointed at Dinky's stick-man. "You see him still wearing he knife out on that piece'a wood, ain't you?" he told Yally, "I done tell'd the boy, he don't need all that carving work for run'way no hag."

Dink kept on carving, ignoring him.

"How?" Yally asked, fascinated and curious, although she did not much care for hag-talk.

"All him need for do," Boo said, wiping the mud from from his face onto his pants and shirt, "is take them same two pebble he putting in for eyes, get 'leven more, and lay them 'cross the bedroom door at night. Everybody's know a hag can't count past twelve. Her get to twelve, she got for stop and start all over again. Her be done stay there all night with the counting, and daylight come, her got for left without tantalizing you. Grandma Risa do that all'a time. That why no hag, they can't cross grandma' doorway."

Making a deep cut alongside the stick-man's side with his knife, Dinky grunted in dissent.

"That don't work unlessen you got you round stone, all'a same size. Finding them more work than carving this-here keeshee. You put any size'a rock in front'a you' door, a hag'll only reckon you just s-s-slack and ain't take t-time for s-sweep."

"You see, ain't you, Cu'n Yally? I does tries and I tries, but c-can't tell that boy, there, n-n-nothing," Cu'n Boo said, mocking Dink's stutter. He was the only one on Yelesaw, or anywhere else, for that matter, who could do that without paying a price.

They chatted for a while at the fence while Yally watched the wrestling, trying to build up interest. Normally she loved to watch the men and boys wrestle, but today her mind was not on it. Instead, her thoughts kept straying back to the wagonpath coming down from the River Road, which was now no longer in her sight, and after a short while she took her leave and returned over the

Bigyard to the house.

To divert herself from wondering why Papa was taking so long
to get back and what news he would fetch when he did, she let her
mind drift. Unshackled, it wandered wide, as usual. She started off
asking herself if Mama was likely to tell her to fix cornbread for
supper and, if so, if there was any crackling left put up in the shed
for the fixings. From there she went on to thinking that if the
crackling was low and with cool weather coming up, a family hog-
butcher would soon be in order. She wondered if any of her
brothers might bring some of the friends to the butchering and
the following feast—not Yay'saw friends, but someone from
cross'oba they might have met on trips over there, not that she was
particularly interested in an oba'dey boy more than a Yay'saw—not
that she was interested in boys at all—it was just that she knew
about every boy on Yelesaw Neck, and even though she would soon
be reaching courting age, none of them had ever seemed to take
any more of an interest in her than she had in them. With no-one
in sight to see what she was doing—she had walked down to the
shed to check on the crackling—she ran her hands around the
shape of her breasts and then lifted them up from the bottom,
bouncing them like bags of rice, to feel their weight. Her breasts
were the only thing about her that had any heft to them, but in the
company of the rest of the women of the extended Manigault
family, she found them woefully lacking, another trait she'd gotten
from the Kinlaw side, across the river. She felt the dampness of the
front of her dress-top from all the walking around in the sun she'd
been doing that morning, and she pulled off her headscarf and
tamped it down beneath her dress to dry off her breasts. Her
thoughts turned to swimming. There was no time for it today, of
course—though she had been doing little all day except marking
minutes while she waited for Papa—and she wondered whether or
not the cold-snap would hold off long enough to allow for one last
visit to the creekpond behind the house, tomorrows, maybe, if she
borrowed somebody's mule to ride down to the ricefields with
dinner instead of walking, and so could get herself back sooner.
She imagined herself stripping to her drawers and slipping into
the cool black-green of the pondwaters, holding her breath and
dropping deep under the surface, so that the sunlight only passed
in dim shafts around her, and swimming that way along
underwater paths without coming up for air, swimming and
swimming and swimming, sleek and black as a mud-eel, through
acres of watery gardens, swimming all the way into the creekmouth

and then out to the junction with the river and then down the
river to the sea—which she had never seen—and all the way under
the ocean back to the old peoples' home, which some of the
saltwater peoples was supposed to had done, back in the slavery-
times, back home to them, but a foreign land to her, a strange
land under strange stars and unknown trees, an orange-green
land, smelling of cinammon and nutmeg and benne, and other
sweet spices...

But always, no matter how hard she tried to avoid it, her
thoughts always returned to Papa and his errand across the river.

Toward the latening of the afternoon, to settle her mind and
keep her eye on the wagonpath out to the road as well, she found
many chores to do outside, around the house. The porch needed
sweeping and the biddies feeding and the yard looked as if it could
use a good hoeing, although you could hardly see a single tuft of
grass poking up from out of the sand. Then it was the quilts that
asked for shaking and waterbuckets filling and by that time the
porch had got all sandy again from her going in and out of the
house filling various chores. Mookie came in back from messing
with the cousins out on the yard, and sat on the back steps for a bit
to talk and keep her company as she took in the wash off of the
line, but only for a bit, and when he went inside, she was alone
again. The sun had dropped behind the trees and it was growing
colder and darker, but still Papa had not come. Finally Eshy came
out on the porch to tell Yally that Mama was calling her for help
with supper, and so at last she went inside.

It was not long afterwards that she heard the clop of Bay-say's
hooves and the wagon pulling around the back, but she was deep
into the supper fixings, and with Mama around, she did not dare
break away to rush outside. She fiddled around with the pot of
peas, growing increasingly anxious until Papa came in, hanging his
coat up on the peg and washing his face and hands in the bucket
on the back steps and saying only *evening* and *is supper ready yet* and
nothing about the news from Jaeger's. They all sat down to supper,
waiting for Papa to speak, but he was uncommonly quiet. Mama
asked him nothing, not even about the board-lumber or the pitch-
tar or any of the list of things he was supposed to have fetched for
her. Yally passed the time in a state of growing nervousness, unable
to properly digest her food, and wanting to chunk something at
Eshy, who was chattering away to Mookie about something or
other, and at Mookie, who was seeming to encourage Eshy,
although he was actually saying nothing in return, only nodding

now and then through thoughtful chews of his food. Both of them were certainly wondering about what Papa had to say as much as Yally was, and it annoyed her that they weren't making a show of it so that Papa would see, and sympathize, and let it out. Just about the time Yally thought she was going to burst, Papa suddenly spoke up, without any warning. "Well," he said, "it looken like what Bonk Jackson say been for-true."

Eshy ceased her talking in mid-sentence, and everyone at the table looked up quick. Yally and Eshy exchanged wide-eyed glances while Mookie cocked his head to the side, blinked his eyes, and stopped chewing on his last piece of sidemeat, momentarily. Mama stared straight across the table at Papa, her eyes beginning to squint, her first, usual sign of annoyancement.

Yally felt that a great pit had opened up in the bottom of her stomach, and everything that had been inside there was sliding out.

"It for-true what Bonk Jackson saying about the flood?" she asked her father.

"If you mean is it for-true, that what Bonk Jackson heard over to Jaeger's, yep, that's true" Papa answered, nodding as he poked between his teeth with a straw he had set aside for just that purpose. "That's all they talking-'bout over to Jaeger's today, the whitefolk planning on damming up the river and making them a lake. But that don't mean that what they all talking about got to be for-true—"

He had not actually gotten the "for-true" part out but was only getting ready to say it when Mama said "Stop" in a voice that was low but commanding, dropping the meaty flat of her hand down on the table as she did, so that the plates and pots and utensils jumped, and Papa's tin cup, which was empty, turned on its side. The children jumped, too, they had been paying such attention to Papa and his news, and Mama's outburst had come so sudden and unexpected. They all turned from Papa to look at her.

"I don't want to hear another word about what no whitefolk is planning," Mama said evenly, still not raising her voice, the muscles of her jaw working in and out as she said it, even though she barely opened her mouth. "Not what they's planning in Cashville. Not what they's planning in St. Paul. Not what they's planning for Yelesaw, and not what they's planning 'bout no goddamn river. Not at my table. Not in my house. I done tol'ded all y'all that already."

Papa looked back across the table at her, his eyes wided up a little bit, but his face otherwise expressionless. His mouth was still open from the uncompleted sentence he had been working on. He started to say something, but before he could, Mama held up her palm towards him. "Not another word, Ben Kinlaw," she said. "Not one." He closed his mouth, abruptly, without saying anything.

Mama stood up slowly and deliberately from the table. She was almost the same height as Papa when they both were standing, and she towered over him while he was sitting down. She also had him by several pounds, and when she stood like she was standing now, shoulders back and thick legs planted, arms held out from her sides, fists beginning to ball up, she looked like she could take any man in a scrap. Yally wondered what might be the outcome if her parents ever had a serious tussle, not a play-play one, when Mama was full-out angry.

They didn't tussle tonight. Instead, Mama turned on her bare heels and left the table, walking across the bigroom to the sound of her footsteps, disappearing behind the curtain-door into her bedroom, the hanging cloth snapping into place behind her with a shimmy of finality.

For a moment, the table was silent. Finally Papa, with a glance at the bedroom doorway, leaned forward, elbows on the table, paused for a moment to look around at his children, and then asked in a low voice, "What y'all reckon you' Mama would'a done-done iffen I'd'a said me another word?"

Yally stifled an explosive laugh by clamping her two hands over her mouth, Mookie gave a little chuckle and went back to chewing on his sidemeat, and Eshy leaned over the table towards Papa and answered, as low as Papa had asked his question, "Grab you by you' ear and take you out back and thrash you good."

Papa drew his mouth down and nodded his head in assent a couple of times. "That what I figure," he said. "That why I ain't say no other word." He pushed his chair back and stood up from the table. "I reckon I'll got out on the porch a bit and catch the cool air," he said. "Seem like it done'd got a little *hotted-up* in here, with all y'all Yay'saw folk up in this house."

Eshy mouthed a silent "it ain't no 'we'" and rolled her eyes toward their parents' bedroom as Papa walked out the front door.

THE REST OF THE EVENING passed peaceable enough, largely because Mama did not come out again from the bedroom, and Papa stayed outside. After the cleanup of the supper things, Yally slipped out the front door, hoping to take the opportunity to quiz

her father in private on the flood-news, but he had disappeared
from the porch and there was no sight of him out in the dark of
the yard, though she looked hard all over for the glow from his
pipe. She walked around the house to the back and found Eshy
keeping company with Mookie, who was chopping logs for
tomorrow's morning fire, his axe rising and falling in steady
rhythm by the light of the kerosene lamp hung from the back
porch hook. Neither Eshy nor Mookie had seen any sign of Papa,
and so there was no telling where he'd gotten to. Yally went back
in and fetched her coat, and Eshy's. As soon as the sun had gone
down that evening, the temperature had dropped. The last warm
times of autumn were over.

The two sisters sat on the back steps in the cool night,
watching their brother at the woodpile, now and then calling out
suggestions on which block to go at next, or how best to line the
next axe stroke. Mookie smiled back at them, and otherwise
generally paid their suggestions no attention, except now and then
to aim the axe in such a way that the log flew at their feet, making
them heist their legs or scramble off the steps to keep from getting
hit. Yally and Eshy talked for a while about whether Mama would
have really boxed Papa if he'd kept on talking, and what he would
have done if she had, but then drifted, like circling moths, back to
the watercoming. But having exhausted all their thoughts on the
subject over the last day and a half, that well quickly dried up, until
the only sound coming from the back yard was the chop of
Mookie's axe biting into the wood-blocks, and the thump of the
splitwood chunks as they flew off and hit along the sandy ground.

Across the yard through the latticed shadows of the
scuppernong arbor, Yally could just see the lights of Grandpa
Budi's house. Someone over there was outside, singing. It was
either Sister Orry or Big Soo, Mama's other sister, but the two
women's voices were so alike from that distance, deep and mellow-
rich, she could not tell which one it was. Mostly it was just the
melody and the sound of the voice that drifted over. Every once in
a while, she could recognize a word or two of the song as they
passed by and through her, not because they had been sung
louder or more distinct, but through some trick of the air and
wind. They were saltwater words, so farback that Yally could not
recognize any of them, or figure their meaning. But from its pitch
she knew it was a mourning song, of loss and leaving. After a while,
she caught enough of the melody that she could hum along. Now
and then, in accompaniment to the song, came the soft tinkling of

Grandpa's bottle-tree, the tree making its gentle music to entice any trespassing spirits into its bottles, where it could trap them and hold them for Grandpa to dispose. Yally willed her mind in that direction, hoping the tree would trap any bad dreams that were lurking around in the night, waiting for her to go to sleep.

After enough wood had been chopped the three of them still did not go back inside, but with nothing else to do, stayed out on the back porch to tell haunt stories. Mookie told the most interesting, with intricate plots and personalities and rich descriptions of spooky woods and bogs ground-holes from deep out of the pockets of his active imagination, but Eshy's were always by far the scariest. Yally stayed outside even when her sister started on the Pennyman, the copper-eyed gafa who wandered the nighttime Yelesaw fields and woods, catching young girl children who strayed too far from their doors. The Pennyman was Eshy's favorite but Yally's particular horror, and she knew it would be sure to give her bad dreams, but she toughed it out, huddling next to Mookie on the bottom step, squeezing her brother around the shoulders or waist until he grunted, or hiding her head under his coat-flap at the scariest parts. Nothing seemed to be able to scare either Mookie or Eshy, and they told their stories deep into the night as Yally leaned for comfort, alternately, from the one who wasn't currently telling the tale, drawing her knees up to her chest and wrapping her arms around them, shivering inside her coat, until the sound of the woodbugs across the yard gradually died out, and the lamp hung from the peg on the outside wall began to flicker for want of kerosene, and whoever had been singing over to Grandpa Budi's house stopped, finally, and went inside.

THE APPEAL TO THE BOTTLE-TREE did not work. Yally did dream that night, a particularly bad one with the Pennyman chasing her through a labyrinth of cornfields that turned into pig troughs and then to work-sheds, and so she was glad when she felt Eshy's finger poking her pointedly in her side to wake her up, even though it was still the middle of the night, and the room was ink-dark.

She sat up in her pallet and tried to get her bearings.

For a moment she could not see a thing, not even her sister. She reached across and patted around on Eshy's pallet, but it was empty.

"Esh?" she said in a low voice.

A low "shush" came from the direction of the curtain-door and so Yally said nothing more, but wrapped one of her quilts around herself and crawled over on her hands and knees to squat down next to her sister, close enough to see Eshy turn and put a hushing finger to her lips.

Papa and Mama were up and conversating. From across the house, they could hear movement and low talking from their parents' room. For a moment Yally could make out little of the words but then Mama, raising her voice, said something distinctly about "them goddamn crackers," and then something that sounded like "fishing."

They did not hear Papa's reply, but it must have rubbed Mama the wrong way against her pelt, because they heard the pound of her bare feet on the floorboards as she stalked out of the bedroom and into the bigroom.

Papa followed behind her, and now they could hear him plain and distinct, but still in low tones. "I ain't think it for no fishing."

"What it for, then?" Mama shot back, as if she were still trying to keep her voice down, but the words were not cooperating, and were raising in volume of their own accord.

Papa answered something that sounded to Yally like "for the 'lectriclight," though she figured at once she must have heard it wrong. The closest 'lectriclights she knew of were all the way to Cashville, and she could not fathom why her parents would be arguing over something the folks were doing down in Cashville so late in the night, especially with such worriation going on about the whitefolks' flood. She wondered if Papa had told her he was taking off early for the fall fish-trip without getting all the after-harvest chores done. That would get Mama's fur up, Yally knew.

Whatever Papa had said, Mama must have misunderstood it, too, but something about it set her off and she shrieked out, not trying to make any effort now to keep her voice low any more. "The *what*?!" she shouted.

They heard movement from the boys' bedroom next to theirs. Mookie slept as hard as any of the Kinlaw children, but Mama's last words had awaken even him.

Papa must have known that they were making too much noise, and his voice dropped again, and they could hear him talking for a bit, as if he were explaining something. His voice receded to a low hum as the sound of their footsteps receded back to the bedroom.

The quiet lasted only for a moment.

Suddenly there was a slamming sound from the direction of their parents' room, and the house shook, like somebody had either stomped on the floorboards, hard, or had kicked their foot against the wall. Something crashed on the floor, either in protest or because it had been thrown, and then came a long string of Mama's cursing. Mama could curse fiercely, artfully, awfully, when she got her temper really up, the words flowing out in a hard stream like a mule pissing, making up phrases as she went along if the regular ones didn't measure up to the heat of her thoughts. Papa must have said something about not disturbing the children, because Mama shouted back at him, the words plain and loud, even coming from all the way out of their bedroom, "The hell with that! They'ga get they disturbements soon-enough when they gots for swim out the back door!" And then she went back to cursing and either kicking at the wall or stomping the floor with her foot again. The house shook each time. Eshy said "Oooo-*weeee!*" under her breath and grabbed a chunk of Yally's thigh with her fingernails until Yally slapped her hand to make her let go.

"What the hell good the 'lectriclight ga' do if we up under the goddamn water?" Mama was shouting. "See the eel?" She said the word 'lectriclight plain enough this time, so that there was no doubt this was one of the things they were fussing over, as well as the whitefolks' flood, but what Mama had said made no sense, and for a moment Yally thought that her mother might have gotten so angry-up, she was beginning to talk out of her head. She hoped that Mama wouldn't go into a fit and get herself sick again.

Whatever Bo Kinlaw had to answer to his wife's outburst, the girls did not hear, but either it satisfied Mama for the moment, or else she had blown out all the hot steam from her spout she intended for that night, and wanted no more venting. The house grew gradually quieter until, finally, no sound of voices or movement came from their parents' bedroom at all, and the only thing the girls could hear was a low hoot of an owl passing by outside.

"Mama something pissed, inna?" Yally said in a low whisper as they made their way back in the dark to their pallets.

"Pissed, sure-enough," Eshy answered, with a giggle. "I been waiting for her to box Papa, good."

"You hear when they been talking 'bout the 'lectrictlight? What they been talking 'bout the 'lectriclight for? You reckon Papa bought some 'lectriclightbulb over to Jaeger's? You think that what Mama been fussing 'bout?"

She could see the dismissive look flash over Eshy's face, even in the dimness of the bedroom.

"You does get the fool in you late at night, sure-enough," she said. "Jaeger's don't even sell no 'lectriclightbulb, and what Papa ga' buy'em for, iffen they did? Put'em on the roof and wait for lightning for hit?" There was a pause as Eshy thought it over, and her tone went thoughtful. "It had something for do with the flood," she said, almost to herself. "But hang if I can figure what." Yally did not offer any more theories, as she didn't have any more. Eshy laid down on her pallet and pulled her quilts up to her shoulders, settling down as if to go to sleep. "Anyways," she said, "I ain't think it ga'happen."

"What? The flood?"

Eshy sucked her teeth.

"No, ass, 'lectriclight for the hog pen. *Yes*, the flood. Ain't no way whitefolk fixing to raise no flood."

"Why you think?" Yally asked, hopefully.

Eshy raised up on one elbow. "Come on. Think about it, Ya'y," she said. "Lam'jackson say they been talking about—what?—flooding all the Basinbottom. You know how many whitefolk live out through there, how many farms and all? Iffen it been nothing but niggers out in the Basin or they been talking'bout onliest the Neck—" here she paused and sucked her teeth again "—shit, they'd flush all the Basinbottom nigger out in a hot minute, and wouldn't add a mourning tear to the water, and iffen it been just Yay'saw, them'd'a throw them a Four-to-the-July barbecue-and-holler party for celebrate getting rid'a we. But all them buckra, all they cousin and auntie and such? Them sure-enough ain't fixing to do that to they own, and you knows that. Grandpa right. Ain't no water coming. I ain't care how much news the Jacksons does carry, or what Papa hear 'cross to Jaeger's. Ain't fixing to be no water. Go-on to sleep. You be done wake up dry as you laid down."

It took Yally much longer to go to sleep than Eshy. She listened to her sister's deep breathing for the longest, trying to hold onto the anxiety of the last two days. She did not want to give it up so quickly, for fear she would be caught unawares if the water actually was coming. But finally she had to concede that Eshy's argument was the best she had heard against the whitefolks' flooding, better, even, than anything Grandpa had said. She laid her head down on the pallet, and slept comfortable and undisturbed by anything, neither from within herself or from the house surrounding, for the rest of the night.

UP AND DOWN the River Road the next day, and back into the sand-lanes spreading out their long fingers across Yelesaw Neck from the settlements down to the ricefields, they talked about Bonk Jackson's news about the damming of the river and the coming of the lake, and what might come of it, and what could be done. As Yally had thought, after a brief turn to skepticism, the majority opinion moved back to belief that there might be some truth to the water-talk this time. There were many on the Neck who worked in cabin and yard and field with eyes darting back and forth between the river and the Swamp and the sky, as if they were afraid the floodwaters were already on their way and would roar out over them from one direction or the other, suddenlike, without warning, and overwhelm them before they could scramble to higher ground. As if there was any higher ground on Yelesaw Neck, and not just low ground and lower.

They did not have long just to talk about flood, however. Before a good two days had passed Sister Orry up and died quite sudden, and after that, there was a whole new set of circumstances to add to the conversation.

# 2

## The Man What Come Looking For Orry

*(Fall, 1935)*

B y the time the wagons started arriving for the first night of
the setting-up it had begun to rain—a cold, cruel slashing
rain—a gray-black winter-coming-on type-of-rain—a rain
that had no respect for the mourners or the mourning and did not
care that folks had to come from all ends of Yelesaw Neck—and a
few even from cross'oba-the-river, as well—to pay their propers at
Budi Manigault's house.

The storm kept up hard-steady for the next three days and
nights. By the morning of the funeral day, the ground could take
no more. In the low spots between the trees in the surrounding
woods, in the bare fields behind the settlements, and in the
sunken parts of the settlement yards, running creeks had emerged
where none had been before, and strings of newly-formed ponds
had begun connecting into shallow lakes that increasingly
conspired to delay passage or block it altogether. The river side of
the River Road, which dropped in a gradual slope down to the
water, had turned in places into a slick running slough on which
no secure hold could be had, and wagon drivers straying too close
to the shoulder were in danger of having wagon, load, mule and
all slide inexorably down the slope, over the banked edge, and
into the unforgiving water. And you did not want to go into those

waters in these turbulent days, even unencumbered. The Sugaree
had become an angry, writhing eel, humping its back and rising
from its bed in unpredictable bursts, dancing to the groan-song of
cracking timber from tree-limbs whipped back and forth by the
wind and the heavy drop-beat of clods of earth torn from the
banks and disappearing into the dark, rushing river-water.

And still the rain did not pause, or even slow.

Through the afternoon of the funeral day, it rained as if the
sky itself was in torment, and all of Tat'Ogoo and Ná'Yamma's
dark children had taken hammers to the dams of all the water-
fortresses of the sky, loosing angry torrents upon the world. The
rain slammed down in rolling sheets, a hard-rain, a det rain, a wula
wildstorm driven by a wudu wind. Mama'Oya in all her anger and
power, driving off the river and out of the woods and Swamp and
over the land from all sides. Swirling. Slamming. Tugging at
everything loose. Howling past the houses and through the bared
trees and across the open harvest fields, making her main assault
upon the wagon processions passing over to the funeral service.
Raging. Shouting. Spitting shards of ice that spattered white on
the uncovered parts of black faces, digging at the gatherers' eyes
with cold-sharp fingernails as they exited their wagons and hurried
inside the safety of the Sambuhouse.

But here at the doors of the Yay'saws' house of spirits, the
elements of the world were held at bay.

The Sambu would permit neither wind nor rain inside, no
matter how much they beat against the outer planking-wood, or
kicked up sand around the foundation blocks, or drove up under
the eaves or shutters to try to dislodge the boards or tin. This was
no baba-hut or swamptrapper's put-up. Squatdown and steady, the
Sambuhouse had been raised by men who knew board and block
as they knew their own arms and hands, and shaped it as if they
expected it to last as long as the spirits it honored.

Inside the Sambuhouse, the mourners shed their wet coats and
hats and piled them in the back corner with the steam rising off of
them, and the warmth of the stacked-together bodies pushed the
cold away, and in the swaying and the stomping and the singing,
they forgot the storm outside, and all that existed in that other
world beyond the closed praise-house doors.

For most ceremonies and other gatherings at the Sambu, there
was more than enough room left open at the front for ring-
shouting and other movements, but for all the people who
gathered to send Sister Orry to the other side, they had to fill most

of the great hall with all the low-back wooden benches from the
shed. The benches ran from wall to wall, with just enough room
along both sides for folks to stand or pass along, and a wider
center aisle. Long before the funeral services began the benches
were all filled, and like rows of tight-stacked sugarcane, the
mourners began lining up two deep against the side walls and
three or four abreast in the center. The latecomers had to fit
themselves in the back of the hall between the last benches and
the door, leaving room enough only for the great stone fireplace
in the corner, its licking fires adding to the growing warmth of the
packed-in assemblage.

In small groups at either side towards the front the attendant
women stood, younger nifá initiates, spirit-women in training,
identically dressed in floor-length white dresses, with bright yellow
headscarves showing they were yolks not yet out of the egg, ready
with palmetto fans or cloth strips dipped in waterbuckets to cool
off those overcome by the heat or the emotion of the occasion.

To one side of the House near the front, on their own special,
cloth-covered benches, were the crossed-over nifás themselves, the
elder women, also all in white, each with no other jewelry or extra
adornment but a tiny palmetto leaf pinned to her chest, and with
the blood-red headscarves that indicated they had passed the
blood-test, and could practice any branch or aspect of spirit-work
in the community. Chewing on cessieroot and sourbark, nodding
and chatting quietly among themselves, one or two of them getting
up now and then to perform or oversee a task, they were not there
for show, but had many jobs to do today: to run the services, to
supervise the initiates, to line the songs, lead the chants, and set
the clap-tempos with their hands and feet and clucks of their
tongues.

Seated in a woven wicker chair just next to the nifá towards the
middle of the font of the House was Ná'Risa Manigault, dressed in
all white as the other spirit-women, except that her headscarf was
white as well. Ná'Risa was not the eldest nifá on Yelesaw Neck, but
as the eldest one in the Manigault family, it was her privilege to sit
in the place of honor at a Manigault funeral and wear the white
scarf. She perched on the edge of her chair like a swamp-bird on a
tree-limb, a small, sapling-thin woman with slender, rope-muscled
arms and legs and narrow shoulders and chest, surveying the
growing crowd of the Sambuhouse with almond-shaped eyes set
wide-apart over high, sculpted cheekbones that defied her age.
Those who were close enough could smell the sweet-smoke about

her skin and clothes, as if she had been hard at the business of burning special and secret things in the wake of Sister Orry's passing.

Just above Ná'Risa and the other nifá—at the head of the house facing the great gathering—was the elder council, a long row of grave, black men seated in carved ceremonial chairs on a wooden platform raised a few feet above the floor. They were all in whitecotton robes, a few white-kerchiefed, gray beards and gray-wool heads mixed with the few darker-haired, the opposing lines of their pale dress and dark skin contrasted here and there by the gold or silver glint of an earring or the yellow-and-red or bright-blue of necklaced beads. Eyes closing now and again in meditation or prayer, faces drawn and solemn, arms folded over their chests or held in their laps in dignified repose, the wise men of Yelesaw presided, tapping the work-calloused soles of bare feet or the bottoms of their canes on the wear-polished wood platform floor, nodding to the rhythm of the old songs, both removed from and simultaneously an integral part of all that was before them.

In the center of the elders, on the largest chair, sat Budi Manigault, stiff as a stone, his face like a black mask carved out of tree bark. He had just lost his eldest child but you would not know it from the way he was carrying himself this day. Head back, grizzled chin jutted out, lips pulled tight, the only sign of movement from him was a slow, measured blink of his eyes, and the occasional slow turn of his head from side to side as he looked over the crowd. For three days family and friends had tried to cover his great wounds with the balm of their sympathy and love, but he held them back with the fierce stare of his one good eye, so that they finally let him be. But when they thought he was not looking their way, many peered over to see if the mourning-lightning had cracked the trunk of that great pine, seeking out any sign that it would set him a-lean, or even make Big Budi buckle and fall. So far, he had done neither.

From all over the Sambuhouse as they waited for the service to begin, without plan or program to guide their way, but only going as the spirit moved them, they tapped or stomped their feet and patted their hands on their thighs and sent up their songs and shouts to gather like smoke amongst the bare ceiling rafters, keeping their gazes on the open space between the first row of mourners and the elders' raised platform, where all the purpose of their gathering was drawn together. There, where this world met the other, in a plain, pinebox coffin built by Tat'Budi with his own two hands in these last days, on top of a rough sawhorse stand draped over with a white sheet, lay the body of Orry Manigault.

With a maroon scarf tied around her head to bring her favor at the cemetery gates and the palmetto frond at her breast to show her spirit-woman status, she was otherwise wrapped in plain, going-away white and set out like a mandi, a cherished one, which, of course, she was.

On the swept and scrubbed planed-wood floor in front of Orry's casket they had placed all of the various tokens and kaffies and other spirit-charms to be sent with her when she was lowered into her grave...bean necklaces and powder pouches...stick figures with thatches of grey moss for hair and black-smudged knots for eyes...polished stones of certain shapes and hues from off the riverbank or out-the-Swamp...glassbottles of all kinds and colors, some empty, some corked and filled with searched-out dirt or fine-ground sand or secret-mixed liquid...long-waving willow-sticks attached with small seed-rattles, or red ribbons, or tufts of colored bird feathers...scarves knotted in special ways for special signs and purposes; wood-and-bone carvings of all kind; bamboo flutes and tiny gourd banjos...packets of greased leaves wrapped around squares of coldwater cornbread or bacon ends or small cuts of sugarcane, Orry's favorite foods. Just beyond the offerings were set several rows of lighted candles, flames dancing in rhythm with the breath blown by the shouts and stomps, spreading slow puddles of warm wax as if writing messages in secret language at their bases. In a small, cleared space in the midst of the candles, on top of a little table, a single, plain-wood bowl of clear water had been placed in which to detain Sister Orry's spirit for a bit, should it choose to leave too early. They were sending her off in their way, the old way, not the way in which they buried the dead over the river, in the cross-stick Jellyhouses of the oba'deys, but the older, saltwater ways from across wider waters, the ways which the Yay'saw grandparents had taught them in the Quarters, in the days before they walked off the plantation at Bethelia.

YALLY WAS STUCK between Mama and Big Soo on the front bench on the opposite side of the hall from the nifá, but so near to the row of candles that she could feel the flicker of their heat on her ankles. She wished she could have managed to get herself next to Eshy, or else Dink, either of whom would have helped ease the weight of the heavy stone that was pressing down on her heart. Even old solemn, serious Mookie would have been a comfort. But

Mookie was on the other side of Mama, and then Eshy farther down past Papa, and then the rest of the Kinlaw family—Lusi and Yito and Dink and all their spouses and children beyond that—so that Yally could not even catch any of their attention without leaning forward in full view of Ná'Risa or the other spirit-women or the row of elders on their platform above or, fatally, in full view of Mama. So she settled herself back on the bench and tried to close off her wandering mind and concentrate on the services.

The formal portion of the service had now begun, signaled first by a clear, high note from Ná'Risa dropping into an ululation, low and carried so long that it did not seem possible that someone so small of stature could have so much reserve of breath. When Ná'Risa's call trailed off at last, it was followed close-on, first by the nifá women, then joined by the elders on their bench, with a common chant-song, close-eyed and rocking-in-unison, and behind her and to either side Yally could feel the dipping of shoulders and heads begin in reply, as if they were all on the same jugalboard, or sitting in a boat upon gentle-rocking waters. Even the Sambuhouse rafters and the floorboards themselves began to shiver and sway in accompaniment. The singing and the foot-patting and the rhythms of clapping hands and shak'ree gourds stirred her in deep places and she wanted to stand and release all her emotions in a dance, as she knew that others might soon do. But Mama was sitting as stiff and firm in her place on the front bench as Grandpa Budi was up in his, and seeing this, Yally fought hard against her own need for release. Trying to emulate Mama's stony ways, she pushed herself back against the bench and held her shoulders still with hard-crossed arms, slipping off her shoes and rubbing the bare bottoms of her feet back and forth against the floor to allow her pent-up tension to flow out throught the boards. She looked around for something in the hall on which to focus that was not in motion. She found it in her aunt in the casket just across the shouting space in front of her, the only one in the House besides Mama and Papa'Budi who remained still.

Death had either changed Sister Orry or else had opened a close-held veil to reveal something she had long-hidden in life. Her face was dark-gray and waxen, and gone entirely were the laugh lines that had once ever-marked her appearance. Instead, her mouth was boxed and turned-down and tight. Her fingers—so strong in life—were bent at the knuckles, even as her hands were folded across the great expanse of her breasts, as if she had been reaching at the very end but could not quite grasp, and so could not take whatever it was she had tried to fetch with her, and that had been a disappointment. Something in Sister Orry's last moments had troubled her—a promise unkept, a deed undone—and it showed in the last expression that had carved itself into her face. And what that unaccomplished thing had been only she knew, because Sister Orry had passed without saying.

Yally was not especially afraid of the dead—not here, at least, in the big day, with candles blazing and the singing and the music and so many of her people all-around. And in any event, she did not think that her aunt would ever attempt to do her any harm whatever the circumstances, wherever she was and in whatever form she existed. Still, the girl could not look long at Sister Orry's face not ten feet away in the casket, partly because she knew it would give her dreams, but mostly because Sister Orry would not have allowed Yally to stare at her in life, and could hardly be expected to change her opinion on the matter now that she was dead.

She'd had a sense about her, Sister Orry had, as if she could see things happening all around, without ever having to stop what she was doing to take a look. She could be standing over the stove, her back to Yally, stirring a pot of okra-and-'matas—as Yally might be silently envying the width and heft of her aunt's buttocks and wishing her own hips would approach the same—when, with no warning, Sister Orry would say over her shoulder, "Mind them eyes don't get so big on my backside, they pop out and fall into the pot and boil-up like sausage. And wouldn't that be something to serve you' Grandpa for supper." And Yally, caught, would slap her palms over her face in horror and then break into giggles at the thought of two eyes floating in the red-green broth, bobbing, staring up at Grandpa as he fished them out with his spoon.

The images of her aunt began to overwhelm her. Sister Orry in her garden or at the clotheswash tub or stripping vegetables on the porch—always working, even while she talked, her thick forearms tireless, the corded work-muscles kneading in and out—a song or a story always in accompaniment, suddenly breaking out in an overflow of laughing for no reason at all, her lips pulled wide, head back, shoulders and big ninnies shaking. "What-for you come-here for *this* time, biddy-biddy?" Aunt Orry would ask when her niece would come trotting across the yard. It wouldn't matter the hour or the task, her aunt would stop what she was doing and attend to some request Mama had sent Yally with, as if helping other people was her greatest pleasure, her only pleasure, and she had nothing else in all the world to do. Thinking of these things now, with Sister Orry's dead body within reach-and-touching distance, Yally's chest rose and became unbearable with the weight, a sob burst out from her without control, and the tears pooled and overflowed in two streams down her cheeks, leaving wandering stains as they dried on her face.

She tried to lose herself in the singing. That, at least, helped to manage her thoughts and quieted her restlessness. She sang along with all the familiar songs until the gathering began to slip into tunes that she had never heard before—old songs led by the white-beard old men and the gray-locked women—songs with 'gola- and guinea- and mandy-words whose meaning Yally could only guess at, full to overflowing with the memory of days and places she had never seen—restless, roaring oceans and swift black rivers running cool under feathered trees, and vast yellowgrass savannahs stretching up to the sun. At these songs, she could only bob her head and backclap along. But all of them gave her comfort, and her spirits began to lift again.

IT WAS A DRAWN-OUT CEREMONY even for the Sambuhouse, where they were never hurried. Soon the space around Yally grew pleasantly warm, and her ears hummed soft melodies that covered her like a winter quilt, and the bob turned into a nod and her head dipped—until she felt a heavy elbow digging into her ribs.

She looked up to see Big Soo glowering over at her, making a sharp upward gesture with her head. Yally quickly straightened up in response. Aunt Soo was slow-going, sure, but you didn't want to rouse her. And Yally was grateful that it hadn't been Mama who had noticed her dozing off. Mama would have pinched and drawn blood.

The singing ended, and one of the older women got up to tell the tale of Sister Orry's death, though everybody by now, of course, had already heard it many times more than once. No-one knew how long Orry Manigault had been sick because she was a healing-herb woman who medicated her own self without consulting others, and who never complained or talked about her own troubles. Though they lived all around her and saw her every day, no-one had noticed her afflictions. Her step had seemed just as firm as always, her arms as strong, her eyes as bright. There were no signs of sickness leading up to her final days that anyone could remember, even with the great vision of hindsight. The last week of her life she scattered feed to the chickens and leavings to the pigs and sang the clothes out on the line every morning and hummed them back in every evening and spent long hours over her cooking and healing pots, the same as she had always done, as ever as they had known her. But something dropped Orry down low just after dark one silver-moon, sliver-moon night and she went straight to her bed as soon as she had served supper to her sister and father. She did not rise the next morning but lay with a wheezling breath and great fever sweat on her forehead and cheeks. That alarmed Budi Manigault to no end, but by the time he'd sent Soo rushing across the yard to fetch Ná'Risa, it was already too late. Orry Manigault wavered between dark and light after that, her eyes fluttering unfocused, unresponsive to queries and concerns, and never said another mumbling word. She died just before daylight four days later, after being roused by a great fit of bloody coughing. What had hurried her off, no-one could guess.

Her mother, Nana'Keece, was long since crossed over to the other side, and Orry herself had never dropped any children of her own onto the warm earth or even took a man-friend, much less a husband, but she had her two sisters to speak for her on this funeral day. First came Big Soo, halting, stammering at first as she always did at public gatherings, pushing the words out of her mouth as if they were strange things that she were encountering for the first time, but her talk growing smoother and more easy as she went along, her full voice finally filling the House as, even on this sending-off day, she found a story to tell about her older sister to make folks hold their heads to the side and smile through their sorrow. When Soo had finished and sat back down, she seemed far more at peace than she had for many days. Then there was a hush and a holding of breaths as Ula Kinlaw arose. Sus'Ula had not spoken in the Sambu in many years, since she'd been a teenaged girl, in fact, and more than a few prepared to hear a talk for the ages over a sister who was the only mother she had ever known. But she only took a step or two to the casket, put her hand on Sister Orry's forehead, paused for a long moment, and then said, simply, "Goodbye, Ree, I'm'a miss you, much" in a voice so hoarse and low that only those in the first few rows could hear it. She stepped back to the bench without turning and sat down, heavily, and that was it. Papa reached over and put a hand on her forearm, holding it there. There was some disappointed grumbling here and there among the assembly that the expected great speech had not emerged, but most understood, and only nodded in sympathy in Sus'Ula's direction.

No-one even ventured the thought that Budi Manigault might speak, it seemed so much of a burden and a strain for him to simply sit there, stiff and straight in the presence of his dead child, and he did, indeed, stay rooted to his seat, unmoving, and only stared straight ahead towards the back of the House into a void whose darkness none of the rest of them could pierce. And so it was left to his brother, Tibo, to talk for the Manigault family.

After that they all began to come up, one by one, the people of Yelesaw, to lay their memories down among the charms and gifts spread out before the casket. Everybody had a good thing to say about Orry, how she had never taken a man's hand, but just stayed right there in her father's house to take care of him and her younger sisters after Nana'Keece had died, and how it seemed like she had tried to take care of everybody else on Yelesaw Neck as well. It was something to hear how many people she had done a good deed for, midwifed many, or set up with others in their sickness, or minded somebody's children for them when they couldn't do it themselves, or sent out a recipe or a healing root, or sewed them a dress or patched a pants or sent along some cabbage or yams, or just sat down with sympathy and a lightening conversation when folks were troubled in mind. It was a wonder how she ever could have done all of the good things people said she did, seeing as how she was a woman who had never in all her life gone so far down the road she couldn't still catch the smell coming from her own cookpot, or hear the snap of the wind in the quilts drying on her clothesline.

The testimonies had ended and the folk had all sat back down, and while the elders on the front platform started a low chant, those with small children began handing them up. They passed the children from one person to the next, up the aisles or across the benches, all the way to the attendant women standing at the front, so that they could be crossed over the casket and body. A few of the children—not many—bigged their eyes in fear or even cried out, and these were held back and rocked for a moment, comforted and whispered secret things in their ears, before they were quieted enough to be moved on to the ritual. The children had to be calm when passing over the dead, or their squirming or squalling would draw over bad qualities from those on the other side, which the child would carry for the rest of its life. There were two or three grown folk walking around the Neck, everyone knew, who had cried out while going over a funeral casket, and who had thereafter ever suffered from bad doings.

Finally the last of the children went over and were returned to their families, and the services were drawing to an end.

Yally stretched her arms and legs as discreet as she could, smothering a nervous yawn. Soon it would be time for the final procession past the casket, and the laying on of hands, and it would all be over but for the burying. As people stirred themselves in their seats to get ready to take their places in line, the House took up another song—a last song—a sadsweet-song—a no-word song, clear as from a single bird, unseen, hidden in the dark woods—a wailing song—a going-away song to send Sister Orry home.

It was in the midst of that last song, as folks were closing their eyes and putting back their heads and giving last thoughts to the beloved spirit taking the first steps in her long journey amongst the gone'ways, knowing when the song ended that her time among them as a living person of the flesh would be ended forever, it was at that time that the thing they remembered ever afterwards and in the stories and legends of their children and grandchildren, it was then when that thing entered the Sambuhouse.

Entered as the beginning murmur of a disturbance in that sad space.

A sort of stirring and a shuffling.

An uneasiness radiating from out of the back of the House that was not noticed at first, except near the door, where it started.

The front door opened and closed, and a low wind entered and did not leave.

There began a whisper of voices from those closest to the entrance, moving slowly back to front, growing steadily louder as it covered more of the assemblage, traveling through the hall like a chilling fog, until it had enveloped the whole of the gathering.

The singing choked on itself, stillborn of spirit, dying away as a low hum of whispering, muttering voices took its place. Above it could still be heard the song-voices of the old men on the elders' bench, who had the most withdrawn into themselves, but even that began to break apart as each of the elders stopped, and frowned, and came out of their reverie, some raising their heads and squinting up their eyes to see what was happening, becoming aware as they did, one by one, of the gathering intrusion.

Yally, noticing the men on the elders' bench had ceased their singing, and hearing, now, the uneasiness behind her, turned around to find what had taken everyone's attention. She felt her mother turn as well, and later, in the quiet hours when she sat and thought of all the events of that day, she remembered feeling her mother catch her breath, sharp, and stiffen on the bench next to her. But that was not what Yally was thinking of now, because of what she saw when she turned to look to the back of the Sambu.

A quiet parting of waters was moving up the center aisle, an undulating displacement of the crowd rolling steadily forward, pushing the people aside as it went. Those who were packed in the pathway, standing up, suddenly found room to press themselves against the benches where previously there had appeared to be no room at all, or to even ease themselves in the laps of the people sitting, or maybe to try and just rise up in the air itself, for fear of something passing by them and through them that they dearly did not want to touch or have touch them. And then, uncoiling, disentwining, disgorging something indigestible, the sea of dark bodies opened enough to permit the emergence of a man.

A strange man.

A raggy man.

A strange raggy man whom none among them confessed to have ever seen before.

A strange raggy man not young, but not looking old enough for the bare oak walk-stick he used as he came on, the ragged brim of a gray slouch hat pulled down almost to his eyes and a tatter-green wool soldier coat buttoned up to his chin against the cold, so that you could see almost nothing of his face above the dark-thick naps and matted tangles of his beard, the shadow was so deep up under his hat.

A strange raggy man making his long way up the center aisle of the Sambuhouse.

And never in all their lives had any of them seen a man walk so painful and slow.

He did not lift his feet above the scrubbed-wood planking, not at all, but scraped the soles of his mudded boots along the boards of the floor, first one foot, then the other, like a man who had been on the road for year and year, without a chance to sit himself down for a rest and a cool drink, and in the hush that now hung over the funeral hall, all you could hear was the slow and deliberate dragging of those walk-wearied feet.

He hauled himself along deliberately, agonizingly, first planting his walking stick on the floor before each shuffling step, each leg in turn wobbling in its knee socket as he gave it his weight, the legs loose as wet cornstalks, threatening to slip out of their joints with every step, legs broken-up like stick-kindling that had been split many times and then loose-tied back together for hauling, and with every excruciating step, the strange raggy man gave out a low exhale of air through his mouth and nostrils, something between a grunt and a moan, the effort was paining him so.

He made his slow way up the aisle to the deep thud of his walking stick and the scrape of his boots and the blowing out of his breath, the steam coming off him like a plowmule, the stormwater running from his hat and coat in long dripping streams, the smell of mildewed tobacco and black bait-earth and wet leaves and mule-rank all about him, step after wobbled step, dragging his broke-up legs behind, holding out his free arm for balance, sometimes reaching out to grasp the edge of a bench-back when it seemed for sure he might lose his equlibrium and tumble forward. No-one in the Sambuhouse said a word. A hundred wide stares followed his slow progress while he himself was looking not left neither right, but eyes steady down, as if he thought the floorboards themselves were going to reach up and slap him on the forehead if he didn't pay them proper attention.

With each row passed the closest got a good look at his face, and you could sometimes hear the sharp take-ins of breaths and see many raised hands up to their faces, some with palms covering mouths, some with two fingers straddling their noses, the ward-off sign, and more than one looked quick-away to keep from meeting his eyes, not turning back until he was beyond them and they were out of his reach.

Not hesitating or pausing, he made his labored walk up the center aisle of the Sambuhouse all the way to the front, not pausing at the first bench where Yally and the Kinlaws and the other close-Manigaults sat, but continuing on, passing through the candles and the tokens, passing the water-bowl set out in case of a wandering spirit, and coming, at last, to Sister Orry's casket. There he stopped. He stood leaning heavily on his walking stick, his back to the congregation, facing the coffin in front of him, near enough that he could reach out and touch it and the woman inside, the elder men seated motionless on their bench on the raised platform above him, waiting, unmoving, like carved keeshe-men, their eyes and all the eyes of the entire congregation focused upon him, but still no-one saying nary a word. They watched as the raggy stranger pulled the slouch hat off his head, showing a mass of dark, wool-nap hair, matted with straw and crushed leaves. He stared deep down into the coffin, studying the body laid out within. Then his shoulders sagged and his head dropped until his chin pressed against the folds of his jacket, his whole body seemed to slump in turn, almost collapsing in on itself, and he put out his hatted hand and pressed it against the side of the coffin to keep from falling. In the silence of the Sambuhouse all around, something that seemed like a sob came out of his mouth.

Head still down, eyes not moved from the body in the coffin in front of him, in a voice not raspy and ragged as everyone had expected, but deep and melodious, as if it were a voice come from another being altogether and not from the broke-up shell of a man in front of them, the raggy stranger said the first words that had been spoken since he entered the hall.

"Who this-here 'uman is? Do anybody here know?"

At first, there was nothing said in reply, the question seeming odder, if possible, than the man himself. But then, from somewhere out among the benches, a lone, brave voice called out in return, "Brother, this-here be Sister Orry Manigault."

The raggy man gave a slow nod of his head in response. Then, ignoring the elder council sitting above who continued to stare down at him, silent, he removed his hatted hand from the coffin and, placing the flat of the slouch hat against the middle of his chest, he bore down on his cane with his other hand to carry his weight and did a slow, shuffling turn on his broke-up legs to face the assemblage.

He took a survey of the crowd as slow and deliberate as his walk up the center aisle had been, looking deep and careful over each face down the benches in turn, row after row, from the back of the Sambuhouse by the door, first, and on towards the front, searching in each face intently, as if he were doing a general interrogation of every spirit, or else seeking out someone in particular. Each person in the House he examined in this brief way shivered in the chill of his stare, drawing back from its unstated questions, and the hands rushed up to their faces again, holding the v-signs steady. Those with babies and young children covered the little ones' faces with their hands, or slipped coats or kerchiefs over their heads.

And still, no-one had said a word since the answer to his query about who lay in Sister Orry's casket.

Now the man's gaze turned toward the front benches, and for the first time Yally could see his eyes direct on, and she knew, at once, the meaning of the ward-off signs the people had made as they looked into his face. He was a mule-eye man, the two brown pupils looking in two directions all at once, the whites pushing the pupils outward, drawing his gaze as far apart as Yally had ever seen, and not even thinking that Mama might be watching, she stuck her own two fingers on either side of her nose, locking her own eyes in place with the tips, so the mule-eyed man's own eyes could not catch them and spread them apart like his.

She knew that the next thing she should do was look away, but she could not, because now the stranger had stopped searching, and was looking directly at her. Or as direct as a mule-eyed man could look.

And so she looked back, into his eyes.

Great, pale-brown eyes, they were outside the white balls, bulging out of hollow sockets, red-rimmed and rheumy, the light of their once-powerful torches now flickering and almost out, pained eyes, lost eyes, eyes of unimaginable sadness peering out from the carved rock of his face. He was the blackest man she had ever seen, coal dust black, eel back black, saltwaterafrica black, as dark as a deepwoods night with the lamp blown out. And in the middle of the pitted black plain of that face were those eyes, like two mudded pools pushed apart by two chalked pebbles, and she felt him drawing her in to them, and the dank smell of him was all over her, and she reeled, and felt herself submerging in deep waters…

Someone was speaking, at last, from the elders' bench, and it broke Yally out of her trance.

It was Tibo. He had stood up from next to his brother, Budi, who was still motionless and staring in his seat. Yally's mind worked backwards, reconstructing Papa'Tee's words from the beginning, which she had heard but not comprehended, even as her mind was deep within the mind and spirit of the raggy man.

"Brother, we is funeralizing this-here 'uman today, we sister and we daughter and we brother-child," Papa'Tee had said in his calm, quiet voice. "Iffen you ain't come here for mourn, then you is free for left, and no harm done. But iffen you done come for mourn, you is more than welcome, welcome." He raised up a hand of friendship. "Iffen you staying, find you a seat, Brother, so's we can continue on, and put this 'uman in the ground, like we's intended."

Tibo Manigault gave a motion with his head to one of the initiate attendant woman, who moved towards the raggy man with her arm outstretched as if to help him to a bench, but at one sharp look from him in return she stopped dead-still before she had gotten ten feet from him, and her arm fell to her side.

Turning the flat of his hat and pushing it out at the attendant as a warning to keep her distance, as if she ever intended to take another step in her life, the raggy man turned his head back to address Papa'Tee.

"I ain't lefting and I ain't setting," he said. "I be here for tell y'all, you must *not* put this-here 'uman in the ground."

The words were so outrageous, there were gasps of disbelief from all around, the spell of his look and looks and his entrance to the hall broken, and then followed a string of loudwhisper conversations between people who had not heard or could not believe what they had heard and people who repeated the raggy man's last statement. Several of the elder men, for the first time, leaned forward on their platform benches as if making ready to intervene. Budi Manigault, however, continued to sit stock-still. Only his brother Tibo appeared to continue to keep his composure, seemingly unshaken by the mule-eyed stranger's demand.

"And who *you* is, brother?" Papa'Tee asked, his voice still calm and measured. "What kind of a man you be, for tell we us'n ain't for put this 'uman in the ground. Where it is you does be from?" It did not sound like a challenge, but as a true question.

"I come from out the Big Bell," the raggy man answered. "And I come for tell you again, *y'all must not put this 'uman down into the ground!*"

Before Papa'Tee could give a reply, from several spots around the Sambuhouse the shouts arose, as more of the people found their confidence and their voices.

"Who you is?"

"Why you say us can't bury her, brother?"

"What'ga happen iffen we does?"

The man turned back to the assemblage. "They's a water coming, ain't you know?" he answered, and his voice was becoming more agitated as he talked. "Water fixing to battle with Earth, and Water gon' win, and cover all the land. This 'uman ain't belong down in that Water. Iffen you does try for put she in the ground, it won't accept she."

"How you does know all these thing?" someone shouted out from the back of the Sambu. Sister Orry's funeral was rapidly breaking apart into a call-out match.

Ever afterwards, Yally believed that the strange man was getting ready to answer that last question and, if he had, perhaps some of the mystery surrounding him might have cleared. He had, in fact, opened his mouth as if to say something amidst the growing clamor of voices around the hall, but never got the chance. At that moment, Budi Manigault stood abruptly up from his seat, his one eye burning fierce as fire across the deadly space between him and the mule-eyed man across the body of his daughter, and in a voice as clear as a trumpet note, called out, as he would have at a stray dog in his yard, "You *git*! You git, right now!"

The shouts and calls from the rest of the House broke off.

The mule-eyed man turned from the body of the hall again and back to the row of elders, immediately finding the figure of Budi Manigault, who had moved to the edge of the platform and was towering above him. For a moment the gaze of the two men locked, as if it were an arc of fierce electricity moving between them, as if no-one else existed in the House, and nothing otherwise but the contest of their great wills.

The raggy man raised his hatted hand and pointed his finger at Budi Manigault, and finger and hat and hand were all trembling, and no-one who saw it believed it was from fear.

"And-I-done-tol'ded-you-I-ain't-lefting," he said, drawing out each word, and now the tremble was in his voice.

Budi Manigault shouted back at him, full in all his wrath now, all thoughts of funeral propriety gone. "AND WHO *YOU* IS, NIGGER, FOR TELL ME WHAT FOR DO WITH MY OWN DAUGHTER?! I DONE TOL'DED YOU, TOO. *GIT*!"

The mule-eyed man slammed the flat of his hand and hat down on the closed end of the casket with a sound that echoed throughout the hall, and if he said something in return to Budi Manigault, there was never any agreement if or what, because what happened next happened so fast, some of it in rapid succession and some of it all at once, that it left all memory in a whirr of confusion.

With Papa'Tee trying in vain to grab the sleeve of his elder brother's robe and stop him, Budi Manigault leaped off the elders bench towards the mule-eyed raggy man below, one hand raised in a heavy fist.

The raggy man raised his walking stick in defense.

Some of the men on the first row jumped up and rushed forward to try to get between Budi and the stranger, some of them, in their haste, stepping on the white sheet set out on the floor.

The sheet went out from under them, sending the tokens and

bowls and the candles over in a tumble.

As several hands caught at Budi and the man, the sheetcloth caught on fire.

And Ula Manigault went into a fit.

She had taken off her shoes and had been drumming the flat of her feet against the floorboards through all the time since the raggy man had emerged from the crowd and she could see him full-on, her body tensed, the rise and fall of her breasts more and more rapid as he made his way to the front and his pause at the casket, and the questioning began, and then the confrontation first with her uncle and then with her father, the trembling of her knees spreading to her entire body as she rocked back and forth, heel to toe, with greater and greater ferocity. As Budi Manigault jumped off the platform at the mule-eyed stranger, Ula's head jerked back with a snap, her eyes rolled up in their sockets, and she let out a single loud whoop that pierced the Sambuhouse like a lightning streak, making the ones closest to her clap their hands over their ears. In the midst of the scramble over the sheetcloth, she rose half-up in her seat, flinging her arms out to the sides, and then dropping down and thrusting her legs forward, bucking and flailing as if a thousand boo-wa's were riding her body, shrieking, and shrieking, and shrieking as she did. Bracing her feet against the floor, she gave a final, savage push, sending the bench over backwards in a fit of tumbling and shouting and confusion, and Yally found herself on the floor in the middle of a tangled circle of bodies, her hands pressed hard on her mother's chest, trying in desperation to calm the wild spasms and stop her mother's shrieking, and shrieking, and shrieking...

THEY WAITED UNTIL the sun had gone down to bury Sister Orry, as was their custom. They had prepared her body and her grave with all proper ceremony and deference to the right spirits, but still, it took the longest to put her in the ground. It was black-dark by the time they had brought her to the graveyard beneath the trees behind the old house where Leem and Effie Manigault— Tat'Budi and Papa'Tee's father and mother—had once lived. The rain had slacked some towards the end of the funeral but now it was rising again, pounding down upon the Neck in a great deluge, the wind whipping back and forth like a crosscut saw, hurling the water into their faces so that they could not breathe, and most who had begun the trek from the Sambuhouse to the Manigault family graveyard could not make it all the way, but had to scramble to the

safety of nearby houses for shelter. Only a few of the strongest men
went on with the casket from the wagon through the narrow path
behind the old homesite. The hissing flames of their torches sent
strange, black shadows dancing into the branches of the trees as
they walked. Twice the wind rose up and lifted the coffinbox from
their shoulders, and the second time they were all sent tumbling
into the sandy mud, slamming Seek Butler sideways against an oak
tree and snapping his wrist. They sent him back to Papa'Budi's
house, his arm bent at an odd angle and wrapped in a dripping
wet cloth. The others continued on, slipping in the slick mud as
they tried to walk, the wind blowing them backwards and sideways
and whichaways on the path, the trees flailing at them with their
branches, whipping their faces as they passed. They came, at last,
to the graveyard clearing, where they found Sister Orry's fresh-dug
grave now filled with brown water that sloshed up and over the
edges in great, belching flows. They fetched buckets and bailed
out as fast as they could, but by the time they got the casket down
into the grave the water was pouring in again down the sides in
great cascades, and the coffin bobbed and bounced and
threatened to tip up and out. The wind gathered itself and howled
out in a human voice, rising to an unearthly wail, and then
snapped off like the crack of a whip to snatch Tat'Budi's hat from
his head and send it spinning in a great arc away into the blackness
of the woods. He stood bareheaded at the edge of his eldest
daughter's grave, leaning into the tempest, squinting against the
deluge pouring down over his forehead, pointing this way and that
and shouting orders that the men could not hear above the wind's
roar. They pulled out the casket from the open hole and Bo
Kinlaw and Ya Manigault jumped in, the freezing water up to their
hips, and they cast out madly with buckets as the mudded water
roared back in around them, washing down the crumbling walls,
overwhelming their efforts. "Iffen you try for put this 'uman in the
ground, it won't accept she." The words of the man at the funeral
ran through Bo Kinlaw's mind as he bailed, but each time he tried
to shout them out to Ya working frantically down in the
gravebottom beside him, the wind-driven water filled his mouth
and nose, and sputtering for breath, he finally gave up the
attempt. They gave up the bailing altogether, as well, when it was
clear they were doing no good, and scrambled out, mud sliding
down into their boot-tops and clutching at their legs, threatening
to pull them back in. Two or three of the others ran to the woods-
edge for stones to put on top of the casket to weigh it down,

wrapping it all with a quilt to keep it in place and then dropping it down into the gravehole again, throwing mud and sand on top with their shovels with a fierceness that matched the fury of the storm. Slowly, against their assault, the coffin stayed down and the mud-dirt gradually replaced the water in the grave, until they finally put their shovels down, numb and exhausted, and stood cold and wet and trembling over the covered plot. They said their last leaving-words above the roar of the wind, and it was finished. As they struggled back out of the graveyard Budi Manigault slipped on the wet mud, and the others had to catch him, and he blinked and looked at them in silent, solemn pain, and for the first and only time they could see into the heart of the great strain he had battled the last three days. The men closed in around him and held him steady with their shoulders and their hands on the way back to his house, walking in the dark, the wind pulling their long coats behind them, so that from the houses they looked like nothing less than a band of black spirits, sailing silently through the night in the beating rain, making their way in a windswept procession across Leem and Effie Manigault's yard.

THE RAIN BEGAN to ease off for good soon after they had buried Sister Orry, settling into a misted drizzle behind a thin, wasting wind. Folks took advantage and did not linger long at Budi Manigault's. The Hill emptied quickly of the carts and mules and within an hour only close-kin remained, and they soon retreated to their own nearby houses. Bo Kinlaw was exhausted, and did not want to talk. He went to bed early, and Ula followed soon behind, grim and distant and silent. Mookie went outside to see how the stock had fared in the storm. Yally and Eshy set up at the table for a while, picking at the cold biscuits they had brought back from Papa'Budi's, having little to say to each other. Each was lost in her own thoughts about the events of the day.

Big Soo had decided to spend the night with them, and could not stay still. As soon as they had come from the funeral, she began to pad around the house on flat, bare feet—from the window to the woodstove to warm her hands—to the door to peep out the crack—then into the girls' bedroom only to emerge a moment later—then back to window and all around the circuit of the house again. She had undone her hair and it spread thick and dark and wild about her head like an animal's horns, her eyes wide and darting from side to side as she walked so that she seemed to be looking at everything and nothing, all at once, muttering softly to herself as all the time. Mookie came back in and went straight to bed, and soon afterwards, Eshy and Yally banked the fire and blew the lamps and went to their room. Big Soo did not follow. She stayed alone in the growing cold of the bigroom, walking the floor in the dark long after the rest of the house grew quiet.

Eshy had dropped off and Yally was just settling to sleep herself when Big Soo came through the bedroom curtain-door, a small candle lighting her way. She fetched her shoes from the corner and her coat from the wall-peg where she had hung it.

"I thought you was staying with we, Aunt Soo," Yally said through a yawn. "We done got you a pallet fixed over there."

"I's staying," Big Soo answered. "But right now, I's going."

"Going where'bouts?" It was a sassy question to be asking a grownup, but after all the strange events of the day, Yally had blurted it out before she thought. She winced and waited for a fussing about no-mannered children and ain't-none-ya-business-and-don't-ask-that-no-more, but it did not come. Instead, she actually did get an answer, though not much of one. "Out." It was more in the form of a grunt than an actual word. Then Big Soo was gone, slipping past the curtain-door again, and Yally heard her aunt's footsteps through the empty house, and the back door open, and then close behind her.

She waited up for the longest, listening for the sound of Big Soo's return among the last drizzlings of the rain and the secret whisperings of the deep-night, but never heard it. She woke to the crowing of the yellow-brown rooster and the barest lightening of the morning in the bedroom. Eshy was still asleep, and Big Soo lay on the spare pallet in the corner, the covers pulled full over her head, her body rising and falling with deep breaths. When Yally was on her way to the shed to gather a load of wood for the breakfast fire, she found her aunt's shoes sitting just under the back steps. Papa's shovel was leaning up against the house next to them, not in its regular place in the shed. Both shoes and shovel were caked with mud. After she had finished starting the fire, Yally went back outside to clean off the shovel and return it to the shed. She did not touch the shoes.

She told Eshy about the incident, of course, and they puzzled over it for a while, trading various theories. Having gotten away with it once, Yally reasoned that asking Big Soo a second time, of course, was courting a backslap to the mouth and, therefore, completely out of the question. Later that day at the table, however, after Mama had gone out to start the clothes-washing,

Big Soo fished into the pocket of her dress and came out with a handful of dirt-streaked healing roots, which she set in front of her and began to clean with a cloth, one by one, and so Yally figured that's what she must have been digging at, and, since that had been one of the first theories she and Eshy had exchanged, she thought about it no more.

FOR DAYS AND DAYS afterward, all they could talk about on Yelesaw Neck was the mule-eyed stranger and the strange events at the Sambuhouse ceremonies and the burial. Except for the barest of necessities—"'morning" and "evening" and "pass the rice," and "close that cold door 'fore we freeze," and such—conversation on other subjects all but ceased. Afflictions went unsympathized, faults uncriticized, other folks' business unminded. No other topic but the funeral day could hold any interest. A different opinion rose up and spread out at every table and on every front porch, in every yard, front and back, and on every stool and chair pulled around a warm woodstove. Wherever wagons met along the River Road or the Rice Way or the wagonpaths and lanes running in and out of the settlements, people would stop their mules while they sat for a while to get up on the news they had not yet heard and to pass on what they already knew.

And the only two things they were certain about were that no-one seemed to know who the mule-eyed stranger was, and everyone wanted to know.

"I come out the Big Bell," he had said when asked of his origins.

But what bell was that?

There were bells at the biggest Black Jellyhouses in Cashville and St. Paul and so probably in other towns further afield, but if there was one thing they could all agree on, the stranger didn't seem like no oba'dey cross-sticker man.

There was a bell, certainly the biggest one in Cantrell County, on the courthouse lawn at St. Paul, used to call the Big Court in session when the circuit judge was in town. Yelesaw folk rarely attended a trial unless it involved a Yay'saw, but there were many at Cashville and other parts of the county who packed a lunch and sat in at every circuit court session, and there were others who had regular dealings at the jailhouse adjacent. None, when questioned, could remember anyone on trial or in the jail or anywhere wandering around the courthouse grounds, for that matter, who had either mule-eyes or broke-up legs like the stranger. It seemed hard to imagine that they might have seen him and forgotten.

There were bells at the trainstations in Georgetown and Florence and Charleston and all the stops to the north or south or west as far as anyone had been, as well as on the engines of the trains that passed through them. But if the stranger had ever worked the railroads or gotten off of any of the nearby stations, none of the county railroad colored men had ever passed on word that they had seen or heard tell of a man as such, either.

Putting aside the mystery of the Big Bell as temporarily unsolveable—but something to be picked up at a later time in case more evidence or information surfaced—there were some who went in another direction, putting out the speculation that the stranger might have been a Yay'saw himself, left home longtime gone and come back broken of legs and so troubled by bad fortune and circumstance as to be unrecognizable.

And so they ticked off long recitations through head-catalogued lists of names and circumstances of men who had left Yelesaw Neck in backaways days, never to return.

Kemba Dingle, who some could remember as a dancing, singing young man who always found bright-colored rags to tie around his throat to attract the young women. Or Big Pessy Brown, who had worked like an ox and hit like a mule and stuffed himself daily like a fall hog. Didi Jackson, one of Bonk's older brothers, was sometimes mentioned as a possibility as the raggy stranger, or else the Washington brothers, Oopa and Oota, the two-twins. There were others. All of them had dropped off from Yelesaw, each in his own way, without word coming back of where they had landed. One after the fight down to Cashville where the whiteman was hit in the head with a pickaxe handle and left drooling-addled for life. Another who went swamp-fishing one daydawn at Deepbottom Down and never came back. They'd mostly thought the Swamp had taken his body to its bosom, but there were some who figured he'd just got tired of the work in the family fields and simply up and left when he had the chance. Then there were the ones, like the two Washington twins, who took up railroad work laying tracks and were never heard from again, or some who had walked down to the docks in Georgetown or Charleston in the hope of finding easy cash-money there, or even a few who looked for their fortunes in Columbia or Charlotte or all the way up the road to the big cities up North and never returned. They were the missing men of Yelesaw. Not a hint of what happened to them had ever come back. Not a message, not word, not a homecoming whistle on the evening wind, though lamps burned nightly in many window corners to light the way, and long-mourning mothers fixed a little bit extra in the pot every day, just in case.

Those that advocated this solution said it solved the most obvious conundrum about the raggy man: did he actually know Orry Manigault and if he knew her, then how?

One drawback to the missing-man-of-Yelesaw theory was that none of the missing was known to have cotton eyes like the raggy stranger, but that did not rule them out as candidates, in the minds of the advocates. There were several ways known that could mule-up a person's eyes. For one, you could take two straws from opposite sides of a pozo nest if you went at a certain hour of the night in a certain phase of the moon, fill them with ingredients which were known but would not be openly named, and then put them on either side under an enemy's bedsheet or all the way under their bed, and, while they slept, the two straws would draw that person's eyes to either side, so that they would mule-out for several days or, with the most powerful potions and potioner, do so permanent.

On the other hand, as to the breaking up of someone's legs like the raggy man's, though the condition of his lower limbs was the most severe any of them had ever seen, everyone agreed that it was still possible for this to happen in any number of ways, on a work site, or in prison, or even over in the France War, hard times and luck being what it was for a nigger out in the world. There were several buckra soldiers in the county who had come back from the war with one leg gone or no legs at all. And though there were no oba'nigger war veterans known of with that particular void or who had even done any actual fighting over in France, many had been in the army in those times and had gone 'cross-the-water to dig ditches and drive trucks and do other things in support that might be benign in most times but were deadly dangerous in the midst of a general shooting. With bombs falling out of the sky all-over and big guns propelling shells through their ranks, as those who returned often told their many stories about, it was always possible that a missing man of Yelesaw had gone 'cross-over and been hit with something hard that had crushed his legs the way the raggy man's were.

Possible, most answered, but not much likely.

But more than anything else, what made the missing man solution a dubious theory for all but a few was that if the stranger had been a Yay'saw, why hadn't he said so, and done with it? Since no-one could water that challenge with a sufficient answer, the Yelesaw refugee return idea withered on the stalk.

Moreoften was the speculation that the mule-eyed stranger was a wudu-man, come to do his moko-work on Sister Orry.

That he had known about the Watercoming was no confirmation. That piece of information was widely being talked about from Cashville to the county line road, and the raggy stranger could have heard it anywhere.

But his warnings about Sister Orry's burial were, of course, disturbing. "This 'uman ain't belong down in that water," he had said. "Iffen you does try for put she in the ground, it won't accept she." Those words had presaged exactly the trouble at the grave, and the fight the men had with water and earth to put Sister Orry's body down. None of the Yay'saw spirit people had anticipated those gravesite problems or suggested or taken any measures in advance to combat or prevent them, not Baba'Zambu, the eldest, nor Buka Brown or Doppy Simmons, who read the bones, nor any of the other members of the elder council, nor any of the nifá, either. There were three possible explanations as to how—more than any of the wise ones of Yelesaw—the raggy stranger could have known so precisely what was coming.

The first possibility was that the stranger had simply put mouth to it, and that the gravesite troubles had occurred not because he wanted it to or from any bad intention on his part, but only because disturbance often came with no other cause than from from the naming of it aloud, in advance. Everyone knew that this was something you ought not to do, but many folks slipped and did it anyway, without thinking.

The second was that the stranger was a prophesier, who could see and describe future things coming. That would be no surprise if it turned out to be true, as many cotton-eye folk were known to have the seer gift.

But the third, and most troubling, explanation was that the raggy stranger was a wudu, possessed of the power to call on such natural forces as wind and water and move them at his direction in the furtherance of his agenda, and had done so on the funerary day. The worst sort of root you could work on someone, without doubt, was to deprive their dead body of a place to rest. What would cause this wudu—if he *were* a wudu—to have so malevolent a grudge against Orry Manigault, no-one could figure, but in his words and actions in the Sambuhouse, many at Yelesaw believed there was proof that he did. There were some who even claimed that while most eyes had been on the men surrounding and restraining Budi Manigault after he leaped off the elders platform, and then the sheet catching afire, and then Sus'Ula going into her fit, they had seen the stranger take advantage of the confusion to slip something out of his coat pocket and into Orry's casket. (A few of the more excitable went so far as to voice the belief that the stranger had set fire to the sheet himself with sparks that shot out of his cottoned eyes, but enough had witnessed the tipping over of the lighted candles to discount that.) Just after the commotion finally ended and order restored, several folks wanted to investigate the casket to see if there had been anything put in there by the stranger, but Ná'Risa forbade it, saying that if a bad charm had, indeed, been deposited, disturbing it might make its consequences worse, or even set it off immediate. She would not let anyone else get close to the casket, but instead herself collected the charms and tokens and tobys that had been scattered across the floor and put them on top of, under, and beside Sister Orry's body, afterwards pulling a covering sheet up to Orry's head before anyone else could take a curious look. Many noticed that Ná'Risa had poked a bit around the body and casket while she was doing all of this, as if surreptitiously searching for something, but none dared ask her if she had found anything out-the-way, and no-one else got the chance to investigate before the coffin was closed and the lid nailed shut. And so if the mule-eyed stranger had tossed something in with Sister Orry, whatever its contents or powers or purpose intended, they hoped that all the powerful Yelesaw charms they had sent her off with would overcome and drown out any harmful effects. Many steps of protection and care were taken across the Neck for several days and nights after the funeral, just in case, none more than in the back room at Tibo and Risa Manigault's home. There Ná'Risa burned a season-full of candles for a solid week, so blazing bright that at night the light of them could be seen all across the Manigault Bigyard and into the woods surrounding. All through the nights of that week, the sounds of Ná'Risa's songs and chants wafted over the trees and spread up into the black sky above, to what destination no-one else knew. By day she went into the woods alone, and gathered herbs and powders and dust from many places from the river to the Swamp, fashioning them into wang'na's which she hung at several points around the graveyard and at Budi Manigault's, so that no-one or nothing could approach either place without passing in close proximity to them. At the end of the week, Ná'Risa doused her candle-flames and emerged from her house and went back to her chores as if nothing unusual had occurred, and the people at Yelesaw mostly reasoned that whatever needed to be taken care of, Ná'Risa had done, so why ask. If the mule-eyed stranger had actually been a wudu-man, most were certain that he had met his match in Papa'Tee's wife.

Some figured that the mule-eyed man might not have been a man at all, which was an altogether different consideration.

Might'a'been he was Cap'n No-Head, the sesh soldier who had wandered the countryside cross-over-the-river for all the years since the Big War ended, searching for his thinking parts, which he had lost in the fighting around Sandy Station to a Yankee cannonshell or a sword-slash or a minié-ball, depending on who was doing the telling. The mule-eyed stranger had a head, sure, but the reasoning went that this was perhaps because he had only recently found it again, or else had t'iefed another he'd found in his travels. Or it could'a'been other familiar county or Lowcountry badspirits—Hairfoots, or Plait-Eye, or Nut-Nut, or Old RawHead, who was known to stalk the islands between Charleston all the way down to Beaufort, but might have come up this far in his wanderings. More often was the speculation that the mule-eyed stranger was the Penny-Man, Yelesaw's resident haunt, with his bright copper eyes and long nailclaws, who soared out of the night sky on ragged black wings to snatch up girls or young children who didn't do their chores. "The Penny-Man come for t'ief you' daughter" was a favorite Yelesaw rhyme for getting children to mind on dark nights.

Maybe, too, the thing that had dragged itself out of the storm to harass the people at Sister Orry's funeral—and "*thing*" was the word that the believers of this theory pointedly used—had come up the abandoned road from out of the grounds at Bethelia Plantation. Overgrown with weeds and rushes, bracketed by two long rows of moss-haired, leaning live oaks, the Old Lane, as it was now called, was a badluck way that no sensible Yay'saw ever entered for any reason whatsoever, and never passed by without marking off a sign in the sand, both because of where the Old Lane led out from, and because its passage over the River Road and out to Old Landing was the only true crossroads on the Neck.

Worse still, was that what came into the Sambuhouse that day could have come there from out of the Sugaree Swamp itself. There were entities gathered down in that Swamp that were known only from the sound of their wails late in the night, so low and thin and hollow that you would have mistaken their hollering and howling for the wind itself, if you didn't know what you were listening to. There were wraiths and shadduhs and rish'uns down there in those palmetto bogs and merepools and blacktar brackenmarshes who danced to quadrilles partnered arm-in-wing with barehead buzzards, and ha'ants and hags and gooby's and fixah's and reefey's and other more frightening creatures as well. And who knew what rent in the sky that terrible storm during Orry's burying may have torn open, and what it may have loosed upon their world? The hours of sleep lost by Yelesaw children— and many Yelesaw old folk, too—listening to such talk by dim lamplight in the days after Sister Orry's funeral could never be counted, not on many hands or toes.

And then there were those who thought they knew the answer, clear and obvious, so that no other solution should even be considered.

The mule-eyed raggy stranger was Orry Manigault's man-friend, they said, case closed, and that ought to be that.

That was Eshy's opinion, which she made plain to Yally and Big Soo as they sat around the table on the afternoon following the funeral, shelling sugarpeas and enjoying the quiet across the Bigyard at Goat Hill again, now that all the folks had gone home, and the excitement somewhat died down. "I ain't know why folk be straining they heads, trying for figure," she said, tossing her own head as if to rid it of any foolish and unnecessary thoughts. "Ain't no other accounting."

Across the table, Big Soo gave Eshy a long, dark look before she answered. "You ain't not for talk about you' Aunt Ree like that."

"Why I isn't?" Eshy popped open a shell and rattled the peas into her bowl with the tip of her thumb, slipping a stray one into her mouth to chew on it. "Aunt Orry were a 'uman, inna? Ain't all 'uman crave them some man, sometime? 'Uman can't never get too old for that."

"What you knows about crave-man?"

"Oh, I knows me enough," Eshy answered with a smile that was meant to appear as if she were letting on some mysterious secret. "I knows enough for handle my courting."

"Shuck, child, any coon can court," Big Soo growled back at her. "I hears them going at it every night in the tree back behind we house."

Yally, fascinated, sat without saying anything and looked over from one to the other of her sister and aunt as they talked across the table. The conversation had certainly gotten fairly interesting, fairly quickly.

Eshy's smile had disappeared, and she gave Big Soo a haughty look in its place. "I ain't no coon, and I ain't no child," she said. She cupped her palms around the sides of her big breasts and pressed them together, pushing them in and out while jiggling them up and down, so that they shook like great, soft melons under her dress. Big Soo snorted air out of her nose and looked away. Satisfied that she had made her point, Eshy went back to her pea-shelling. "I's a 'uman-grown," she went on, "and I knows enough about courting mens for marry one, when I wants."

Yally winced and hunched her shoulders in anticipation of something flying across the table from Big Soo's hand—there were some particularly hard and dangerous things within close reach—but if their aunt caught Eshy's dig at her own long unmarried status, Soo chose to react another way, giving out an incredulous, hooting laugh.

"Who fixing to marry a rank old split-tail girl like you?" she asked.

Eshy opened her mouth to answer, paused, and then closed it again without saying anything. She was not one to boast about the army of boys lined up in the Kinlaw yard for the privilege of a Sunday sitting with her, even if their numbers hadn't been obvious to anyone observing. They were legion.

Thinking that Eshy's failure to answer was an expression of weakness, Big Soo pressed her point.

"You talking about marrying that old long-shank Dingle boy?" she asked "Hmmmph. I wouldn't mate him with Mosby's lame mule. That boy got him foots long as a jackrabbit."

That one got to Eshy.

"Foots ain't the long I'm looking after," she shot back, her eyes glowering as Yally widened her own eyes and gave a sharp intake of breath at the most obvious, and most scandalous, meaning of her sister's words. Eshy herself did not pause. "And I could be done marry Nu Dingle this year here, iffen I wants to, and be living in St. Paul with a house and a husband and all. And then good-bye, sweety pie, to all y'all countrified Yelesaw folk."

"You studying on marrying Nu?" Yally broke in before the meaning of the "foots" and "long" comment caught up with Big Soo.

"Iffen he skillet fit my burner I might, sure-enough," Eshy said, still glaring across at Big Soo, who had stopped paying attention to the conversation and had gone back to work on the peas. Eshy gave their aunt a last, long look and then turned to Yally. "If not, they's plenty more boys on Yelesaw. Plenty offen it, too, if I want. Mama marry a oba'dey. It ain't do she no harm."

If she had hoped the mention of Mama marrying someone from across the river would get another rise out of Big Soo, it didn't. Their aunt was now fully engrossed in her work again. Eshy drummed her fingers on the table, thinking, still galled by Big Soo's slam at her friend-boy.

"You ever had you a man-friend for you' own self, Aunt Soo?" she asked, finally.

Big Soo looked back up, briefly, and then dropped her gaze to her pile of peas again, clucking her tongue and saying nothing.

Eshy, being Eshy, would not let it go.

"You ain't never think about marrying nobodys?"

"I ain't studying no mans," Big Soo answered, finally, and, emphasizing the word "childrens," she went on, "and I ain't studying no no-manners childrens, 'specializing ones what sound like they done got to smelling theyselves." Although her bowl was only half full of peas, she apparently decided that it was time to quit the table. She pushed back with her chair and stood up with emphasis, walking deliberately around the table to the counter behind Eshy, rattling the pea bowl in front of her. She poured a measure of water into the bowl from the bucket on the counter, sloshed it around with her fingers for a bit to get the peas clean, then walked to the back door and flung the water deliberately out into the yard, keeping one big hand flat over the peas to keep them from escaping with it. Eshy sat at the table, watching her intently all the while. When Big Soo went back to the counter to do a second washing, Eshy pushed away her own bowl and stood up herself, walking over to the back door with exaggerated steps to get the broom, passing so close by Big Soo that she nearly brushed the back of her aunt's dress, bigging her eyes at Yally as she did. She began sweeping around the kitchen with noisy strokes, smiling and humming to herself, satisfied that she had clearly won that round.

While Eshy and Big Soo settled into an unstated truce, Yally's thoughts drifted as she let her fingers work on the pea-shelling on their own. If Sister Orry did ever have a man-friend, as Eshy said, whether it was the stranger at the funeral or anyone else, why had she never mentioned it? Such a thing had never occurred to Yally before, as she had never considered Sister Orry in a courting light. In Grandpa's yard, or up on their porch, or warming at their woodstove fire, Yally had heard her aunt talk long mornings or afternoons away telling Trickster-Rabbit stories, or recounting old times on the Manigault Yard when she and Mama and Big Soo were just little rope-skip and sand-swallowing girls. Sister Orry had given her niece hours of advice explaining where to look in the woods to find the right plant to boil to stop a gripe on the stomach, or the best way to cut the wild smell out of a possum before you tossed him in the pot, or how to line up a pattern on a quilt or boil lye soap, or the right way to grind rice or meal, or similar such. After Yally had gotten big enough, Sister Orry would sometimes ask her if *she* had a friend-boy, and when Yally always answered no, not as such, her aunt would smile and tell her "Well, don't worry over it, none, honey. Time bring all thing to you what coming for you, iffen you ain't try for hurry it" or things like that. But Aunt Orry never made mention of how friend-boys might come to be, or what Yally might do with a boy when she got one. And never in all those times of longtalking had Yally ever heard Sister Orry say a word about a friend-man of her own.

"I don't figure Aunt Orry," Yally said, finally, coming out of her thoughts.

"Don't figure Aunt Orry, what?" Eshy asked from her sweeping.

"Don't figure her worrying over no man." Though Eshy was being especially free with the word this afternoon, Yally could not bring herself to use the term "crave" in relationship to their aunt.

"Why *ain't* Aunt Orry?" Eshy said, in what was both an answer and a question. She stopped sweeping and stood with one hand draped over top of the handle of the broom, the conversation having grown interesting again. "Sister Orry weren't no child." She gave a quick smirk at Big Soo, who was still at the sink washing peas. "Anyways, why else you figure that broke'ded-up, rag-ass old man come out in a storm like that, looking after she?"

Big Soo made a low humph deep in her throat. "Shows what you know," she said into her bowl of running-water-and-peas.

"I knows what I knows," Eshy answered. "What else would a man want but craving, in all that hard-rain?"

"Like I just said, shows what you know. That weren't no man at-all."

"Him weren't? What him were, then, Auntie Soo, iffen him weren't no man?"

"A gafa. Or a kisi," Soo said, giving the names of both kinds of bad-spirit things in a way that was both familiar and wary, a way that brought them through the door and into the kitchen to hover around the sink and table, making a shiver run across Yally's shoulders and down her back.

It didn't have the same effect on Eshy, who only sucked her teeth and went back to her sweeping. That only lasted for a moment as she thought on Big Soo's answer briefly and then stopped again, abruptly, standing in the middle of the floor and spreading her legs, the broom paused in the air in mid-sweep. "Anyways, what sense do that make?" she asked. "Iffen that man was a gafa or such, why him walk around on them busty-up leg like that? That'a'be fool. Why him ain't just fly on up inside the Sambuhouse on him two big wing, like him had some sense?"

Finished with a peas-washing that had taken far longer than necessary, which should have shown Eshy the extent of her growing agitation, Big Soo drained the water out of the bowl into the sink, set the bowl on the sink with a loud clatter, and walked over to the woodstove. She jerked the stove door open and began stirring around in the fire with a stick of wood to air it out, doing it with a studied deliberateness, talking all the while as she did. "You ain't know nothing about no men-friend and you ain't know nothing about no 'uman-craving and you ain't know nothing about no gafa, Eshu'Kola Kinlaw," she said. "A gafa ain't got him no wing, and a gafa don't fly. They comes straight out the graveyard and walks the ground."

"That make *less* sense," Eshy answered. "Truth-to-tell, that don't make no sense a'tall. What-for him drag he old bent-up ass out the graveyard ground, then, iffen that where him come from? They been fixing to bury her out there, in a minute, anyways. Why him ain't just wait for she for come to him?"

"Ain't him say him ain't want we for bury she in the ground?" Yally put in, but neither her aunt nor her sister were paying her any attention, now, intent as they were upon their battle.

Still poking around in the woodstove with the stick, Big Soo did not say anything for a moment. "I ain't talking about no gafa no more," she said, finally.

"I ain't got to talk about no gafa," Eshy answered, airily. "I weren't talking about no gafa. You the one been talking about the gafa. Me, I been talking about Aunt Orry and she men-friend."

"Then don't talk about Orry no more," Big Soo said.

Holding the broom in one hand, Eshy propped her other

hand, elbow akimbo, on the round of her hip in defiance. "Why I can't?" she asked. "Her my mama sister and this my mama house, and I be done talk about Orry Manigault iffen I wants to, anytime I wants to. Ain't my fault, her had she a ring through that man' nose, pulling him all'a way through the rain from she coffin—"

That did it.

Big Soo straightened up and made two steps for Eshy, the stick of wood—sparking with embers from the fire—raised up in her hand as if to either throw or strike. Before either could happen, Eshy had dropped the broom and was out the door, the broom clattering on the floor even as her bare feet were scrambling across the porch. She leaped out into the yard, Yally close behind her.

They stood down by the corner of the shed out of sight of the house, gasping at breath, peeking around to make sure Big Soo hadn't followed. When no large, dark figure appeared at the front door of the house, Eshy began doing a little circle jig-dance in the sand, twirling her index finger in the air and singing.

*Cotton-eye Joe*
*Cotton-eye Joe*
*Where you done come from?*
*Where you does go?*
*Ain't'a been for that nigger*
*With the cotton-eye*
*I be done marry*
*Bye-and-bye*

"Why you mess with her?" Yally asked, holding her chest to slow its heaving.

"Her need for stop stirring my stew," Eshy said, stopping her dancing and frowning up. "Soo ain't got no right for talk about Nu Dingle' foots like that. That ain't none'a Big Soo business. Iffen she act less wild and comb out she hair once-to-the-while, maybe she'ca catch some man sheself 'fore her get too old."

"I thought you said a 'uman don't get too old."

"I said they ain't get too old for crave. But just 'cause you can crave don't mean that you can craft." Having impressed herself with her own word-smithing, she gave out a raucous laugh.

"Yeah, but now we got for stay outside 'til Mama get back," Yally said a little mournfully, sitting down heavily in the sand and leaning her back against the shed.

By the time they dared to go back inside the house the day was waning and the smell of cooking peas-and-hocks on the woodstove was beckoning, and Mama was still not home from visiting her

oldest daughter far up on the other end of Yelesaw. Big Soo had
spread a quilt over the table and was mending patches with a
needle and thread. She paid the girls no attention when they came
in.

For all her bravado, Eshy kept out of Big Soo's way that
evening, working extra hard on the inside chores, keeping quiet
until Mama did get back, finally, hoping that her aunt would let go
of the afternoon's events, and not tell on her, which was what
happened. Big Soo was not the tattling sort. She took care of her
business her own self.

MOST OF THE FOLKS ON YELESAW NECK agreed with Big Soo,
thinking it impossible that the stranger at the funeral could have
been Sister Orry's secret lover. Why would she want a mule-eye
man like that, having passed over so many more agreeable and
able? And anyways, even if he had appealed to Orry, where would
he have met her, and they not heard, and how? This was not
Jaeger's or Cashville or St. Paul, where any tramp or drag-ass could
come out of the woods and plop himself down on the porch of the
first pretty-up 'uman he came across. Business with obas was
conducted strictly 'cross-over in the county, so it was impossible for
one to be wandering around Yelesaw uninvited. There were
oba'niggers who had courted and even married Yelesaw women,
like that Kinlaw man had done with Budi Manigault's youngest
daughter, but such courting by an oba in a Yelesaw house could
only be carried out by asking, in advance, for the father's
permission. While some Yay'saw women met and courted
oba'nigger men across the river, true, Orry Manigault had never
spent enough time in the county for any courting to have
happened, making only brief visits to the store over at Jaeger's or
the shops and outdoor market down to Cashville, never dawdling,
returning to the cable-barge crossing and coming back over to
home as soon as she had finished buying what she had come for.
Orry had been a handsome 'uman, true, with her mother's good
looks, and would have certainly attracted the stranger if he'd seen
her from afar, however briefly, somewhere over the river. She had
sure-enough attracted many Yay'saw men in her time, though
none had ever figured out to get around Budi Manigault's
imposing opposition. But say that raggy man had seen her at
Jaeger's or in Cashville sometime, and had found out that she lived
across the river, and had somehow got himself across without
using the cable-barge or otherwise being noticed, learned enough

about Yelesaw to find Goat Hill and the exact house he was looking for without having to ask for directions, been able to walk the River Road, down the Manigault wagonpath, and slip past all the houses on the Hill with without detection from man or 'uman, child or dog, and finally make it to Budi Manigault's door, it would have to be in the night to do it, and Budi Manigault himself would be home. You didn't slip past Tat'Budi and his porch dogs even in the dark, one-eye or no, even if you *had* met Sus'Orry someplace before and had managed to arrange in advance for her to ease you into the back of the house or to meet you out in the yard somewhere, and if Budi Manigault had caught a man trying to sneak-court one of his daughters, oh, Da!, that would have been the end of it, right there, done, go, and thanky Popo. No one on Yelesaw drew down a shotgun better than Big Boo. While that would have been the most logical—and satisfying—explanation of the cause of the damage to the raggy stranger's legs, since no-one had ever heard of a mule-eye oba'nigger being shot by Tat'Budi for any purpose whatsoever in Budi Manigault's yard or pen or shed grounds in back or in the woods immediately behind, and since they could not imagine such a shooting happening without the shots being heard by someone in the houses nearby on Goat Hill, and since they could not imagine the shots being heard by someone on the Hill and that person not running immediate to tell everything they knew to everyone else across Yelesaw Neck, they could not imagine such a thing to have ever happened at all.

THERE WERE TWO people on Yelesaw who some folks thought may have actually known something more than speculation about the identity or the purpose of the mule-eyed stranger. But if those two knew, they didn't share it with anyone else.

A few who had been close to the front at the funeral, and therefore supposedly had gotten the best looks, expressed the belief that they had seen a recognition between Budi Manigault and the stranger when the two had confronted each other over Orry Manigault's casket. Where Tat'Budi and the raggy man might have met each other before, and under what circumstances, the advocates of this particular assertion did not try to speculate, but only advanced what they thought they had seen in the Sambuhouse. If there had been such a recognition, Budi Manigault himself did not acknowledge it, since as far as anyone could ascertain, he never talked about any of the events of that day once the funeral was over and his eldest daughter was in the ground.

And why the appearance of the mule-eyed stranger had so affected Ula Kinlaw, she did not tell, either. Yally wondered about it a lot in the days following, but Mama was not the kind of person whose private thoughts you probed, especially if you were one of her children, and so Yally's curiousity went unsatisfied. Eshy was a different sort of Manigault child, however, and she bolded herself up to try it once, some months after the funeral. Catching her mother at the supper table in a talkative mood one evening, she asked off-handed in the middle of a general conversation amongst the family, as if it weren't of much matter, if Mama remembered that mule-eyed stranger—as if he could somehow possibly be forgotten—and if she had ever come across him any time in the past, before Sister Orry's burying day. The clatter of fork-on-plate around the table grew eery-still as Mama turned to her middle child with eyes as dead as early morning coal, said nothing for the longest, and then went quietly back to her eating without uttering a word. No-one else in the family made the attempt to ask again and Mama, like Papa'Budi, never offered her thoughts about anything concerning the funeral.

The one person who it was definite sure could answer the riddle about the mule-eyed stranger, of course, was the mule-eyed stranger himself. But they could not ask him, because he was not there. In the turmoil at the end of Sister Orry's services, the stranger had disappeared from the Sambuhouse, somehow making his way through the crowd and out the door and back into the storm from where he had come, without anyone ever remembering having seen him during his passage out. And where the stranger went after that was something nobody on Yelesaw knew, or if they knew, they did not say.

In the wake of his departure, considering both the storm and his words and then the disruption of Orry's burial, the belief began to rise again among many that had previously doubted that maybe, after all, there might be something to all of this talk about the Watercoming and the whitefolks' plans to flood the Basinbottom, the Swamp, and Yelesaw Neck.

# 3

# For T'ief You' Daughter

*(Fall, 1935 To Summer, 1936)*

On the night the Bighouse at Bethelia burned, even while the flames were still flaring amongst the falling timbers, the Quartersfolk—they had not yet come to call themselves Yay'saws because they had not yet claimed Yelesaw for their own—walked off the plantation grounds and down through the deepwoods to the Goma Tree to decide what next to do.

The Goma was the oldest tree on Yelesaw Neck, by far. Standing in a wild area deep in the woods at the Swamp's edge, it was set on a landmound that rose up from behind a convoluted labyrinth of interconnected ponds. There was no way to approach the tree directly, if even you knew what it was you were trying to get to. Because of a thick stand of mangroves that filled much of the pondwaters and blocked the view, you could not see anything of the Goma's massive trunk or lower boughs from across the water in front, only a hint of its topmost branches that gave no hint of its majesty. The mangroves also blocked access to the Goma Tree land-mound by even the smallest skiff. If you tried to get to the tree by circling completely around the ponds and creekwaters and crossing over from dry land at the rear, you'd discover no land that way dry enough to walk on, and quickly find yourself bogged or, worse yet, hopelessly turned around and lost and in danger of

being led down into the Swamp itself. The only way to reach the
Goma clearing was along a narrow, convoluted path that at first
showed no sign of its ultimate destination, but coming out of the
woods several hundred yards north of the tree site, wandering
north to south through deep tree groves and between sawgrass and
palmetto braces, skirting the brackish, oil-black edges of the
pondwaters, hopping over the narrowest spots across the creeks,
never facing the Goma at all but running first far below it and then
doubling back on itself to go far above, then taking several sharp
and confused turnings until, finally, the pathway suddenly rose up
and opened out onto the sandy land-mound. There, past a final
screening copse of trees, many of them marked with grim
guardian-masks long-ago carved into knots sticking out from living
bark, in the middle of a flat, open circle devoid of grass, sat the
Goma. It was an ancient live oak, knotted and gnarled from years
of contemplation during its long time in the world, bearded with
long thatches of gray-green moss, heavy with a fat garment-and-
crown of green-brown leaves, its trunk as big around as six grown
men, the upper branches so thick and crowded together that you
could not see their tops while standing directly underneath, the
lower limbs so load-weary that they rested their elbows on the
earth amidst a cushion of innumerable seasons of their own leaf
and acorn droppings.

It was sometimes said that the Sugarees—the once and former
inhabitants of the area for whom the river and swamp were
named—had used the Goma for their spirit ceremonies in the
backaway days before the white-eyes came, and if you dug deep
enough into the sandy soil around the base of the tree, evidence of
that theory could be found in the form of buried pots and
polished animal teeth and an occasional broken string of beads.
But even if the Sugaree had been persuadable to give up the secret
of the location of their Father Tree to anyone outside of their own
people, they had disappeared from the land behind the river by
the time the first white settlers were moving into the county
beyond, and the very existence of the Goma was lost to human
knowledge for a time. It was rediscovered by the African captives
first brought across the Sugaree River, who kept it secret from the
masters, claimed it for their own, and gave it the name of Goma. It
was here that the Quartersfolk often slipped away in the deep
nights to hold secret gatherings and, like the vanished Sugaree
before them, practice their private spirit-work. When the Freedom
Time came and there were no more masters or drivers from whom

to keep secrets, they built the Sambuhouse in a clearing at the head of the path leading down to the Goma guarding pools, and it was at the Sambu they now held their ceremonies and celebrations and general meetings and gatherings. But the Goma Tree they still reserved for their most important decisions, and it was here, on a cold October morning about the time the first frost set in, that the Yelesaw elders called an assembly to answer the general concerns about the Watercoming, and to report on what they had decided to do.

All of Yelesaw was there, old folk and breast-babies and those in between, led by Zambu Dingle, the oldest living of the 'Thellywalkers, they who had walked off Maw'se Grady's plantation at the burning. Baba'Zambu had to be carried to the Goma gathering laid in a rope hammock, because he could now only walk a trembling step or two without support.

Only a handful of the gatherers were not descendants of the 'Thellywalkers, in one way or another. Bethelia had been the largest and the grandest of the plantations between the Sugaree and the Swamp, and many of the hands and servants of the smaller estates had already intermixed with the Bethelian Black Folks before slavery-time's end. Many more did so afterwards. In addition, in the troubled times immediately following Freedom, when Yelesaw had been a refuge from white night-rider terror and so lowered the barrier of oba'dey prejudice against the Yay'saws, several Black individuals and families had moved across the river from Cantrell County proper. Most of them at first established a community of their own in the upper part of Yelesaw above the Crossroads, but in the marriage intermixing and husbands moving in and wives moving out that thereafter followed, the oba'dey nature of that settlement was gradually lost. In a generation or so, anyone's cross-over-the-river origins were either generally ignored or totally forgotten. Almost everybody now living on the Neck could trace some part of their family history—smaller, larger, or total—back to Bethelia.

Now they returned to the place where the Bethelia folk had come for spirit and succor, gathering in front of the great tree in a large semi-circle, several hundred of them, spreading far out over the clearing, a sea of dark faces in the early evening, flopped hats and colored kerchiefs abounding, coats turned up against the cold, the damp wind pulling at their clothes, all waiting in quiet expectation by the light of the warming fires set out around the Goma, the reflection of their images doing a ghostly dance in the black waters surrounding. A few of the more ambitious and bold perched in the lower branches of the tree itself for a better view and hearing, dangling their feet above the crowd like so many flocked crows.

The elders had sent a delegation to meet with the State Senator and the County High Sheriff and the Probate Judge, and received the word that what Bonk Jackson had heard was true. Yes, a dam was being planned to be built across the Sugaree just north of Cashville that would flood the bottomlands above. Further, the delegation was told that all who were living in a wide circle of land roughly between Cashville and St. Paul would soon be receiving notices that must leave their homes and farms no later than the beginning of winter next, a little more than a year from now.

The delegates also learned that the County and the State were buying up land nearby where the people of the Basinbottom and Yelesaw Neck were to be invited to resettle. Every family moving would be promised a fair trade—an acre in the new settlements for every acre they gave up in the homes they had to vacate. And if folks couldn't find anyplace in the set-aside properties that fit their fancy, that was no problem, they were told. The evacuees would be able take the trade in cash-money alone and thereafter move wheresoever they wished, even all the way up the road to New York, if that's what they wanted. Wherever they eventually ended up moving, however, the high officials of Cantrell County made it unequivocally plain in the delegate meeting that everyone now living on Yelesaw Neck had to pack their things and move. By springtime next, the dam would start going up, the river would begin to rise once it was fully closed in, and soon thereafter a lake would form where solid land now stood. There would be no dissenting or even delaying argument considered, not even the normal leeway that Cantrell County whites often allowed to coloreds. Both the details of the dambuilding and evacuation and the dates they were to be implemented had been decided upon, not by anyone local, but by whitefolk at the highest levels up in Washington, in close consultation with the governor and members of the legislature and, like the dam itself would eventually be, those decisions had been hard-cast in stone and set down so deep as to be unmovable.

All this was related to the crowd around the Goma as an unsettled stirring picked its way through the crowd.

A three-quarter moon had risen above the trees, but as if it were listening from another room, it hung discreetly back behind a thin bank of clouds.

Someone began to sing, but when no-one joined in, they thought better of it, and their voice trailed off in echoes before disappearing into the swampy woods.

From his seat of honor on a quilt at the center of the base of the tree, Zambu Dingle tapped his walking stick on one of the exposed Goma roots to get their attention, then raised it in the air and waved it back and forth in an unhurried arc over his head.

He was too weak to stand, but he did not have to. The troubled murmurings around the clearing dropped into steadily thinning whispers, hushed themselves, and blew out. All around the Goma Tree grew quiet as they waited for Baba'Zambu to speak.

Wrinkled and rheumy, his eyes yellow and sunken in the hollow runnings of his face, he leaned forward on his narrow haunches and looked around for a moment at the great assembled crowd, seeing in their familiar faces a line extending both backward and forward in time—from beehive villages on long-ago green shores to a future—where?—forever in this narrow stretch of lush land between the river and the Swamp, or oba'cross the Sugaree in the county, or even somewhere beyond? Baba'Zambu shook his head and blinked, scratching in his cotton-white hair with the long fingers of one bent hand. He was not sure if his olding eyes could see that far, but in any event, that did not matter. That would be someone else's task. These were his last days on this side, he knew. His focus, this evening, was on the more close-at-hand, on things he could grasp and shape.

He motioned to one of the men sitting beside him. A wooden bowl was immediately set down in his lap and someone poured it half-full with milk from a tin jug.

Baba'Zambu cleared the phlegm from his throat and began to speak.

"Y'all know me," he said. "I ain't just come-here. I been-here." He paused to let that thought sink in among them, and then continued. "I were there, at the Kamba'wora, when they put my papa' papa into the ground." He spoke slowly and deliberately, picking his way through the words, his voice so raspy and low that only the ones closest to him could hear, and they had to pass the message along to the ones further back and out.

He stopped talking again to dip one hand into the bowl and pull out a cupped palm of milk, holding it up so at least the ones seated in the front could see.

"Dufa!" he said, gesturing with his milk-filled hand in a half-circle, calling out his grandfather's name.

There were nods and murmurs all about, not another among them actually remembering the old man themselves, but most of the gathering knowing the name, and holding it in reverence as one of those elders who had held their community of people together back in the bullwhip days.

Zambu Dingle cast his arm out like a person throwing seeds, turning over his palm and opening his fingers wide, fluttering them, letting the milk flow out from between them, to patter over the sandy ground in front of his quilt.

He dipped his hand back into the bowl, lifted out another palmful of milk, held it up again.

"E'diye!" he called out in his wavering voice. "My papa' mama." He cast out the milk over the ground, again, covering some of the spots where Dufa's damp marks were already sinking in.

More nods and murmurs followed.

"Numu! My mama' papa. Om'bela!" He repeated the gestures with each name said, and the assents from the crowd each time followed in response.

Again and again, Zambu Dingle dipped his hand into the bowl and cast the milk out onto the ground, each time calling the name of one of the old-time people buried in their hidden plots deep in the Yelesaw swampwoods. Uncles and sisters and cousins and half-cousins and other kin of the gatherers, a few of them a living memory for only a handful of the most elder under the Goma that evening, but all of them well-known, familiar figures in family histories, community stories, and praise-songs.

The names of the far-back elders completed, Zambu Dingle paused once more to let his gaze roam over and through the waiting faces of the gathering to mark the transition. After a moment, he continued. "And I were there, at the Kamba'nangy, when they put my papa into the ground." He pulled out a palmful of milk, held it up, called out "Tumba Dingle!" After spreading his father's milk on top of the others, he pulled up another palmful and called out his mother's name. "Yu-yu Dingle!" He continued with more names, but now the nods and murmurs were more animated, as here he was talking of people who had lived past the slavery days, had taken on last names, and were buried in the graveyard behind the houses at Kanuza'kimbi, what the younger ones called the Dingle End, where the Dingles and their kin now lived.

The milk grew low in the bottom of the bowl, and a thin, white puddle slowly spread across the ground in front of where the elder man sat. He stopped, finally, and a fit of coughing took him. Two men held his arms from behind to give him support as his thinning body wracked with spasms, battling against itself. The assemblage waited in quiet patience, many looking in other directions, not wanting to stare at the Eldest in his discomfort. Someone gave him a sip of water. He caught his breath, held his palm against his chest, and began speaking again, forcing the words out, his voice now barely above a gravelly whisper.

"I ain't fixing for my peoples to be no walkin-'rounds, no poma'kiya," he told them. "Walkin'round, walkin'round, wandering 'cros't the land, with no kinfolk they can find. When *my* peoples come back for 'wisit from t'other side, I fixing to be at my cabin, with 'wittle for them set out propers on the porch." Here his filmed eyes wided up, and he fixed them all with a long, steady stare, as many as he could see in his dimming sight, his hands now trembling almost out of any control. But he was determined to make these final points, which were the whole purpose of his talk. "Iffen you want for honor you' peoples like you done been taught, y'all'a do the same. I don't care *how* much water the buckra say coming down off'en that river." He raised his body up from its seat on the ground, his voice rising as well. "I ain't fixing to go me *nowheres!*" Worn out both from the long speech and the strain of that final declaration, he broke out in another coughing fit that now could not be stopped.

But he had already said as much as needed to be said, and the gathering at the Goma Tree ended soon afterwards. After lighting torches to show their way in the nighttime dark, they walked the path between the pondwaters back the way they had come, through the deepwoods between the Swamp and the settlements, across the empty fields, and returned to their homes.

BUDI MANIGAULT HAD GOTTEN AN EDGE TO HIMSELF in the days following Sister Orry's funeral, turning brooding and bitter and sometimes even flat-out mean. The Manigault men working with him in the family fields noticed it first, and whereas immediately after Orry's death they had kept their distance from him out of respect for his feelings, now, gradually, they began to stay out of his way with more of a care for their own. He caught quarrels with everybody within reach, but most especially with Big Soo, who was the last daughter left at home and had now taken over all of the household chores. It was understood all around that this was a difficult transition for Papa'Budi. Orry had managed his house for more than four decades, taking over at the age of ten at Mama U'Keece's death, and people knew it must have been hard, this late in his life, for Budi to lose a housekeeper who was not only sunnily efficient, but was particularly adept at anticipating his wants, his needs, and his moods. Big Soo was the harder worker between she and Orry. She did what she was told to do, without complaint, and felt that this should be enough to satisfy anyone concerned. For all of her life, that had been sufficient. It wasn't sufficient any more, not nearly, now that Sus'Orry was no longer around to serve as a levee for Budi's stormy waters. Further, Soo was often moody and silent in the evenings after her father came back from the fields, withdrawn into her own contemplations, little company for Papa'Budi, providing him with none of the interesting stories that Orry had or Mama U'Keece before her, never engaging him in the lively conversations and spirited back-and-forths that he required, not even listening to his monologues with the correct "yessir"'s or "them did *what?*"'s in the proper places that showed just the right level of interest in what he had to say. And when Big Soo did speak, it was with an ingrained gruffness and bluntness that Budi mistakenly took for sassiness and disrespect. The sum of it was that Pap'Budi began to pick at his middle daughter not long after his first daughter's funeral, constantly, beginning as soon as he hit the back steps after the day's work, continuing through supper and the after-sittings until either he or she retreated to the porch or their respective rooms for the night, picking up again in the morning where he had left off, as if there had never been a break. Soo had been nothing but respectful to her father all her days and she did not disrespect him now, not fussing back, but taking his many criticisms with a stoic acceptance. That was not what he desired. He wanted arguments to fuel his fires, and so his complaints grew more heated, in particular concerning the quality of Soo's cooking, which he claimed did not suit his tastes. Sometimes, when he worked himself up to an especial state of agitation, he would take to skimming pots, tin plates and cups, or utensils across the kitchen floor, whatever was close at hand and not breakable, the sound of things crashing against the wood boards and the far walls the only thing that seemed to satisfy his anger. Finally, one morning, after he threatened to brain her with the fry-pan—hot grease, frying sausage, and all—because he claimed she was purposely letting his breakfast cook too long, Big Soo put her broad foot down. Never raising her voice, she looked at him straight and fierce and declared he could eat hay with the milkcow if he liked, but she would fix his meals no more. And she didn't. Instead, she began making her own plate in the mornings before he got up and the evenings before he got back home, vacating the meals table altogether, eating alone in her room.

It was left to Ula to come up with a solution.

At first she sent her father board and fare from her own house, but that only lasted for a short while, as Papa'Budi soon refused to eat any more food cooked in pots or on a stove other than his own. He said it made him feel like a road tramp begging at the steps of his house, which he had built with these two hands right here—spreading wide his big fingers out in front of him—and had always worked *can't-to-can't* to bring home all the victuals needed for himself and his family, and had no plans for stopping now.

Since Ula did not have the time to operate both her father's kitchen and her own, she next decided to lend out one of her daughters to go over to their grandfather's house to cook his meals. Her eldest, Lusi, would have been the best for the job, matronly and settled and unexciteable, the most pleasant of her children as well as the most like Orry in her efficient handling of a household. But Lusi was long married and living far up on the other side of Yelesaw with her husband's people, too busy with her own family chores to make the necessary regular trips down to Goat Hill. Eshy was close by, but she was out of the question. She was never a slacker for work but with her high-spirit ways, too much like Papa'Budi's own, she and her grandfather were certain to clash as bad as he had with Soo. The task fell to Yally, the grandchild who had always been Papa'Budi's favorite. Two or three times a week, thereafter, the youngest Kinlaw daughter walked across the yard to her grandfather's in the early afternoon to fix him enough food to last for several days. Often she stayed until he got back from the fields or the stockpens so that he would not have to eat his supper alone. Afterwards, if there was nothing pressing to do back home, she sat with him by the fire until late in the night. Her presence loosened the tight cords her grandfather had bound himself up with, and for brief periods, he even got back to being the old self he had been before Sister Orry's death. Shielded from her father's anger by another presence in the house, Big Soo would sometimes come out and work on quilting or other chores in the same room with them, and once in a while even resumed her place at the supper table, though between the two—Budi and Soo—there still remained a deliberate and pointed silence. It was a delightful time for Yally, not the least because it allowed her to question him on something she especially wanted his thoughts on: the whitefolks' flood.

Despite what Baba'Zambu had said at the meeting at the Goma Tree, the Watercoming was still very much on her mind. One evening—it had turned less coolish enough and they were out on the porch—she took up the subject.

"Grandpa," she said, "what iffen the whitefolk serious about flooding up the Basinbottom and Yelesaw?"

He regarded her balefully with his good eye.

"And what iffen they is?"

"Well," she said—she had thought about this part of it a lot, but could come to no conclusion on her own—"you reckon if we ain't leave like Baba'Zambu done say, them would just dam-up the river anyways, and flood we all out, don't matter we still be here? You think them mean enough for do something like that?"

"Oh, Old Buckra *mean* enough, sure-enough, if it'a come to that," her grandfather answered. "But it don't follow, them does means for do it."

As he so often did, he made his point with a story.

*Cu'n Rabbit and Cu'n mole lived out on the edge of a beansfield in the middle of a big farm up on the top of Cantrell County. Cu'n Mole had taken his time and dug himself out a warm den to live in, but the rabbit was of a trifling kind, and slept out under a tree, and the only thing he liked to work was his jaws chewing up and down on something that belonged to somebody else. But it was coming up on winter and Cu'n Rabbit had to get himself inside somewhere. He didn't want get his brown paws all scarred and scratched up digging in the dirt like a field-hand, and the mole looked so cozy and comfortable living in his house down under the ground. So old rabbit tried to figure out a way to get the mole away from that den and that den away from the mole.*

*One day, the rabbit went off into the woods and stayed a while, and when he came back, he was running lickety-lickety, like something bad was close on his tracks. And while he was running, he was hollering all the while.*

*'Oh, Da! Oh, Da!' Cu'n Rabbit kept hollering. 'Here come the farmer with he shovel-nose dog! What poor us'n gone' do?'*

*And the rabbit stopped right in front of Cu'n Mole's door, huffing and puffing to beat the wind.*

*Now the mole, he didn't study that rabbit, and he didn't move. He was sitting on his doorstep sunning himself, not worrying about anything, not farmer or dog. That's because the mole knew that if anything came up threatening him, all he had to do was duck back into his hole, where he knew all the tricks and turns, and nothing bigger than himself could follow behind. But still and all, he got curious about what Cu'n Rabbit had to say about the shovel-nose dog, which the mole had never heard of before.*

*'What kinda' dog that be?' the mole asked him.*

*And the rabbit said, 'You fixing to find out soon-enough, bro'. That a dog what got a nose flat and hard as a shovel, and he can dig with that better than you can with you' front and back foots. The farmer can set him loose on the back-end of you' hole, and him dig he way all the way through, flushing you out, and the farmer, him stand out here in the front with he shotgun, and when you runs out the hole, there you be, and there you was.'*

*Well, that got the mole's attention. He hadn't ever heard of a shovel-nose dog before, but it sounded like a dangerous sort of creature, and Cu'n Mole didn't see any way to get away from him. So he said to the rabbit, 'You'se the smart one, Cu'n Rabbit. What must we do?'*

*And the rabbit said back to him, 'You ain't got to worry, my brother. I got me a plan what will save we both.'*

*'Then tell it quick,' the mole told him, because he thought he could hear the dog and the farmer coming through the woods, close to his house. He had only imagined it, of course, but that was the power of the rabbit's talk.*

*'Since I be the quickyest of we two,' the rabbit said, 'I'll get up on that ridge and watch out for the farmer and he dog. As soon I sees them two coming out'the woods, I'll holler out loud, and then you and me both, we'll light out into the beansfield and hide under the vines before they can see we.'*

*The mole shook his head at that, no.*

*'I ain't think that'a do we much good,' he said. 'Dog ain't need for see, him can smell we out in that field good enough for find. And you might can outrun him, but my little legs, they don't work as fast as you'rn do up on top of the ground.'*

*But the rabbit just smiled and patted the mole on his shoulder.*

*'No, Cu'n Mole, you wrong,' he said. 'Iffen it been a terry-hound or a niggerdog what the farmer had with him we'd been in trouble, all both, 'cause either one'a them could smell a sparrow on the other side of the pond. But that shovel-nose dog ever got he snout holes plug up with dirt for the digging, and him couldn't smell mule shit iffen him step in it. No, all that shovel-nose know is for dig. And when him get tired of*

moving ground when ain't no mole or nobody's else in there for move out, he and that old farmer be done gone'd back to they own house for they supper soon enough, and you can go back home.'

The mole asked the rabbit why they didn't the both of them just run into the beansfield right now, before the farmer and the dog even got there. But the rabbit said that wouldn't work, because the farmer might trick them and circle around and come at them through the beansfield, and they had to know that way was clear before they took off.

That relived the mole of his worries, and he agreed to the plan, which he thought was a good one. So the rabbit went up on the ridge, and the mole waited in front of his door. After a while, the rabbit hollered out, 'They's coming out the woods! They's coming out the woods!' and the mole took out as fast as he could go on his little legs, over into the beansfield, where he hid out in the deepest patch of vines he could find. The mole went so fast, he must have outrun even the rabbit, because he didn't see or hear anything of that old rabbit behind him. He kept thinking how good a friend the rabbit was, and brave, too, risking himself to stay on that ridge to warn the mole, instead of keeping on running and getting away clean. The mole hoped the rabbit hadn't gotten caught by the farmer and the dog, but was hiding himself in another part of the field.

The mole stayed out in that field most of the afternoon, waiting for the shovel-nose dog to finish his digging. After a while, the day got late, and he got good and hungry. He called out for the rabbit in a soft voice, but the rabbit didn't answer, and even though the mole searched around in the beansfield for a while, keeping as low under the vines as he could, he couldn't find any trace of the rabbit to get his advice. But since the mole didn't hear anything of the dog or the farmer either, even though he listened hard, he decided it was safe to go back home. As a matter of fact, he hadn't heard anything of the dog and the farmer at all since he'd run out to the field, but he didn't think about that at the time.

When the mole got out of the beansfield and back home, he found a sight he hadn't expected. There was no trace of the farmer of the shovel-nose dog, which was what he had hoped. But what he did see was Cu'n Rabbit sitting on the mole's doorstep, picking his teeth with a pinestraw and grinning to beat Bob's band. And the rabbit right then and there invoked the first law of animal property, which is that nothing belongs to any animal permanently, even his own house, and if he walks away from it too long, any other animal can come and lay claim to it, and it will be his. Old mole was disappointed in the rabbit, and told him, 'I thought you been a friend, Cu'n Rabbit. I thought you was looking out *after me.'* And the rabbit answered, *'I is looking out after you. I be looking out after you from right inside my new home.'*

So the mole had to go and dig himself another house, and be satisfied with that, and if there ever was such a thing in the world as a shovel-nose dog he never saw it, although he used to look for it every evening just before it was getting dark.*"

Papa'Budi leaned back in the porch swing and folded his arms across his chest to signify the end of the story. Giving his granddaughter a hard look out of his good eye, he asked her if she understood the point.

"Yessir," she answered after a moment, nodding her head.

"What it be, then?"

"Well," she said, hesitating a little, "what I reckon it mean is, the whitefolk just be trying to fool we with that water-talk. There ain't really fixing to be no dam or no flood or no lake or nothing like that. It all just talk. All they want is for fool we off Yelesaw so's they can come over the river and take we land, just like that rabbit did mole."

The fierce look in Budi Manigault's eye softened, and a hint of a smile hit the corners of his mouth.

"I reckon we might make a Yay'saw out'ten you yet, iffen we tries hard-enough," he said. "'Spite where you' pap come from."

He began to rock in the porch swing, picking out a song softly to himself, the first time she had heard him sing since the funeral.

*Run, rabbit, run*
*Maw'sa Grady got he gun*
*If you hops up in a tree*
*Best be sure that him don't see*
*If you hides out in the pen*
*Gots to look like you's a hen*
*If you jumps down in the cut*
*Ask Big Da to save you' butt*
*If you makes it to the woods*
*You be done gots away for good*
*But if him catch you in the grass*
*Cousin, that's you' rabbit ass*

HER GRANDFATHER'S MOLE STORY did not completely dry up all the concerns she continued to have about the Watercoming. Papa'Budi, after all, had said all along the news of the dam was nothing but a whitefolks' trick to get the Yay'saws off their land, merely the latest, in fact, in a longrunning series. His latest strong words, therefore, while a comfort, did not actually change anything. Her fears, meanwhile, were not at all helped by the talk of past floods and their accompanying tragedies currently being carried on back and forth across Yelesaw Neck by anyone old enough to have a personal memory of any such event. Everyone over twenty years old had tales of their own personal experiences with deluges of various size and intensity and duration, of waterlogged barns and ruined crops, ponds sprung up where roads and fields and yards should have been, moccasin-snakes swimming up to the back steps to ask "Please, ma'am, can I get me some supper? It ain't nothing in this-here water for eat."

The flood-stories kept up the nagging unsettlment Yally had been feeling over the dam news since the day Lam Jackson had almost run her down out on the Ricefield Way. When she let her thoughts drift, more often than not they would eventually seek out a body of water to immerse themselves in, water never at the same speed and never the same color or type. Sometimes it was light-blue, fresh and boiling, a creek rushing over rocks. Sometimes it was rank-black, fetid and troubled, a marsh-pond creeping up over its banks in a winter rain. Sometimes it was salt-green and miles-deep with frothed waves crashing, the ocean she had never seen, except in her dreams. Regardless of what type of water it was, she always found herself sinking down in it, but, thankfully, never over her head. She would always break out of her reverie, automatic, just before that happened. At other times, she found herself picturing what it would be like if a real storm came up like none that had ever happened in her lifetime. Rain and rain and rain for days on end. Torrents of rain. Buckets of rain. Barrelful after barrelful dumped down without pause on the land. She saw the water overflowing the Sugaree River and the Swamp and rising, rising, nothing holding it back, covering the Bigyard and then the porch steps and all the porches, then whole houses up to the tops of the chimneys, washing over sheds and chickenyards and chickenpens and all the fields out back. Blackeels and golden minnows and rainbow crappie passed by in the dim light of murky waters, gliding in and out of open windows, swimming into cupboards in search of food, the eels trying to open pea-jars by screwing their tails around the lids and squeezing. These visions would become increasingly disturbing, and with the saving act of a part of her mind that was still keeping vigil somewhere close enough, she would give her head a sharp, animal shudder—and often her shoulders and all of her back as well—to set herself on dry and solid ground again. She wished there was a way to discipline herself so she wouldn't see such things at all, at least not in the big day. She knew she had no control over her night-dreams, but she certainly didn't want these kind of disturbing ones to keep drifting into her daylight hours.

There was one person on Goat Hill who Yally wanted to talk with who might be able to ease away what was becoming something of an obsession with water and flooding—Ná'Risa—but the girl could not figure on a way to do that.

Papa'Tee's wife was the resident conja'uman on the Hill, whose candles and charms graced sills and shelves and mantles and bedsides and porch steps in almost every Manigault home, and many others beyond. She was the person most often consulted on the Bigyard on all matters of the spirit. But that was by grown folk, not children. Though Yally had often seen her great-aunt in front of somebody's house or at the Sambu giving out advice or admonitions to some young folk or other, or sometimes even just passing the time, this always seemed to be at Ná'Risa's initiative, and not by request from the children themselves. It was not hard to figure why. While Ná'Risa was always pleasant and ever greeting with a broad smile that extended all the way to her missing back teeth, there was something reserved in her demeanor that did not appear to invite frivolous approach.

Yally did not think what she had to ask Ná'Risa was in any way frivolous, but she thought it best that she come up with a way other than a direct approach.

Except for close-kin such as Grandpa Budi or Sister Orry, who she visited on her own, the usual way in which Yally had always had contact with Yelesaw adults—such that she might be able to slip into questions or even conversation with them, if it came to that—had always been through her mother. Mama was ever receiving cousins or friends at the house for visits, and she sometimes took Yally along with her when she made visits herself. But while Ná'Risa was one of the few women on the Hill who Yally had never heard her mother talk against or call out of their name, and who Mama had always treated—either in Ná'Risa's presence or out of it—with respect, Ná'Risa was also one woman who Mama never visited, and who never visited the Kinlaw house. There was something of both a tension and an understanding between the two of them—Mama and Ná'Risa—that Yally could feel but not figure. And whatever the case, while Mama had never forbidden her youngest daughter any contact with Ná'Risa as she had with a few other Yay'saw women, she had never done anything to facilitate it, either.

Yally could have asked Eshy for help. Were it almost any other situation, she certainly would have, but not this one. Eshy was bold enough to simply walk up to any grownup on the Neck—or to any oba'nigger or whitefolk off it, as well, for that matter—and ask any question or strike up any conversation, whatever came to her mind. That would be her first and only advice to Yally, but that was advice Yally couldn't take, as she had already rejected the direct approach. She could ask Eshy to come with her to Ná'Risa's—Eshy would clearly be game for that—but then it would be Eshy who would open the talking, and so it would be Eshy's conversation, and Yally might never be able to steer it back to get the questions answered she wanted. But what finally caused her to look for another way to get to Ná'Risa besides Eshy was that Eshy was one of those—like Papa'Budi—who had adamantly dismissed any possibility that any more water was coming to Yelesaw Neck than was already there. But unlike Grandpa, who teased up to a point and then stopped, Eshy had no such scruples, and would tease her unmercifully from the moment she said that the reason for the visit was her fear of drowning in the whitefolks' flood. And on the subject of the Watercoming, Yally, right now, did not feel much like being teased.

She studied hard on it for several, days, trying to figure out some way to get her concerns before her great-aunt. Ná'Risa's image first began to intertwine with the water in her mind, and then to overshadow it. No plan came to her, and after a time, she began to slowly resign herself to the fact that nothing would come.

She was delighted, therefore, when she happened on Ná'Risa one afternoon coming back from taking supper to the men at the ricefields, and had the great and unexpected fortune that while she was fumbling around thinking of some way to open up a talk, Ná'Risa, out of the blue, asked her if she could come by her house that evening on a fetching errand.

SHE WAS THERE as soon as supper was over and the kitchen cleaned up, telling her mother only that she was going for a walk out on the Bigyard. She had not wanted to risk saying that she was going to Ná'Risa's. She was not worried that Mama would directly tell her that she could not go, but instead had the feeling that Mama might come up with several chores that suddenly needed doing that would prevent the visit. She figured that if Mama later

found out she had been to see Ná'Risa, she would say, but only if
pressed on the point, that her great-aunt had asked her over. It was
not exactly a bold-faced lie, only a bit of twisting. She *was* walking
out on the Bigyard, as she had said, and Ná'Risa *had* asked her
over. That the asking had come first and had preceded the walking
by several hours and was, in fact, the cause for the walking—well, if
Mama didn't directly ask, then Yally didn't feel she was directly
bound to tell. She buried that bit of hypocrisy deep inside her
immediate, to keep it from making her feel bad about getting the
chance to tell Ná'Risa her concerns about the flood and to get
Ná'Risa's advice.

Papa'Tee and Ná'Risa's was a house thick with scents. Often in
the warmer months, when their doors and windows were open,
Yally would slow down just enough when walking past to be able to
pick out the vast collection of smells wafting out. She could
sometimes even pick out the individual aromas—the sweetness of
sage and cinammon, mint and ginger, the pungence of crushed
camphorweed or the bite of red pepper. Even all closed up in the
winter, the Tee-Risa house had a slight fragrance of spices to it,
which you could catch if you passed by close enough. Smelling
Ná'Risa's house fragrances on her way on other errands had always
been one of the highlights of her day. But now, sitting inside at the
table while the elder woman stirred at a collection of black-iron
pots in their sweaty, steaming array on top of the wide woodstove,
Yally felt herself overwhelmed by the assault upon her nose. Two
rows of candles placed along the flat stones in front of the
fireplace, one set of them thick and black, the other slender and
deep-red, sent shafts of musky smoke rising from their flames. The
fumes from pots and candles all blended together in one
thickening cloud that spread across the ceiling and then slowly
settled back down again to fill the room. Yally's head began to
grow light. It was certainly unlike Sister Orry's kitchen used to be.
Aunt Orry had believed in blending potions one at a time "'fore
they won't take to scrapping with each'n other and then turn on
you," as she would often say. Ná'Risa's way seemed to be to do as
many as she could at once, going to each mixture in turn for
attention as they matured or needed a new ingredient. But Sister
Orry had been an herb-healer and not a conja, like Ná'Risa, so
that might be the reason for the difference in the way they worked,
Yally figured. And Ná'Risa had been at it for much the longest.

She looked around for Papa'Tee but he was nowhere to be
seen. Instead, she found her attention—as much as she could

retain—caught by the row after row of jars on the shelves along the side kitchen wall, each with its own collection of individual blossoms or leaves or roots or bark bits or clear or colored liquids inside. As she tried to figure at what the identity of each might be—most of them she had never seen before and, therefore, a complete mystery to her—she felt herself growing sleepy, and her head to nod. Before her chin hit the top of her chest, however, she was startled into alertness when she found that a cup of hot, pale-colored tea had been placed in front of her. Yally had not seen how it got there, though she did not think she had ever actually closed her eyes, and Ná'Risa looked as if she had never moved from the woodstove or her potion pots. But the elder woman had a way of shifting places like that even when you weren't nodding off. Ná'Risa was like a little dried-up sun-lizard who sat still on a rock, the only sign of life the bright brown eyes that watched you constantly, until suddenly there was a quick movement, a snap of apron like the flick of a tail, and she was somewhere else, you never quite noticing how, she had done it so quick. Her skin was like a lizard's as well, stretched tight and leathery dark over her tiny frame, thin but certainly not frail, the tight cords in her neck and arms showing the underlying foundation rods of her strength. Watching Ná'Risa at her fixings-work, Yally thought of the saying "a lee-little bit of leather, but her well put-together." Whoever had first said that, must surely have had Ná'Risa in mind, or somebody like her.

The girl sniffed at the steam coming out of the teacup her great aunt had given her and immediately her senses began to clear again. She took a deep sip, trying to guess at its contents, as Ná'Risa gave her pots a last looking over and then sat down at the table across from Yally with a cup of her own.

"Well, how you for do this afternoon, child?" Ná'Risa asked her, smiling broadly enough to show the dark gaps behind her front row of teeth. It was the first time she had really spoken since Yally had arrived. "Everything going alright?"

"I'm doing good, thank'y ma'am, yes'm," Yally answered through sips from her tea. Life everlasting was in it for sure, which she recognized from long hours at Sister Orry's. But there were other ingredients in it that she could not identify.

She looked up from her cup to find Ná'Risa regarding her thoughtfully, the elder woman turning her head as she did, slightly, from one side to the other, so that each eye got a better look, as a bird might do. Yally lowered her own eyes immediately, picking at some of the residue at the bottom of the teacup with her finger, trying to do it in such a way that it did not seem as if she was deliberately avoiding Ná'Risa's look, which she found to be much too penetrating. Ná'Risa had never paid this much attention to her before.

"I ain't know," Ná'Risa said, finally, blowing over the liquid in her teacup and then tasting a little of it. "You 'pears like you's troubled in you' mind, child. You worry-up over something?"

"No, ma'am," Yally said, looking back up too quickly, and then back down at something she suddenly found of great interest set out on the table. She felt like kicking herself. Here the opportunity to talk out her feelings and fears with Ná'Risa had been handed over to her like a present on her birthday, and she wasn't taking advantage. She began to think that it might have been a better idea to bring Eshy along. "Well," she ventured, allowing her eyes to raise up again only briefly, "maybe I is."

"You is, what?" Ná'Risa said it in a warm sort of way, not insistent, as if she were really interested in what Yally had to say, and not throwing out a criticism for being reticent. It gave Yally encouragement to speak on, although she still kept her eyes on the table and her cup.

"Worry-up, ma'am," she said. "A little. Over something."

"Over what?"

Yally took a long breath and blew it out again before going all in. "Over what folks is all talking 'bout. You know. 'Bout that flooding."

"Oh. That." Ná'Risa let her head go back and gave out a little quick, high-pitched laugh. "You worry 'bout the buckra and they water? Reckon you be like some of them on this yard, they be thinking Old Buckra got him the power for flood-up all the county and going down to Georgetown, iffen him want."

"You ain't figure so?" Yally asked it in a voice that was small but growing hopeful. She found herself looking up again, but this time allowing herself to be held in the elder woman's gaze.

Ná'Risa gave a dismissive snort. "Oh, Old Buckra, him think him can take them a sip out the world anytime him want for loose the cork," she said. "But him can't hardly blow up no storm as biggity as all *that*."

She looked at Yally, first out of one eye and then the other, smiling as she did, the intensity of her gaze having diminished greatly, as if she had already seen as much as she needed to see.

"Anyways," she went on with a little shrug of her narrow

shoulders, "ain't no need for worry over it. Flood ain't nothing for fear after, child, 'til him come. And when him do come, you can't do nothing but run for what higher ground you can find, and try for dry-out after him left. Ain't nothing else you can do. You' folk never tell you about the Ha'woola?"

"Yes'm." She had heard the story before, about the Death-Rain, the hurricane and then the bigflood that came in the early morning hours several years after the old-timey folks came out of the old plantation at Bethelia. "Mama done told'ded me all about that."

Ná'Risa cocked her head to the side and grunted, and the smile temporarily left her face. "Well, you' mama ain't been'ded there back in that time," she said. "I were. I remembers it, good."

*It come in with a hollering like it been something out there living, and in the terriblest of pain. Rain two day straight, 'thout the first break. Couldn't see out the window or the door for the water falling. Couldn't hear nothing but the thunder and the water banging on the tin roof and the houseboards. Tornadoes running with it like dogs running in a pack. Some folk' roofs flewed all'a way away. Some porches and whole sides of houses, too, the folk what ain't built them proper. Some house all'a way gone'd, ain't matter how they been put up, like a train run down the track straight through'em. Me and Tee been marry then. We had we a good house, and solid. That old man can't do much right, but he can put up a tight-built house, when him got a mind to do it. But still and all, that old howling wind slam-up against we shutters so hard and long, it finally up and blowed them in, and rain come a'pouring all through the house. Tee took a rope and lash us all to the chimney, me, the chaps, dogs and all, and that where we stayed 'til that storm pass over and blowed itself out.*

*When it were finish, all from the River Road down to the ricefields, that been done cover with water, most places more'n a foot deep. Some say it done been higher than that during the raining, but I ain't stick my head out the door for see. My Pap gone down to the river where the bank had been, and him tell me the water been high-up as his waist, and he been a tall-up man. My Pap put a stick-post up on the bank and marked it at the water line. That stick is still there, I reckon, out near Old Landing, if it ain't rotted up by now. I went out and seen it, some year back. Anyways, the water been so high after that storm, onliest ways you could get up the River Road up through the Crossroads, you had to take you a boat. All the crop done wash'way, and the farm creatures with it, all too. Tee and his brother and his Pap and some'a he uncle and cousin, they took them pitchforks and hay hook and gone'd out and catch hog and chicken out the water that first day after the storm broke, been so many floating by, they foots in the air and they tongue hanging out, blue. That's all there been for eat, and we butcher and smoke all we could get. They kept on floating by every day for a week or more but after that first day, but we didn't fetch'em out the water, they been rotted up, stink. Some folk did, they been so hungry, and they paid for it, sure-enough. After that, we ain't had nothing to eat for weeks but root and old potato we dug out from under the mud. It been a hard time, let me tell you.*

"Now look at me," Ná'Risa declared, her story now over, throwing her arms away from her body and poking out her meager chest, from which no rise of breasts were visible.

Yally looked at her, but could not understand why she had been asked to do so, and the expression on her face showed her puzzlement.

"Look at old, thinny-up me," Ná'Risa went on. She raised one slender arm, made a circle around her wrist with the middle finger and thumb of her free hand, and ran it up and down her forearm, easily, from just below the joint of her hand to just above her elbow. "You see that?" she asked. "I ain't got as much meat on me as a field sparrow. Never did. But old poor-bone'ded me come through that bad woola, and it ain't drown'ded me out, and it ain't blowed me away, neitherways. Now, look at you, child. Look how healthy you be, next to me."

She reached across the table and gripped Yally's forearm with the hand with which she'd been circling her own. Though Yally had always thought herself skinny, she realized that she was actually considerably built-out, if she compared herself to Ná'Risa. Up until that moment, she had only thought she was in competition to blood-born Manigaults. This was something she hadn't considered before.

Ná'Risa let go of Yally's arm and patted it, then leaned back to her side of the table. "Ain't nothing them buckras can t'row acrost that river can come up to what Nana'oya stirred up against we back in them old peoples' time," she said. She took a sip of her tea. "And they sure ain't got nothing for knock down no hefty girl like you is. Now I know you' Mama ain't let you left the house without finishing you' supper, but let's see iffen that old man ain't etted up all the cornbread or pie in the cupboard, we can even fatten you up some more."

Yally went back home that evening considerably lighter in spirit than when she had left. All her anxiety had vanished.

Normally, such stories of horror as Ná'Risa's flood tale would have kept her awake for many nights afterwards, afraid for the dreams it would bring. But none came in the aftermath of her visit. She felt a strange contentment for several days afterwards as if, after all, there really wasn't anything to fear, even if the flood did come. And it wasn't until much later that she remembered that Ná'Risa had neglected to give her the fetching errand for which she had been invited in the first place. She wondered if that had simply been an oversight, or if there had, in fact, been some other purpose for her summoning. If so, Ná'Risa had not told her and, unfortunately, did not summon her again, so she had no way to ask.

YALLY WAS NOT THE ONLY ONE on Yelesaw Neck whose fears were easing over the whitefolks' water. Once Zambu Dingle had spoken at the Goma Tree, the threat of an imminent flooding had already begun to fade in the minds of many other Yay'saws. While the water might come it didn't look like it was coming anytime soon, and if Eldest was not worrying, why should anyone else? And so gradually, as the whitefolks' plans to dam the river became olding news and as the excitement over it waned, other interests took its place. There were babies to be birthed and winter storm damage to be repaired and preparations needed making in advance of the spring planting and much more, all of the various chores and challenges and concerns of any farming community. In February, Yally had her sixteenth birthday party. Recorded in one of the bound books in the office of the county clerk in St. Paul was a date of birth listed under her courthouse name, the date probably wrong and the name undoubtedly misspelled, none of which mattered to any Yay'saw, since all of that writing down was for the benefit of the whitefolks and whatever possible use they might have for it, and not used or acknowledged or the details even remembered on Yelesaw. Yally had been born in the new moon, and so that's the time of the month they always held her celebration. Papa'Tee killed a hog for the occasion, and Lusi came down to help Mama and Eshy fix up the biggest feast they would have until the fall harvest, including, of course, the hog divided into several dishes, plates of fried chicken, collards and blackeyes, both sunk down in small mountains of rice, cob corn, sheets of sweet cornbread, and cakes and cobblers and all. After supper, they cleared the bigroom of all furniture, it being too cold to go outside for long, and danced to clap-and-stomping songs. Lam

Jackson rode over with his younger brother, Dokie, and a couple of their Sheffield cousins to provide energetic arrangements of music on their banjos and clackers, with Yally's father helping out with his fiddle and Uncle Ya pitching in on the mouth-harp. Even Papa'Budi played, which they had not seen much of his doing since Sister Orry's death. Dink and Cu'n Boo had brought a jug or two of corn liquor with them, and they and some of the men kept going out back behind the shed to sip on it, slipping out the door in one's and two's so Mama wouldn't notice. She did notice, but chose to let it continue, just this once, so as not to spoil her youngest's celebration. Because she was sixteen and a child no longer, Dink and Boo encouraged Yally to come outside along with them to take her full measure of the jug. It was not the first time she had ever taken a drink of liquor—Eshy had discovered the location of their grandfather's hidden shine stash three summers before—but it was the first time she had done it with her brother and cousin's approval and that, indeed, made her feel that she was really growing up. Afterwards, she danced with every man in the house until she was giddy-silly, and had to sit on the floor in the corner, giggling uncontrollable, waving others off until she could get her breath back. Almost all of her dance partners—aside from the Jacksons and Sheffields and Eshy's latest friend-boy, Nu Dingle—were relatives of one sort or another, but that hardly mattered to her. It was the best party she could ever remember, which made it most certainly the best party she had ever had.

As they were waving to the last of the guests leaving and already beginning in with the after-cleaning, Papa came over to her at the doorway, put his arm around her shoulders, and said, "You be sixteen, now, Bit. I reckon it's time you start taking company." Though it excited her to hear, she did not actually expect any company, and so, as the weeks passed and no company came, she was neither surprised nor especially disappointed. She knew that she was not the kind of girl that boys much noticed, especially living as she was in the shadow of her big sister's bright flame.

Actually the house and yard should have been filling up with boys about now, not come to see Yally, but to get Eshy's attention, because Nu Dingle's time with her was about due to expire.

That bright flame of Eshy's attracted boys like so many moths, and they flitted around her in thick, fluttering packs the instant she shone her light their way. And just like moths, the ones who actually managed to win exclusive rights to her affections and attentions discovered that while Eshy's fires were even more golden than they seemed from the outside, the flight into the source of them could be fatal to the flyer. Though few looked back upon the experience of keeping company with Eshy Kinlaw with regret, and some ever afterwards even thought it the brilliant highlight of their lives, eventually and inevitably, without exception, all fell to earth finding themselves burnt out, burnt up and cast off. Now it had come to the end of the normal allotted span of the Nu Dingle era in Eshy's courting cycle, and the others at the Kinlaw house looked every evening after work for the expected sign, the absence of the familiar mule-cart from the yard. To their surprise, both mule and cart stayed beyond the end of the shift, as well as Nu Dingle.

Around the time of the first hard freeze that winter, instead of beginning to ease off his visits as the first step towards break-up, Nu Dingle started showing up more regular at the Kinlaws', and courting Eshy more seriously than before. On Saturday afternoons, after he had stayed a respectful enough time at the house to pay his propers to Mama and Papa, he and Eshy would leave together in his mule-cart, sometimes not returning until late in the night. Often they would go out to the impromptu fiddle-and-blowjug gatherings the Jacksons and Sheffields held up in Jacksontown or the Sheffs' Field on Saturday nights, but once in a while, when there was a big dance across the river in Cashville, they would ride over on the cable-barge to attend. At first on the nights the couple went out, Mama sat up at the table working at some project or other with the lamp burning high until they returned, as she had done with all the rest of Eshy's beaux and with Lusi's before her. But after a time, Yally noticed that Mama did this less and less with Nu Dingle's visits until she finally stopped it altogether, retiring to her room at her regular time, whether the two were still out or no, leaving it in Eshy's hands to keep to her curfew. And though Eshy had conspired to break almost every rule her parents had made for her over the years, now she meticulously managed to get herself back home on time every night she was out. When Yally pointed this out to her and asked why that should be, Eshy gave a thoughtful frown and said, "I reckon when you ain't got for do something no more, it take all the fun outten not doing it."

When Eshy did return, in their room afterwards, Yally would lay propped up on her pallet in the dark with chin on palms, sucking on boiled peanuts she had squirreled away for just that purpose, listening for an hour or more to Eshy's stories of the

night's events. Most especially she liked her sister's stories about
the dances at Pooky's Palace, the dance-joint in Cashville where
singers and players came from as far away as Columbia and
sometimes even Augusta, Georgia to perform, because Pooky's had
a piano and all, and could always be expected to produce a big
crowd. Sometimes, still excited from the evening and not yet ready
to go to sleep and put the experience to an end, Eshy would light
the lamp and get up and heist her gown and repeat the dances she
had done—the shine and the syrup hips, the blacktop and the
pelican dip—around and around the pallets, keeping her feet
from hitting the floorboards too hard so as not to wake up Mama.
If it was Pooky's she and Nu had been to, she would sing in a loud
whisper all the new barrelhouse blues songs she could remember
from the festivities. The next day, in between chores, Eshy would
take Yally into the middle of the bigroom or out in the yard and
teach her the new dances, marveling at how quickly her baby sister
picked them up, telling her she would be the best dancer in all the
Cantrell County joints and clubs, once Mama and Papa let her go
out.

"You sixteen now, you should ask them iffen you can go over
with we, next time there's a dance to Pooky's," Eshy told her. "Or
at least come when the Jacksons play to they place." But sixteen or
not, Yally was sure her parents would never approve a trip to a júk
joint across the river, nor over to the Jacksontown or to the Sheffs'
Field, either. Cashville was simply out of the question, far beyond
her reach, and though there were few places on Yelesaw Neck
barred to Yally, Mama was not especially fond of the Jackson boys'
mother or of most of her Sheffield kin, either, and so Yally never
asked.

In those late nights after Eshy came back from her outings
with Nu Dingle, Yally would see the glow that remained on her
sister long afterwards and she would mark, all over again, how
unpretentiously beautiful Eshy was, tapered as a spring calf, eyes
large and nut-brown and almond-shaped, her dark hair braided in
thick plaits that reached far down her long neck, skin a brilliant
black. The Goat Hill women all said that Eshy had gotten the best
of the Manigault side and avoided the worst of the oba blood, and
was easily the most beautiful of the three Kinlaw daughters.
Without any envy, Yally knew it to be true. Lusi had taken on a bit
too much of the Manigault heaviness, even before she'd begun to
have her own children, while Yally claimed the Kinlaw ganglies.
Eshy, on the other hand, was the pride of the litter, and that was

all that needed to be said. It was no wonder all the boys flocked to her and jockeyed for her attentions.

For her part, Eshy was too preoccupied with life and living it—and especially, now, with Nu Dingle—to dwell much on her own qualities.

Instead of just Friday and Saturday evenings, Nu began to come over on weeknights as well after work, staying around the house those nights nearly as long as he and Eshy would stay out on the weekends. On nights less cold they would sit out on the porch, but when it got too frigid outside, they would camp out on the sofachair in the bigroom. Either way they would spend hours in each others' company, Eshy doing most of the talking, Nu content mostly to listen, his long legs stretched out in front of him, sometimes making low remarks to Eshy that often made her break out into extended fits of laughter. Eshy laughed more *with* Nu Dingle—as opposed to *at* him—than the family had seen her do with any of her previous courters, and one evening when the couple had just left to go out for a drive, Papa remarked at the table that he knew the secret.

"And what you reckon that be, Ben Kinlaw?" Mama asked him, a little disinterested, over a late cup of coffee she was sipping.

"He know exactly how to set that plow. Right down the middle row. The boy don't veer left neither right. That the way to do it with that girl."

Mama frowned up a bit in mild annoyance, but still did not seem to be taking her husband's observations very seriously. "What you mean by that? Eshy ain't pay no attention to how that boy work he papa' farm. Her don't spend 'nuff time over she own chore for know how farm work supposed to be done."

Yally, who was on the sofachair across the room, tried to make herself as small and unobtrusive as possible, so that she could escape her parents' observance and hear the rest of the conversation. For the time being, at least, it seemed to be working, as they gave her no notice, but continued on.

"I ain't talking about no farming," Papa said. "I mean, that the first boy what don't moon over Esh like a old yard puppy. But you notice, too, he don't butt heads with her like no goat, neither. He done figure out just the right way to catch him a Manigault girl." He thrust his hand in front of him, fingers and thumb pushed together and pointed forward, like a plowshare. "Don't straight one way or t'other. Just go straight down the row."

That got Mama's attention. She stopped drinking her coffee in mid sip and gave Papa one of her Mama looks over her cup. "That how you figures you catched-up me? Like I been a patch of dirt for you to plow?"

Papa shook his head, vigorously and quickly.

"Uh uh. No, ma'am. That wouldn't a worked with no Oolie Manigault," he answered. "You had done put so many rock in the row for trip up all them Yelesaw boy what been chasing after you, I had to come at you around the back acres and then through the woods. I knowed you been a old sour-face thing what ain't know nothing about smiling with nobody, so's I tried for kept you laughing much as I could. And time you stop up laughing and figure out the trick, we been already all tie-up and moved over here and making baby."

"You figure that how it worked?"

"Must'a. We working on the grands, now, and you ain't pack and left, yet." He turned his head towards Yally and gave a wink in her direction, his way of telling her that he, at least, had known she was sitting there all along, and that she was old enough, now, to stay and listen to grown folks talk.

"Well," Mama answered, dryly, "don't think that bucket done drain out yet. They's time left in the evening for me to put clothes in a sack and to go back to Budi Manigault's house."

"Well, I hope you don't, Ula Kinlaw," he said. He paused, thought about it, and then added, "and so it don't come up again, Sus'Kinlaw, I'm putting it out right now that I ain't said nothing—and I ain't mean nothing—'bout you being no patch of dirt. That been you' word, and not mine, but to keep peace in this-here house, I'll take'em back right now, even though I said them, the first. You accept my apologize?" He got up and walked around the table and hugged her neck.

"Go on, man, 'fore you make me spill this coffee and I t'row the rest on you," she said, pushing him away from her, cutting her eyes at him as she did. "Plow the row," she said under her breath, as he walked back to his seat. But there was a flicker of a smile playing around the corners her mouth after she said it, the first time Yally had seen her mother smiling since they'd heard the news about the Watercoming, and then Sister Orry had died.

Some days later, when they were alone back at the stock pens, Papa gave Yally a different explanation as to how he believed Nu Dingle had managed to keep up a courting of Eshy. "I be thinking that old grand-uncle'a his'n done give him a holding-on potion to slip in that girl' drink every night. That why she can't turn him go." He said it with such a serious face that even though she knew her father's ways well, he had long turned his back on her and walked over to the other side of the pens before she realized it was one of his jokes, and she spent the rest of the afternoon trying to think of how Baba'Zambu might look sitting on the ground somewhere back off in the woods, feet in the sand, stirring up love potions in a pot, putting some on his tongue with a long spoon to see how it tasted.

But however Nu Dingle was managing Eshy, it appeared to be satisfying the toughest critic in the Kinlaw house. After her conversation with her husband about the best way to catch a Manigault girl, Mama took up a humming as she was straightening up the kitchen before bed. And the next day, without explanation, she brought out the whitecotton dress that she had worn when she jumped-broom with Papa on a warm June day in the yard in front of Grandpa Budi's house, and for days after that she worked on it in earnest, altering it to fit Eshy's slightly leaner frame.

THE WINTER OF '36 wore itself out in one end-month February blow, one ice storm after the other, leaving the bare tree-limbs leaned heavy towards the ground with long strands of icicle hag's hair, and the alternate freezing, thawing, and refreezing turning the roads and wagonways from hard as city paving to slippery-muddy and impassable as a marshbog and back again. But by the first week in March the weather broke. Green buds began sprouting up all over the Neck, and men and mules were already out in the dewey-wet dawns breaking up field ground, making ready for spring planting. On the week when the pink and white blossoms burst out all over the dogwood trees, Eshy married Nu Dingle in the front yard of the Kinlaw house in front of family and friends. Grandpa Budi proudly presided, and even Baba'Zambu made a rare trip to Goat Hill to lay hands on his grand-nephew and his bride. When the ceremonies were over and the last of the celebration candles snuffed out and the last stray reveler departed—satisfied, finally, that there was nothing left sweet at the bottom of the many pots for eating, and nothing else in the jugs for swigging, and no more songs to be sung or dances to be done—Eshy got her packed canvas bag from the bedroom, mounted the mule-cart with Nu, and rode away to move in with him in the new house at Kimbitown.

It was the loneliest time of Yally's life.

She had never been apart from her sister before, not for a full day and night, ever, and she did not know how she was going to cope. It was Eshy who had started her on her sums and letters long before she went across to Jaeger's Cross to the sessions at the county colored school, and it was Eshy who taught her where to find the best blackberries along the ditchbank, and how to make dollbabies from tree twigs and moss-hair, and combed and plaited her hair in the mornings and again before bed after Mama had long given up, for the twisting and the squealing of her tender-headed last child. It was Eshy who knew the rope-songs, and sand-games, and swamp-stories, and a thousand-thousand other such things that passed the days and evenings and nights around the Kinlaw house. It was Eshy who would nudge Yally in company, secretly pointing out some child's rough-brushed heads and ash-streaked legs or flapping shoe-soles or holes in parts of clothes that revealed secret places to the light of day, so that Yally was left with hands clapped over her mouth, bursting with bottled-up giggles and cut-eyed by angried-up grown folks who did not know the cause of the merriment, and would have sometimes appreciated it even less if they did, since Eshy's fingers were more often than not pointed at children of theirs, if not the grown folks themselves. And when the thunder beat fists upon the roof of their house and the lightning exploded and split trees in the blackwoods behind, it was Eshy—not Mama or Papa or Lusi or any of her brothers—to whom Yally scooted for comfort and protection. In the next minute, of course, it was also Eshy who would shriek "Ooooo!" in her little sister's ear, or poke a cold finger in her side, sending Yally screaming back to her pallet in fear. And when the storm was spent, and the rain just a drizzly patter on the tin of the roof, it was Eshy who would rag her unmercifully for being such a scare-teeny. That was big sister Eshy. She had been Yally's ever and always, but now she was married and gone.

Yally thought about her sister much, and missed her more. In the long, warming days following the wedding, she tried to figure what Eshy was doing right then, right at that moment, and what life must be like for her on the Dingle End. Was she having to wash Baba'Zambu's feet—with toenails thick as a mule's hooves— and spoon the food into his mouth and then wipe the snot and dribble off his chin, like all the Dingle girl-cousins supposedly did? Yally could not figure any way under the sun that Eshy would consent to such, but what would they do to her over there to try to make her? And how was her sister getting along with Nu's mama and with *his* sisters, Ta'wala and the little cripple-arm Nigli, and the rest of the Dingle peoples? For that matter, how was Eshy getting along with Nu Dingle himself, now that they had stopped courting and were sleeping side by side every night? Had Nu changed, like most men were supposed to do on the other side of the broom, with all his sweetness and deference and solicitation changed over into bossiness now that possession had supplanted pursuit. It was not so much a question of how Eshy would take to being bossed as it was how soon, in what manner, and to what height and reach would she blow. There was no Eshy around to give answers.

Of course, by day there was plenty of work to keep Yally busy, and when the work was done, there were cousins to keep play with all across the Bigyard on the Hill, and Grandpa Budi to continue to cook food for and keep company. But in the evenings after supper at her own house, or when she had come back home from eating at Papa'Budi's, when it got too late to go back outside, there was no-one in the house to talk with. Mama was mostly tasks and orders these days and when she did take time out to talk it was just that—to talk—and not much to listen to what her youngest might have to say. As for Papa, spring-planting was his busiest time, as it was with all the Yelesaw men. When he wasn't working he was in the bed sleeping, or stretched out in the swing-chair on the front porch as much close to sleep as you could be without actually being it. When Mookie wasn't asleep himself—worn out from the planting—he kept his own thoughts and company, as ever. And so much of the workday and at night as well, behind the curtain-door of their little bedroom, there was only Big Soo.

YALLY'S AUNT HAD MADE her final break with Papa'Budi, but in a decidedly convoluted way. She had stayed at the Kinlaw house during the last couple of weeks leading up to the wedding, helping Mama out through the days and into the late evenings with the many preparations. It was something of a puzzlement to Yally why her aunt couldn't have given the same help while making the short walk across the yard from Papa'Budi's every day, since she did not bring anything with her but washup things and a change of underwear, and returned home every couple of days anyway for clothes. Big Soo was not one to offer explanations for her actions, however, and Yally didn't ask.

Yally assumed that once the wedding was over, Big Soo's extended stay would be over as well, and her aunt did, in fact, return to her father's house once the celebration cleanup was completed. A day or two later she was back, however, sleeping for a couple of nights on Eshy's old pallet in the girls room before going home again. She was back at the Kinlaws within a week for another round of overnights, with no pretense this time that the purpose had anything to do with helping Mama out. She ate her breakfasts with the Kinlaws and then walked back to her own house to do her chores, returning late in the afternoon to help with the supper fixings, and then for supper itself. Neither Mama nor Papa seemed to think anything strange about this arrangement, and it got to be so regular that on the nights when Big Soo did not show up at the supper table, Mama took to asking Yally if she knew if her aunt was coming, so they'd know whether to delay serving the food. For his part, since Big Soo had refused to cook his own food any more, Papa'Budi had maintained a studied indifference to anything concerning his middle daughter, and whether she was in his house when the last door for the night was closed or not seemed to have no visible effect upon him. But it did not appear to Yally that any new argument between father and daughter was the cause of Big Soo's absences from Papa'Budi's house. As far as she could see, the two of them were hardly speaking to each other at all.

Big Soo's puzzling pattern of on-again, off-again overnight visits of various duration and time in between—puzzling only to Yally, apparently—continued down into the early summer, when everything changed on the night of the dog-shooting.

Yally and Grandpa Budi had been out on the porch, trying to catch a cooling breeze in a particularly warmish evening. Big Soo had remained indoors, braving the heat. Yally had turned from her seat on the steps to ask something of her grandfather—she never afterwards could remember what—when he suddenly stiffened on the swing, bracing his feet against the porchboards, and turning to look out into the dark towards the side yard, he put his hand up to shush her. She turned to the direction he was looking at but could see nothing in the wide expanse of the pitch-black of the yard beyond the little circle of the porch lamp.

"What wrong, Grandpa?" she asked him.

He frowned slightly, shook his head, and continued listening for a bit. "You done hear that?" he asked back, finally, in a low voice.

She concentrated, dropping her head and turning one ear towards the side yard, but the only thing she could hear was the little bit of warm wind in the far trees, some crickets from under the house and peepers out in the tall-grass, the flapping wings of a nightbird or two flying by, and laughter and faint music coming from one of the houses across the yard, the normal sounds of the summer night. She did not think any of that was what he was referring to, so she answered, "Nossir."

"That som'bitch been sneaking around here, of a night," Papa'Budi said, grumbling the words under his breath. He gave his head several affirmative shakes. "I'm'a catch him, though."

"Catch who?" she asked him, and then, not certain of what he was talking about, she thought it might have been more appropriate to ask "catch what?" But either her grandfather did not hear her question or had decided to ignore her, and she wasn't certain that he had even been saying it to her, and not just to himself. Turning back to him, she watched as he sat, poised and listening on the porch swing, his attention out in the side yard.

"There he be's again," he told her, finally, still in a low voice. "You ain't hear?"

She had still heard nothing, and she shook her head.

"Damn girl' ear must be done stop up," he said.

Automatically, without thinking about it, she put the point of her index finger inside one of her ears to see if it did need cleaning it out. While she was doing that, cautiously and deliberately, to keep the porch swing chains from squeaking, he got himself up to his feet and walked across the porch and into the house. He was back out again almost immediately with his shotgun cradled in the crook of his arm. He sat back down on the swing— still careful not to make it sing out—and set the gun on his lap. While Yally watched in fascinated curiosity, he fished in one of his overalls pockets and pulled out a single buckshot shell, held it out briefly in front of his face for examination, shook it a couple of times and then gave it several light blows of breath to remove any stray lint or dust, broke the shotgun open in a single, quiet motion, slipped the shell into the barrel, and then eased the gun closed again, careful to make sure it locked but did not issue out a loud snap. Still not saying a word or making hardly a sound at all, he turned his body and feet to face out towards the side yard, adjusting the shotgun so that the butt-end was against the well of his shoulder and the barrel resting on the porch railing. He sat and waited. Then, without any warning whatsoever, with no attempt at a sighting or an aiming but only a slight adjustment of the direction of the barrel, he squeezed off the shot. There was a bright spurt of flame from the shotgun barrel and a sharp, explosive crack. The girl jumped and, much too late to have any effect, cupped her hands over her ears.

Papa'Budi stared out into the dark of the side yard for a while more. Now it was deathly silent out there. Even the laughing and the music from the far houses had ceased in the wake of the shotgun blast. Yally herself did not dare say anything, even if she could have figured out something in any way appropriate to the moment to say.

The silence was broken when Big Soo came storming out of the open front door, fists clenched, mouth open, clearly trying to figure out what had just happened. She stopped abruptly as she saw her father sitting quiet and at peace on the porch swing, eyes closed, the shotgun now resting comfortable in his lap. Big Soo took a deep breath and dug her fists down into the fat-muscles of her upper hips.

"What you out here shooting-at, Papa?" she demanded of him, all semblance of respectfulness temporarily vanished.

He opened his eyes slowly and regarded her briefly, as if deciding whether or not her question needed an answer.

"That old yellow-ass dog of Isa Brown, him been at them chicken again," he said, finally. "You ain't got for fret no more about him. I done gotted him good, this time. I done shotted that yellow bastard."

Setting her mouth closed and firm as if she did not believe him, Big Soo went to see. She stepped off the porch past Yally and walked out into the dark towards the chickenyard out behind the house, disappearing for a moment from view.

"Lookit where that ignorant girl going," Papa'Budi said to no-one in particular.

There was a squawking of disturbed chickens from back that way, and then Big Soo called out. "Shotted him where? I ain't see no dog out'chere."

"Ain't at the pens," Papa'Budi shouted back to her in disgust. "I ain't said nothing 'bout shooting no dog at no damn pens." He pointed the shotgun barrel out towards the side yard. The metal glistened dangerously in the light of the porch lamp. "I shotted him out that way, out'cross that field."

Yally could not see Big Soo out in the dark of the yard, but Big Soo apparently could see the direction Papa'Budi was pointing the gun, because after a minute Yally heard her going through the fieldgrass past the side yard where Grandpa had shot, muttering to herself as she did, then a rustling now and then from different points as she made a circling investigation of the field, still keeping up some sort of running commentary whose words Yally could not make out. After a while the sound of the talking apruptly stopped, followed by a single, loud, "Oh, yi!" from Big Soo. Afterwards came a long, silent pause, and then Yally made out the big figure of her aunt coming back from across the field, through the yard, and into the range of the porchlight, walking with long, deliberate strides. She stopped when she got to the side of the porch and, without saying anything, looked up over the railing at Papa'Budi, who looked back at his daughter indifferently.

"Tol'ded you I gotted him," he said with a note of triumph in his voice. "Weren't no need for you to check up after me."

"You gotted him, yes you did," Big Soo said back, evenly, nodding her head several times as she did. "You done gotted we milkcow."

Papa'Budi narrowed his bad eye to get a better look at her with his good one, sniffed, and sent a spray of tobacco-spit out of the corner of his mouth just past where she was standing. "Girl, I believe you done gone raccoon fool," he said. "You think I ain't know a big-ass milkcow from a yard dog?"

Big Soo kept her temper, but Yally could see she was not going to be able to do so much longer. Her aunt had begun raising and lowering herself on the balls of her bare feet, the sign that normally meant you needed to clear out of her way.

"You want for go out there and see for you'self?" Big Soo asked her father.

That made Papa'Budi explode. "What the hell I want for go out and see what I done shotted?!" he asked. "I knows what I done shotted! I done shotted what I shotted at." He lifted up the shotgun and slammed the stock end down on the porchboards, making them shiver all the way down where Yally was sitting on the steps below. "The hell if I need some sassy-ass child for stand up in my face and tell me what I knows I done shotted!" He then went off into a fearful round of cursings and invectives, some of them said directly to Big Soo, some of them said about her and apparently aimed at whoever he undoubtedly believed were now listening to his words from across the yard, some of them, perhaps, for Yally's benefit, his tirade peppered with many "no-mannered"s and "uppity heifer"s and "ain't got no respect for she papa"s and much more like that. The veins in his neck and at his temples began to bulge, and he leaned over to slap the porch railing in front of her with the flat of his hand, his voice rising in pitch as he spoke until it reached a high squeal. Yally had never heard him curse Big Soo like that, and she was now deathly afraid that her grandfather was getting out of control, and was working himself up to leap off the porch at Soo as he had at that stranger man at the Sambuhouse. And with none of the men around to stop him as had been there on the funeral day, she could see no other end but either blows or bullets. But through it all Big Soo did not flinch, standing stiff and unreacting in the yard below him, her legs spread, their agitated moving now ceased, her arms folded across her chest, a grim calm about herself. When the storm of invective had finally blown its course, and Papa'Budi could think of nothing else to say to her or about her, he sat back in his seat and merely glared at her, the upright shotgun still clutched in one hand, pushing off on it to begin swinging. As if that were a signal for her to move, Big Soo turned abruptly on her heel, walked around past where the wide-eyed Yally was sitting, up the steps and, in quiet dignity, past her father and into the house, never looking over at him or saying a solitary word. The sound of things tumbling around inside followed immediately. Grandpa Budi stared straight ahead, unmoved, while Yally peeked unsuccessfully through the doorway to try to find out what was going on. Then Big Soo was out on the porch again, several sheets and a quilt folded under her arm, a boxwood trunk clutched by the handle with her free hand. She walked past Papa'Budi again, still without a word to him, then down the steps and out across the yard in the direction of the Kinlaw house, disappearing into the dark.

For the longest, Yally did not know what to do in response. She could not think of anything that it was possible to say. Going into the house seemed impossibly awkward, besides which there was really nothing for her to do in there, with the supper things already all cleaned and put away, and she did not want to leave so soon after Big Soo because it might seem to associate herself with her aunt's departure. So she simply sat in silence, keeping herself busy by breaking off splinters from the edge of the porch. For his part her grandfather acted as if absolutely nothing had happened, swinging quietly for the longest in the porch swing as he ever did, offering no comment himself. After a while, however, he got up to put the shotgun back into the house and that broke the spell, and before he had gotten to the door to go inside, Yally was up and saying her goodnights and rushing off home herself.

Much later, when she visited Eshy on the Dingle End and told her the story, her sister—who almost never took sides with Big

Soo—said she thought Papa'Budi must be going fool, and didn't blame Soo at all for up and leaving. "I'm surprised her ain't box him 'side his head," she said. "That'd end all that cursing out." Eshy soon turned the incident into a song, putting new words into a children's rhyme they had often sung on the yard:

> *Grandpa shot the milkcow*
> *'Clare him heard it bark*
> *Grandpa can't see nothing*
> *When it out there in the dark*
> *Here come Soo*
> *With a frown on she face*
> *Now her gone and move she thing*
> *Down to Mama' place*

Papa'Budi himself never said a word about the incident as far as Yally could tell. Yally noted, however, that the next day when she checked on it herself before Papa'Budi came home from the ricefields, no cow carcass was present out in the field beyond his house. Clearly, however, from the blood and matted grass left behind, some large animal had bled out there the night before. And there was fresh beef for supper at her grandfather's for several meals afterwards.

And as far as she could tell, this time Big Soo's move to the Kinlaws was permanent.

THE BOXWOOD TRUNK that Big Soo carried with her from her father's house did not contain much: a brush and comb and metal mirror, a handful of dresses and underwear and headscarves, a heavy blue-black sailor's coat, much patched, a pair of overused work boots, some sewing things, a small collection of necklaces, anklets and braclets that Yally had never seen her wear, a hand-made doll, a much-used wooden cooking spoon that had first belonged to her mother and had passed to her through Sister Orry, the only thing of Mama'keece that she had, and a small miscellany of other items. But Big Soo brought with her one other thing to the Kinlaws that was more important to her than all the other things combined. She also brought her root-sack.

About the size you could fit two or three potatoes in, Big Soo's bag was of patched-together burlap and canvas irregularly cut from several different sources, with a circle of black and red beads sewn around the base and just below the neck. In addition, she had pasted small bits of glass-mirrors at intervals all over the outside. The folds of the burlap and canvas and the undulations of the bag as it moved set the mirrors off each at a slightly different angle, so that they often reflected numerous views of the same object from a multitude of perspectives, and if you looked at the bag direct on, it had the disturbing way of seeming to look back at you from with several pairs of your own eyes. The bag bulged with items inside, but what those items were, Yally did not know. Generally the root-sack was hidden inside the folds of Big Soo's dress, suspended from the cloth rope she habitually tied up her waist with, and on the few times Yally had seen it out before Big Soo came to live with the Kinlaws, she never got the chance to see its contents. But it was clearly for root-work, not just from the obvious look of it, but because of the falling out that occurred between Mama and Big Soo not long after Big Soo moved in.

It happened one afternoon, just before supper.

They had been weeding the peas and greenbeans beds in the garden out back behind the hogpens—Mama and Yally and Big Soo—and late in the day, Mama and Yally had gone back to the house to do the final fixings for supper, leaving Soo to put the tools away in the shed. Yally was coming back out with the slop bucket to feed the hogs when she saw it—Big Soo sitting on the ground under the chinaberry tree on the far side of the barn, dress hiked above her knees, legs spread, the root-sack set down in the sand in front of her and open at the mouth. Yally stopped in mid-stride midway across the yard to make sure she was seeing it right. Yes, Big Soo was digging her hand deep down into the bag and bringing something out, and not only that, had already spread several items out on the sand between her legs. But it was too far away to for Yally to be able to identify them.

For a brief moment, she considered simply walking up to get a look—it was directly on the way to the hog pen, after all—but rejected the thought immediately. Since Big Soo had never once volunteered to show the inside of her sack, Yally was certain her aunt would simply put the things away before she got too close. She came up with an alternate plan. Taking care to make no sudden movement or to kick up any sand with her feet, she turned and walked into the barn, hoping she could find some opening in the slats to see what Big Soo was doing under the tree outside. For a long while she searched up and down the wall opposite where Big Soo was sitting outside, her curiosity rising, but Papa had built the barn too well to leave any spaces between the boards, and there were no knotholes she could peep through. She could only hear Big Soo talking in a steady voice from over at the chinaberry tree, either to herself or to the things in the bag or to some other entity, unseen, the words so low and muffled that Yally could not make them out, even when she kneeled down and put her ear close-up against the wall.

Giving it up, finally, as a lost cause, she had picked up the slop bucket and was just about to walk out of the barn and go on with her chores when suddenly here came Mama, striding across the yard from the house in purposeful anger, past the barn door opening. Just in time, Yally ducked back out of her sight. Mama was talking to herself as she walked by, the words rumbling low under her breath, so that all Yally could catch of it was "I done tol'ded she 'bout all that before…" and then Mama disappeared from her view in the direction of the chinaberry tree where Big Soo was sitting.

She could hear none of what Mama said to her aunt out there under the tree, even though she got as close to the barn door opening as she dared, but she had no doubt that it was about the root-sack. And it was clearly a fussing out, from what she could make out from the harsh tone of her mother's voice. "Poor Soo," she said to herself. "Looking like everybodys' done riding she this summer." This particular riding did not last long. In a moment Mama walked back across the barn door opening in the direction of the house, the quick cadence of her steps showing that while some of the steam had come out of her, she wasn't completely finished with her fuming. When Yally was certain that her mother had made it up the back steps and into the house and out of view, she slipped out of the barn and went the far way around to the hog pen, on the opposite side from the chinaberry tree. She needn't have bothered. By the time she cleared the barn and looked over that way, Big Soo had already collected her things from under the tree and was gone.

After that day, Yally saw Big Soo's root-sack several times more, but never anyplace there was any possibility that Mama might see it as well.

BIG SOO HAD NEVER BEEN MUCH for frolic, but now, after Sister Orry's funeral, she had become a great, brooding presence in the Kinlaw house, somber and moody, her thick brows forever tamping down over her big eyes in deep thought even as she went about her work, flicking her bottom lip in and out under her teeth all day and deep into the night while she talked to herself in a murmuring, running monologue.

Yally found herself paired-off often with her aunt on chores
around the house and yard. Soo was an ox of a worker, slowsteady
and meticulous, bearing down on each job with steady purpose,
moving methodically from task to task, one behind the other, with
nary a pause, so that many days by the midday meal they had often
accomplished more than Yally and Eshy would have taken a day to
finish off. With hands almost as big as Papa'Budi's, Big Soo was as
strong as many of the men at Goat Hill, plowing with a mule as
straight and deep and steady as any of them, making the wood-logs
leap in the air as they exploded in half from the power of her axe-
cuts, pounding down the butter churn or the grain-pestle for
hours at a time, stopping only now and then to wipe the sweat out
her eyes with a rag and then back at it again. When it was time to
water the stock, the most Yally had ever seen anyone do, even
Papa, was to fill two buckets and carry them, one in each hand,
from the well behind the house down to the barn and pens. For
Yally and Eshy's part, any more than three-quarters full in the
buckets, and more water ended up along the pathway than did in
the stock troughs. Yally watched in undisguised admiration one
morning, therefore, when Big Soo filled four buckets just under
the brims, slid the bucket handles onto the ends of an old yoke
center stick, two on each side, hoisted the yoke onto her broad
shoulders, and toted the whole load across the yard with nary a
tremble in her step and without spilling a drop.

Sometimes, if only to get a breath and a small break from the
steadiness of working with Big Soo, Yally would try to engage her
aunt in a conversation, any conversation. Eshy, of course, had
needed no prodding on that accord. Eshy could talk for hours on
end as she worked, flowing like the Sugaree from topic to topic,
joke-telling, gossiping, fool-cutting, an opinion on every subject, an
answer for every question, a constant source of fun and
entertainment to pass the day's time. Big Soo was none of this. For
most of her niece's questions she grunted out an answer of a word
or two and nothing more. Sometimes, she would ignore Yally
altogether, but would continue muttering or lining out rhymes or
full-out singing as she worked along as if no question had been
asked, with Yally never being able to tell whether her aunt had
simply heard and chosen not to talk, or was lost-away in some
distant thought and hadn't heard at all. When she did actually sing
aloud and wasn't just talking under her breath, most of Big Soo's
songs were ones Yally had often heard from the women on the
Hill, work-songs and trouble-songs and man-songs and spirit-songs,

and some that did not have easy placement in any category. One of
Big Soo's most-repeated songs was one that Yally herself had sung
many times along with Eshy and their girl-cousins out on the
Bigyard. It was a song about the Pennyman, and the Yay'saw girls
used their version as a rope-jump rhyme:

> *Run, Sal*
> *Run, gal*
> *Run you'self, back to the Quarters*
> *The Pennyman coming for t'ief you' daughters*

Then they would count jumps by marking the daughters stolen
away by the Pennyman until the jumper mis-hit:

> *ONE daughter!*
> *TWO daughter!*
> *THREE daughter!*
> *FOUR daughter!*
> *FIVE daughter!*
> *GONE!*

the "GONE!" ushering the old jumper out and sending in a new
one to take her place.

Even though the rhyme was about Yelesaw's most feared
resident haunt, it was all good bright-day fun, and safe in the
protected circle that was the common yard in front of their homes,
they gave it no more thought than the other jump chants they
used in their play.

But Big Soo's rendering of the Pennyman song was different, a
decidedly grimmer construction, with a chilling turn to it that gave
Yally a shiver across her shoulders and back the first time she
listened close enough to be able to figure what her aunt was
singing, the more disturbing because of its kinship with the jump-
rhyme:

> *When the black crow talk*
> *Like him ain't' oughter*
> *And the snakeskin lay*
> *Up in the larder*
> *And the fish swell-up*
> *On top' the water*
> *When the moon drip sweat*
> *Can't get no hotter*
> *Then the Pennyman come*
> *For t'ief you' daughter*
> *That-when he come*
> *For t'ief you' daughter*

> *Run, Sal, run*
> *Get back to the Quarter*

There were many more verses, each seeming more frightening than the last, and Big Soo always ended by giving out three dry spits and a wipe in the form of an "x" with the ball of her her foot along the ground or the floor over where she had pretend-spitted.

Yally told Eshy about Big Soo's Pennyman song the first time her sister finally came back to Goat Hill for a visit following the wedding, repeating as much of the chant as she could remember. Eshy, of course, thought it powerfully funny, going into a fit of laughter so that she almost lost her water, and making Yally repeat it several times until she could commit it to memory. But Yally did not think it amusing when the words would sometimes come to her late at night in the room, after everyone else had gone to sleep, or, worse yet, when she had to go out in the back yard by herself to use the outhouse.

MORE THAN THE Pennyman rhyme, however, which her aunt usually sang in the broad day, it was at night, with everyone retired to bed and the lamps all blown that Big Soo spooked Yally the most. Most nights Aunt Soo lay down on her pallet on her side, pulled the quilt up to her shoulders, and, exhausted from the day's hard work, went directly to sleep, the soft sound of her heavy breathing filling the bedroom space like the sound of the wind sighing through the woods. While Yally missed the long, bedtime conversations that had almost always happened between her and Eshy, she quickly learned to look forward to the nights when Big Soo dropped into immediate sleep, and did nothing but sleep.

Some nights, instead of going to bed and simply sleeping, like any normal person would do, or else sitting up half the night telling jokes and stories, as Eshy and Yally had so often done, Big Soo acted as if she were laying down, dead, in a coffin. On those nights—which came at odd intervals, with nothing particularly different in her actions that day or evening to give advance notice—she would set herself flat on her back on her quilts and, no matter how hot the night, pulled the covers up over her entire body, face and all, so that they draped her like a funeral shroud. And that's how she would lie for the longest, so absolutely silent and deathly still that Yally was convinced Big Soo had either voluntarily or deliberately ceased breathing. She would not lie that way all night. An eternity of time would pass while Big Soo lay seemingly drained of all life, until, without any warning, she would suddenly draw the covers down from her face, take a deep, gulping breath with mouth wide open, turn on her side, settle into her pallet, and apparently immediately go to sleep.

If it was of conscious intent by her aunt, the purpose of Big Soo's death-breath dance—as Yally came to call it—the girl could never figure. She could not even tell if it was deliberate or something induced by bad dreams. She only knew that the first night it happened, it startled her to no end, and long after Big Soo dropped into her normal dormant breathing, Yally lay awake in her pallet a few feet away, holding her own breath, waiting for it to happen all over again. Eventually she came to understand that the pattern of catatonia, revival, and then regular slumber never presented itself more than once in a night, and so, on those nights, she learned to wait until the dance was over before dropping off, herself.

But other of Big Soo's actions in the nighttime bedroom either jolted Yally out of a deep sleep, or kept her awake for hours.

Every once in a while, far into the night, when all the house had settled and no other sound could be heard, Big Soo would suddenly rise up in her pallet without any warning, the covers dropping in loud whispers to the floor from around her, and sit up like that for the longest, saying nothing and seemingly simply staring out across the blackened room at something only she could see. The sudden movement so close beside her would immediately awaken Yally, and she would lay on her own quilts, silent and still, the racing of her heart gradually slowing back to regular as she realized the cause of the disturbance. How long the two of them actually stayed there like that, watchful and listening, Yally never knew, since she found the marking the passage of time in the silent, dark night impossible. Then just as suddenly, Big Soo would lay back down again in her bed, going back to her slumber, and Yally, after a time, following.

On other nights, Yally would awaken, confused, to small sounds from the side of the bedroom where Big Soo slept, quiet scrapings of something being moved back and forth over the floor, or a muffled clink or clack now and then as one hard thing hit lightly against another. At first it would seem like a mouse or a small possum had found its way into the room and was tumbling around seeking out food, until Big Soo's low mutterings would identify the source. Yally was certain, at those times, that Big Soo was going through the things in her root-sack as she had done under the chinaberry tree the day Mama had fussed her out, though she never could confirm it. And though the girl held her own breath and strained hard to hear what her aunt was saying, she could rarely make out the words, or gain much sense from them when she did, since Big Soo seemed to be speaking in the oldest of old-time Afficky mandy-talk, of which Yally knew only smatterings. Every now and then, though, one plain word would come through the dark from across the room. "Ree." That was Big Soo's favorite name for Sister Orry.

There was no discernable order to these night-time set-ups— sometimes happening several times in a single week, sometimes spaced out at unpredictable intervals, and once, early in the fall, holding off for almost a month—and so they never ceased to be unsettling to Yally. Apparently not to Big Soo. However her aunt spent the hours when everyone else in the house was still and 'sleep, she was always the same the next morning, ready for a day's work, full and hard. For Yally's part, though she gradually became used to the disturbances, it cost her many a full night's sleep, and she often found herself stifling yawns late in the afternoon, and sometimes had to slip away and hide in the hay at the back of the barn to get a few minutes of nap-time so she could make it all the way through the rest of the day.

FOR HER PART, Eshy missed Yally as much as Yally missed Eshy. The chores of newmarried life kept her busy, and it was too far from Kimbitown to just pop over whenever she wanted. Mama, too, had warned her that in the first year of marriage, she must avoid being away from her house and yard too much, otherwise she would always pine for the old home and never fully accept the new. Eshy stayed put, and had a fierce love for both her husband and the new little place he had built for her, but that did not stop her from pining for Goat Hill. One drip-sweat night in early June, when she had been married less than three months, she found herself unable to sleep, thinking both of her mother's bacon cornbread and of something she needed to share with her little sister, each of which reason seemed to get more and more pressing as the night hours moved on. Nu was sleep-breathing loud and peaceful in the bed next to her, unaware of her torment. Finally, when she could stand it no more, she eased herself from under the sheet, put on her clothes in the dark, slipped out the door, untied the mule, and set off riding at a trot back to the Hill.

It was very late when she got there. She tied the mule at the head of the wagonpath and walked across the yard on foot to the

Kinlaw house. The dogs came out from beneath the porch as she got close up, whimpering in recognition, and beating their tails against her legs until she shushed them and sent them back. She hadn't planned her visit out any further than this, and so she stood on the top front step for a moment while she studied on what best to do. She didn't want to wake up Mama for sure. Mama would first think something terrible had happened between her and Nu, and then would fuss to all getout when she found out nothing had. Big Soo would fuss with her just for waking her up, regardless of the cause. If it weren't for Big Soo in her old room, Eshy knew she could tap on the shutter and wake up Yally, and Yally would get from the kitchen whatever good had been left over from supper, and they could take it down under the scuppernong arbor and trade stories for a while. If it weren't for Big Soo.

If it weren't for Big Soo, laying big and stank and sleep in Eshy's old spot.

Well, while there was no way for her to get Soo out of her place in the old bedroom, there had to be a way to make her pay for the intrusion.

A wicked plan came to Eshy's mind.

Quiet and careful as she could, she dropped off the stairs and slipped around the side of the house, her feet barely a whisper on the white sand. When she came to the shutters of her old room, she dropped down on her knees, pressed her body against the houseboards so she couldn't be easily seen by anyone looking out, and reached up with one hand and tapped sharply on the board under the windowsill.

She had to put her hand over her mouth to stifle a snicker.

At first, no sound came back from inside.

She put her face close to the board and cupping her hands around her mouth so that they formed a bullhorn, she gave out a wail that was deep and low and mournful.

"Ooooooweeee. Ooooooweeee. Owoooooweeee."

Eshy stopped and listened, but there was no answer from inside, only the hopeful whining of the dogs from under the house, wondering if she had changed her mind about sending them away, and might be making a call for late supper, or early breakfast.

She waited another moment in silence, and then tapped under the sill again, three sharp taps, and then two more "Ooooooweeee"'s.

Inside the house the sound, muffled against the boards, was

like something coming up out of the damp earth. Big Soo awoke and sat straight up on her pallet.

"Who that is?" she asked.

The answer came back from the veiled darkness along the bedroom's outer wall in a raspy, muffled voice. "I's the Pennyman," the voice called out. "You ain't know me?"

"*Who?!*"

"I's the Pennyman, I done tol'ded you!" came back the hollow answer. "Oooooweeee. Oooooweeee."

"I ain't care who you is!" Big Soo shouted back at the wall. "You stop bothering peoples sleep in they beds and just *get!*"

Yally had herself awakened by then. In the bewilderment of coming so rapidly out of her sleep, she could not fathom what was going on in the room, only that Big Soo was sitting up in her pallet, shouting and waving her fist in the dark.

Yally groaned, thinking that her aunt's nighttime fits had now advanced from muttering to hollering, and there would never be any more rest in the room. Just then, the hag-voice came wailing from beyond the outside wall.

"I's the Pennyman, Sudi Manigault," the voice wailed through the houseboards, "and I sees you with my copper eyes. I ga' fly down you' chimbley and snatch you-up and take you 'way to the woods with me. Oooooweeee. Oooooweeee. Hide all you' daughter'."

There was a sudden, swift motion inside the room.

Big Soo was on her feet and at the wall with something long in her hands, the axe handle, maybe, and where had she gotten it from that fast, Yally couldn't figure in the confusion of the moment, except maybe she'd been sleeping with it under her quilts. But there it was clutched in her fists, and she was beating on the wall with it so that the booming reverberated and shook the whole house. BOOM! BOOM! BOOM! And now the dogs were out from under the house barking up a racket to wake Goat Hill and maybe all of Yelesaw Neck, as well, and here came Papa busting through the curtain-door into the room, barelegged in his nightshirt, Mama and Mookie close behind. The dogs' barking now turned to a baying like trumpets calling out soldiers for battle, and Big Soo was bellowing out, "YOU GET-WAY FROM HERE, OLD *NAY-NAY!* YOU GET-WAY FROM HERE! YOU GET-WAY!" and beating, beating, beating on the bedroom wall with the end of the axe handle with all of her strength until Papa and Mama and Mookie had to grab her by her arms and around her waist to pull her back and keep her from knocking the whole house down. It was all the three of them could do to hold her.

By that time, of course, Sister Eshu'Kola Dingle had long disappeared from behind the Kinlaw house. She didn't much care about getting caught. The chance to poke-tease at Big Soo was well worth the talking-to it might get her, and because she was a 'uman-grown and married and living with her husband in her own house, the time was gone when either Mama or Papa could put the strap to her. On the other hand, she figured that if Papa didn't know what was out there in the dark he might shoot, and so she sprinted across the yard until she came to where she'd tied the mule at the end of the wagonpath, and not taking the time to mount it, she drove it in front of her as she went, and she did not stop running until there was a screen of trees between her and the Bigyard. She heard a single shotgun blast behind her but did not hear any pellets hitting the tree-limbs or trunks, and so she figured Papa must have come out on the porch and fired the shotgun up in the air to scare-off whatever was out there. She let the mule run on by itself up the path, big-eyed and braying, while she allowed her own self to collapse, holding onto a trunk for support, trying to catch her breath while laughing and laughing until she almost made herself sick.

# 4

# For T'ief We Land

## (Winter-Fall, 1936)

T hey had waited out the winter of 1936 watching cautiously and quietly across the river for some sign of movement towards the building of the whitefolks' dam.

Tacked on the front of Jaeger's Store, in between the metal signs advertising Beech-Nut Chewing Tobacco, Luzianne Coffee, and Royal Crown Cola, among other things, a map of Cantrell County had been posted to show the proposed boundaries of Lake Pinckney, as it was now officially being called. It was a duplicate of the map hung at the courthouse at St. Paul, with another on the announcement board in front of the County Extension Building in Cashville, one at the Roberts Feed & Grain Store in Sandy Station, and a fourth at the Grange Hall in Porterfield. There were several more on display inside various public buildings and the largest churches and workplaces around the county, so that no-one could say they had not been properly notified, or warned, according to how they took the news. All of the maps showed a small rectangular box, pearl-gray in color, set astride the Sugaree River just above where it passed through Cashville, and identified in bold lettering as the "Cashville Dam." With the exception of those with some sort of engineering background, most of the county residents who came and scrutinized the maps looked for the proposed location of the dam, noted it, and then paid it scant more attention. The site where the dam was actually planned to be built was not of general concern, once it was ascertained that it did not involve either occupied land or favorite fishing spots. Of vastly more interest was the mark-off on the map of where the new lake was supposed to come. Outlined in ominously-heavy black and then shaded-in with an airy blue, as if to lighten the effect, the proposed flood plain covered what the Cantrell County people commonly called "the Basinbottom"—which stopped at the bank of the Sugaree—as well as Yelesaw Neck and most of the Sugaree Swamp on the other side. It was the perfect place to put a lake, if that's what you had a mind to do, a natural hollow sunk down in the center of the county, running roughly eighteen miles north to south from just below St. Paul to just above Cashville, and then, at its widest point, some twelve miles or so from the town of Sandy Station to the west out to the Porterfield community far bank of the Blacksnake River.

The Yay'saws who came to look at the Jaeger's Cross or Cashville maps took particular interest in the position of Yelesaw Neck inside the shaded-off lake boundaries, which confirmed in draft-and-print what had already been asserted by word-of-mouth. Marked as Adams Neck—Yelesaw not being a name recognized on the oba side of the river—the community sat on the map between the Sugaree and the Blacksnake like either a bottom-heavy gourd distended to one side or the torso of a narrow-bosomed pregnant woman standing sideways, seven miles from top to bottom, four miles at its thickest, dropping from the narrow, impassible bushbrakes where the two rivers came close but did not quite meet, widening at the belly as the Sugaree made a great, curving sweep to the west before turning back eastward where it met the Blacksnake and the rivers converged, marking Yelesaw's bottom end. More than one of the Yay'saws who came to see the map ran the tip of a finger across the light-blue shading covering Yelesaw, as if they thought by doing so they might be able to feel the wetness of the whitefolks' lakewater. They went away without commenting, at least while they were standing in the general public, in front of the map.

In the meantime, there was plenty of comment from other county residents, colored and white, with questions, debates, discussion, and expressions ranging from delight to disapproval to despair to disdain, rising and falling all day at the map-gatherings as each new knot of gatherers formed, reformed, and then drifted away to spread the word and continue the deliberations through the rest of the county.

Bo Kinlaw made several trips to Cashville and Jaeger's Cross on business that winter into the summer, and each time he returned, he would bring with him a new copy of the county newspaper, *The Southern Call.* Now that it was settled that the Yay'saws would not be uprooting, Mama tolerated water-talk around the house, and so, after supper, Papa and the children would sit around the fireplace while one of them would go through the paper, reading aloud all the articles that touched on news of the dam. While Mama offered no objections, she always sat apart from the others while the readings went on, hearing but ignoring what was being said. Mama had not had any county schooling of her own and had never learned to recognize more than a handful of words, and the *Call's* sudden saturation with the flood project confirmed her long-held belief that reading was entirely unnecessary and unwanted in her affairs. "What I want for wear out my eyes for over all that word-writing, ain't got nothing for talk about 'cepting that dam-news," she would say. Eshy and Yally, of course, immediately agreed that what their mother was almost certainly saying was the "damn news."

Most weeks there was more than one article in the paper on the Watercoming, some of them under the continuing heading of the "Cashville Dam Progress Report" that regularly appeared in the same spot every week, and mostly repeated official pronouncements and information. But many other accounts detailed the public reaction to the project. Some of these reported on the growing controversies between whitefolks in the county and beyond over who should build the dam, or whether the current proposed location was the best place to build it, or what area the lakebed should cover or leave untouched, and even whether the dam should be built at all. Yally listened in fascination when one article noted that some of the white farming men from out of the eastern end of the county had actually gotten themselves arrested for breaking up an information meeting at the Grange Hall.

> "As one of their members so colorfully told this reporter from behind the bars in his cell at county jail, he and his kinsmen 'will be d...ed and go straight to h..l and take plenty of others with us before we let some some Washington Yankees and Columbia scallywagons drive us off our family

land.' The highly agitated gentleman added that
'my granddaddy toted arms at Cold Harbor and
Petersburg, and I ain't too proud to do the same
right here back in Cantrell.'"

One of the Porterfield men got tussled up some by the High
Sheriff's men during the arrests, the *Call* article reported, and
there was a big row over it, and worries that there indeed might be
gunplay, everybody knowing how the Porterfield people were,
white and darky. Afterwards, Yally found the paper where Papa
had folded it up and left it on the table, and took it into her
bedroom and read the article to herself, all over again, several
times. She had never seen curse words in a newspaper before, not
even dotted out.

The editor of *The Southern Call* itself was somewhat skeptical of
the lake plan. In one editorial with a heading in big letters reading
"SHOULD WE CALL IT BUTLER'S FOLLY?", he wondered aloud:
"Is Governor Jim Butler pushing the Cashville
Dam Project so hard because he wants to win
Washington favor for the job he's rumored to be
seeking in the Roosevelt Administration?"

The *Call* went on to charge, in several follow-up articles, that
the State Senator and High Sheriff also had "dirty hands," only in
league with the plan because of what the paper described as the
"fat labor contracts" for the land-clearing of the proposed lakebed
they were trying to line up for the county prison farm. The
editorial and articles made something of a stir, and caused the
State Senator to tell a reporter from *The State* newspaper in
Columbia that he would not deign to answer the charges made by
*The Southern Call*'s editor, who the Senator said was "imported
trash, not even from Cantrell County," and who "hid like a
bluebelly jackanapes coward behind a desk and a pot of black ink."

Others at Yelesaw monitored the *Call* articles as well, and
copies of the newspaper made the rounds from house to house up
and down the River Road. A consensus began to grow, as the
winter weakened and broke into the new planting season, that with
the whitefolks fighting so fiercely with each other, the plans for a
dam across the Sugaree River might only be a storm of little more
than dry clouds and bluster. It would not be the first time that
whitefolks' grand plans had come to nothing. That is why the
Yay'saws did not pay it much mind when they found out about the

Sparman, who had come down to Cantrell County from Columbia to set up shop.

HE WAS A THIN, YOUNGISH WHITE MAN with owl-round glasses and a sad, studious expression ever on his face, and who, regardless of the heat, always wore a forest-green tie and starch-pressed soldier-type khaki shirt and pants, often with a khakhi-colored jacket as well. The whitefolks and the obas called him the SPAR man because of the round patch he wore sewn onto the shoulder of both his shirt and jacket. Around the top curve of the patch was a silver fish jumping over a spot of blue lake between what looked to most Cantrell County residents like a factory spouting white smoke on the one side and a telegraph pole on the other, the two divided by a yellow zig-zaged lightning bolt. It was actually an electrical power plant and a power pole divided by an artist's conception of a line of raw electricity, but Cantrell County wasn't yet fully used to those. Around its bottom curve the patch spelled out the letters S-P-A-R for the Sugaree Power and Recreation Authority for which the Sparman worked. That logo was printed on all the official papers he passed out, which were many. He was truly a paper-pushing man. Some of the folks on the county side of the river referred to him as Mr. Sparky instead of the Sparman, referring to the spark in the center of his uniform patch. The Yay'saw's quickly changed that to Old Socky, because Socky was the old-time name for a thief, and in the Yay'saws' opinion, his only purpose for coming to Cantrell County was to t'ief their homes and land.

He had begun working out of the SPAR office in the courthouse at St. Paul sometime in the late winter, and by early spring had moved into the County Office Building in Cashville. Soon afterwards, handbills began appearing on vacant walls and telephone poles and tree trunks throughout town, and then out into the Basinbottom communities where the lake was supposed to be coming, passed out and around in dry goods stores and on the flatbed trucks carrying laborers to the fields or the pulpwood mills, in barber shops and beauty parlors, on the steps of a hundred churches, and in any other place where the county people might be congregating or passing through.

The handbills announced that a dam was going to be built on the Sugaree River sometime soon—as if there were anyone left in Cantrell County who wasn't aware of *that*—and provided a map of the towns and communities that were marked to be vacated. The handbills invited landowners to come to the Sparman's office in Cashville to sign up for something called "the fair land trade," or renters to survey drawings of the new-building homes and land tracts that were being set up for them. Several groups of obas went—no Yay'saw's, of course—and they were told that any land or homes they owned in the areas to be flooded could be swapped for land just to the south and west of Cashville, away from the bed of the new lake.

Most went to the office out of curiosity, or boredom, or for the coffee and cola drinks and cigarettes and chewing tobacco and packs of nabs that were provided, free of charge, at the Sparman's office. But early in the spring, several families, both colored and white, from the Hollyfield community just up above Sandy Station, announced that they were making the move. No-one in the county was surprised, these being Hollyfielders. The spring planting that year had been particularly bad for them, and anyplace the state might offer was better than the dry, yellow scrub-and-sand land where they presently lived and farmed. The Hollyfielders packed up quickly enough, not having much to carry with them, and on the day they came into Cashville in a caravan of several wagons and flatbed trucks, many obas and a few Yay'saws went out with packed dinners to sit on the roadbank and watch the spectacle. The Yay'saws came back saying it was better than the circus parade that came every year to St. Paul.

As expected, the Hollyfielders' decision did not sway any others of either race in the projected area of the lakebed to follow their lead. Weeks passed, and as the days went by in an increasingly empty office, the Sparman decided to take his pitch on the road.

He worked his way over the St. Paul-Cashville Road in a battered black roadster truck, stopping like a traveling tent preacher wherever he found three or four gathered together who might hear his pitch. Unrolling his collection of maps and schematics and architectural drawings out on tabletops or porches or benches or the hood of his truck or just smooth spots on the ground, he pointed out the land that the new lake would take, marked off the plot areas set aside for the relocations, showed the configuration of the new houses and farmplots, talking to many, convincing a few, signing up less. But he knew the pressure would be mounting for people to move, as SPAR-related activites increased on all fronts. Just this week, the surveyors had begun to travel in earnest around the Basinbottom in their logoed white trucks making a systematic analysis of the flood plain, peering through instruments across houses and fields and woods, recording the angles and rises and sinks in their books, taking up soil, putting down stakes, adding to the growing impression that, brother, this dam-building and land-clearing, indeed, was going to happen and happen quite soon. And so he let chapter and verse percolate amongst the congregation while he turned his attention to what everyone was telling him would be the most difficult barrier to breech, that community of coloreds living over on the swamp-edge across the Sugaree.

THEY CALLED THEM THE NECKERNIGGERS and they were a favorite topic of conversation among other county residents, both colored as well as white, none of it particularly encouraging. He learned that while they were regular and responsible traders in town, good workers when you could get them to work off of their enclave, and not known to be especially raffish or prone to stealing—not when compared to the no-'count niggers of St. Paul's Trackbottom Downs district or of Jumptown in Cashville— the Adams Neck coloreds could be stubborn and argumentative, and even subject to violence, if they got it in their minds they were being crossed. These were stiff-necked, bull-headed nigras, for sure, and for that reason, had been left to their own devices practically since the Yankees came through Cantrell. "Even traveling salesmen don't travel over there," the Sparman was told, more than once. If a white man had business with an Adams Neck nigger, up to and including the High Sheriff himself, he rarely crossed the Sugaree to do it, but sent word for the darky to meet him in town. And when you did business with the Neckers, you'd best bring a translator if you weren't familiar with their speech. They talked a gibberish all their own that even most regular Cantrell County darkies couldn't understand. And they called Adams Neck by their own made-up name—Yay-lay-saw or something such, if you could imagine—which was either red Indian-talk or Congobabble, you take your pick.

The Sparman listened with interest and respect, took in everything he heard, and mentally threw out the chaff. He'd seen most of the errors white men usually made when dealing with the coloreds, and if there were going to be mistakes made, they would originate with him. He had his own ideas on how he'd handle the Adams Neckers, much of which he had learned from his father, a circuit revival preacher who had worked extensively and successfully among the Lowcountry darks, and knew their ways as much as any white man from Savannah to Charleston.

One of the most important things he had learned from his father was that a white man couldn't simply trust in his own innate intelligence and abilities when doing business with a darky. Planning and preparation were the key. And so he made it a point to be around the feed stores and markets in Cashville when the Neckers came in to do their business, listening unobtrusively as they shopped or bartered their stock or produce, to see what their dialect was like. Within a short time, he knew he'd have no trouble understanding. He'd grown up around darktalk, and while the cadence and pronunciation of the Neckerspeak that seemed to so confound the Cantrellians took a little bit to get used to, it wasn't much worse than what he'd regularly heard in the backroads and fields back home. Most white men didn't understand colored talk because they didn't think it important to try, his father had often told him. One thing in particular he did that day around the market was to learn how the Adams Necker coloreds pronounced the word *Yelesaw*. He didn't care where it came from. But he was going to make sure to only use that name during his visit across the river—and use it as the Neckers spoke it—so that he could present himself as a sympathizer and a friend in a way the Cantrell whites almost certainly never had.

He was also not worried about the main thing he had been warned about, the famous Adams Neck hoodoo. "Every nigger on this side of the river *go* to a rootdoctor," he was told by the Cantrell whites, "but every nigger over on that side *is* a rootdoctor." The Cantrell blacks, by way of confirmation, assured him that he would be hit with an assortment of spells, bewitchments, and unholy hexes the moment he set foot across the Sugaree, and he was offered an assortment of charms—for a price, of course—for protection. He declined the propositions with thanks. While he knew many white men who believed in the power of black folks' magic, he wasn't one of them. He had traveled with his father along the tent-holler circuit through a countryside—from Beaufort down through Jasper County and into the outskirts of Savannah, as well as on the adjacent islands—that was thick as ticks with an abundance of voodoo practioners, colored and white, known all over the South. He'd seen them work many a spell, some of them tried, in vain, on his own father, who had learned all the protections and countersigns in his spare time and who would sometimes throw back a bit of sorcery at the ones who had tried to sorcer him "just to see," as he'd say, with a chuckle, "how many inches them niggers could bug their eyes out of their heads without them falling out altogether, and how far they could jump back-a-ways without turning their feet around." The Sparman knew these jinxes and whammies and evil-eyes worked only on the weak-minded and the initiates and believers, and he was hardly any of those. On the other hand, even though sitting down and eating in the open yard was one of the best ways to draw a crowd of coloreds and get your message out to the largest number of people, he wasn't about to accept any of the Neckerniggers' food. You didn't have to believe in poison for it to kill you.

One afternoon late in June, he crossed the Sugaree River to take his own preliminary look at Adams Neck.

He had left his roadster at Jaeger's Cross and hired a horse from a nearby farm. That would slow him down, of course, but it couldn't be helped, as he'd been told that most of the roads and pathways on the Neck were too narrow and muddy to be suitable for autos. He was also somewhat hampered by the fact that there were no up-to-date maps of the land between the river and the swamp. The latest ones he could find either inside the county or out had been drawn by Yankee topographers on their hasty way through during the time of the Late Troubles, and showed only those things which the generals were interested in digging up, blocking off, or blowing up. It rankled his sense of organization and record keeping that the good local white citizens had not abandoned their avoidance of all things Adams Neck long enough in the past seventy years for new maps to be made. Still, he had the sense of landscape and direction that came from a civil engineer's training, and figured he would manage. On the way across the river on the cable-barge, he got some general directions on the lay of the Adams Neck land—Yelesaw Neck, he reminded himself—from the older colored boy operating the barge, and that got him from the landing up to the main road, a rough, sandy lane that paralleled the course of the river. Turning the horse onto the road, he started up it at a leisurely trot, taking his first look at the land he had come to conquer and clear.

AT THE FIRST HOUSE HE VISITED, set in a small yard carved out of the woods just aside the road, a little colored girl with uncombed hair answered the door. Seeing a whiteman standing on the porch, she slammed the door again and ran whooping through the house and out into the back yard to her mother, who in turn came rushing around to the front, hoe held high, as if her child had been threatened by a snake. Seeing a whiteman on this side of the river was clearly going to take some getting used to for them.

He did not tarry at the first house, staying only long enough to introduce himself and get the woman's feathers down, so that she could be assured that he was no threat to her child. But by the time—not long afterwards—he had reached the next house a hundred yards or so up the road, and at every house thereafter, the reception was decidedly less dramatic, a clear sign that word of his arrival was preceding him, as he knew it would, and as fit his plan. He was often met out in the yard as he rode up as if the people had been both expecting and waiting for him. At each of these, he said who he was and briefly told his purpose—though clearly they all knew that information by now—noted their names, and briefly asked if they might want to sign on the spot the moving papers he kept buckled up in his saddlebag. He would have been shocked if any did. Though he had a calmer atmosphere in which to talk, the actual results were no different than at the first house. He was listened to politely, nodded to at the right places, and then sent on his way with an "'afternoon, to you, Cap'n" or a "thanky, sir, we'll study on it," and nothing more.

This did not faze him in the least. He was only conducting a preliminary probe, and he had fully expected either spirited dissension or sullen resistance or mannerly indifference, one, all of which were common among the coloreds. He began to try out several variations on his approach for future reference, flattering at one house, cajoling at another, sometimes gentle ridicule, or at other times, outright baiting. Though he didn't expect it today, generally, eventually, one of those things always roped the coloreds in. All he needed was one break in the dam. Smiling at himself that this might not, in fact, be the proper analogy for the current situation, he rode on.

Once in a while, he would come across a farmer plowing in a field beside the road, and those he generally passed by with only a wave. What he was really looking for today were places where the larger crowds gathered, so that he would know where to concentrate on his next trip over. There he would find the leaders, the ones he needed to convince and recruit to his cause, who would then, in turn, bring along their followers. The cleverest among them—the ones that you really wanted on your side—did not immediately identify themselves as the ones in charge, in order to scope out potential rivals to their rule. But he knew how to cull them out, once he discovered where the herds were.

As the afternoon passed, he looked for the signs of activity leading down to the places he knew they were gathered at, the road houses or fish-holes or even convenient shady spots under the trees, the lounge spots where the coloreds always congregated. Coloreds loved their lounging, but out of habit almost always did it out of a white man's sight, to keep from being scolded or shamed or ordered back to work. In Cashville and Sandy Station and the other settlements he'd been working, it was easy-enough to find guides to take him to those hidden holes. A bite of tobacco or a bottle of beer would do in payment, and sometimes, not even that. But today, on this side of the river, he had come across none of the indolent and slack-jawed who would slide up to him as soon as they saw him walking in the colored parts, asking if he needed any help, and so the idling locations, so far, had escaped him.

Finally, late in the day, he found something better than what he had been looking for.

The largest collection of houses he had come across so far during his ride was two or three set together in a common clearly visible from the main road down a short stretch of pathway. But when he came to a somewhat larger wagontrack whose end he could not see because it made a sharp turn and disappeared into the trees after only a few yards, the well-worn condition of the wagonruts gave him hope that maybe there might be a somewhat larger settlement down there. To his delight, it was much, much more than that.

After the first turn, the wagontrack ran fairly straight through a thick pine forest for a bit towards a screen of trees that blocked the view ahead. It now began to look as if this might be a logging road, and though that wasn't as good as a settlement, there might be men down there working who he could talk to. He continued on. Just before running into the blocking line of trees, the track made a sharp turn to the left and then, after a short stretch, back to the right again, and then suddenly came out of the woods and into a wide, sunny clearing that could not be seen until you actually made the last turn and came up on it. It was not the clearing, however, that got his attention. Midway across it was a large collection of houses, something over 20 or 25, he figured, not even bothering to count, he was so pleased at the discovery. Trust your woods-sense, he said to himself. It always takes you where you need to go, even if you're too dumb to acknowledge it.

There were also people back there, he was glad to note, coloreds, of course, mostly girls and aunties, some with children in tow, standing and talking or going about their chores around the periphery of the houses. They did not see him at first, sitting on horseback a distance away, still under the shadow of the pinewoods, and so he had a chance to examine the settlement before the inevitable stir hit.

The houses themselves were of the usual colored type, bare of paint and tin-roofed, a few of them narrow shotgun shacks, some of them cabin-sized, but several considerably larger. That was no different than you'd normally see in the colored sections of town. But unlike the nigger rows in Jumptown or the Trackbottoms, these houses were not packed together slavequarters-fashion. Instead they were clearly separate homesteads, widely spaced, each with its own identifiable yard devoid of any hint of grass or bush, separated here by a strip of garden, there by a copse of fruit trees or palmetto bushes, the front of the individual yards opening seamlessly out into the large front clearing. Behind the houses, he could also see the stock pens and farm buildings and beyond them, open fields that dropped back into the woods on the back side of the settlement. The house plots were of different sizes, the distance between them varied widely, and they were staggered up and back in a sort of a zig-zag, with no obvious pattern to the staggering. Despite that, their arrangement did not seem at all random, and something suggested to the Sparman's engineer's knowledge a uniformity of planning and purpose as well as some sort of social hierarchy whose logic he could not quite figure out. After his initial surprise, he began to look over the settlement with a trained eye, internalizing all the details, so that he could sketch and study them at his leisure when he got back to his office. Then it hit him. If he ignored the fact that the houses were not on a line with each other, he could immediately see that the settlement was still set out in a row, left to right, in a sort of rough semi-circle, all facing the clearing, and all but the very center houses angled slightly inward towards each other as well. He had found the leaders. He'd bet a gallon of gas to a gopher hole that they'd be living in the houses right at the center, like Guinea grass-skirt kings surrounded by their subjects.

Smiling, satisfied now, he kneed the horse forward and started it at a walk towards the houses. Halfway across the clearing, before he reached the outskirts of any of the individual yards, he turned to the left and rode down the settlement's length, keeping at a distance that deliberately showed he was making an inspection and an appraisal. His appearance coming out of the woods was immediately noted, and he gave a nod or two of greeting their way, but otherwise ignored the people as they stopped what they had been doing and stood in the yards and stared at him, agape, joined by others who came quickly out of their doors or from around the back. He rode at a measured pace until he came just level with the last house on the row, where he stopped again. From there he could see at the far edge of the clearing a well-beaten, open pathway that passed through a grove of trees and out into a second, similar settlement beyond. Hell, he'd come up on damned Indian village. He turned his horse back. He'd seen enough.

He rode at the same slow pace the opposite way past the houses again, but angling across the clearing towards the opening in the woods and the beginning of the wagontrack. The girls and old aunties and their children—along with a handful of old uncles—continued to stand in their yards and on their porches and stare at him. At the track he paused, turned in his saddle and dipped his head towards the houses, and then started up the pathway. There was still plenty of daylight left, but he had done exactly what he had come to do, and he was through for the day. Leaving the community of Neckers to wonder what he was up to, he returned to the cable-barge, and then back across the river to Jaeger's Cross and then Cashville. Fully satisfied with himself, he spent the next couple of hours going over papers in his office, humming softly to himself.

IT HAD BEEN THE SPARMAN'S INTENTION to go back to Adams Neck the next day, to capitalize on his discovery, but another piece of good news intervened. A delegation of ministers and business owners and big farmers from out of Sandy Station had come to his office while he'd been across the river, leaving word that they were ready to use their influence to facilitate the land sale and relocation signups in their area. He spent the next three days following up, and the breakthrough resulted in a packed community-wide meeting at Sandy Station's Methodist church. The Sparman's presentation was well-received and supported by many of the community leaders, and afterwards several families signed up. He got the impression that soon there would be many more. The signups kept him busy with paperwork for several more days before he could finally get back on the rented horse and be off on the road down to the cable-barge to cross the Sugaree again.

It was a muggy and thunder-rumbling morning, with billowed gray-black clouds over the western woods threatening rain. On the way over the river he struck up another conversation with the rangy older colored boy who operated the ferry—Lem Washington, he called himself—who had been willing to give out a little information the first time the Sparman had used his barge services. Washington apparently did little all day but piddle around his shack down near the water's edge, catch fish and cook the fish he caught, while he waited for people to come back and forth across the river.

"You can make a living like that?" the Sparman asked him.

"Sure, Cap'n," Washington answered with a lopsided, grizzled grin. "Folks pays me with fish, when they does gotted'em. And when they ain't, I manages."

The bargeboy was talkative and interested in the Sparman's purpose and progress in his work, the only person on Adams Neck so far who appeared to be such, and so the Sparman took the opportunity to get the lay of the Yelesaw land from a Yelesaw himself. Though he now had an important key with the discovery of the village in the woods, he knew not to rely upon that completely, at least not until the lock was opened and the door cracked. And so he told the bargeboy he was interested in meeting the most respected and influential citizens on the Neck, adding that he was sure that Washington, whose job brought him in contact with everybody doing business on the other side of the river, would certainly know who such citizens might be. The flattery worked. The bargeboy was more than happy to oblige, holding the Sparman on horseback at the water's edge for a half an hour or more as he gave out a complicated and dizzying recitation on Yelesaw families that the Sparman at first tried to keep up with and write down in his notebook, but found he could not. Seeing his morning already beginning to slip away, and the rainclouds continuing to make their slow drift in his direction, he took his leave from Lem Washington and started along the road beside the river on his horse, and then onto the wagontrack through the woods and down into the village.

There was no surprise registered when he rode out from between the trees this time, as if they were fully expecting him at that particular day and hour. No-one came rushing out from the back yards or the houses to see the spectacle. What looked like the same colored girls and old aunties and a few uncles were out in the yards doing their same chores, with their same pack of children scattered around them. They all watched him with blank faces, keeping their eyes on him while they kept at their work or play. He walked his horse across the clearing and then angled towards the far end of the village, nodding to each of the girls and aunties and uncles as he passed, which they returned with nods of their own. There was something a little disconcerting in the way they did not drop their gazes as most coloreds did when a white man looked at them direct, but there was nothing angry or defiant or dangerous in the way they watched him, as you might see in the worst nigger sections of Savannah or Charleston, so he did not think he would have trouble handling that. Avoiding the center houses where he had figured that the leaders lived, he went directly to the last house in the line, and there he stopped for his first introduction and chat. His strategy was to make the leaders come to him, and by so doing, make them and their followers understand that it was he, and not they, who were in charge.

He got off his horse, and walked up to the colored girl who was sweeping off her porch with a broom fashioned from a palmetto stalk and fronds. He figured her to be in her early 30's, but it was hard to tell exact ages with the coloreds, of course. She stopped her sweeping and looked at him with eyes that were barren of any revelation of what she was thinking. A little boy was sitting on the edge of the porch not far from her, swinging his bare legs and feet in the air.

"Good morning," he told her, with a smile.

"Morning, sir," she told him back, her own mouth moving only enough to get the words out before it settled back into its firm line.

His smile increased rather than diminished, broadening over his entire face. He went into his performance. "I'm from the Sugaree Power and Recreation Authority," he said, pointing to the badge on his shoulder. "You've heard about us, I reckon. We're out here to bring y'all some electricity. You ever been inside a house with electric lights? Let me tell you, sister, it's a sight. You turn on all those lights, all together, ooooweee, it give God a good run for His daylight, and old Satan wishing he had some to get in those dark corners down in Hell. You know how to read?" Without waiting for an answer, he handed her a brochure from the packsack he had taken out of his saddlebag. She took it in her hand automatically and held it out in front of her, a small frown creeping into her face, looking at the brochure as if it were something foreign and slightly peculiar. "Don't matter if you can't," the Sparman went on, leaning forward and flipping open the brochure in her hand with the point of his finger. "Just look'it those pictures. They tell it all. We knew a white lady down in Hardeeville—my father was her minister—and her husband had fool her to get into bed every night and then tie her up to keep her there, she was so excited about getting electricity. Used to stay up until the chickens got up, doing her sewing, it was always too dim for her to see the stitches when she had kerosene. Don't you want your house all shine-up inside like that at night?"

He took off his glasses, buffed the lenses against his sleeve, and held them out in front of him while he squinted at them, waving them a bit as he did, all done with big gestures so that they might catch both the light and the attention of the ones he knew were watching his theatrics from afar.

"I had to do my studies by tallow 'til I was 14 and we got our lights," he went on. "If we'd had 'em before that, I wouldn't need to look through these things now."

He turned the glasses around in his hand and extended them towards the little boy swinging his legs on the porch edge.

"You want to see through my glasses, boy?" the Sparman asked him.

The little boy seemed eager to do so, ready to slip off the porch and come running, but after a glance at his mother standing above him—the Sparman guessed it was his mother—he froze in his spot, and shook his head as vigorously as he was swinging his legs. The Sparman gave an indulgent smile at the boy and put his glasses back on, giving them a last little wave in the air before he did.

Southerners colored and white alike, he knew from long experience and practice, were all of a curious sort, and from his evangelist father he had learned all of the tricks of drawing a crowd without seeming to be doing so. The raising of the voice at certain spots so that folks afar could catch some tidbit, followed by an all-but-conspiratorial lowering to a loud whisper as if some secret was being shared. The drawing out of laughter from a selected few because nobody, after all, can tolerate not knowing what others are laughing about or at. The unrolling of documents and then quickly rolling them back up again before anyone can get a good look, the shuffling around in your pocket to find something but never bringing it out, the pointing of a finger at nothing in particular, the waving about of metal or glass objects sure to catch a glint of sun so that their nature could not be determined from a distance, but only by coming up close and examining. All were designed to draw others into the circle, straggling first, but increasingly coming in droves, until eventually a meeting was in session without ever being called. The Sparman had never seen this fail, in his father's traveling ministry or his own work in assistance back in Beaufort and Jasper, or in the last few weeks in Cantrell County.

But it did not work here in Yelesaw village.

He came to the end of his presentation to the colored girl, and the three of them—along with the little boy—remained distinctly by themselves.

He was careful not to show any disappointment. That was one of the other tricks. Never let them see you dispirited.

"Well, you just keep that paper and look it over and think about what I said," he told her, the smile never leaving his face. "Show it to your husband, and share it with your friends. You need a couple'more to pass around?" While she was shaking her head no, he continued without a break. "And if you're studying it at night and all you have is a kerosene or candles to see by, think of how much better you'd be with electric lights."

"Yessir," she told him. She tucked the brochure into the folds of her dress and went back to her sweeping, keeping her eyes on him while she did so, as did the little child. He had not mentioned anything about selling land or moving, and did not intend to unless asked. He knew it was on the minds of the colored girl and all the silent watchers, and eventually they'd start asking him instead of him bringing it up first. That's how you got them talking instead of hanging back. Leave out the one thing they were dying to know. He gave the girl and her little boy a wave of his hand, then took the reins of his horse and led it down to the next house, raised the theater curtain, assessed the audience in front of him, and went into his act again with the two gray-haired aunties who were out in the yard.

Slowly, as the summer stormclouds worked their way across the sky, he worked his way down the line of houses.

He knew as he talked and gestured and cajoled, he was being carefully watched from the adjoining dwellings, but none stopped their chores to come over, only purchasing their tickets when he actually came into their particular yards, and so he was forced to go through his act over and again, to the smallest of audiences, as he went from house to house.

He confirmed the observation he had made of the age and nature of the visible population when he first saw the village from across the clearing. Of working-age colored boys or older children, he saw almost none. Mostly he found girls that looked to be in their 20's to 40's doing home chores, and older aunites tending gardens or cooking, or older uncles doing yard work or other light tasks. A few—but very few—sat or lay in the shade of porches or trees, taking a break from the heat that grew more sultry as the morning wandered towards noon and the clouds pressed down lower. After initially giving the Sparman all of their attention, the little children began to lose interest when the obviously-expected excitement did not follow, and gradually came to ignore him and went back to their play, only resorting to their watchfulness when it was their yard he invaded. Their shouts and laughing and chanting slowly made the sounds of the village come back to what he believed was some semblance of normal. There was none of the shouting and chatter and music, however, that was the regular fare of a colored quarters. Even though they, too, were ignoring him now, his presence in the village certainly hadn't slipped the minds of the older folks.

The only residents who seemed excited about his presence were the packs of dogs that came gamboling out from under porches and trees and behind sheds and barns at every house he visited, barking and hallooing furiously, surrounding him even before he could get off his horse. His plan for the dogs worked considerably better than the one for their owners. He had a butcher wrap of meat strips in his saddlebag especially for yard dogs, and he tossed two or three of the scraps in the middle of each horde as they reached him. The dogs—as he knew they would—went off in a furious scrum over the pickings and when they finally returned to him, it was with all tails a'wag, and an eagerness to be his friend.

He'd often seen such tactics work with coloreds, but these Adams Neckers were clearly of a somewhat different sort.

As he talked with them, one by one, house by house, making his slow way through the village, he kept one eye on the two or three center houses in the row, where he had figured the leaders were living, but he found no special sense of scrutiny coming from that way, only the same disinterested interest he was getting from the people in the other houses. And when he finally came to them, the people in the middle homesteads seemed—on the surface—no different than the others, acting no differently, asking no special questions. All were polite, respectful, but noncommittal, neither their eyes nor any gesture revealing either their status or the thoughts that were going on inside those wooly heads.

With a growing belief that he might not be able to smoke the big chieftains out on this, his first real day in the village, he began to add on a couple of different tacks so he'd be able to go back to Cashville with something more than simply seeds sewn.

First, he tried to find out where the rest of the people were.

"I know there's more folks around here than y'all," he would say. "Everybody out in the fields?" He'd give a look out towards the back of the houses. "Where the fields at? I didn't pass any coming in." To the younger girls, he gave a special dig. "I grew up on a farm out from Ridgeland. You know where that is? It's down on the Georgia border. My Daddy was a good man. Wasn't a harder working man in Jasper County than him. But a day like this, with a good rain coming, he'd get the wander in him, and take off, and Mama would have to send me to look for him. Wasn't but two places he'd be, down at the fish-pond or back at my uncle's still. I know you won't tell a government man where your stills might be—" there he'd give a wave of his hand and a conspiratorial little laugh, as if he and this colored girl were sharing a secret that he, of course, would never reveal "—but I'm not that kind of government man, so no need to worry. But I *am* a fishing man. I got that from my Daddy's side. I'd be obliged if you'd let me on to the good fishing spots, I can get some in before I have to get back across the river. And if I see any of the boys down there, I'll be sure to tell them their girls are looking for them, and send them back home. And I could use a beer in all this heat. You got a place around here that sells beer?"

"Oh, folks be around somewheres," he was told in response with a wave of the hand in several different directions that gave no clue where the somewheres was. Sometimes, if they wanted to be especially helpful, the respondents would add, "They be's back directly. I ain't for certain when, though."

He also began to ask about some of the people whose names he had written down in his notebook from the recitations of the cable-barge operator. He quickly found the information he'd been given was fairly useless. Many of the so-called influential people were dead, some of them long-dead, apparently. At other names mentioned he was met with confused stares or frowned-up shakings of the head, so that he could not tell, even by the asking, whether there was disagreement over the leadership status of those

he was seeking or merely the problem of misunderstanding who it
was he was trying to identify. And making himself understood, and
understanding the speech of these coloreds on this side of the
river, was more of a chore than he had anticipated. He had grown
up just outside of Beaufort and knew the Lowcountry colored
dialects well, which was one of the reasons he had been chosen for
this job. But even he found the Adams Neck—the Yelesaw Neck,
he had to remind himself—way of talking challenging, at least
down in this village, and he found himself squinting and cupping
his hand to his ear and asking for a repeat of something said, or
being asked to repeat himself, more than had ever happened in
his life.

That was one of the reasons he was having so much trouble
identifying the people he was talking with. One of his plans had
been to take a census of the village, but he quickly disabused
himself of that idea. Asking for a name while he stood with pen
poised over his notebook, he would get back something absolutely
incomprehensible. Asking to repeat the name only made him less
certain of what he thought he'd originally heard, and more than
once he believed that he was given an entirely different name the
second time around than he'd been given the first. He knew not to
ask for a spelling. Eventually he stopped asking for identification
altogether and contented himself with notations such as "girl, m-
30s—two children" or "uncle and aunt—60?" beneath the
individual houses he was sketching out in a rough-draft chart,
leaving it for his next visit to fill in the blanks.

When he came to the end of the row of houses, he went
through the little pathway to the second village on the other side
of the trees. Though laid out somewhat differently, he found it
essentially identical to the first in its most important features, and
gave the same impression of deliberate arrangement. The results
at the second village were a mirror image of those at the first, as
well. He came away with nothing in hand.

He hoped these two villages were an aberration and his time
would be more productive in other parts of Adams Neck.

It was nearing mid-day when he rode back across the clearing
and up to the main road. Knowing what signs to look for now, he
found several more wagontracks running off the road and back
into the woods. Some of them led to dead ends or work sites—
unoccupied unfortunately—but several came out into more
villages. Yelesaw Neck seemed to be honeycombed with them. He
spent the rest of the day like that, searching out the villages and

then working house to house when he found them, continuing his sunny promises of an electric future while riding ahead of the rainclouds, resigning himself to the fact that this would be a day of planting rather than harvest.

Along those lines, he put up a collection of handbills dominated by a picture of an operating electrical power plant, announcing the dam-building project underneath and promoting the electricity benefits and giving out the location of his office in Cashville, tacking them up on trees every few yards along the main road. He knew that many of the coloreds here had no knowledge of reading, and of those that did, he did not think it would induce any of them to come across and visit him. But because the white people of the county had for so long abandoned this side of the river to the coloreds, the coloreds over here had obviously come to believe that they could do whatever they wanted in this isolated little spit of land, and could ignore a white man's word with impunity. He wanted the handbills to serve as notice that regardless of how much they had resisted in the past, those days of resistance were done. They might not be able to read, but they would know who put them up on the trees, and the message they intended to convey. This white man was not going to give in to field-hand slacker foolishness.

Still, he had to be honest with himself. He would send in a positive report of the large numbers of Yelesawans he had contacted that day, and give an optimistic prediction of what he believed would be the ultimate results. But he knew that this was not going at the pace it needed to, and he wished now that he had crossed the river sooner. Clearly there were far more people over here than he was actually seeing. There was no accurate count of the Yelesaw Neck inhabitants. Since the plantation slave rolls had closed out and the white folks had evacuated the community, there had been no incentive to do such a count. The best, broad estimate he'd been able to get from the admittedly incomplete census figures, notations of birth, and other records in St. Paul was that somewhere in the neighborhood of five hundred people lived on this side of the river, but it could actually be something north or south of that. At the rate he was visiting individual houses, he figured that he might end up seeing a fifth of that in the time he had allotted for Yelesaw, with no guarantee he was talking to the right ones, and therefore no guarantee that it was making any difference. They were like a mule digging its hooves in the dirt, hoping to slow things up so much it would halt the day's work. He would have to think of some way to speed things up.

Coming to a bend in the road beside the river, he stopped his horse and looked back over the ground he had covered that day, distinctly less upbeat than when he had crossed over in the morning. Was he a blind man groping about for a dropped coin inside a sack of fresh-picked cotton, which offered no resistance as he bumfumbled his way through, but which kept its secrets by an accumulating weight of soft obscurity? Probably not, but right now it certainly felt that way. Receiving neither assent nor disagreement nor even simple curiosity from the coloreds he had encountered, he had the sense of having gone a great distance while having gotten himself nowhere so far.

To add to his miseries the storm broke late in the day, and it rained on him, hard, all the way back to the cable-crossing, and he had to stand for a while under a tree, the rain dripping off the bill of his hat, waiting for the cable-barge operator, who was not at his post.

IT RAINED OFF AND ON FOR THE NEXT TWO DAYS, just hard enough and unpredictable enough to keep him off the road, giving him some time to revise his plans concerning Adams Neck. The catalyst for his change of strategies he found inside his rough maps of the villages, which he propped up in a row, one beside the other, against the books and reports on his desk and studied, periodically, during breaks in his other tasks. When it finally came to him, the revelation was so simple that he wondered why he had not seen it all along. The patterns of the village houses had been confusing to his eyes because they were not planned patterns at all, but transitional forms. Deprived of contact with whites for two full generations, the coloreds of Yelesaw were losing the benefits of civilizing influence. The "villages" he had seen in the Yelesaw woods were exactly what you would expect to find in a devolution from the regularity of slave quarters cabins back to the chaotic haphazardness of a true African village. The "Neckerniggers" were going in reverse, reverting to their roots.

That conclusion led directly and inevitably to the next steps he must take. He had originally planned to spend the following couple of visits searching out the remaining villages, both to complete his rough survey and census, but also in the hopes that one of them would provide the breakthrough that would turn the others. But if the "Yelesaw problem," as he had come to characterize it, was caused by a dearth of white contact, concentrating a renewed contact—not dispersing it—was the most obvious cure. You didn't shatter a hard rock by hammering it with the flat of a shovel, you cracked it with the point of a pick, so that the pieces fell away from each other, and you could then move them out of your way at your leisure. He decided to return to the first villages he'd discovered, and hit the point over and over, until it broke.

It was with that plan in mind that he went back across to Yelesaw as soon as the rain slackened up, his spirits renewed.

The first thing he noticed as he rode down the main road was that none of the handbills remained on the trees where he had tacked them three days before. He was not certain if this was a good thing or bad. It could be that the coloreds had taken them back home to read and study them, those of them that could read, or simply to look at over and over because they were impressed by the confidence in the typeface and the white smoke billowing out from the power plant, those that didn't know their letters. On the other hand, it could mean that someone had come behind him and destroyed them all.

While he was riding at a slow walk and sorting out the implications of each possibility, and what he should do to either handle or capitalize on the one or the other, he heard a noise on the road behind him, and turned on his horse to see what it was. Five or six colored youngsters had taken up behind him, walking about fifteen or twenty yards arrears. They seemed to be about seven or eight years old, mostly, along with a couple of smaller tykes of maybe three or four in hand. Gaunt and sallow-faced and hollow-eyed, their clothes hanging from their narrow shoulders and waists like shrouds, they looked almost like a little band of black wraiths. He thought little of their appearance. The towns and countryside were full of such children, colored and white. You couldn't take a step around many communities since the Depression started without seeing such youngsters who were going without food and practically without clothing. He thought, though, that none of the children he'd seen in the villages on his first visits had looked quite so bescragglish.

At first he thought that they were simply traveling along the road on their own business, but when he stopped his horse to let them catch up so he might find out where they lived, the little band of colored youngsters stopped as well, standing and waiting in the middle of the road at a distance, arms limp at their sides, except for those who were holding the hands of the two littler ones.

He smiled and put up his own hand, beckoning them to come up. Instead, they stared at him solemnly in silent contemplation across the length of separation.

"Catch on up, y'all," he called back, and when that got no response, he fished down in his saddlebag, and came up with a bulging paper sack. He had brought along penny suckers and licorice for just such a purpose, in the hopes that he could break down the intransigence of the adults by getting their children on his side. "See what I got?" he called out, taking out one of the suckers and waving it in the air back and forth. "Y'all want one? I got plenty."

The youngsters stared back at him like dead souls come up out of the graveyard, and did not say a word.

"Well, suit yourselves," he said, shrugging. As he put the sucker back in the paper sack, and the paper sack back in the saddlebag, he called out, "They're right here, if you want'em" and turned in his saddle and continued on his horse up the road.

He turned down the wagonpath that led to the first village he had visited. The youngsters turned behind him, and followed in the trail of his horse until the wagonpath made the final sharp turn before opening out into the clearing. There the little ragged band stopped, out of sight of the houses, and when he looked back, it seemed like they had turned and were walking back towards the main road.

Shrugging, he put the children out of his mind, and rode across the clearing to the first house.

HE HAD BEEN DOING MORE than simply pondering his own drawings in the days since he had last been on Yelesaw. He had been doing his research, calling around the state to friends and associates and old schoolmates, trying to find anyone who might have more useful information on Yelesaw Neck than had been given him in Cantrell County.

He'd gotten something useful, very useful, during a telephone conversation with one of his old Clemson Ag engineering professors. The professor had become quite excited when he'd said he was working Adams Neck, saying that this was the location of the old Bethelia Plantation lands, which were quite famous and important, and didn't the Sparman know anything about them? He didn't until he was told. James Grady, Bethelia's only owner, had been something of an engineering and agricultural pioneer, the professor said, having come up with a method of rice cultivation combining tidal and artifical irrigation methods unique to the state. Grady had written a pamphlet on his innovations, and they were mentioned in several newspaper articles and other books, all of which had been the subject of study at Clemson College at the turn of the century, although by that time the ending of slavery knocked the bottom out of rice planting in the state. But it was the early application of groundbreaking engineering principles to agriculture that was of such great interest, not the agricultural component itself. And the Bethelia ricefields had been so successful in their time that they were often visited by both educators and other rice planters alike to study James Grady's methods during the years when the plantation was in operation. Even though they must be sadly dilapidated and out of repair since his death, with only the unsupervised nigras working them now to get out a rice crop, the remnants might still be of engineering value, and something to behold, with some traces of the old dikes and sluiceways and intricate series of gates remaining where a good engineer might discern an old echo of the genius of thought that went into their construction and use. The professor told the Sparman it was his only regret about the Cashville Dam Project, the loss, forever, of the Bethelia Plantation ricefields for on-the-ground study, and asked the Sparman if he could visit them and preserve them in technical sketches and—if at all possible—in Kodak photographs.

While the Sparman had no interest in making sketches of plant life—power production had been his specialty in school, not agricultural engineering—the talk of the ricefields had given him a clue as to where he might find the missing Yelesaw coloreds who so far had been avoiding him. It was well past planting time for every crop he was familiar with. But he had a vague idea of the rhythm and timing and intensity of rice cultivation and that it was singularly different from other agricultural work, so that droves of people could well be out in those fields during times when other crops could be left to grow with less intense attendance. That's where the Yelesaw Neck crowds might be. And so he had come over this time with one of his tasks the finding of those ricefields.

He also changed the tenor of his presentation in this, his second real visit to the Yelesaw Neck villages.

While he did not abandon his friendly demeanor, no longer was he the folksy door-to-door salesman playing up the virtues of electric home living. He mentioned the brochures he had left, and asked if folks had a chance to look at them and think about what electric lights would mean on their farms. But from there, he transitioned immediately into an Old Testament prophet. SPAR, for whom he worked, was building a dam across the Sugaree River at Cashville at the behest of the good people of South Carolina, to benefit those people in general, and the citizens of Cantrell County in particular. The dam was coming, and some people had to root up and go. That was the unfortunate nature of progress, but SPAR was not leaving them out in the cold. He talked of the new communities outside of Cashville that the agency was providing when they left their homes, but one thing he made plain, leaving they would be.

He was not certain if he expected a different reaction from his first round of presentations in the villages. If so, he didn't get any. The looks they gave were just as blank and unrevealing, the "yessirs" just as polite. When he pressed the point by pulling out his folder of applications and asked if they wanted to sign up right now to get the process going, a "nossir, not right now" was the general reply. "Alright," he would answer, pleasantly enough, pointedly showing them that their answers did not disturb him, "but you're going to have to do it soon, and your neighbors and folks over across the river will be taking up the best spots when we trade them into their new places. I'm just letting you know."

At each house visited, he also made it a point to ask about the ricefields, and directions for where they were located. The answers he got back were more deviously disingenuous than what they'd been telling him on other subjects, if that were possible. No-one denied the existence of the fields or knowledge of how to get there, but they might as well have been reached by ascending Jacob's ladder or a ride on the back of Jonah's whale for all the good the information he was given did him. They were somewhere off through the woods to the east, he was told, but the best he could decipher the information he received was that the only way to them seemed to be through the Bethelia Plantation grounds, but no-one ever went that way. The first time he heard it, it struck him as an amusing darky construct, like you'd hear out of the rabbit in an Uncle Remus tale. You can't get that-way from this-way, Cap'n. Then how is it that everybody from here got themselves to be over there? The Bethelia dodge became increasingly annoying the more he heard it, as he knew it was being used to deflect without open defiance, a not-so-amusing darky practice. And although the people he talked with would stand or sit with him politely through his presentations, never giving an indication they were in any sort of a hurry to do anything else, they would all, without hesitation, declare they were too busy with work to guide him down to the fields themselves, but were always helpful with the name of someone else, at one of the other houses, maybe, or just down the road, who might be available to show him. And always, of course, the person suggested was either equally not available, or not home at all. Moreover he was cautioned, more than once, not to attempt going out to the ricefields without a guide, as they lay along the edge of the Swamp, into which no-one of good sense would possibly want to stray.

He did try it four or five times, taking—for a short way— smaller pathways that led out from the eastern end of the settlements, away from the direction of the main road and in the direction where he knew the Swamp lay. He knew enough about the location of the ricefields that they were not along the river, but lay somewhere back on the swamp-side. A couple of the pathways eventually opened out into other villages, and the others simply seemed to meander around towards no destination in particular, none of them showing the kind of heavy wagon use that he knew would be necessary for the hauling of the rice crop back out. After finding himself seemingly simply going deeper into the woods, he turned back on those pathways and returned the way he had come in.

Far up the main road, he came to what was obviously the old lane into a plantation grounds, possibly Bethelia. It was a broad avenue, wide enough for four of the old horse carriages running side-by-side, and still lined with magnificient, mossed and low-hanging liveoaks. He rode down the lane for a bit, but the roadbed was badly overgrown with weeds and briars and palmetto plants, some of it difficult even for his horse to traverse, and certainly showing no use of any kind whatsoever since Lee laid down at Appomattox. The only sign of life he encountered was a swarm of fat, blackbottom mosquitos of a different kind he had never seen before, and larger, as well, their bellies so big that they felt like small sweetpeas and squirted out his blood in a puddle when he swatted them against his skin. Clearly either the village darkies had lied about Bethelia being the road down to the ricefields, or they got into the plantation grounds another way, or this lane did not lead to Bethelia at all. Not wanting to waste much time in unproductive wandering, and hoping to escape the mosquitos, the Sparman turned back without going to the end of the lane, convinced that, at least in this instance, his informers had been telling him the truth, and you really couldn't get there from here.

He was tussling with the last of the mosquitos that had trailed him all the way back into the main road when he noticed that the band of nigger children had taken up behind him again. They must have been standing somewhere in the woods waiting for him, he guessed. He had been seeing them periodically since their original appearance after he first came over the river.

"I see y'all are back," he called back at them.

They walked steadily along in his wake, saying nothing in return, as they had said nothing to him all day.

It was well past mid-day by then, so he stopped under a spreading live oak tree by the side of the road, tied the horse near a little free-flowing stream that ran alongside, and sat down in the shade to eat his dinner. The little spook-band—he had stopped thinking of them as children by now—halted by a pine grove some distance up the road, squatting amidst the pine needles and looking over at him. Pushing his hat back on his head and swatting at the mosquitos, as well as at some nitties and a couple of yellowflies that had joined them in the hunt, a smile of understanding slowly spread across his face. Maybe this was the answer to it all. He'd never known a nigger child to turn down candy, but maybe it was food that they wanted. They were just hungry.

He waved a chicken sandwich in their direction, beckoning them once more to come closer.

They continued to sit and stare, and did not move.

He did not try again. Instead he chewed noisily and enthusiastically until he had finished his sandwich, put the empty paper sack in his saddlebag, got a last swallow of water from his canteen and then took off his hat and poured a little over his head, to compensate for the sun, filled the canteen from the stream, untied his horse, swung up on it, and started up the road again. He did not look back to see if the little spook-band was following him. He did not have to. He could feel them behind him, their eyes on his back as he rode.

They spent the day following him like that, along the main road and partway down the paths into the villages, almost like the rag-tail of a makeshift parade, but always halting before they came in view of the settlements themselves, reappearing from somewhere out of the adjacent woods or fields when he had finished his talks and was on his way out. One thing he noted, unlike what they did on the wagonpaths down to the villages, they had not followed him onto the plantation lane at all, not even a step. There was some significance to that, he knew, but with no other information, and unable to get any answer out of them, he had no way to figure it out. Meanwhile, he noticed, too, that when he had come up on several travelers on the road, walking or riding mules or in carts, the little spook-band seemed to have already stepped off into the trees and disappeared before the other travelers had come into view. They had done the same when he rode past the few farmers working in the fields beside the road as well, appearing again only when he was far down the road and farmer out of sight, and then they seemed to come out of nowhere and get back in line in his wake. He figured, finally, that they must be beating off from work, and were taking care not to be spotted and sent back home. As to why they were following him, though, he had no clue, except perhaps that he was the great attraction and curiosity of the day, a whiteman riding around on Yelesaw Neck.

And there was another peculiarity. Although the numbers in the little following pack seemed to be about the same, somewhere between five and seven, perhaps, it was not always made up of the same members. Looking back now, he remembered that there had been only two very little ones when he first saw them behind him, and now there were definitely three. The tallest girl, he knew, had been back there all day—he remembered her gangly, ashy black legs coming out of a red-and-white polka-dot dress—but one of the boys, with a ragged plaid shirt and a straw shade hat, he was sure he had not seen before. Later the plaid shirt boy was no longer there, though he had never seen him leave, and only one of the little ones rather than three, and a boy and a girl who he may have remembered from earlier in the day, but had not been in the pack for a while. Like a relay race at the carnival, he thought, though nobody was racing, and what was the finish line going to be?

The sticky heat beginning to get to him, he talked at decreasing length to each new set of dark village residents he visited. By the end of the day, when he had turned back, finally, towards the cable-barge crossing, he had grown testy and weary. The results today were no different than the first extended trip. For all the response he got, it was about as productive as talking to a pile of flat rocks. He looked for the little band of followers behind him, but they had disappeared for good, a fact which he noted with wry regret, since they appeared to be the only ones in these swampy lands who were paying him any real attention.

In place of the pickaninny band, a small flock of bearded black crows followed him down the cable-barge road, flitting from tree to tree just behind, calling their bawdy crow-comments down on him as he rode. Just before he got to the river, annoyed, he stopped and got down off his horse and picked up a couple of large stones, throwing them into the trees with force and scattering the gaggle, which scattered in a flutter of black wings and hoarse curses.

IT WAS IN THE SAME WEEK that the Sparman came across the river the second time that Mama and Yally went down the River Road to Mama's favorite hole to trawl for crawfish. On the way they met Sisi Brown going up the other way, and they stopped their wagons side-by-side under a brace of trees, the mules nodding and munching grass and rubbing their flanks together while the two women fanned the hot air with their scarves and traded talk and Yally got out to fill up her own headscarf with blackberries from a nearby patch.

"I hear y'all had 'wisitor your way," Mama told Sis'Sisi.

"Old Socky? Yeah, that boy come-by for chat with we," Sisi Brown said. "Him just full'a the talk."

Sisi Brown went on for the longest about what the Columbia buckra had told her about "that damn old dam," as Mama was now regularly calling it. She was particularly dismissive of the electric lights the Sparman had been so enthusiastic about. "You 'magine me 'ondressing in the bedroom with that bright old light and that old Candy Brown staring at me, all two both?" she snorted. "I ain't want that nigger for see all my twist and turn, I ain't care how long we been done marry."

Sisi had heard that Old Socky had caught Baki Simmons out in the field, plowing, and had tried to sell him on the merits of the land across the river in the new settlements, which the whiteman had said he had helped supervise the picking out himself, and promised it would grow cotton and corn and collards tall enough to make you cry. When Bak' had asked him about ricing, and if there was water enough to support that crop over there, the Sparman had told him he did not think that was important. "Ricing is over," the whiteman had declared. "I know you've been rice-growing all your lives but there's no future in it as a cash crop. Takes so many hands to put it in the ground and grow it, you can't feed all them with what you end up harvesting." Sisi Brown took a big pinch of flesh out of her fat rump. "How that cracker think us been feeding we'sef all these year done gone if it ain't with nothing but rice and anything else you can scratch up out the kitchen? I seen them old skinny-ass buckra out to Sandy Station, them look like them been a'miss plenty meal in all that good ground him'a talk about." Mama nodded her assent. The Sparman had gone on to say that people in Florence and Georgetown and Berkeley counties were putting in tobacco, where there was good money. That made Mama give out a horse-laugh and ask, "And when you' babies done crying for something on they plate, you supposed to toss'em a chaw?"

Sisi Brown leaned over between the wagons and gave out a conspiratorial whisper. "But that ain't the worstest of what that old buckra done tell'd me," she added.

"What been the worstest?" Mama asked her.

"Him say when we does move, they must even come over and help dig-out we cemetery, iffen we needs it."

Yally, who was listening from the road-edge while she munched on her blackberries, had thought there was nothing the Sparman could say that would surprise Mama, but this seemed to have set even her aback.

"What that fool man want for dig-out we cemetery for?"

"For take up the dead-ones and carry them 'cross'oba-the-river with we," Sisi Brown said. "Him say that-what some of them oba'dey folk fixing for do."

Mama stared across at Sisi Brown for a bit after that, her eyes widing up and her mouth half-open, and for one of the first times ever, Yally found that her mother apparently could come up with nothing to say in response. But after something like that, after all, what could possibly be said?

IN FACT, Mama did not say anything about the conversation with Sisi Brown during all the time they were down at the crawfish hole, or much of anything at all, seeming pensive and distracted and deep in her own thoughts. Yally bore it as long as she could but on the wagon ride back home, took the chance, finally, to ask her mother what she thought might happen.

"What might be done happen, which?" Mama asked, flicking the mule reins absently, still in reflection.

"Iffen we ain't leaving, ain't the whitefolk fixing to try for make we?"

Mama gave a shrug. "Them can try," she said. "Wouldn't be

the first time."

"Grandpa always talking 'bout the whitefolk trying for fool we off we land."

"You' grandpa know what him saying. But I ain't talking 'bout doing no fooling. I'm talking 'bout the time them come and try for *take*."

"Take?" Yally tried to picture that, but because she had never seen more than one or two whitefolks at a time on Yelesaw Neck in her life, she could not. "When that been?"

"Oh, back-a-way in *my* grandpa' time. Near back to slavery-time, what them say. Old Sesh still been around."

"What happen?"

Mama didn't say anything for a while, only watched ahead at the little tufts of road-sand kicked up by the mule's heels. Yally thought that Mama had either forgotten the conversation or had decided not to answer, but after a while, her mother said, as if she had been watching a scene play out in her mind that had just finished, "Them been mens in them days back then. Tough mens. Grandpa Leem and him brothers and them other ones. Them ain't take no guff neither gall offen nobody's, not offen Old Sesh, not often Old Maw'se kin, not offen nobody's." She pursed her mouth and gave a little sideways nod of her head. "They's still some mens on Yelesaw Neck," she said. "Ain't such'a many. Ain't so tough. But they's still some left. And some womens, when the mens don't do." Now she looked over at Yally, and her eyes were dark and hard. "Ain't nothing for fret over," she said. "Ain't nobody's leaving noplace."

THE SPARMAN DID NOT come back across the river again for several days, and there were some among the Yay'saws who thought he might have given up on Yelesaw for good. He had not. In fact, he had come under considerable pressure to step up his activities across the Sugaree. Several top Cantrell officials—the State Senator and High Sheriff chief among them—had begun to express concern about his lack of progress.

"We all know Adam's neck gonna' be a tough one to wring," the High Sheriff said over a cigar-and-crab-salad lunch with the director of SPAR, "but it don't seem like that boy knows how to catch up with the chicken."

According to his submitted reports, while the Sparman was doing reasonably well in other parts of his territory, he had so far not signed up a single Adams Neck family for the move, and that was causing a problem. A rumor began to run its course that a deal had been struck with the Adams Neck niggers so that their homes would not be flooded at all, but that the Neck would be banked up with dikes and form an island when the lakewaters came in, so that alone among the people in the original boundaries of the lakebed, they would not have to move. "Be goddamned if I'm going while them Neckerniggers is staying," became a popular saying, and people across the Basinbottom, colored as well as white, began using it as a reason for dragging their feet on the signup. Legal action could be taken on any intransigent landowners, of course, wherever they lived, but nobody wanted that, not the local officials who would stand for election next year, nor the SPAR leaders who were still sparring with Congress for their money. For the Cashville Dam project to move forward on time, and perhaps to move forward at all, the Adams Neck blockage had to be broken, and broken fast.

The Sparman was called up to an informal meeting at the State Senator's plantation, where he spent several sweat-sodden hours fighting off suggestions from the Senator and his boss that perhaps he was not the right man for the Adams Neck portion of the job, too young, maybe, and not possessing the experience or temperament to handle such a a stony crop of niggers. Might not a heavier hand be needed, a driver, rather than a gatherer?

He lost several pounds in the heat on the State Senator's front porch, and exhausted all the persuasive powers in his sack, but when he drove back to St. Paul that evening, he still had Adams Neck in his hand. He was on notice that it was only a temporary reprieve, and reorganization only held off to see what he was able to accomplish in the next week or so.

It would have been easy enough for him to give up Adams Neck, but he could not do that. It galled him to think about those darkies over there, sniggering as they saw his replacement ride into their yards, maybe on the very same horse he had rented, knowing they had beaten him down.

"Blue-gummed black bastards," he said under his breath.

That's what his father had called them sometimes, after a day breaking his back and his health, trying to bring them to Jesus and Jesus to them. He didn't often use words like that, but sometimes the old terms were the best terms, and they had a better ring and rhyme. And it certainly made him feel better.

By the next morning, he was back in Cantrell County and riding the Adams Neck roads, his demeanor set and serious, his signup sheets ready. He had no different plan this time, only a grim determination that whatever the coloreds of Yelesaw Neck threw in his direction by means of resistance, he was going to drag them out of their dirt this day.

That is, if he could find them.

THE LITTLE SPOOK-BAND OF CHILDREN which he had seen on his last visit did not reappear this time to dog his steps. That did not disappoint him. Wherever they disappeared to, however, they seemed to have taken their kinfolk with them. He did not see more than three or four people on Adams Neck that whole morning, and that included the colored fellow who operated the cable-barge. It was as if much of population of Adams Neck had withdrawn itself into the woods.

He went from cabin to cabin in village after village, knocking on doors and then waiting, vainly, for an answer, walked around the back through the gardens and the chickenyards and hogpens, hailing "Hello!" at barns and sheds and over fences and out into vast and empty fields. Even the dogs that he had seen on his first trips now seemed to have disappeared. The only sound he heard in return was the cackling of chickens, and the creak of old boards turning on hinges, or the wind tinkling through the hoodoo bottle-trees in front of several of the houses. The clinking of these bottles against each other had never bothered him before, he had heard them so often back home, but coming as it did in this sudden emptiness of people, it did so now. There was a meaning the niggers attached to their bottle-trees, some symbolism he'd had explained to him years before, but could not exactly recall now. Darkies had so many meanings attached to things, a sane white man could hardly keep up. He gave spur to his horse, setting it off at a trot in an effort to to outpace the willies. The two or three people he did see were at a distance, while he was out on the main road, and they turned off and disappeared into the woods or fields before he could get to them, giving no indication they had seen him, though clearly they had.

This new turn of events had come so unexpected that he had nothing prepared to counter it. What acts of enticement or coercion or threats could work upon people who were not there? Early on, he was of the suspicion that the people were not very far off, but were watching his movements from someplace in hiding, withdrawing into the woods when he came into a village, to return again as soon as he left. He took several measures to counter this, doubling back, quick, after leaving a settlement yard, or backtracking to places he had been an hour before. Once he came back around through the woods to eat his dinner behind a grove of trees just out of sight of a row of houses he had recently visited, spending a half an hour sitting there, on the chance that the he would catch them coming back. None of this worked. The houses and yards and gardens and pens remained vacant of habitation, and as the day began to drift into afternoon, with no more people in sight, he began to believe that the darkies might actually have withdrawn themselves to some location for a great meeting or religious gathering.

He would have even welcomed the pickaninny parade if they had shown up again. They, at least, had displayed some interest in his activities, however perverse. But he looked in vain for their reappearance. Even the little, ragged children had deserted him.

INTO THE AFTERNOON he began to see a few more people than he had in the morning, several of them around their homes, but with no more success.

This wasn't the sullen, lip-poking foot-dragging that he'd so often witnessed among the coloreds back home in Jasper County trying to duck out of work they didn't particularly want to do. Senagamulishness, his father had called it, the worst combination of mule-headedness and black African stubbornness, and he'd known of more than one white boss-man driven to drink and losing his sleep and hair and worse trying to drive such niggers.

If anything, the type of resistance the Sparman was seeing today was worse.

Whereas in his first three days on Adams Neck, the darkies he'd talked to had met him with blank politeness, on this, his fourth day, they did not even bother to disguise their desire to be rid of him. The few he did happen up on all had excuses for cutting off the conversation in mid-presentation—stock to be fed, supper left on the fire, a sick relative to attend to down the road.

Late in the afternoon, he rode into the yard of a woman he had already talked with the last time he had visited this village. She was washing clothes out of a tin tub at the side of the house. She glanced up at him with what seemed like a look of simple annoyance, of all things, then back down at her work, putting one open hand up even before he reached her, waving it back and forth, palm out, while she continued to scrub a piece of clothing against the washboard with the other, shaking her head as she did.

"Don't even get offen that horse, mister man," she said to him, as if he were a salesman peddling insurance door-to-door, and there was no mistaking the irritation in her voice. "I ain't got time for talk with you today. I got for finish my work before my husband get home."

The woman was right on the border of rebellion, but he decided to ignore it and push through. This, at least, was better than the open avoidance he'd been meeting all day.

"Well, when *is* your husband coming home?" he asked her. "He's really the one I need to talk with." He patted the saddlebag where his knapsack was stored. "I've got papers, here, he needs to look over and sign."

The woman straightened up from her washtub, soapsuds and water dripping down the dark muscles of her arms. Her eyes narrowed as she cocked her head to the side, and she stared up at the Sparman, straight and steady and direct in *his* eyes as he sat on his horse above her. She did not look away as he stared back and showed *his* annoyance. "Him be coming back when him finish with *him* work," she said in a tone that was not defiant, but bordered on dissdainful. "That what us'n mostly does around here. Us *works*. Ain't non'a we got the time for ride'round 'wisiting and asking folk question *like some folks does*."

That did it. All of the frustration and rising pressure of the past several weeks dealing with the Adams Neck niggers rose up inside his chest, all at once. His composure galloped away from him on flying hooves, and he snapped.

"Do you know what I'm here for, girl?" he asked her, his voice rising in step with the redness rising up his neck and into his face. "This ain't no darktown dance y'all can walk away from when your feet get hurt. You know they're getting ready to build a dam down to Cashville and Y'ALL—GOING—TO—HAVE—TO—LEAVE! I got to get these papers signed!"

The woman pushed her shoulders back and pressed the knuckles of one hand against her hip. She was a large woman, not fat but tall, and clearly work-strong, and now the muscles in her forearm were even more evident as she gave him back a smile with no humor to it while still meeting his gaze without a flinch. Then a bit of air came up from her chest and blew in a single, hard puff out of her nose like a mule might do, making her whole upper body give a small jerk, almost like she had given out a hoot at his sudden display of temper and what he had just said.

"Mister man," she said, "onliest thing *I* gots for do in *my* yard and in *my* place right now is to finish with this-here wash, like I done'd already tol'ded at you, and then I got for finish fixing supper so's my man will have something on he plate when him get back from *him* working. What *you* got for do is you own business. I'd appreciate it if you'd 'low me for tend at mine."

Except in pointed emphasis on a handful of words—*I* and *my* and *him* and *you*, her head bobbing forward slightly as she said them—her voice had not risen in pitch or volume to match his own outburst, but if anything had dropped lower and more even, spacing out each word to make sure she was not misunderstood, and that made him angrier.

The first thing that came to his mind was to get down off his horse and slap her across her face for her sassiness.

The second thing that came to his mind, quickly following, was immediate regret and shame that he could have considered doing such a thing, striking a woman in her mouth, colored or not, and the devil died within him before he made a move to carry it out.

Meanwhile, without him having noticed her coming, he now saw that an older girl had come out onto the front porch and was standing there, eyes wide, mouth agape. Another woman, larger than the first, now came around the house from somewhere in the back and stood just behind the woman at the tub, rake in hand. All of them had all of their attention on him and he saw, now, that the girl on the porch had a black fry-pan held loosely at her side. He could not tell if she had brought it with her inadvertently, because that's what she'd been working with when she heard the commotion outside, or if it were for some other purpose. He thought, suddenly, of how deep into the woods he was right now, and how long a lonely ride it was back out to the crossing.

He rose up in his stirrups to recover as much dignity as he could, and nodded down to the woman at the washtub. He got control of his voice, so that it projected that he was not flustered, but completely in command both of himself and of the situation.

"I'll come back when your husband is home," he told the woman.

The woman gave a little sideways nod of her head, pursing her mouth as she did so. "You be done does that, mister," she said. The three of them continued to watch him as he backed his horse up from them, turned it, and walked it, slow, with as much poise as he could muster, out of the yard and across the clearing towards the wagontrack beyond.

SOMEONE WAS CALLING HIM but he was distracted and so he didn't, at first, react.

He was trying to concentrate and think of what next to do but it was not working well. The chest and back of his state-issued khaki shirt stained dark with sweat from the heat of the day, he had been riding on the main road—how long he could not be certain—out of the bright-burning sun and into the muggy shade under the overhanging trees and then back out into the sun again, mirroring the alternating patches of thoughtfulness, melancholy, inspiration and depression that his mind was traveling through at the same time.

He was at his most efficient in solving a problem when he was able to plug in all of the data and then allow the deeper part of his mind free rein to mull over a solution on its own terms, while he moved on to other things. But now, each time he loosed a tight grip on his thoughts, invariably they would return within a few moments to the scenes of his confrontation with the woman in the yard, replaying themselves in random order in a recurring and increasingly louder loop, like a badly-edited newsreel, until they threatened to overwhelm him, and he had to shake his head, violently, to make them stop.

He could hear, over and over, the dismissive, disdainful tone in her voice, see the defiance in the high way in which she had held her head or anchored her legs in the sandy yard and spread them, pushing hard and tight against the fabric of her dress, stretching its limits, as if the dress represented the old bonds of obeisance which her body itself was determined to split asunder and cast off onto the ground. He was angry with her for having challenged him in such a humiliating way, even angrier at himself for having let her bait him, breaking through his professional poise and getting him to embarrass himself out there in the broad daylight, in the middle of that nigger village. A hundred times or more he had seen his father handle such women so easily, sending their dark bodies and minds into a paroxysm of ecstatic religious fervor, simply through the cadence of his voice, or the touch of his palm upon the flat of their foreheads. He wished now, not for the first time, that he possessed his father's powers and could bend these people to his will...

The calling voice on the road behind him intruded upon his thoughts and no longer could be ignored. Someone was calling after him, "Cap'n! Ho, Cap'n! Wait up!" over and over. He turned in his saddle to see a mouse-tiny little colored man on muleback, spurring his ride by repeatedly digging his knees into the animal's sides, waving a wide hat in the air to get the Sparman's attention. Seeing that the Sparman had finally noticed him, the colored man's face widened into a grin, and he slowed the mule to a trot, fanning his face with his hat as he did.

The Sparman's horse had been gradually slowing its walk as the Sparman had paid it less and less attention while he rode and thought. Now, as if understanding the colored man's call, the horse halted on its own without command, stopping in the shade beside a patch of sweetgrass, which it bent its head over to munch on. In a moment, the colored man and mule caught up.

"Afternoon, Cap'n," the colored man said to the Sparman, still grinning widely as he plopped his hat back on his head, the hat only stopped from engulfing the whole top of his face by the largeness of his ears. "Sure is hot, ain't it? Ain't a day for riding out on the road like this, outten in this old sun. Should be down to the pond, fishing. But here I is."

"Yes, indeed," the Sparman said to him with a wryness in his voice, giving a look around the woods and road, which were empty of any other people but the two of them. "Here we is."

The colored man's grin faded a bit at the coldness of the reception, but he did not abandon it altogether. "You ain't rememorize me, Cap'n?" he asked.

"No, I don't reckon I do," the Sparman answered. While a part of him was mildly curious about the colored man's excited demeanor, the major part had grown terrible weary of the Adams Neck niggers for the moment, and he had been appreciating the time they had left him to himself and his thoughts.

"Pookie Prioleu," the colored man said, his grin widening again. "You come at my house, a week, or so, back. You been asking me about them ricefields. You ain't a'member?"

"I believe I do," the Sparman said, although he wasn't sure that he did. The colored man's face was not familiar. He thought he would have remembered the big ears and the stupid grin, if nothing else.

The colored man did not let the hesitation in the Sparman's voice deter him. "Anyways," he prattled on, not taking a breath or a pause between what should have been sentences, "you been'a ask'ded me about them ricefield and how to get down there, but I tol'ded you I ain't know at the time—which'in-while, I *still* ain't know, I ain't general' go down too near that old swamp—I ain't no rice-man, myself, I puts down a little corn and such, but I don't mess around with growing no rice, I just eats it—anyways, I been a'talk it with one'a my cousin, after you left out that day, and him a rice-man—him *been* done been a rice-man, all he life—and my cousin say iffen you want for go down there, *sure*, he take you down there and show you them ricefield, easy, next time you come back'oba, iffen that where you want for go—'course, him ain't know why-for anyone want for see them old field this time'a the season, ain't nothing much down there for see 'till the rice come up, good, but iffen you want for see'em, he be happy for take you. Anyways, that-what my cousin done tol'ded me, Cap'n, so that-what I'm'a telling you. You still want for go see them ricefield?"

The Sparman struggled to follow behind the rapid train of the colored man's words, but what was clear—because it was repeated so many times—was that he was being offered a guide to go down to the fields where the bulk of the Adams Neck niggers undoubtedly were. All of the misgivings and disappointments of the day vanished from his mind as he struggled to keep his face stiff and mask any eagerness in his voice. He took a glance up at the sun, which had begun its lowering arc towards the western treeline. "Well, it's a little late in the day," he said, slowly, as if he were really considering the issue. "How far is it, to the fields?"

"Oh, I ain't exactly know, Cap'n," the colored man answered. "I don't usual go that way, I done tol'ded you. But my cousin' house, it ain't far. Him the one what fixing to take you down there."

"Let's go, then," the Sparman said.

"Yessir, Cap'n, let's go." The colored man turned the mule with the pressure of his knees—he had no bridle, and only held the tuft of its mane in one balled fist—and they took off on their mounts at a half-trot back down the road from the direction the colored man had come. "It a good time for go down there," the colored man said as they rode, taking off his hat and mopping his forehead with the brim. "Sun ain't'a be so bad, now." The Sparman nodded, but said nothing in reply. They turned at the first wagontrack they came to and rode back through one of the villages, still eerily empty, that the Sparman had visited earlier that day. They passed between two houses and then through a jumbled collection of sheds and hogpens, crossed a weedy field, and dropped down into a single-lane footpath into the pinewoods behind.

Riding now Indian-file in back of the colored man, the Sparman asked him his name again, which he had forgotten during the man's rapid monologue back out on the main road.

"Pookie Prioleau, Cap'n," the colored man called back. "Everybodys over this side of the river knows me, and I knows everybodys and just about most things, too. You needs anything on the Neck, anything, you just asks for old Pookie. If I can't serve it up, I be done know'd the one what will."

The easy-going darkyspeak he was so used to hearing in the colored quarters back home lifted the Sparman's spirits, and signaled a possible reversal of what had so recently seemed such dismal, dwindling fortunes. To check how much things might have actually changed in his favor, the Sparman called back up to the colored man, "Haven't seen many folks out today."

"You ain't?"

"No, not many, not as many as I've been seeing," the Sparman said. "You reckon where they all might be?"

The colored man pushed aside an overhanging branch and holding it, so that the Sparman could catch it before it snapped back into his face, he said, "I suppose most of them, they's all down to the ricefield. That-where folks usual be, this part of the year. That one reason I ain't no rice-man. Too much'a the work. You got for work all the time in that rice." The colored man turned on his mule and flashed a grin behind him. "It ain't like I'm a'feared'a no work, Cap'n, but everything bad for you, iffen you overdoes it. Fellow need a little water for drink with he meal, but you gets *too* much water in you, you be done drown'ded you'self in it."

Behind the colored man's back, the Sparman allowed himself a brief but triumphant smile as well as a last thought of that nigger woman out in her yard. Her defiance no longer burned. Instead, it was pleasant to think about how her face would fall, and to wonder what she would say when she discovered this old cracker had cracked open the great Adams Neck secret. He was sure the ricefields were where all of the leaders and influentials had been hiding all along. When they found that he was a rat terrier who could follow them all the way down into their little hole... The day, which had seemed his worst, now appeared to be threatening to break though into his most promising. God's blessing and reward, his father would have said. God's blessing and reward for those who persevere, and do not lose faith, or take their hands off the plow. He wrapped his feelings of elation into a little package, tied it with a loose bit of twine, and put it in his pocket for future pleasure. For now, he began to plan the strategies he would use once they got down to those elusive fields.

THEY SOON came out of the pinewoods and into a sweetclover field, which the little colored man crossed straight over after stopping to let his mule take a mouthful or two. The sweetclover field seemed to be only a small break in the middle of the pinewoods, which they entered again on the far side. The pathway now appeared to bear a little more to the south than the straight eastern direction they'd been riding in up to then, but after a while, as the pines gave way gradually to oaks and sycamores, the path began to wander a bit, as woodspaths do, to avoid the thicket-patches that began to spring up. The woods ended at the edge of a field of spring corn, which the colored fellow skirted around its leftward edge. The cornfield turned out to be a series of cornfields, four or five of them, set at different angles to each other, which the two riders crossed in a zigzag pattern along their boundaries. At the far end of the last cornfield they came to a creek that was narrow but looked somewhat treacherously deep in the middle, and the little man led them up the bank a ways until they came to a spot where their mounts could step across to a wide tanglebrush field and then into the woods again. The colored man was keeping up a running commentary of something or other of which the Sparman could only hear snatches as he rode in his rear, but all of it seemed self-contained and not designed to elicit any response, since the colored man never stopped or looked back to get a reply. The Sparman was not thinking about the colored man's conversation, in any event, as it was taking all of his concentration to keep up with their line of march.

He possessed a good sense of direction, and despite the twistings and turnings they had made along their way, he kept a watch on the westering sun. More often than not it bore down heavy on his back no matter how circuitous their route, and so he knew they were heading generally towards the east, where the Sugaree Swamp lay, and on whose edges the ricefields would be. It would have been impossible for him to try to make his way back out again on his own the same way they'd come in, of course, but he was definitely not lost, because he could always follow the sun back out, if it came to that, because the sun *was* still high above the trees. The growing lateness of the day bothered him for another reason. He realized now that because of the length of time it was taking to get down there, he would hardly have time for more than a cursory look-around by the time they got to the fields, unless they were going to make the return trip in the dead, country dark, which he did not relish. But he comforted himself with the thought that this was the breakthrough he'd been looking for, and he was already making plans to secure the Prioleau man for tomorrow as a guide, both through the Adams Neck landscape and into the heart of its elusive peoples.

HE HEARD THE SOUND OF LOUD TALKING as they were going through a thick patch of oak-and-magnolia woods, and for a moment he thought they were coming up on the ricefields at last. The ground had been dropping steadily down as they rode for the last mile or so, and in the last several hundred yards came the faint but distinct smell of rank and plant-rot that marked the proximity of the swamp. But when they came out through an opening in the trees, he was disappointed to find that it was not the talking of field-workers he had heard. There was no field at all, in fact. Instead they had come to a little cabin in a small clearing thick with patches of greengrass, beyond which the land fell off immediately behind it and on both sides into a blackwater pond. The pondbank was lined with cattails and palmettos and rushes, the water itself stagnant and oily and partly covered with matted patches of long-dead leaves, and its far bank disappeared into a series of marshgrass islands and cypress stands. The bog-smell from out of the pond was heavy in the back of his nose. There was no doubt they were at the beginning of the swamp, the deepest the Sparman had yet penetrated into the heart of Adams Neck. Despite his disappointment that they had not yet come to the ricefields, he felt a thrill roll over him, knowing they were very close.

A little distance from the cabin a narrow, wooden landing jutted some distance out onto the surface of the pond. On it were lounged several indolent-looking colored men, sitting cross-legged or on their hams around some activity of interest that was going on in the middle of them. One of the colored men had laid himself full-out on his side, his elbow resting on the landing planks, the palm of his hand holding up his head. Black'a'jacks, the Sparman's father would have called them, the kind of no-work niggers you saw hanging around the colored section of every Lowcountry town and crossroads, but which the Sparman had not, until now, encountered on Adams Neck. They were the source of the loud talking he had heard, the running conversation broken up by wicked laughter and triumphant shouts. As the Sparman and his colored guide rode up to the foot of the landing, the Sparman could see that what was holding their interest was a peculiar card-game, peculiar because instead of money, the men appeared to be using live fish. Each of them had a bucket in front of him from which he pulled wriggling crappie or goggle-eye or catfish, tossing them into a common bucket into the middle as he bet, sometimes the fish missing the bucket altogether, sending two or three of the men scrambling across the landing to catch it before it slithered back into the river, whooping and laughing as they did. They were passing around a chipped and well-worn earthenware jug, obviously full of some sort of liquor, each one taking a long sip from the spout before passing it along to the next. There was a row of fishing canes set out at the end of the landing, their lines trailing far out into the water, and one of the young colored men got up and wandered over to check them as the riders came up.

The Prioleau man hailed them while he was getting off his mule and the card-players looked up only briefly and hailed back, neither stopping their card-playing nor their conversation as they did so, seeming not even to acknowledge the presence of a white man in their midst except by sidelong glances that caught the Sparman's eyes and held just overlong enough to be slightly uncomfortable to him before they lazily looked away. This was strange. Whether old-time darky or new, coloreds usually treated white people with deference or resentment, but never this combination of indifferent scrutiny. He was not quite sure how to react, and so, when the Prioleau man bounced up onto the landing and stood over the card-players and began to exchange the usual back-and-forth of colored country small-talk with them, he did not follow behind as he normally would have, taking immediate control of the situation, but instead got off his horse and then stayed next to it, the reins held in one hand as he flicked them over and again across his thigh, one eye on the men on the landing, the other on the sun, which was still above the western trees, but dropping faster now. He was not surprised by the rudeness of the fact that he was not being introduced to the card-players. Nothing these Adams Neck niggers did could surprise him now.

He was trying to figure which one of the card-players was the cousin being sought—and about to intervene to speed things up—when the Prioleau man, seeming to have sensed his growing impatience, said to the men in a louder voice than he had been talking in before, "Well, us-here ain't got time for bullskate like y'all does. Us'n—" with a slight nod of his head in the direction of the Sparman "—got business for tend. Kezzy up-there in the house?"

The card-players all gave general negative grunts and one of them jerked his thumb out in the direction of the pond. "Nope," he said. "Gone out checking him line."

"Done say when him coming back?" the Prioleau man asked him.

The card-player gave a noncommittal shrug as he slapped a fish hard against the common bucket, sending a misty spray of water over all the other players, which they ignored, and then tossed it inside. "Directly," he said, and then put his full attention back on the card-game.

The Prioleau man nodded, cocked his own head to the side, seeming to be considering something for a moment, then walked back to the edge of the landing and squatted down on the boards in front of the Sparman, who was standing on the ground just below him. His great-getting-up-morning grin as broad and sunny as ever, as if this had been quite expected, he asked, "Well, Cap'n, what you wants for do, now?"

The Sparman gave a puzzled look back. He had been following this Prioleau nigger through the woods for what was certainly more than an hour now, letting him take the lead, and he was not quite sure what had happened that had abruptly put him back in charge again. During their long ride he had pointedly resisted looking at his watch, but now he held up his wrist to see that it was closing on 6 o'clock. They had about three hours more of daylight, perhaps, to work with, and that included getting back out of this wilderness. "I don't understand," he said. "Where's your cousin?"

"Done gone'd out on the water. That what them boys done said."

"When's he supposed to be coming back?"

The Prioleau man gave a shrug to his shoulders.

"I couldn't say to the certain of it, Cap'n, but I don't believe he be gone'd out on that water after dark." He gave a shake of his open palm at the pond. "That ain't noplace you wants for be, when it get dark. Him only checking on him trapline. Them say him be back directly."

The Sparman looked out over the pond, empty of all visible life except for a string of ducks paddling across. He looked at the vast tangle of underbrush and bog into which the pond disappeared on its far side. He looked at his watch. He looked up to mark where the sun was sitting above the trees.

"We're close to the ricefields?" he asked.

"Pretty close'by, yessir."

"Why can't you take me there, from here?"

Having asked the question, the Sparman immediately realized how dumb it was. If this darky could get him to the ricefields from here, there would have been no need to look up his cousin.

The Prioleau man agreed, shaking his head. "I mought could get us there from here, Cap'n, but then again, I mought could not. You gots for go down through the Swamp a'ways for get to them fields, and me, I don't go up in that Swamp, not without somebody's showing the way what know it. That Swamp, he got him a tricksy nature to heself. Him don't run the same way two-times twice't in the row. You can get down in there easy-enough, but you can't never be sure you can get you'self back on out."

"What about those boys, there?" The Sparman gestured towards the card-players out on the landing, still intent on their game.

"What about them, Cap'n?"

The Sparman took a long breath to settle his annoyance. This was like peeling skin from a catfish. It should have been easy, except you had to keep detouring around all the thorns.

"Can't one of them take us?" he asked.

"Them boys?" The Prioleau man gave a brief glance at the landing behind him, and then let out a derisive snort. He leaned down towards the Sparman standing on the ground below him and lowered his voice so that the men on the landing could not hear. "Oh, no, Cap'n. They might could get there, but them lazy-ass ain't going nowheres. Only way you could get them boys for walk offen that landing is iffen you set fire to the pilings. They be out there with them card and them fishpole 'til the moon come up, or later."

The Sparman looked at his watch again, though only a minute or two had passed since he looked at it last.

"How long will people be out at the ricefields? Couldn't we just wait and catch them on the way back? Do they come through this way?"

The Prioleau man shrugged his shoulders. "Us's could wait, sure, iffen that-what you wants, Cap'n. But ain't no telling iffen any of them would come back on this side. Them gots all sorts of trails they can take for get back home. And anyways, you don't want to be out here *that* late, not in no dark. Folks don't left the ricefields this time a year just 'cause the sun get tired and want for go to sleep. Them got laying-out work for do. Them be out there under the torches, 'til they finish."

That was the only bit of encouraging news since they'd come up on the pond and the cabin and the card-players.

"So what are the options?"

"Op'uns, Cap'n?"

"You asked me what I wanted to do. What are my choices?"

"Oh, choices. Well, we can wait for my cousin, here, 'til him get back. Ain't fixing to be too long, I don't reckon. Like I done said, him don't stay out on the water too long when it getting toward the dark. Or iffen you likes, I can take the pirogue out and find him and fetch him back right away. He traplines ain't far up in there. Or you can go back cross'oba and we can come back tomorrow for catch him. Or any day you wants for come back. It don't matter with me. I be's around 'most all the time, iffen you need me."

"*You* can take the pirogue out? Why not both of us?"

The Prioleau man shook his head and laughed. He pointed to the other side of the landing where a little skiff was tied, sitting low in the water. It was hardly wider than a foot-tub and not long enough for a set of legs to stretch fully out, scarcely big enough to fit one grown man. "Cu'n Kezzy, him always take the big boat out. We could try the two of us in that'n. We might make it over to that first patch of cypress. Might not. It a nice evening for swim." He looked back at the Sparman expectantly. "What you want for do, Cap'n?" he asked again.

The Sparman made a quick pursing movement with his mouth. There really wasn't any decision to be made.

"Go ahead and get your cousin," he said, slapping the horse reins on his thigh with authority. "I'll wait for you here. And don't be too long coming back, and don't get in any conversation with him about his fishlines, or anything else. I *do* have business to attend to."

The Prioleau man beamed back at him, as if he'd been given a task he'd been looking forward to all day. "Yessir, Cap'n," he said, "I'll do what you done ask'ded me and won't do what you done ask'ded me not." He bounced up from his squat and started down the landing towards the boat. "You make you'self at home over to the cabin. Ain't fixing to be long at all. Like I said, me and my cousin, we'll be back directly. You look after the mule for me, inn'a?"

He was still talking like that over the water as he rowed away, the Sparman standing on the bank and watching him duck in and out between the water-rush islands and the cypress stands, his wide hat the biggest thing on him, parting the lilypads and scattering the ducks until, finally, boat and man disappeared into the sun-dazzle and waterbrush on the far side, presumably into a feeding creek. For a while after he was gone, the sound of the Prioleau man's running soliloquy—the words themselves increasingly unintelligible—continued to carry back across the black water as the wake of his passing settled over itself and the pond surface gradually smoothed out to a flat, the voice fading away into nothing.

THE SPARMAN CONSIDERED, briefly, going up on the landing and doing some landswap talk with the men who were out there playing their card-game, but almost immediately decided against it. Although he would not admit it, even to himself, the memory of his exchange with the woman down in the village was still a fresh wound, and these sporty-hat darkies playing fish-poker, or whatever it was they were playing, seemed cut directly of the same cloth and just as likely to give him backtalk. Although only a few hours ago he would have jumped to have a crowd of them like that all together to speak with, another verbal challenge by a sass-ass nigger would probably set him boiling over the top. And now that he was so close to the elusive ricefields and the bulk of the Adams Neck coloreds who had been hiding from him out there, he had his mind set more than ever on those men—and, yes, those women, too—whose age and bearing marked them as landowners and community leaders, and who could be persuaded to join the program and bring their flocks with them, en masse. He reasoned that at this late date, a couple of names on the signup rolls from this side of the river would not be enough to stave off disaster. He needed news of a major break to bring back with him to Cashville tonight, and he felt a measure of confidence that a major break would be the outcome. If they were hiding from him, it meant that they knew he would win them over and win, when he caught up with them.

He gave a glance over at the colored men out on the landing, but after giving him the fish-eye when he and the Prioleau man first rode up, they had stopped paying him any attention, and were concentrating on their game, shouting and catcalling at each card played and each bet made. Clearly they were having too good a time to worry about the fact that this landing and this clearing and little hideaway cabin and all the land surrounding would all be under water by the end of next year, and they'd be picking out a living for themselves on the far banks of a new lake. But what did they care? Darkies!

Putting the colored men out of his mind, he led his horse and the Prioleau man's mule over to the cabin and tied his horse to a nearby sapling. He had nothing with which to tie the mule, but knowing how mules generally acted, he did not believe it would stray away too far from the horse, and so he left it loose. He took his worksack out of the saddlebag and went around to the front of the cabin and sat down on the bottom step, out of sight of the colored men and their card-game. He did not want that distraction. He had some careful writing to do, and needed all of his concentration to do it.

He had begun to realize that the day was going to end up a bust, even if he made it to the ricefields and the field-hands were still out there, and everything went as well as could be reasonably anticipated. The most he could accomplish this late in the afternoon was to tally a list of names of the people he had talked with, and he had already turned in three days worth of uncommitted names. That was not going to be enough. He had to write a report that would show progress where no real progress had yet been made, with enough promise to hold off those who were rattling at the reins for someone else to take over his work, but not so much promise that if he could not deliver a mass of signed moving agreements by his next trip over, it wouldn't be just the final excuse needed to take him out of Adams Neck altogether.

It was a narrow row to hoe, but he thought he could manage it.

And there were other considerations as well, political considerations. There were local and state and national politics involved, and racial politics, as well. The governor, the state senator, and the sheriff all had a personal, political stake in this. And there were white people in Cantrell County who were looking for any excuse to turn the bulldozers loose on this side of the river and knock over a few houses, and maybe knock in a few heads as well. Maybe a lot of heads, and put some holes in some bodies and a rope or two around a neck, if they could get away with it. The Sparman had noticed a deep resentment of the Neckerniggers by some powerful people in the county, white *and* colored, who seemed anxious to mete out punishment to them for some old transgressions, the exact source of which he could only guess at, though he could easily see their point. Nobody likes uppity niggers, even other niggers. It upset the order of things. SPAR was deeply worried about potential violence in the land clearing, and finding ways to avoid it had been a special point of emphasis in their training for the Cashville Dam project. There were people up in Congress who would use such violence to cut back on future funding, or even halt the dam-building altogether. If he failed in facilitating the Adams Neck evacuation peacefully and it came to beatings or shootings or lynchings he knew he would catch the blame, even if he were no longer on the scene, and it would shatter his career at SPAR, or in any government service. That was the nature of government service bureaucratic politics.

The framework surrounding his report now set in his mind, he took out his notebook and pen to begin to write.

He had not been at it long, however, when he noticed that a silence had come down over the late afternoon. He had been consciously working to keep the loudtalking and shouts and laughter of the card-players out of his mind, and when the noise of them was suddenly gone, it was like a man leaning against a door that is opened inward, without warning, from the other side.

Out of curiousity, he got up and made a pretense of walking over to his horse to get something else out of the saddlebag. From there he could see the landing. The card-game had ended, and the card-players were reassembling on the bank below and were making preparations for a meal. A fire had been started, and one of the card-players was kneeled down at the edge of the water, washing out cooking gear, while another was going through the fishbucket, making selections. None of them looked over at the Sparman when he came into view around the side of the cabin, but only continued about their arrangements.

The sight of the beginnings of a fish-fry made the Sparman realize that he had not eaten for many hours, and would not be sitting down to a real meal for several hours more. He got a candy bar out of the saddlebag and went back to the bottom step and his work, out of sight of the card-players and their mealsite again. Soon, the sound of grease sizzling in a pan and the smell of frying fish coming from around the side of the cabin was a far more difficult thing to block out than the shouting and laughing had been. He dabbed the point of the pen against his tongue to get the ink flowing better, squinted his eyes behind his glasses, and wrote on.

THE REPORT WAS AS COMPLICATED A DOCUMENT to produce as he thought it would be. It resisted him until he admitted to himself two truths. The first was that the Adams Neck darkies had surprised him. He had expected resistance, of course, but resistance he could put his hands on. So far, everything on this side of the Sugaree River defied grasping. Nothing he had learned of these people in Columbia or St. Paul or Cashville had quite prepared him for the reality. Everything he had known about turning a community had hinged on applying one of two strategies.

One way was to break down the weak points around the edges, drawing away the followers from the leaders until most or all of them were with you. At that point, it little mattered if the leaders came over, because they were no longer leaders. The other way was to go directly after the leaders, winning them to your side, so that the rest had no choice but to trot after you in their wake. Neither way had worked on Adams Neck because the followers had held firm, and the leaders had so far successfully eluded him.

That brought him to the second point. If he wanted to be realistic, the breaking down of the Adams Neck resistance was going to take time, more time, certainly, than his superiors at SPAR or the politicians had figured on. He needed time for the old strategies to work themselves out, or time for new strategies to be formulated. It was as simple as that.

Neither one of these admissions could be put in the report, of course, but they formed the foundation of its purpose and structure. Time was what he needed. He needed to win himself more time.

He alternated sucking at the blunt end of his pen with scratching in the notepad balanced on his thighs, doing more sucking than scratching at first, but gradually getting into the flow of the writing until his thoughts came out onto the paper in the familiar, easy stream. When he was finished, he had filled five full pages. He did not bother to read them back over. He knew it was good work, in a draft that would be polished and typed tonight after he got back to his office. While never explicitly saying it, the underlying message in the report was that in the four days he had worked on Adams Neck—and he was projecting some sort of success at the ricefields this afternoon—he had begun to gain the trust of the inhabitants. They respected him, in fact, for his tenaciousness against their intransigence. Not only did he have the skills to get the job done over here—his superiors had recognized that when they had given him the toughest assignment in the land acquisiton office—but replacing him at this stage might give the foot-draggers the belief that their resistance was working, and they could get rid of any of the SPAR agents who opposed them and perhaps even stop the building of the dam itself, if only they held out long enough. It also would mean the man coming behind him would have to start from scratch and would be even more resented by the locals, and that would set the entire project irretrievably back. He liked that hint of irreplacability, even though he knew that no-one, in actuality, was ever irreplaceable. No matter. What was important was that his superiors at SPAR were convinced that it was imperative that he stay. He stretched his arms to relieve the kink that had developed in his back from too long sitting and hunched-over writing, feeling much better about himself than when he had sat down on the cabin steps. His confidence was beginning to return.

He closed the notebook with a movement of finality, put it away in his worksack, and stood up. He realized at once that he had spent more time at the writing than he had reckoned while it was in the doing, and while he had sat there on the porch steps, the day had grown late. Without his realizing it, he had put all thoughts of the Prioleau man out of his mind while he was concentrating his mind on the report, but now they returned with a vengeance. More than likely Prioleau and his cousin had returned off of the water, seen him working, decided not to disturb him, and were around there with the card-players, stretched out on the ground eating fish or sucking on the end of a jug. Darkies and their sense of priorities and time! He walked around to the side of the cabin already manifesting the sight of them into actuality, preparing the scolding he would give.

There was no-one around to scold.

The horse and the mule were where he had left them, standing, their heads bowed in unison, munching absently at the lush grass patches surrounding. The rest of the pondbank was empty of any other presence. The place where the card-players had made their fire was now only a small patch of dark cinders, carefully stamped out, from which no smoke arose. The card-players, the cards, the buckets of fish and the poles, all were gone. The pirogue was not tied up at the dock. Out upon the pond he could see no returning boat or any life at all, except for a long-necked white heron soaring gracefully and silently into the growing dark that was rapidly enveloping the cypress stands across the water.

The Sparman found it was suddenly difficult to capture air for his lungs, as if the great expanse of water and woods were slowly compressing in upon him.

IT WAS SOME HOURS LATER that they heard it, long after deep dark had fallen over Yelesaw Neck, a baying or a whooping or something akin, with a human kind-of sound to it, coming through the thickets and across the fields behind their houses like the Palmetto Limited had jumped its tracks and crossed the river and was barreling through the woods out there trying to find its way back. They thought at first it was a ha'ant running rampant, except that it was making far too much noise breaking up the underbrush to be a spirit. But by the time they figured that out and worked up the nerve to peek outside, some with shotguns at the ready, whatever it was had already gone, with only the high-howling drifting back to mark its passing, and the trumpeting of startled dogs in its wake.

It was only Soos Brown, then, who actually saw him, and so had the privilege of telling the full tale. He had been out night-hunting, and was on his porch cleaning his rifle when the Sparman came bursting out of the stickle-burr patch on the side of the house. Soos Brown would later say, as often as anyone would listen, "And him'a scare me-up so, I like'ded to shot that old buckra 'fore I knowed what it were coming at me." It certainly hadn't looked like the clean and pants-pressed whiteman Soos Brown had previously seen on horseback out on the River Road. His hat was gone, and his hair was wild over his head. His face and neck were scratched as if he had come through bramble-thorns, and there were several rips in his shirt and one great rent in his pants that left the fabric flapping around his bare, pale leg. His clothes were mudsplattered, and the pants water-soaked up to the thighs and all in all he looked, as Soos later told it, like a man who'd run several footraces with a rabbit "'twixt't'ween the mudbottoms and the briars." In the first telling, the Sparman's eyes were big as bo-dollars, gradually enlarging to pie-tin plates in the later versions, but always popping out like duck's eggs, and he had lost his glasses. He bounded across the yard and took the front steps at one leap, bursting past the startled Soos Brown and his rifle and through the open front door, stopping only when he had pasted himself, backsides first, in the farthest corner of the room.

Soos Brown braced his feet and turned his rifle out towards

the stickle-burr patch and waited for the horrible thing what must have been chasing the Sparman, but seeing nothing stir out there for a while, he went into the house to see what was what. By then the whole family had gathered in their nightclothes in the front room, wide-eyed themselves, watching the strange whiteman in the corner, bent over and trembling, his chest heaving as he fought to catch his breath. It took some time for him to get enough of it to be able to talk, and when he did, he would not say what had been after him, but only called for a ride down to the cable-barge.

Soos Brown was more than happy to oblige, if only to get the man out of his house.

All the way in the wagon out to the River Road, the Sparman would not sit still but turned on a swivel in his seat "like him been'a try for screw heself right down into the wood," peering into the trees and the underbushes from left to right and then back into the dark of the road behind them, as if he expected something to be close by following and preparing to leap into the wagon. Soos Brown had his rifle laid across his lap and continued to try to discover what might have been chasing the buckra, wanting to be ready for it himself, but the Sparman would only answer his queries with "get me to the landing, goddammit, just get me to the landing" over and over, and nothing else. His agitation appeared to increase as they turned down the cable-barge road and came up into Lem Washington's yard, and he did not bother to holler for Lem or knock on his door, but jumped out of the wagon while it was still rolling and sprinted over to the landing. Soos Brown thought at first that crazy and spooked as he was acting, he was going to try to run out the cable-barge himself, and was getting ready to get out to try to stop him, but the Sparman made straight for the boats tied up at the dock. He jumped into the first one he came to, casting off even as he was sitting down, propelling the craft out into the river with hard strokes on one oar, not even bothering to give Soos Brown a word of thank-you for the ride. The last time Soos saw him, the Sparman was paddling furiously across the black Sugaree waters, the spray shooting out on all sides of the boat, his anguished pale face gradually disappearing into the gloom of the night.

"Well I'll be chicken'," Soos Brown said to himself. He could not wait to tell somebody the tale, and so he walked up on Lem Washington's porch to knock on his door and wake him up.

THERE WAS GREAT AND LONG SPECULATION, of course, and

many interesting stories, over what might have driven the Sparman
so suddenlike off of the Neck that night. Most often mentioned
was the Pennyman, but in close competition was the man who had
shown up at Sister Orry's funeral, who was fast on his way to
becoming a permanent part of the pantheon of hags and haunts
and hobs thought to wander the nighttime Yelesaw woods.

The most important source of information was Pookie
Prioleau.

He had his own story to tell, differing in key points from the
actual events. While he left it somewhat ambiguous as to who had
approached whom that afternoon out on the River Road, Pookie
said that he had agreed to take the Sparman out to the ricefields,
and had led him down to the fish-landing and the cabin at
Deepbottom Down. That you had to deliberately bypass several
backroads and pathways leading to any of the Yelesaw ricefields to
get to the Deepbottom was never questioned by any of his
listeners, as it would have interrupted the flow of an entertaining
tale. And two key items were altered from the events at the pond.
There was no mention of the fishing men playing cards out on the
landing, nor of Pookie's cousin Kezzy, either, who everyone knew
did not live anywhere live Deepbottom Down. Instead, according
to Pookie, it had been at the Sparman's insistence that Pookie had
taken the pirogue out into the pond—the reason for the errand
over the water being somewhat vague, and changing, slightly, with
each telling—and Pookie, not being familiar with the Down, had
immediately gotten himself lost up in one of the byways. It had
taken him longer than expected, he said, to make his way back to
the bank and the cabin, and by then it was already dark. There he
found the mule and horse still waiting, but the Sparman had
already gone. He neither saw nor heard nothing else on his way
back home, and only learned of the Sparman's flight through the
Yelesaw woods the next day. Pookie kept the Sparman's rented
horse for several days, riding it across Yelesaw as a visual prop for
his story until finally and somewhat reluctantly taking the animal
across the river to Jaeger's Cross and returning it to Mister Tom
Butterfield, from whom the Sparman had rented it.

It was from Tom Butterfield that Pookie's identity got back to
the High Sheriff's office, and a deputy sheriff came over in a day
or so and sought Pookie out to tell his story detail. The deputy
sheriff listened attentively, writing out notes in his pad as he did,
questioning at key or vague points. Despite those questions, in his
summary of the story to the High Sheriff, the deputy still had

trouble relaying the train of Pookie Prioleau's tale, Pookie's memory having clouded up at various times. The High Sheriff stopped the deputy in mid-explanation and instructed him to write out a general report that concluded that the Sparman "had been frightened by an unknown something out in the woods." No other investigation followed, and the matter was left at that.

FOR MANY YEARS AFTERWARDS, whenever there was a strange disturbement coming from out of the woods, a Yay'saw would often say, "Well, there go Old Socky," and everyone hearing would smile, and understand.

SEVERAL DAYS AFTER the incident at Deepbottom Down, word came out to Jaeger's Cross, and thence across the river to Yelesaw, that the Sparman had broken camp, cleaning out his office at the county building and his room at the hotel in Cashville, packing it all in his black roadster truck and leaving out on the highway without much of a word to anyone in town. There was talk that he had returned to the SPAR headquarters in Columbia, but wherever he went, he was definitely gone. Though the exact events that had caused his flight were never fully known, people in the county were not surprised by his sudden departure after spending so much time with the Neckerniggers. Four days had been the longest any white person had spent on Adams Neck since the Grady family had left in the time of the Yankees, and everyone in the county knew—or was quickly told if they didn't know—the story of how the Gradys had ended up. "That would drive a sane white man loony," many said, "and you know that SPAR boy was always wound up a little too tight, from the start."

In any event, though the Sparman was gone, his office in Cashville did not stay vacant for long, as SPAR sent another man down to take his place in land acquisition and resettlement for the Cashville division.

They called him Boss Ben and nothing else, and it fit him like the belt stretched tight around his big belly. He dressed in white shirts and a tie and pressed slacks and tool-stitch-pattern black boots, with a wide planter's hat sitting flat on his broad head. He took off his hat often to wipe his thinning hair with his handkerchief or the perspiration off his forehead. But it was not a worrying kind of sweat, because he displayed little worry about anything. He smiled Cheshire-cat-style at everyone and everything, the smile of a man who was good at his job and lived secure in the knowledge. Neither the office clothes nor the planter's hat fooled anyone. One look at his hands told the real story. Boss Ben hadn't come up in no office. He had blacksmith's hands, big, meaty hands, with the fingers so thick that they crowded each other out for space when he gripped something, the palms and fingertips horn-yellow with callouses, and he had forearms as big and knotted as bull's thighs that stretched the fabric of his shirtsleeves. He walked on massive legs with a rolling swagger that displayed a confidence that in whatever manner he approached the ground, it would always prepare itself to hold him. It was clear from the testimony of Boss Ben's body that he had started life out as a working boy, either in mill or factory or field, most likely all three. And from his demeanor and ways—the easy bluster in his walk and the note of barked command in his voice that underscored its deep and lazy drawl—it was also clear that Boss Ben had bulled his way up from carrying loads to driving other men to do so. Thus, the name Boss.

He was as unlike the lanky, intellectual Sparman as could be imagined.

He did not live in Cashville, as the Sparman had, but drove the fifteen miles every day down from St. Paul at high speeds, passing slower cars whenever he could, blowing them down with his horn when he could not, waving at people with the bottle of Coca-Cola he usually clutched in his hand. He drove a tan and white touring car, the latest Ford model, which he took care to have wiped and shined every morning by the colored boy at the Lee & Longstreet in St. Paul where he took his rooms. On the job in the countryside around Cashville, he never went door to door, seeing that as a waste of time and talent. He attended organized meetings at churches and halls and other gathering spots, and there he made his pitches, enticements and threats. He had the barrelly voice of a camp meeting preacher and the salesmanship of a potion peddler and under his direction, families slowly began to stay after the meetings and cautiously, one by one, sign up for the move, convinced that SPAR meant business if it had hired a man like Boss Ben.

He never crossed the river to Adams Neck, not for any reason. When asked by people in the Basinbottom why they should sign up for the move when the Neckerniggers were not, Boss Ben would tell his colored audience, "They got one foot in the bog over there, and sinking. You ain't going to let them hoodoos drag you down with them, are you?" And to the white folks he would say, "I seen a lot of things in my travels, but I never seen a Carolina white man let a nigger take the lead of him. But maybe y'all different down here to Cantrell, and can't do nothing until the niggers do it first."

Not content with mere persuasion, Boss Ben had new signs printed up.

> This is to announce that court proceedings may be initiated at the discretion of the Sugaree Power and Recreation Authority, the State of South Carolina, and/or the Federal Government of the United States of America against any landholder within the below census tracts of Central and Southern Cantrell County, South Carolina, who have not made preparations to surrender their dwellings and/or real property and vacate said premises by August 31, nineteen hundred and thirty-six.

He paid a crew of boys to nail the new signs up all across the Basinbottom, sometimes side-by-side with the already-yellowing ones that had been posted by his predecessor, sometimes laid out on top of them. Crowds gathered around the signs, interpreters were called in to read and explain the legalese, and there were long and heated discussions by Basinbottom residents over what must be done. One sign went up on the pole at the cable-barge crossing on the county side. It disappeared from the pole within hours, and was rapidly passed around Yelesaw Neck, so that three days had not passed before everyone interested had seen or touched it.

At first, the new SPAR signs caused a stir on Yelesaw Neck. But when Boss Ben showed no interest in coming over the river, and nothing seemed especially imminent in the threats lined out on the signs, concerns about the coming water and the new whiteman from Columbia began to wane again, and their attention turned to other things. There was much to do that summer. The year ripened fat and oily like a sweet pecan, rolling over bright emerald green to sand-dust brown, stretching itself out and cracking open sweet in the sun. The rice-shoots drove up like growing grass, and they worked by torchlight many nights to keep up with them. Rain came and went at just the right time. Crocus-sacks and baskets of fruit and garden crops hung heavy in their hands, and the cane grew so high even the tallest among them could not touch its leafy tops. Potatoes were big as stepping rocks in a pond, the melons and cabbage the size of small boulders, the carrots and sugarpeas and tomatoes the sweetest anyone could remember, okra the most tender, corn ears so weighted to the ground that the bending stalks called out to people passing by to please ma'am, please sir, hurry and pick them things off, it was too much a strain to try to hold them up. The fall harvest was fat and yellow-deep, the wagon-axles crying and groaning and hardly able to hold their loads coming out of the fields. It was a fall of many healthy babies born, and few accidents or illness, and fewer elders passing. It was the best growing time in a generation or more, and with the days rolling on so well, who among them could imagine leaving the land of their fathers and mothers?

5

## What Go In The Swamp

*(Fall, 1936)*

I n the years before his oldest daughter died, it had been Budi
Manigault's way—once the fall harvest was in and the ricefield
repairs finished—to load up his shotgun and fishgear and a
jug of homemade liquor and take off walking with his best
huntbitch and favorite traveling companion, his black dog, Du, to
clear his thoughts.

Early risers would see him ambling along out on the River
Road in the washed-pale light of the early sun, his bare feet and
ankles hidden in the morning field-mists, whistling, canvas
dufflebag slung from one shoulder, shotgun and cane poles over
the other, boots tied by their laces and hung around his neck,
bucket handle looped in his belt, the bucket itself rolling across his
thigh and bouncing out with each step, Du ambling up ahead and
behind and then in and out of the thickets on either side of the
road, hunting up something interesting. On these mornings
Tat'Budi walked like a man who was not in any particular hurry,
but would not stop to talk, either, only calling out greetings and

waving a hail to anyone he met or passed on the road, and walking on.

Somewhere up above the Old Crossroads, he would cut off from the River Road and cross over into the trees, skirting the old plantation grounds and making his way, by long-overgrown paths, up to the edge of the Randwoods, the great track of thickets running between the Sugaree and the Blacksnake that marked the northern boundary of Yelesaw Neck. Budi Manigault always maintained that during the rainiest times, the many creeks that interspersed the Rand merged one into the other, connecting in a convoluted string to complete the work of the rivers, so that Yelesaw Neck became an actual island. There were not many who tried to dispute him on this point, as there were few others on the Neck or off who traveled those woods as he did. And in any case, the Rand was so thick and pathless and virtually impassable that no-one ever traveled that way between Yelesaw and the county but instead used the river crossings, and so for all intents and purposes, Yelesaw *was* an island.

On the edge of the Randwoods, Budi Manigault would make camp for the night, sitting next to his fire and Du, chugging from a corn liquor jug until he got sloppily, happily drunk, singing rollicking songs up into the stars, loud enough to reach the folks in the upper settlements.

> *Oh, a oba'dey farmer plant a muleshit row*
> *Toss out the seed wheresover him go*
> *And where the mule shit*
> *That where he crop grow*

Those that heard would turn to one another on their porches or in their beds and say, "That old Cu'n Budi, can't you hear him? Wondered when he'd take his break this year." And Budi would sing and sweat out the cares and toils and troubles of the year deep into the night, until he drove himself into a deathlike, dreamless sleep.

In the morning he was finished with the foolcutting, and afterwards the trip was all business.

He would walk across the Rand by ways only he and a handful of Yay'saw men knew, hunting for smaller game, taking them down with a single shot from his rifle, stopping only for Du to fetch and for him to skin them and throw the carcasses into his crocus-sack. The Rand was thick with deer and though he usually sighted many, he would let them go on these particular trips, as he was not going straight back, and had no way to tote all that meat along the paths he planned to travel. "Not this time, Cousin," he would tell them, smiling and wagging a finger at their shining eyes, or the sight of their flags or antlers retreating into the trees. "But wait here 'til I gets back, iffen you wants, and I'll accommodate."

It would take him a day and a night, generally, to make it across the woods and to the banks of the dark and oily Blacksnake at one of the few places where the river ran free of the Swamp. There he would stop to light-smoke the game he had brought down, and to cut down a dozen small trees or so and lash them together with vines to make himself a flatboat. He would then put out on the river, he and Du floating down its wandering, weed-strewn way with the current. At the place they called the Dimba Downs, the sunken acres where the swamplands melded into the Blacksnake river-waters on both sides, he would get off the flatboat again and disappear for days into a trackless land of bogs and creeks and soggy sawgrass fields and canebrake pools and cypress grove lakes that was the Sugaree Swamp.

It was this part of the trip, especially, that Mama did not like.

Once when Sister Orry was still alive, Yally had heard her mother fussing about it with her older sister, worrying over their father wandering around back there in what Mama had called "that bad-ass place," wishing if he did have to go in there, he would take someone with him.

Sister Orry had laughed off Mama's concerns, her big breasts shaking with mirth.

"Him don't take nobody's cause him figure them be done scare off the creatures and the fish. 'Too many niggers make for too much'a noises,'" Orry had said, mimicking their father's voice, adding that he tolerated Du only because she never asked to share his tobacco, and had sense not to piss in the boat. At that, Yally had to stifle her giggles to not let on that she was listening.

And when Mama had protested, "But why him got for go up in that old Swamp? They's other place for fish and hunt," Sister Orry had shrugged and said, "Uly, you been'a fussing about Papa going back in that-there Swamp since you been a biddy. Mama been'a fuss about it, too, 'fore you been borned. But iffen you think it'a do some good, why you ain't bring it up with Papa? Why you coming to me?"

"I been thinking you mo'ught put in the word with him you'self," Mama had said. "You the only one him'a listen at."

Sister Orry had snorted at that and said, "Oh, you knows that big-old man don't study nothing I does say," and Mama had answered, "He did once't."

But it was just then, to Yally's bad luck, that Sister Orry had noticed her playing out in the back yard below the kitchen window where they had been talking, and changed the topic, immediate, and Yally never found out what it was that Papa'Budi had listened to Sister Orry about.

WHAT BUDI MANIGAULT DID back in the Sugaree Swamp besides hunt, and why, only he and Du knew. Whatever it was, and however long it took, when he was finished, he and the dog would get back on the flatboat, the sack now bulging fat with smokemeat, and from there they would make their way down the slow, muddy crawl that was the lower half of the Blacksnake. It was on that portion of the trip that Papa'Budi would start his fishing, stopping here and there in quiet pools and byways or in the main body of the river itself to drop his line in the dark waters for an hour or two, sometimes for as long as a full morning or an afternoon, continuing on his way not necessarily based on how many fish he was catching or had caught, but when the spirit moved him. He would stop fishing completely when his bucket was heavy overflowing with bream and crappie and goggle-eye and cat, and that was it. At that point he would put out into the center of the river and make for home, down the Blacksnake to the Junction where it met the Sugaree, then back up the Sugaree to New Landing. He called it the Circuit, making the entire round of Yelesaw Neck along its watery perimeter, and sometimes it would take him as long as two weeks to do it. When he came back, they knew it long in advance, because they could hear his singing for miles as he poled up the Sugaree, his voice booming through the half-tunnel of the overhanging trees:

> *Sugaree, Sugaray*
> *Him'a running to the water*
> *And the niggerdog' won't catch him*
> *But them damn mosquito oughta*
> *Yi-yi-yi!*
> *Got me squirrel and alley-gator*
> *Fire up the grease, Yu'keece*
> *We save the coon for later!*

And the low-hanging willows and wateroaks and river birches would boom back echoes in accompanying chorus:

> *Yi! Yi! Yi!*

Then he'd make the last turn just below the cable-crossing,

tobacco-juice dotting the river with round brown coins floating in his wake, Du sprawling with her paws and head out over the water, tongue hanging, panting, exhausted and eager to get back under the house, the flatboat dipping in and out of water level, heavy with whatever had been killed and caught. Papa'Budi would walk back up from the landing to the house at Goat Hill, singing his arrival along the way, but Mama'Keece would always know of his coming long before, and was already clearing the kitchen table and getting the smoke-fire going behind the house before they heard his booming voice coming down the lane. In the early days—before Ula was born—Orry would ride back to the landing with her father in the wagon to pick up the game that was too heavy for him to carry. Soo, even then, did not much care for the company of Tat'Budi, and always stayed back at the house with their mother to help prepare for the fixings. But after Ula was born and Mama'Keece had passed on, it was Orry who stayed at the house to take their mother's place with the preparations and the cooking, and little Ula, when she was big enough, who would go down to the landing. Like Mama'Keece, Ula could tell when Papa'Budi was on the way back, even while he was still out on the river, and more than once she had trotted by herself down to the landing to greet him at the dockside, grinning, little dark feet dangling in the water.

They always held the big hog-butcher of the fall when Budi Manigault got back from his harvest hunt, supplemented with the load of fish and game he brought with him. Once it was an actual alligator, which Budi said had crawled up on his flatboat to get at his bucket of fish, and he had bashed it to death with his pole because the gator was between him and his gun. Another time it was two big bucks, who he said he had come upon in a clearing, antlers locked together, so intent on fighting over a doe, they didn't even notice either him or his dog. He'd had no intention of hunting deer, of course, but this was too tempting an invitation to pass by. The doe was standing at the edge of the clearing herself, watching the battle, and according to the story Tat'Budi told with great relish and many hand-gestures, he walked over and stood next to her for a while, finally turning and telling her, "Sister Kimpy, you picks you out the buck you likes the best, cause I'm fixing to shoot the other." And Budi would say that the doe looked back at him out of the side of her head—the only way a doe could look, he was quick to remind them—sucked her big teeth, and told him, "Shit, ain't neither one'a *them* fits my fancy. *My* buck's down at the waterhole. I were just watching 'til him get back." So Budi, of course, had shot them both.

There had to be some truth to the story, since Budi actually did bring two bucks back with him that trip, cutting them up into quarters and then lugging them, piece by piece, out to the River Road, where he stashed them until he could fetch a wagon. The two sets of interlocked horns with heads attached, ever after, stayed nailed up over the door of his shed. It was the first and only time he had ever cut a harvest hunt short, coming straight back without making the Circuit down the Blacksnake and into the Swamp.

And however true and however many times he told it, everyone agreed it was a good story. No-one could ever figure what drew friends and family to the fall hog-butchering at Budi Manigault's more, the food or Budi's tall tales. For that matter, nobody cared, since whether it was Mama'Keece cooking or Sister Orry in later years, and with Budi steady running his mouth, both food and talk were among the best on Yelesaw Neck. The corn liquor from out of the shed didn't hurt much, either.

It went on every year like that, year after year, in a comfortable and comforting rhythm for as long as anyone on the Neck could recall. In all that time, Budi Manigault had only missed one harvest hunt since he had started them in his youth: the year that Sister Orry passed away and was buried in the soggy ground at the back-end of Goat Hill. He had gone into mourning in those days, and the time for heading back onto the Blacksnake had passed with his gun remaining on its rack and his fishpoles tied and stacked above the back porch. But he had suffered as much deep loss as any in his life, the death of his wife in the birth of their last child, the older brother who had bled out in Budi's arms after a tree-cutting tragedy, to name among the saddest, and knowing Budi's fierce, one-eyed resilence, they all figured he would pull out of it in a bit and be his old, tornadoish self again.

But he did not.

He spent that next year like a mound of sand in a soft rain, quietly dissipating, parts of him melting off, piece by piece, in gray, tiny rivulets, even as they watched. He rarely talked out at the ricefields any more, and almost never sang with the rest of them as they worked, and more and more, he began ceding the decisions to his younger brother, Tibo. When the day's tasks were done, he did not stop by anyone's house or wander the yard chastising the children as he had in times past, instead mostly returning directly home to feed his dogs and stock and then retreat to his porch, and those who passed by found him carving absently on branches of wood, or going through a box of old things set between his legs, or simply sitting with big hands draped over his knees, staring out at the trees toward the River Road with his one good eye. Sometimes he would lift a hand when they hailed him as they passed by. Sometimes not. Only the whitefolks and their talk of evacuating Yelesaw seemed to rouse him into his old bouts of invective, but even that was only for a short time. Afterwards he seemed like a motor that had either spent all of its fuel or, worse yet, had been submerged in water, and sputtering into silence, he sank down even deeper into himself, brooding, languishing, picking at some inward sore.

For the first time in his life, he was living by himself, and it was wearing on him.

He had taken to eating, cold, the extra two or three days of food his granddaughter, Yally, had been fixing for him at his house since Big Soo had moved out and noticing that, the girl had begun coming over every evening just to light a fire in the stove and warm his supper up. She did it not only for the food itself, but because of an inherent feeling she held—unspoken and not even consciously acknowledged—that the stove was the home's heart, and her grandfather's house felt dead and already crumbling into its grave when its fires sat permanently silent and cold.

After Papa'Budi had eaten, she would sit with him inside by the fire or, on warm nights or even nights that were not-so-warm, out on the porch. She would share the news of the day and ask him many questions, trying to get him to talk as of old, or even deliberately doing something mildly provoking, so that at least she might get a rise out of him enough for him to chastise her. Generally, he was not aroused. Mostly her grandfather responded in single words, often only in monosyllables, even to her provokements. Every once in a while Tibo, his only surviving brother, or else maybe Ya, Papa'Tee's youngest son, would come by for a visit, and on those nights Grandpa Budi would grow more animated and join in the bootjacking and storytelling for a while, slapping knees and cackling-laughing and filling the air with tobacco-spit and it was an echo of the old days again, before Orry died. Papa'Budi would pull out his mouth-harp and Papa'Tee would bring out his, and if Ya were there, too, he would set the tune on his banjo. Often as not on those nights, Bo Kinlaw would hear the playing from across the yard and come over, fiddle and

bow in hand, and they all would go at it out on the porch for a
while. But it would be only for a while, and the laughing never as
loud and unencumbered and the spit never as far-traveling and
wide-spattering and the tunes never as long-lasting as they had
been in past years, and if Yally stayed on after her uncle and
granduncle and father had left, she noted that her grandfather
would lapse back into silence before the visitors had even passed
the scuppernong arbor, putting his mouth-harp back into his
overalls pocket and not bringing it out again until another night
when the men came back with their own instruments. He never
played alone, now. And gone, too, were the high-pitched work-
and-saltwater songs that had been Budi Manigault's staple and
regular fare for all his years.

A few of the other men in the community sometimes stopped
by, now and again, but not nearly as many as had come in the past.
They engaged Papa'Budi in brief and semi-formal talk—over the
weather or the state of this year's crop or the latest news about the
dam-building project and such—never staying long, but taking
their leave as quickly as they could, saying that what was best for
him was that they continue to allow him his space. This worked up
something of an anger in Yally, that folks seemed to have deserted
her grandfather, now that he was down. All before the folk on
Goat Hill and all up and down Yelesaw had respected Budi
Manigault, crowded around him, listened to his words, and
followed his lead. Now they were like the man in the story who
would not slow his walk for a new-crippled friend because he could
no longer keep up the pace. On many nights, when Papa'Tee or
Uncle Ya or Papa did not come over at all and Yally had run out of
things to say, the only sounds around her grandfather's house was
the tinkling of the wind passing through the bottle-tree out in the
yard. The old Manigault house was now a lonely place, in a
lonesome time.

Mama always invited her father to their house for Saturday and
Sunday suppers and at first he came, seeming to enjoy the
company and attention of his children and grands and great-
grands. But the only time after Orry's funeral he appeared truly
happy was at Eshy and Nu Dingle's wedding, sitting in a special
cane-wove chair in the place of honor in the yard, dressed in all
white, a blood-red scarf tied around his neck, annointing the
newlyweds' heads from a bowl of clear water and sending them
into their married life and their home across to the Dingle
settlement at Kanuza. But after the wedding he came to supper at

the Kinlaws less and less frequently, until by the summer he had stopped altogether.

He kept up his work in the fields as always, on his old schedule of labor—when it was necessary—from can't-see-the-sun in the east when you leave out in the morning to can't-see-it-again in the west by the time you get back home, but that marked the end of his day's responsibilities. He ceased most other work around the house altogether, and would generally only find someplace to sit once he had come back from the fields—at the fire or on the porch or under a tree out in the yard—and there he would generally stay for the evening unless someone came by to rouse him to activity, until it was time to go to bed. The old homestead began to fall into disrepair, and Uncle Ya and Papa had to come by regular, or send their sons, to patch a hole in a fence, or to put back up something that had blown down in a wind. Yally's daily task now—along with the cooking and the cleaning of the house— was to feed the chickens and the mule and the hogs and the dogs, which her grandfather had all begun to neglect, as well as to clear the weeds and grass that were springing up with regularity in the yard. Budi Manigault would join in with the men in their repair work when they came, sometimes directing the efforts, more and more leaving it to Ya or Bo to decide what needed to be done, and how. And if they did not come, he would not call them over neither do the work by himself, so that when they were not keeping a hand on him to hold him up, both the old man and all that was directly around him seemed to be falling irretrievably inward, as if into some unseen and unfathomable and undefinable hole, even as they watched.

ONE NIGHT AFTER SUPPER, just at the end of the harvest season, when the sacks fat with rice grain had been brought from out of the fields and stacked to the ceiling in the sheds behind the houses, Bo Kinlaw told Ula that he thought things might be changing, and looking up for her father.

She was sitting on the bed with her back against the wall, already in her nightclothes, brush and comb and grease can in her lap, tying up her head in a scarf, while Bo sat on the opposite side, pulling off one of his boots. Ula turned to him with a hopeful look.

"Why you be thinking that?" she asked him.

Bo finished with the first boot, held it balanced in the palm of one hand, measured with his eyes and then gave it an easy toss, so that it somersaulted once in the air and landed upright in the corner, toe pointing out. He had gotten to where he could do that four times out of eleven or so, and he was proud of the accomplishment. He leaned down and started on the laces of the second boot.

"It just look like he had him a good attitude about hisself today, is all," he said. "Ain't been hanging back, like he been. And he kept up a talk with the boys 'most all day, telling story."

Ula tossed her head back to get the scarf material out of her eyes and held the ends out in mid-tie. "What kind of story?"

"Story about you' grandma and you' grandpap and he brothers and sisters and the like, and things what he done when he been a boy. He gone all the way back to the plantation-times. It been a long time since I heard him talk like that. It been good to hear. The boys like'ded it. And I believe he done found hisself a friend-girl, somewheres."

Ula gave a dismissive laugh deep in her throat and went back to her scarf-tying.

"What my papa would do with a friend-girl 'cept lay down on he side and watch she sleep?" she asked. "Last 'uman my pap court been my mama, and her been in she grave these forty year. What make you tell that bold tale like that on a old man?"

"He told me tonight him fixing to go and visit with one."

"'Wisit with a 'uman—so? Every time you eat corn, don't mean it's cornbread. Which 'uman him'a tell you him be fixing for 'wisit? Pro'lly one'a he cousin out there to Simmonsville. Him come up with them. You does got you a habit of getting everything all twist-up sometime, Ben Kinlaw."

Bo had hoped the news about her father's uplift in spirits—which hadn't been nearly as much of an uplift as he was asserting—would actually be a catalyst to lift his wife's own. She'd been running on low fuel lately, and he was worried about her. Instead, the only spirit it seemed to be raising in her was a fighting one, and he didn't feel like fighting with Ula tonight. He tossed his second shoe over in the corner, trying to get it to land side-by-side with the first, but the shoe hit the wall and lay at an odd angle on its side.

"Weren't nobody out of no Simmonsville, unless she done move," he answered as he got up and walked over to the corner to straighten the shoe out. "Some 'uman name'a Timbi, I believe he said, offen the Blacksnake, or somewhere nears."

Behind him he heard the comb and brush clatter on the floor, the can of grease close after, the can rolling on its edge until it hit the far wall and stopped. He turned his head quick, now, to see what had happened. His wife had half-risen off the bed, one hand bracing herself against the mattress, one foot on the floor, an expression on her face that seemed a cross between horror and shock.

"What wrong with you, Ula?" he asked her, alarmed.

It took a moment for her to find her voice and when she did, it barked out at him.

"*What 'uman you done say?*"

He felt as if he had done something terribly wrong, that he should have caught something immediate when talking to Papa'Budi, but hadn't, and couldn't figure out what it might have been.

"Timbi, I reckon that who he said," he told her. "Something wrong with him going to see Timbi?"

She ignored his question.

"*What my papa say about Nana'Timbi?*"

"Said he was fixing to go fishing back on the Blacksnake, and might go visit some 'uman name' Timbi while he were back there," Bo answered, thinking hard, now, on exactly what his father-in-law had told him as he tried, at the same time and so far unsuccessfully, to figure out the cause of his wife's sudden upset. He repeated Budi Manigult's words, slowly. "'I got me a mind for might go visit with Sus'Timbi, this time around.' That what he said. I figured she was some old girl lived over on the county side of the Swamp. Ain't she?"

Ula continued to push past his questions without answering them. "Go fishing *when?*" she shot back at him, the words sharp as a meat-cutting blade.

"Soon. I ain't know. He ain't say. Who the hang this Timbi is, anyways?" He didn't think Papa'Budi visiting an oba woman should have caused this much of an upset, with his wife since, after all, she had married an oba man. He had a sudden flash that he had gotten it all wrong, that the Timbi woman might not be from over on the county side at all, but might be a Yelesaw free woman living out near the Swamp, that men paid nighttime visits to that they did not care to let the womenfolk in their families or the community know about, and Bo had made a terrible error in mentioning it to Ula.

His wife was not paying him any more attention. She stood all the way up now and went quick to the dresser, opened a drawer and began to pull out a dress. Then, of a sudden she stopped again, standing with the dress half-out, as if torn between two thoughts. He had never seen his wife hesitate like that before, and it worried him more than anything else she had done in her reaction to his news. Now she shook her head, violently. "No," she said, aloud, as if she had been arguing with herself. She turned back to him, all resolute again. One side of the argument had prevailed.

"Bo," she told him, her hand still clutching her dress, her voice now changed to dead-even adamance from the explosiveness and hesitation of a moment before, "go-on over to my papa house and tell him he must not go fishing out on the Blacksnake tonight."

"What I'm'a tell him that for?"

"*You just tell him! You hear me?!*"

The tone in her voice left him no alternative, and he fetched his boots from the corner and sat back down in the chair to put them on.

"What I mean was, what reason I'm'a give him for not go?" he asked as he began to lace up his boots. "Papa 'Budi ain't fixing to stop nothing just 'cause I done tell him he shouldn't. He sure gonna' ask me why. Tell him you ain't want him for see this 'uman Timbi?"

She cut him off sharply.

"No!" she said, shaking her head again. She pulled off her nightclothes with one swift yank and slipped her dress over her head. "*You* think of something, Bo Kinlaw. My papa listen to you more than you know, man. You just hurry and get over there and do like I done ask'ded you. Just hold him to the house whiles I go fetch Papa 'Tee."

A HARVEST MOON hung low outside, the sand in the yard glittering white under its pale light. Bo took his time walking past the scuppernog arbor, still wondering why his wife didn't want Tat'Budi to go and see this Timbi woman—whoever she was—and alternately trying to figure out a reason to give his father-in-law to keep him from going. Neither train of thought was moving along especially satisfactorily and finally he gave up the attempt at the latter one, reckoning he'd just stall his father-in-law until Ula got back with her uncle. Papa 'Tee was about the only one on the Hill who had a chance of talking Budi Manigault out of anything.

When he got to his father-in-law's house, it was dark and silent. He went up on the front porch and knocked on the door, calling out Budi's name. No answer came, so he called out again, adding, only half-humorously, "Don't shoot, Papa'Budi. It be me, Bo." And then, thinking his father-in-law may have been drinking, he put in, as insurance, in case Budi might have somehow forgotten, "Ula' husband."

Two or three of the dogs came out from under the house, sniffing at his boots and pantslegs suspiciously and then giving expectant whimpers as they recognized his scent. Otherwise, around the house and yard, all was silent and still.

Bo shuffled his feet on the porch, and tried to figure out what to do. You tumbled too much around Budi Manigault's house at night and startled him out of his sleep, he *would* shoot, for-true.

Shrugging his concerns off, he got down off the porch and walked around the house to the back, all of the time calling out, over and over, "Budi Manigault. Hey, Budi Manigault. It be me. Bo Kinlaw." The dogs trotted behind him in a hopeful little parade. When he came to Papa'Budi's bedroom window he knocked on the sill, hard, and called again. He stopped and listened, but no sound came from inside the house. The wind stirred across the yard, and the bottle-tree tinkled as the glass bottles brushed against each other.

Something of his wife's reaction in the bedroom came back to him, and for the first time, he began to be worried more about Papa'Budi's absence than in waking him up and having to explain his visit.

He walked back around to the front porch and paused at the door to holler, "Budi Manigault. It Bo, Bo Kinlaw, and I'm coming in." Then he took a long breath, opened the door, and walked inside.

The house was hard-heavy with quiet, and black-dark. Not even the light from the full moon penetrated past the porchboards.

"Papa'Budi," Bo called out again.

There was no answer, but he didn't need one. The feeling of Budi Manigault's absence was overwhelming. "Anyways," he said to himself, "he ain't done dead up in here. That's something good."

He fumbled around for a moment in the unfamiliar dark, found the lamp on the front table, lit it, and took a quick tour of the house. The shotgun was missing from the bigroom rack. Inside the main bedroom, the bed was made, and empty. On his way through the kitchen, he stopped by the woodstove to feel its side. It was cold, with no hint that there had been a fire for a while. He blew the lamp out, set it on the table, and went out by the back door. By the moonlight, he could see that the fishpoles were missing from the back porch. The dogs had gathered around the back steps, and he looked among them for Du's familiar brown-and-white spotted coat and rheumy eyes. Not seeing her among the pack, he stepped off the porch and leaned down and whistled for her under the house, just to make sure, calling out her name once or twice. She did not come out. Although it was not needed from all the other mounting evidence, that was the clincher. Budi Manigault had already left for the woods and the backriver.

For a moment, Bo thought he might wait for his wife and Papa'Tee, but decided against it. If he was gone when they got here, they'd know that Papa'Budi was gone, too, and where, as easy as he could tell them, by checking for the gun and the poles as he had. Now, without knowing why, he began to feel full-on his wife's urgency to stop her father.

He took off across the yard, angling behind the arbor towards his own pens and sheds, picking up the pace as he went. At the barn he considered taking Zelly, who was the faster of the two mules, but was also known to get her ignorant up if she thought she was being overworked, and she would certainly feel overworked if he took her out again after a day out in the fields. He did not have time to struggle with a bull-headed animal on the road tonight. He found Bay-say, who was older and slower but the far more reliable. He threw the bridle over Bay-say's head in the dark, and in a moment he was up on the mule's back and out into the yard again and off at a trot, kicking its flanks to urge him on as he turned his head up across the yard towards the wagonpath and the River Road beyond.

IT WAS VERY LATE by the time he finally turned the mule down the road into the cable-barge landing. He had ridden all the way up to the Crossroads and had even gone a short distance up the old plantation lane, calling out his father-in-law's name every few feet into the haunt-lit night. The road had been forlorn and empty all the way up and back, and only the night creatures—owls and whippoorwills and the occasional fox howling from a distance— answered him back. In his hurry he had forgotten to make an appropriate sign when passing over the Crossroads the first time, and he made sure he did so, twice, on his way back over. He rode back down the River Road slower than he had ridden up, because he was certain, now, that he was too late to catch his father-in-law, and went out to the landing only on a whim. Ever before, Budi

Manigault had always started out on his end of the season fish-and-hunt trips on foot, but this had long ago seemed something different from his annual trips, and so perhaps, Bo thought, he might have chosen instead to take his boat. Even so, Bo did not think that Papa'Budi would have lingered that long down at the dock, but he went out there anyway just to check, because there seemed nothing else to do.

At the Landing, he got off Bay-say and walked out onto the planks, listening as he did to the sound of the quiet lapping of water against the pierboards. At the edge of the Landing, he looked for his father-in-law's boat among the row of tied-up crafts bobbing noiseless in the black water. It was missing.

He cursed himself quietly for not having thought of this earlier, and coming to the Landing first, before he went all the way up to the Crossroads.

He cupped his hands around his mouth and called out, "Papa'Budi! Papa'Budi!" first up the river and then down, twice in each direction, then stopped to listen.

The river whispered wetly back to him.

"You ain't never fixing to see that old man again, Bo Kinlaw," his own voice told him, inside his head. "You should'a been quicker. You should'a knowed, when he told you where he been going."

He shook his head to clear those thoughts. There was no way for him to know anything, just because Budi had told him he intended a visit back in the woods to a woman named Timbi. Not for the first time, Bo Kinlaw grew angry at the idea of all the Yelesaw secrets that were still being kept from him, after so many years married and living on this side of the river. If they had not been so intent on hiding so much, he might have known. His anger faded and then dissipated, as quickly as it had arisen. There were other things to be done besides getting angry at things that would never change, and which did nothing to help to track his father-in-law down and bring him back. He considered for just the briefest moment about getting into his own boat and heading out on the river to look for Papa'Budi, but stopped himself immediately. His father-in-law had probably been gone for hours. And besides that, even had he gotten out close behind, looking for Budi Manigault in Yelesaw waters would be like trying to follow a crow in the dark after it t'iefed a crumb of pie off your plate and flew out the window. It would take someone who had grown up over here, and knew Budi's ways. He was a stranger in a strange land, amongst people whose ways he could only barely fathom.

He got back on Bay-say and began the long ride back out to the River Road and then home, singing to himself, as he did, an old song, remembered from his church days on the other side of the river.

> *I am a pilgrim*
> *And a stranger*
> *Trav'lin' through*
> *This lonely land*
> *Come down Jesus*
> *Have pity on a stranger*
> *Help this trav'ler*
> *Lend a hand*

You should have stayed in church, Little Bo, he could hear his grandmother saying to him. Stayed in church and married a church 'uman and not gone off across the Sugaree to live amongst them hoodoos, them damn root-workers, them *shay'ree.*

And he answered, to his grandmother, and to himself, and anyone else that might be listening, that he hadn't never cared much about church, anyways, what-with the things he'd seen church-people do when the spirit wasn't on them, and even when it was, and beyond that, he'd been crazy about that big-eyed, big-legged Shay'ree girl the first time he'd seen her looking at fabric at the store in Cashville, and he'd been crazy about her every day since.

He sighed, thinking about Ula, and wondered how she was going to take the news that he had missed her father.

He was almost back home when the thought came to him that it had been in the harvest time a year ago—in fact, almost a year ago to the day, if he recollected rightly—that they had buried Orry Manigault in the graveyard behind Leem and Effy Manigault's old house, and Budi Manigault's slow, downward spiral had begun.

HE FOUND ULA even more unsettled when he got back than when he'd left. She hadn't come back with Papa'Tee, who had not been home when she'd gotten there, Ná'Risa neither. That was not unusual since Ná'Risa often was away in the evenings on spirit-missions and on the longer trips, Papa'Tee frequently drove her so she'd have company, but it certainly hadn't been what Ula had wanted. And then, when Bo had not returned from her father's by the time she got back home, she went over to Budi's house herself, and so had learned that Bo must have missed him there, since the fishpoles and shotgun were missing. She was pacing the house from back to front when Bo got back from the cable-barge landing, and Big Soo was up as well, fixing either a very late supper or a very early breakfast at the stove. Soo appeared unworried by her father's absence, but given her rocky relationship with Papa'Budi, that was hardly surprising, and certainly not indicative of what she, herself, might have been thinking about Budi's mission out on the backwaters.

Ula grew more agitated after Bo told her of the missing boat, and it took him some time after that to get her calmed down enough to go to bed. He only got her into their room, finally, with the promise that he would go over to Papa'Tee's at first light. If Ula slept at all that night, it was in a state of tossing uneasiness, murmuring unintelligible things into the darkness.

BO WAS UP and dressed and out the door while the sun was still waking, leaving Ula asleep in their bed. By the time he got to Papa'Tee's it was just beginning to dawn, but the old man was already up, out in the back spreading out leavings in the hog trough, whistling as he did.

"You over this way mighty earlyish, young man," Papa'Tee said above the clamor of the pigs over in the outer pen. "You taking a break from my niece, or you got business for tend?"

"Business for tend. Papa'Budi done gone'd out fishing on the Blacksnake and Ula worry sick over it, for some reason."

Papa'Tee did not pause in his work spreading out the leavings. "And—?"

"And... And ain't nothing much'a else but that. Ula ask for me to come over and let you know."

"You mean for tell me, you done got out you' warm bed and rush you'self all'a'way over this side and beat the sun to my yard just for tell me my brother gone'd out fishing, 'cause it bothering at you' wife? You'se a better husband than I am, young man, you certainly is."

Bo put his palms up in the air and rolled his eyes in a what-could-I-do gesture. It sounded silly, hearing it like that, but he knew he'd had no choice. There would have been no living in the house with Ula today if he hadn't come over to Papa'Tee's, first thing.

The hogs and pigs were making a rising racket on the other side of the gate between the two pens. Papa'Tee tossed the empty leavings bucket over the top of the outer fence, climbed up on the railing, and kicked the gate-lock open with the toe of his boot. The gate swung open and the hogs and pigs tumbled over themselves to get to the trough.

"Anyways, you ain't had to be like the Jacksons, running over for pass-news that my bubba done gone'd fishing," Papa'Tee said, setting himself down on the top pen railing with legs straddling. "Budi tell'ded me that yesterday down at the fields. Asked me for tend to his stock and dog 'til him get back. Ain't be nothing wrong with them animal already, is there? My bubba'll pitch a fit with me, iffen they is."

"I ain't look at the stock, but the dog, they alright."

"I better go check on them, soon's I get finished with my childrens here," Papa'Tee said, indicating with a wave of his hand that he was referring to the pigs. "Hand me that next bucket there, will you, young man?" He took the full bucket from Bo and began tossing loads of it out across the heads and backs of the pigs. There was a furious knot of squirming below him as they tried to snatch pieces out of the air or from each other's mouths, diving and grubbing and fighting over whatever managed to fall into the muddy pen grounds.

Bo was feeling a little better about the fact that Papa'Tee seemed so unconcerned about his brother's fishing trip, but at the same time, he did not look forward going to back home to Ula with a "Tee-say-everything-be-alright" speech.

"You ain't reckon we should take a boat out and check on him?" he asked.

Papa'Tee let out a quiet laugh, shook out the last of the leavings from the bucket and tossed the bucket out on the ground outside the pen next to the first one. He let his legs swing back and forth on either side of the top railing like a little boy while looking down at Bo with a broadening smile. He began whistling.

"You know where Budi going out fishing, right?" he asked.

Bo nodded, yes. "I told you. Back on the Niggerfoots. The Blacksnake, I mean."

"I know what y'all calls it cross'oba," Papa'Tee said. "Blacksnake or Niggerfoots, it don't matter what the name is. It don't change the river none. And you telling me now, you want for go out and track my bubba back there?"

"Not me doing the tracking. I were hoping you would. It sure would make Ula feel better."

"Might make Ula feel better, but it ain't Ula what'a be out there in that Swamp looking for Budi," Papa'Tee said. "It don't really matter which, it be you or me or Aunt Hani's ha'nt. You couldn't follow my bubba 'round a tree back in there once he done got out of you' sight."

Finished with the last of the leavings, the pigs and hogs began to sniff around each other for any stray food. One of them stood up on its hind-parts and sniffed at Papa'Tee's boot, and the elder man nudged it away with a gentle kick.

"See how my childrens does treat me?" Papa'Tee said, with a wan smile. "Iffen I ain't got enough for them for eat, them try for eat at me." He swung his leg over and slid down the railings and onto the ground, putting one hand on Bo's back. "Come on and walk with me, young man. You can skip yard chore when you wants and go 'wisiting, but that old lady what live up in the house there, her done got to chunkin' thing at my foots when I does shirks my work, and I ain't so good at gettin' out'the-way like I been'ed." He gave a little skip-step to demonstrate and grinned, and Bo— knowing it was obvious that he was out here early in the morning on an errand for his own wife—laughed both at the elder man and himself.

They walked back towards the barn, Bo marveling—again—at how different in temperament were the two brothers, Papa'Budi and Papa'Tee. Born in slavery to the same parents, one only two years behind the other, raised in the same house by the same parents, both come out of the old plantation together and married and then lived for the rest of their years side-by-side, close enough so that you could throw a rock through the window of one of the houses and it would hit the sideboards of the other. And yet, so different.

Papa'Tee s went through a succession chores as he talked, first feeding the mules, then the dogs, then checking the fences around first the chickenpen and then the garden, never missing a beat on his story, Bo following dutifully behind, assisting with the work whenever he could.

"I'll tell you 'bout my bubba and that Swamp," Papa'Tee said. "This been after the slavery-time, but we still been chaps. One night after we'd all gone'd to bed, the High Sheriff come'a knock on we door. Had him two strange buckra with him. Yankee buckra, I think, from they look. Old Sheriff, him say the two'a them, they been with a hunt party down along the Blacksnake, and one of they friend had got hisself losted up in there, and them been powerful worry-up him might'a gone'd up into the Swamp. Sheriff say he would take it propers if Papa could spare the time to go up in there and fetch that white boy back out, which-in-while everybody knowed that Papa knew the Swamp better than anybody in Cantrell County, nigger or white. So Papa said he would go, but he had a boy what knowed the Swamp better'n him.

"Now Mambu and Tutu been done marry and living close'by, and Woo, him been still in the house along with we, but Papa ain't fetch for neither none'a them. Him fetch for Budi. I couldn't't'na been no older than ten year, so Budi, him were twelve at that time. So when my bubba come out the house, all bone-and-britches-and-burr, them buckra give the High Sheriff the eye like them thought him been'a fool. But the High Sheriff ain't do nothing but put he arm around Budi shoulder and tell him, son, if you' daddy say you the best going into that Swamp, when us gets down in there you lead the way, and I be done follow you.

"But when they got out to the Dimba Downs, Papa wouldn't let the High Sheriff go with them, them strange buckra neither, just gone'd up in there in a boat with Budi and a .22 rifle and a kerosene lamp, and Papa' best dog. Bo and Papa and the dog been up there all that night, and just about first light, them come back down the branch with the lost buckra fellow in the boat, draggle-wet like a old puppy done drag-ass in the river. And Papa ever always said it been Budi what find that buckra, not Papa, not that dog, and that Budi spend so much time in that Swamp and knowed so many ways back up in there that even the Cu'n Kuta and Cu'n Rabbit used to stop him when he going through, sometime, to ask him for direction."

They had finished the round of chores and come back to the barn and stopped there, just outside the door, while Papa'Tee tamped a wad of tobacco into the bowl of his pipe, lit a match on the seat of his overalls, and sucked on the fire for a moment until the bowl glowed orange.

"Say we was to foll'y what you' wife done ask we for do, young man, and go hunt for my bubba back on that river and into the Swamp," he went on. "Few days pass, you' pap-in-law be done put he boat in at the Landing and come walking across the yard, there, with he fishbucket full, asking what all the wailing and crying was about going on over at you' house and mine, all both, and find out that *we* the ones what lost'ed, now, and 'stead'a him getting in he soft bed and sleeping off he weariness, him got for turn right-back-'round and go back up in there and fetch out *we*. You *think* you done hear him cuss before! 'Sides which, if you' wife feeling frantic over she papa missing, how you think she fixing to be iffen she papa *and* she husband both gone, all two."

Bo cocked his head to the side and began to see the wisdom of Papa'Tee's reasoning.

"I reckon that make sense," he said. "But could you come over sometime this morning and tell Ula that, you'self? She'd take it better, coming from you."

"And save you a fussing, I reckon, and put it on me," Papa'Tee said. He smiled as he said it, though, as Bo nodded, a little sheepishly. "That's alright, I'll come by," the old man said. He made a gesture with his head towards the house. "I done had year and year of practice taking a fussing. Hogs. Wife. Mule. Dogs. Seem like everybody on this yard got they 'pinion on how I does handle things, and ain't none'a them good."

They talked on for a few minutes after that while they leaned against the barn and Papa'Tee smoked, about a farmer's favorite subject—the weather—and the plans for the ricefields for the winter and the planting season next spring, the price that rice and other commodities were fetching over in Cashville this month, the nature of the illness of Ná'Risa's relative that she had gone to visit the night before, the progress of the dam-building project and the land acquisition across the river, and other minor subjects. After a while, Papa'Tee said he'd better get in and look after the mules. Bo took his leave and turned to go, but had not gone more than a step or two across the yard when he stopped, slapped his head at the remembrance of something he should not have forgotten, and turned back.

"We ain't got to search for Papa'Budi," he said.

Hand on the barn door, Papa'Tee gave him a patient smile. "I know. I thought that what I been trying for tell you, young man, these last twenty minute."

"No, that ain't what I mean. I mean, I know where Papa'Budi going."

Papa'Tee frowned up, now, at this restatement of what had seemed the obvious. "Out on the Blacksnake," he said. "Him tol'ded me. Him tol'ded you. You tol'ded me. I'm glad for see it getting through. You better than the hog, young man. Usual take me a half-day or more, to get a understanding outten them."

"No, I mean 'xactly where he going. He told me he might be going to visit a girl back there. We ain't got to hunt. We could find him there." In all the confusement and worriation over missing his father-in-law the night before at both the house and out on the road, and then trying to get Ula settled down when he got back home, it had slipped his mind.

"Budi meeting a girl back on the Blacksnake?" Papa'Tee gave out a horse-laugh. "What lie my bubba done tol'ded you 'bout meeting some girl back on that river? Budi ain't meeting no girl, and iffen he were, it wouldn't be back in them itchy woods. And you done believe him?"

"He ain't said 'meet,' he said 'visit,' so I figured she lived back up in there."

"*Live* on the Blacksnake?" Papa'Tee threw his head back and laughed even harder. "What girl him tell you *live* on the Blacksnake?"

"Some woman named Timbi."

Papa'Tee stopped in mid-laugh, his mouth open, but no sound coming out of it. He froze where he was standing for a moment, the expression on his face changing from tolerant bemusement to concern, with just a bit of a furrowing of his thick eyebrows as he narrowed his eyes. He started to put his pipe into his mouth, paused, and then lowered his hand again. It was almost the same reaction Bo had gotten when he had said the name to his wife the night before.

"Bo told'ded you him going back for 'wisit with a 'uman name'a Timbi?" Papa'Tee's voice had dropped to low and firm, all the funning and time-passing gone out of it.

"Yessir," Bo said. "I forgot all about that. I should'a told you, the first. That's what got Ula all worry-up when I told her. Who this Timbi 'uman is?"

Papa'Tee ignored the question. "When him told'ded you that?" he asked.

"Last night, after we come out the field."

"What him tell you, 'xactly?"

Bo fumbled, again, to get it exactly. "He ain't made no big thing about it. Just said he had a mind to go visiting with her whiles he was out hunting, is all. Said 'I'm thinking I might make a visit to Timbi, whiles I'm back up in there.' Who's Timbi? Ula had a fit last night when I called out her name. I thought first it been a old friend-girl of his'n, and then, maybe, a oba'uman on the county side of the Swamp, and then I was thinking it might be some old whorish girl back up in those woods."

Tibo Manigault was no longer ignoring the question. Instead, he did not seem to hear it any more. Instead, he turned and looked past Bo across the yard in the direction of the woods, far beyond which the Blacksnake and then the Swamp lay, his mouth boxed up and pulled in tight, his eyes now only small slits. Bo waited, saying nothing. Finally, Papa'Tee's gaze snapped back into focus, and he gave Bo a steady look.

"I believe we might just go out on the river and take a look for my bubba, soon as I get these chores done," he said, finally, and then, with no more ceremony, opened the barn door and took a few steps in.

He had not gone far when he stopped in his tracks, half-turned, and said quietly and evenly and seriously over his shoulder, "Bye-the-bye, young man, I know you ain't mean no harm, and you ain't know no better, but Timbi ain't no whorish girl, and best you ain't do no talking like that no more." Then without saying another word, he continued back towards the mule pens. Bo watched him walk away, more puzzled than ever.

BY LATE THAT AFTERNOON, Papa'Tee had put together a searching party to look for Budi Manigault out on the Blacksnake River.

He picked three to go with him. Ya Manigault, his youngest son, who knew the Swampwoods as well as any. Bambo Saunders, the rope-slender, axe-handle-strong man about ten years Ya's senior, who hunted more than he farmed and whose owl-biggity eyes were better for nightwork in the woods than sun-soaked days in the middle of a corn or ricefield, and who was known as the best tracker on Yelesaw Neck. There was room for one more in the search-boat, and many volunteered, all with good credentials. Papa'Tee turned them all down with thanks, and without explanation. Most were more than a little surprised—and more than a few were genuinely offended—when the person Tibo picked for the fourth slot on the search party was not known as an expert huntsman, by Yelesaw standards, and was, in fact, not even a Yay'saw at all, but an oba. Nobody was more perplexed at the choice than the person picked, himself.

"Me?" Bo Kinlaw said, when Ya came over to the house to tell him early that evening. The two men went out on the front porch to chat about it, sitting on the edge of the boards and looking out at the reddening sun dropping down into the western treeline. "Why you reckon your pap want me to go?"

Ya shrugged. "I suppose him know you'se a good man in the woods. Him know we general' does hunt together, and I ain't never come back with no complaint."

"Not over in *them* woods, not on that Blacksnake. I ain't never

even been up in there, Ya, not the first. They's plenty what know
them woods back there, what could be more help than me. Kezzy
Prioleau for one. He up there all the time, fishing, ain't he?"

"You ain't want for go?"

"It ain't that," Bo said. "I just ain't want to be no burden.
Finding Papa'Budi, that the main thing."

Ya gave a quiet grunt. "Oh, we'll find him," he said, hoisting
his feet up on the porchboards and wrapping his arms around his
doubled-up legs. "Truth to tell, Cousin, I ain't got idea the first
why my pap picked you. I just know us ain't need nobody else what
done familiarize with that Old Blacksnake. Kezzy a swamp-running
nigger, for true, but him don't beat me and Pap and Bro'Bambo,
not back on the 'Snake. You could put any one'a we in a boat,
blindfold, and run us up and down that river half a day and then
take the blind off, and we could tell you 'xactly where we been,
down to the bush and boulder. Kezzy couldn't do nothing like
that. And anyways, him a sort of nervous-kind'a fellow. Make me
nervous being 'round him. Maybe Pap reckon you ain't the
panicky type, no matter what we come'cross back there. You
married Cu'n Ula, inna'? That took some courage, I'm'a tell you.
And you come over and told my uncle you' intention, face to face,
on he own porch. Shit, son, that took nuts big as a boarhog."

"Truth is, I been'd something feared for talking with
Papa'Budi, but I been more feared of not talking with him, once I
done promise Ula we was fixing to marry."

"True, true," Ya said. "Weren't no backing out of it then, son.
'Most Uncle Budi would'a done would be to light you' ass up with
birdshot. Uly would'a loaded up with buck."

The two shared a laugh, the first one Bo'd had in several
hours. Ya bit off a chew of tobacco from the plug in his shirt
pocket and worked it around in his mouth, staring out to where
the sun had now disappeared, its red afterglow still painting the
western sky.

"What time we fixing for left?" Bo asked him.

"We be by for fetch you 'bout three-thirty to the morning,
thereabouts," Ya answered. "Pa want to hit the junction at first
light. You ain't want for be running down the Blacksnake in the
dark."

"Thought you said y'all knowed it blindfolded."

"Hmmmph. I said you could blindfold all three'a we and run
us up and down there. I ain't said nothing 'bout *everybody's* being
blind-up in the boat. I's foolish, but I ain't fool. That Blacksnake

don't run like the Sugaree. Him old and slow, but that just he trick. That how him sucker you in and pull you over. Don't you never forgets that, Cousin, when we's back up in there."

"How long you reckon we'll *be* up in there?"

Ya made a small dismissive gesture with his mouth. "'Til we come up on Uncle Budi, or him come up on us, or 'til we get tired of looking. Who know?" He handed his plug to Bo, who took out his pocket-knife, cut off an even slice, and handed the plug back. Turning the slice over and again in his fingers, thoughtfully, Bo said, "You ain't seem too worry-up about Papa'Budi."

Ya yawned.

"I don't come from the worry-up side of the family," he said. "That the side what you marry into."

"Papa'Tee, he seem to get concern' over Papa'Budi after I said he been talking about visiting up with this Timbi 'uman back there."

He watched Ya carefully as he mentioned Timbi's name, so he could judge the reaction. The other two he had said that name to—his wife and Papa'Tee—had acted like lightning had hit a tree in the yard, just missing them. Ya's response was somewhat different. He stopped in mid-chew but said nothing, blinking slowly and then turning his gaze towards the darkening trees out in the direction of the road. He grunted and shrugged his shoulders, neither of which had any meaning to them, and then went back to chewing on his tobacco.

"Who she is, Ya?" Bo asked. "Everybodys I ask, they don't seem for want to say nothing about her."

"Sus'Timbi?" Still not looking at Bo, Ya pursed his lips and then chewed both on the tobacco and the name. "Timbi were a 'uman what lived out in the Swamp in the slavery-time. That what the old folks say."

"Back in the slavery-time?" Until this moment, Bo had thought that this Timbi was a woman living somewhere off the Blacksnake right now. "Iffen she lived back in the slavery-time, what Papa'Budi mean about going back there and visiting her?"

Ya turned now and looked long and searchingly at Bo sitting next to him on the porch, almost as if he were deciding something, and then looked away again with a gesture of dismissal. "That ain't nothing a oba'dey could understand, Cousin," he said.

Bo felt himself growing angry over the opening of that old wound. He tried to hold it in and steady himself and make his point.

"Look, *Cousin*," he said in an even voice, leaning forward so he could catch Ya's eyes, "every one of my childrens is Yay'saw. My grandchildrens, too. I sleeps with a Yay'saw 'uman every night. When I goes back over the river on the Creek End and Millen Pond with my folks, they calls me Shay'ree, and they won't eat close-up next to me, lest I put something in they food. I done live 'cross this river more years than I lived on the other side. How long you figure it gonna be 'til I's a Yay'saw? If I ain't that now, I ain't know *what* I is."

Ya grunted and turned his head to the side to spit a patter of tobacco-juice out in the yard again away from Bo. He turned his head again to look Bo straight in the eye.

"You up-and-down with me, Bo Kinlaw, you know you is," he said. "You done marry my baby cousin, and ain't a day or night y'all been living together, I could ever say you treated her harsh. You'se a good man, and a good father. You take'd to rice-farming better than I expected, and you takes in more game than lots on this side of the river. You closer to me than many what's blood kin. But you been born a oba and you ain't gonna' be no Yay'saw, ever, and ain't nothing 'bout that is fixing to change."

Bo said nothing in return, only sat on the porch and stared back at him.

Ya paused and then added, "I ain't know if this help or hurt, Cousin, but my Pap wouldn't never consider taking no oba'dey with him out on the Blacksnake. So you ain't no Yay'saw, but I guess you ain't no oba no mores, neitherways. Hell if I knows *what* you is, exactly, son. Maybe you'se a new kind of something." He reached out a hand and put it on Bo's shoulder, squeezing it a little and then giving him a small shake, smiling as he did. "Now. You done marry into the worriation side of the family, but that don't mean you gots to worry with the rest of them. Best you just get you some 'wittle in you, and then some sleep. We got a early start and a long haul in the morning. You gonna need you' strength."

He started off the porch but then paused, turned back, and added, "Oh, and pack you fiddle with you, too. You might want to saw on it, a tune or two, back there."

"We fixing to have time for that?" Bo asked him.

Ya smiled again. "You ain't thinking we fixing to be banging at the bushes night and day for Uncle Budi and nothing else, is you? We got for camp. And if we plays loud enough, him might come out the woods with he mouth-harp and set-up with we. Or else ask we for stop, 'cause us scarin'way him squirrel and catfish."

Waving his goodnights, Ya took off across the yard in the direction of his house, the dark growing around him and causing him to quickly disappear, leaving Bo alone on the porch, staring after him out into the gloom. Funny, he figured, every time the name of Timbi came up in a conversation, folks was either sending him away or walking away from him themselves. She must have been a powerful woman in her time, he thought, to provoke such reactions. Anyway, he guessed he had his answer, such as it was. Since Timbi was a slaverytime woman, any visiting Papa'Budi was going to be doing with her would have to be done at her grave. Though why that should cause such concern in the family, he still did not know.

DESPITE YA'S ADMONITION, or maybe because of it, Bo Kinlaw worried over the trip the rest of the evening and even after he had retired early to his bed and should have been asleep. His thoughts kept returning to the Blacksnake, a river the Millen Pond folk and Creek Enders never visited, not for any reason. The Niggerfoots River, they called it. Water so black that if you looked it dead-on so's you could see your own reflection, it would turn your face blacker than it already was. It had the power to turn whitefolk into niggers and niggers into creatures even the night would shun.

*Why they call it the Niggerfoots, Me'Mama?*, the children on the porch would ask Grandma Butler. Or, *How that water get so black?* And Bo's grandmother—ever out on the front porch in her rocker, a quilt over her legs down over her slippers and pulled up under her narrow bosom, no matter the weather—would squint across at the crowd of grands and great-grands, lower lip quivering and dribbling with snuff, throat heavy with phlegm, and grunt out,

*"Once't to the time that Niggerfoot water been clear as a spring. That how God first made it, and you could drink it like milk. But then old Devil, he chose that spot for his back stairway down into Kingdom Hell. Dug it down right there on the riverbottom where the water could run over it. Every time old Devil stir up confusion in the world, he jump into the river and run back down through that hole, and God' angels couldn't catch him, 'cause there been cattail and frog-rug over the hole what hid it from seeing. But one day Gabriel, he been God' top soldier and Devil-tracker, he come down out the sky and send'ed a lightning bolt and burn-up the cattail and frog-rug all on that part'the river, and you could see right down through that clear water, straight down the old stone stairway, right into Hell. And the Devil say if I don't cover up*

*that doorway, them angel going to catch me for sure. Right then, the Devil seen two-three nigger girl coming down to wash the whitefolk's sheets in the river, and Devil ask them, why y'all down here washing them sheets? And them nigger girl, they too dumb to know it been the Devil, so they answer, them sheet done soil, and they washing them to get them back white. So old Satan had the idea, and he told them, seem like that water is magic water, and iffen it can get them sheets white, like you done says, then can't it whiten up a nigger, all too? Seem like if you could gets down in that water you' own selves with the sheet and cover-up all the way, you be done come out snowy white all over, tip to top, same as the whitefolk, and wouldn't have to work for nobody's but you'selves every afterward. And them nigger girl, them been so backwardy, they tries to get down in that river water, but old Satan, him had draw'd offen most' the water right when they gone to touch it, so the only part them girl could get wet were the bottom of they foots. So they scrub 'til they scrub 'til they scrub, and the more they scrub the more that black come offen the bottom of they foots, and the bottom of they foots got just as white as whitefolk, but where that black done fall into the river, h'it turn that water coal-dusky and hide the Devil's stairway from the prying, and that-why they calls it the Niggerfoots Water, and that-why it turn everything what touch it stone-black."*

But that was only Grandma Butler's talk for little children. Among themselves and the older children, the old folks around Millen Pond and Creek End talked of darker things about the Blacksnake, of hoodoo-land and spell-country, and folks going down on the river and never coming back, of a place where the Shay'rees danced with horn-headed, hoof-footed demons on moonless midnights, and made their pacts, and learned their secrets and gained their powers. The Blacksnake River was a place where haunts and hags made their homes, where they flew back to hide in the early dawn hours after tormenting the countryside all night. It was a place where dry bones came to life and walked the land. It was a place where jackrabbits played four-hand dominos and rolled dice, and buzzards and crows wore cloth coats and breeches and top hats, and the snakes walked on two legs in high-boots and talked like natural men. It was a place where teeth grew out of the knots on trees, and fingers and toes on ferns and palmetto bushes, and eyes out of the ends of the willow wands. It was a sinkhole to which all evil in the county was drawn, the black and oily fount from which it spread back out. It was a place where the most powerful of spells carried in your pocket and hung around your neck were not enough to keep you safe. It was a place that tested God's protection, and so a place where Christian people dared not and did not go.

And the Blacksnake, of course, ran right down and through the heart of the Sugaree Swamp, which was worse than the river, fifty-'leven times over.

Bo Kinlaw lapsed into a dream-troubled sleep that night with the thought that this was the place where he was going before daybreak in the morning, to hunt for his wife's father.

In the bed beside him, Ula Kinlaw did not sleep at all, but only lay unmoving, her hands crossed under her breasts, staring into the blackness of the ceiling above.

THE FULL MOON WAS LOW IN THE SKY as they set off in the boat the next morning, floating easily on the bosom of the Sugaree with the current. In the woods back inland, the leaves were already falling and stripping the tree-limbs bare, but here along the riverbank the branches were still thick with them, the last memory of summer past, so that the moonlight could only come through here and there in soft shafts, tossing out shimmering circles that rose and fell gentle with the lapping waters. Before they had gone far the moon fell off behind the trees, leaving only a last hint of its soft glow behind, and the river and the bank, both, slipped into a half-darkness. Ya sat in the prow with an oar held ready in his lap, peering into the gloomy waters in front of them. Papa'Tee had torches lit and held one aft while Bo sat in the front just behind Ya and held the second one high, an autumn-cool breeze blowing the flame back over his head in sputtering gusts. Instantly, the shadow outside the torchlight deepened into nothingness, and it seemed that they were traveling along in a void, with nothing before them and nothing behind and nothing to either side, only the four of them in the boat within two small circles of yellow light that bobbed and danced upon diamond-sparkle black waters, a compacted world being born and quickly destroyed and then born again anew as they passed through it in the night.

There was nothing for them to look for until they made the turn from the Sugaree into the Blacksnake, far down the river, and so each rode preparing for the morning's search in his own particular way.

When Bambo Saunders had nothing better to do, he generally spent his time sleeping, and he did so now, dropping off almost immediately in the middle of the boat as they got out on the river, hands folded loosely in his lap, head dropped down over his chest, mouth falling open, snoring slightly.

Ya sat in his place in the prow, his knees doubled up to his chest, watching the river ahead intently. Every now and then, as the current took them too close to one bank or the other, or bore down on a fallen tree or protruding rock or small island out in the middle of the waters, he would slip the oar from between his knees and chest and push at the water or the obstruction, moving them out of the path of collision. He did it without effort, automatically, almost dreamily, as if the oar was there just for show, as if he were riding on horse or muleback and guiding with his knees and a dip of his shoulders one way or the other, or even that the river and the boat were one, and he was moving within them with the force of his mind alone. Bo had been out on ponds before in the night but never on moving water, realizing that in worrying about the Blacksnake portion of the search, he had forgotten the real danger of this first leg of the trip. He watched Ya's navigation in fascination and admiration, both in its execution and in the fact that Ya seemed to take its operation so for granted.

Papa'Tee sat in the back behind Bambo Saunders, one hand resting on the edge of the boat, the other holding the torch aloft, watching in the direction of the passing banks, which he could not see in the dark, his thoughts clearly someplace far away. When a black water-moccasin floated alongside and raised its head to peer into the boat, the old man did not move his hand, or show in any other way that he had noticed. Bo looked back just in time to see the snake riding along in the water, watching Papa'Tee intently, its tongue forking in and out, its yellow-green eyes flickering in the torchlight, before it turned its head suddenly and dove, disappearing into the black of the river. Bo shivered his shoulders and back like a mule shaking off flies, not sure if it was a bad sign that the snake had shown them so much attention, or a good sign that it had let them pass.

His mind was racing across a thousand steppingstones, each a thought or a question he wanted to give voice to, but none of the others seemed in a talking mood, besides which, talking seemed somehow inappropriate as they passed through this silent, gliding, rippling world of a constant opening and closing void, and so he kept his thoughts to himself, and concentrated on keeping the torch held aloft and not snagged in any overhanging branches along the way, trying to convince himself over and over—because there was so much evidence to believe otherwise—that this was a real world they were riding through, and not a vision or a dream in which, any moment, the light from the torches might disappear altogether and the firmament open up before them to lead them sailing away into nothingness, without return.

IT WAS STILL BLACK-DARK NIGHT when they had passed the point where the Sugaree took a wide, sweeping turn first west and then back east, finally to be joined by the Blacksnake and they became one river running southeast down out of and away from Yelesaw. They pulled the boat high up on the sandy-beach clearing that was southernmost point of the Neck and stopped to make breakfast and wait until dawn, when it would be light enough to make the turn into the backriver. They ate quickly in the dim grayness by the light of a small cooking fire, ricecakes and a small knot of butts-meat washed down by black coffee. While they were eating, Bo sat a little ways from the others to look at the little packet his sister-in-law, Big Soo, had given to him the night before. She had put it in his coat pocket while Ula was in the bedroom, just as he was walking towards the door, giving him a deep look and telling him in a low voice, "You ain't lost that, you hear? It'a protection you over in that Swamp." She'd given a quick glance at Ula who was coming back into the bigroom, and then turned away with a grunt without saying another word, a sure sign that this was a secret between her and him, and definitely not to be shared with his wife. He had never understood why his wife so shunned root-work. It was not one of the things she talked about voluntarily, and Ula was not the type of woman you sat down at the table and interrogated. All Bo knew for certain was that her aversion was certainly not on his account. She'd had it went they met and, further, he himself had no special dislike for hoodoo, not if it was being used for his protection.

He lay down with his back to the fire and the other men and took the packet out from his pocket and held it by its leather cord. It was a small, crocus-fabric pouch sewn up at the neck, so that you could not open it up to see the contents unless you cut the thread or sliced a slit in the cloth. He rolled the pouch between his thumb and forefinger. It seemed packed tight with dirt or sand, but there were some solid things inside as well, two or three tiny stones, maybe, and what might have been a shell, as well as something more elongated whose shape he could not figure, but had the pliance of a plant. He held the pouch up to his face, rubbing it up and down between his palms, regarding its meaning.

It smelled slightly of stale liquor and cinammon. He slipped the cord over his neck and pushed the pouch down into his shirt, making certain it did not show from the outside. Whatever its powers, the thought that Big Soo had taken the time to put it together for him was a comfort enough. His sister-in-law had always been a closed door to him, behind which was a wide room he knew might have held warmth and light, but never—until now—for him.

All the next day, as they passed up the Blacksnake, he rubbed the toby now and then, with the tip of his finger, through the fabric of his shirt, and the touch of it always made his spirits lift, even if only for a moment.

THEY DID NOT STAY ON THE BEACHPOINT for long, only until it became light enough to distinguish the mist rising out of the water and the bank-brush from the river and woods themselves. Then they were back in the boat, turning it into the thick water of Blacksnake, and on their way again. Ya moved now into the middle of the boat, pulling the oars against the slow current with his powerful arms and shoulders, keeping up a regular pace that sent them steadily upstream.

Bo could see now how the backriver had gotten its name.

Only a few hundred yards up from the junction with the Sugaree, the Blacksnake took a deep turn to the left, a hairpin turn, almost, so that they were headed back in the direction from where they had come. Just as quickly, the river doubled back on itself again, and then went through a series of slow coils, first to the left, then to the right, then back to the left. They were traveling through a tall canebrake growing down into the water from either bank, almost like going along a winding hallway, with only the still-dark sky immediately above to be seen. Sitting behind Ya with nothing to do, now, Bo tried to keep track of the direction they were going as the river continued its winding, snakelike wandering, but could get no bearing on where the sun was rising. He quickly gave up, seeing that charting their path—at least for him—was neither possible or necessary. There was no way for them to get lost so long as they remained on the river and it did not break off into any branches and, besides, it wasn't his job to keep them on track. He wondered, once more, exactly what his job and purpose were supposed to be on this trip. He figured he would learn, soon enough.

They came out into an opening in the canebrake, the banks

spreading out on either side in a lush, marshy meadow, the daylight enough that he could now see the surface of the river. It was different from the water in any creek or river he had ever seen before. It was black-colored, but not dead black or coal black, rather it held what looked like an oily dark sheen over its surface that absorbed all light, making it impossible to see anything beneath.

Like a blacksnake, he said to himself. A blacksnake, yes indeed. Quiet and both lovely and deadly in the dim hush of the morning, and ready to strike.

He was sitting in the back of the boat next to Bambo Saunders, who was no longer asleep but up and squatting on his hams, his head swiveling back and forth from one bank to the other, wide eyes bright and intent, like a lake bird looking for the slightest surface ripple in the water denoting a potential meal below. Every now and again Bambo would tense and lean out over the edge of the boat, peering at something that Bo himself could not see, no matter how hard he looked in the same direction. Then, almost immediately, Bambo would relax and settle back on his haunches and return to his scouting. He was looking for some sign of Papa'Budi, clearly, but how he could see anything of value amongst the still-dim rushes and thickets and woods they were passing on either side, Bo had no idea.

Papa'Tee was up in the prow, attent like Bambo Saunders, but his attention on the river immediately ahead as a look-out for Ya. Occasionally he would give a short, sharp command—"Rocks ahead, boy, bear little right," or "Mind that limb there. Break left. Break left. That's it."—that Ya would immediately follow.

Other than Papa'Tee's directions, they pulled up the river in deep, respectful silence, as if they did not want to disturb anything unnecessarily, and only the sound of the slow parting of the water, and its deep, lazy lap against the banks, marked their way.

Once in a while, Papa'Tee would put his hand up and give it a quick shake, and then Ya would tamp back the oars and bring them to a halt in the middle of the river. During these stops, they would make as much noise as they could, banging with horseshoes or hammers on the bottoms of the castiron pots Papa'Tee had brought along for that purpose, clanging around inside of them like they were bells, hallooing and calling Budi Manigault's name over the water and back into the woods. Several times, the sudden sound startled flocks of birds that had stopped to rest in trees or had hidden down in the marshgrass, sending them off in a swift rise of beating wings and hearts. More than once, as well, the disturbances brought out something larger that leaped away from the riverbank, either into the water or into the woods, disappearing before Bo could get a fix on what it might have been. Their calls and pot-clangs brought back nothing more, the sounds of them dying off immediately, smothered amidst the lush green of the landscape and the black muck of the river-water as if it had never been. Leaving these holler-out spots, as Bo began to think of them, they continued on up the winding river in deep silence again, broken now and then by the clatter of clickbeetles and the humming of hideybugs which the rising morning sun had awakened out in the cattails and waterweeds.

The further up into the Blacksnake they rode, the more they began to pass logs and whole trees rising out of the waters, their raggy edges and dead branches reaching over to try to snag both the boat and its passengers and hinder their passage. Bo had never seen a river so clogged with debris, and he realized, after studying for a bit, that it was the sluggishness of the current that caused it, too slow to move the larger residue along. At the same time, the passageway up the water itself began to narrow to near choke-points, the banks moving in until Ya, if he had wanted, could have reached out and touched them with the ends of his oars on each side, simultaneously. At these points, they found themselves traveling through the smallest of aisles of open water between the rushes and vines and waterbushes, the tree-limbs growing so close and low on both banks that the boat-riders had to keep a close lookout and duck in time to keep from being hit. It began to seem—to Bo, at least—that the river was purposely seeking to impede their passage and keep them from penetrating into the deep, black heart of its secrets, in a way that felt disturbingly alive, almost conscious, and near-human. Once or twice the logs themselves actually did come alive, turning before Bo's eyes from inanimate wood, floating in the water or buried in the bankmud, into the bodies of alligators, betraying their true form only by the twitch of a limb or the blinking of yellow eyes, watching the boat in lazy menace as it passed. More than ever, Bo began to understand why the folks at Millen Pond and Creek End avoided this part of the world.

In the absence of a clear view of the sun, which had only appeared two or three times in between the corridor of treetops, and with the inability for him to know exactly how much territory they had traveled or how fast—or slow—they were traveling, it was difficult for Bo to mark the exact passage of time. After what seemed to him that they had been on the Blacksnake for a couple of hours, Ya looked up at Bo and asked if he wanted to take a turn at the oars.

"Glad to," Bo said, with a grateful smile. "I been feeling sort of use'a'less."

They lodged the boat against the bank, and there was a general shuffling of places. Ya got up in the prow to take the river-watch from Papa'Tee, while Papa'Tee got in the back to help Bambo Saunders scout the banks. Bo got in the middle and pulled the boat back out into mid-stream, and immediately saw that rowing up the Blacksnake was much more difficult than he had imagined, even while watching Ya. Bo was stronger than he looked, that kind of lanky power that didn't need bunched-up muscles to get the job done, and he was a good hand at rowing, but this was a rowing different from what he had ever done before. The problem was not the current, which was slow and not especially strong, but rather the water itself, which seemed to have a heavy substance to it, not so much flowing as pushing its sluggish way against the point of the boat, like the slow spread of thick mud running along the ground after a good rain. Now that Bo had direct contact with the river through the oars, it did actually seem like a living thing, like something that was raising itself up from the innards of the earth and digging its way along, devouring the riverbed in its path, throwing up a foul, dark, clotted refuse in its wake. Bo braced his feet against the deckboards and put his back into it, and the sweat began immediately to form on his forehead, soaking his hat and flowing down his face.

He took them into another of the river's innumerable turns, this one appearing no different from the others, but actually marking a distinct boundary in the country into which they were traveling. Immediately as the boat came around a bend—marked like a gateway by three or four cypress on one bank and by a massive, ancient willow on the opposite—both water and land widened out in front of them. They had entered a new world. Instead of pressing inward, the woods began to fall back on either side the further up they traveled, the narrow river corridor slowly giving way to open mudflats and reed-marshes dotted with stands of stately mangroves and stunted palmettos. The light of the sun, so long diffused, spread its warming fingers out in all directions, sparkling the waters, exploding the landscape's colors. Great congregational gatherings of pelicans and white herons watched them from a distance with unblinking eyes as they pulled by, and the riverlands, which had until now been closed-in and silent and oppressive, now suddenly came alive with chatter. Bo was too busy with the rowing to do much more than pay it a passing attention, but it was clear to him that they had come into the middle of the Swamp. Sometimes a great, gray-green immensity spread on both sides as far as could be seen, the reed-waters of the river opening up into vast ponds and bays, so that at points it was hard to tell where the river ended and the Swamp began. Then again, the cattails and lilypads once more pressed inward, the actual riverbed narrowed and threatened to choke itself off entirely, closing in so tight that now they could actually touch the weedy banks on either side with their hands at the same time. Alternating opening out and closing in on itself, the river and Swamp ran on like that for several slow hours.

Once they found evidence of someone's recent landing at a grassy willow grove, perhaps Papa'Budi, perhaps not. It was Bambo Saunders who spotted the signs from the boat—broken rushes and faint impressions in the muddy ground—that Bo could hardly recognize even when they got close-up. The rest sat in the boat while Bambo got out searched the rim of the grove like a hunt dog, back hunched, bright eyes darting over the ground, but he came back saying nothing, only shaking his head, and they moved on.

Several times at Papa'Tee's direction, they turned the boat up into creeks and wider waterways leading back into the Swamp itself. At one, they docked the boat at a spot that seemed no different than all the rest. They went aways on foot, crossing single file over a narrow sand levee between two fetid ponds, slapping at mosquitos as big and black as the tips of their fingers, making their way through places where the rushes grew so high and the tree branches dropped down so low that they could push both of them away from their faces simultaneously as they went. A half a mile or so back—it was hard to tell how far they had gone, the way was so twisty and tortured—they came upon the edge of a tree-choked lake, and there they found the remains of a camp and a blackened patch of cinders.

"Uncle Budi?" Ya asked Papa'Tee.

The old man nodded. "This one'a he spot," he said. "You know them big catfish Budi always'a bring back—from he secret water?" They all nodded and smiled. Everyone knew of Budi Manigault's famous catfish. Papa'Tee made a gesture towards the lake. "Well, that-there them secret water. It ain't Budi' secret, though. Papa fetched us here, all we bubbas, when we been just chaps, and Papa used to fish it all the time 'fore him got too old for come back here. I ain't know if Papa found it on he own, or got it shown to him by the old peoples. I do know one thing. Budi gonna pitch a natural fit when he find out I done showed it to y'all." He gave a hollow, mirthless, almost noiseless laugh. "Papa ever said, what go in the Swamp, must stay in the Swamp. And Budi figure just the same."

"It don't matter, far as I's concern," Bo said, looking around at the tangle of trees and bushes surrounding. "I could find my way back here if I needed, but I ain't. I wouldn't come back on this end iffen the catfish sent word they'd done already laid theyselves out in the pan, and please just bring the salt and bread and something for light the fire with."

Ya and Bambo laughed at that, the first time since they'd started on the water that the solemn mood had lifted. Bo was glad at that. It made him feel that he was making a contribution, however small.

Papa' Tee did not laugh, however. "No, I don't reckon you would come back this way," he said, his mind clearly somewhere else. He bent over and picked up a pinch of cinders between his thumb and forefinger, and put it to his nose. "Him ain't been back here," he added, almost to himself. "Not on this trip." One hand on his hip, the other rubbing at the cinders, he took a last look across the lakewaters, receding into a gloom under overhanging trees. He took off his hat and wiped the sweat off his forehead and out of his hair with his shirtsleeve, blew air out of his nose, and then absently slapped his thigh with the flat of his hat as he tossed the remainder of the cinders in a wide sweep. "Let's get back to the boat," he said. "Us got lots more ground for cover."

THEY CAMPED THAT NIGHT on a dry, sandy beachhead a few yards up the bank from the river. After supper, they all pulled out their instruments—Bo his fiddle, Ya his banjo, Papa'Tee his mouth-harp, and Bambo Saunders a flute-like thing carved out of bamboo—and they pushed back the dark night with their music. While they played, Bo stared up at the long highway of stars in the narrow, black corridor above him between the trees, and felt a puzzlement flowing over him.

He could not remember a time in which the Blacksnake River and the Swamp had not been an unsettling presence on the edge of his life. It had never been a present and immediate threat to him because its dangers and demons were confined to its boundaries which—until now—he'd never had any intention of crossing. Instead, it had been more like the abandoned well-hole in the neighbor's yard which the old folk always warned the children to avoid lest they fall into it to their deaths and, consequently, the children, fascinated, were ever drawn to its edges to see if any in the neighborhood had suffered that fate. The Blacksnake and the Sugaree Swamp's very menace was its attraction. The Millen Pond and Creek End folk had used it often as the evil backdrop to their porch-step stories, or as the pastoral villain in their morality fables and folk sayings. Bo Kinlaw had rarely thought about the Swamp straight-on—as a child it had been too frightening for that, and into adulthood he had retained that habit—but instead it came into his mind obliquely, unbidden and at angles—in the daytime and sleeptime dreams that dominated his youth, a grim, gray-green kingdom where haunts and devils roamed, a shadow-land of death and the dead that could only be dimly perceived at the soft edge of consciousness, and never in the full light of lamp or day.

Last night at home in bed with Ula—was it only last night?— his sleep had been disturbed several times by thoughts of the Blacksnake and the Swamp, and he had awakened with the sweat clammy-cold on his face, the image of moss-laced, bonewhite fingers reaching for him still vivid but slowly dissipating, retreating from the tail-end of his dream. His stomach had been in a turmoil all the long ride in the boat down the Sugaree River in the early morning hours, and after they had stopped at the point where the two rivers converged, and when it had come time to get back into the boat and begin the trek up the Blacksnake and into the heart of the Great Swamp, he'd had to take a strong mental hold upon himself to keep from falling into a panic, and to force his arms and legs to move. And Bo Kinlaw was not a man given to panic. Several times, he had caught himself fingering the little bulge of Big Soo's toby through his shirt-front.

But tonight, in their actuality, the Blacksnake and the Sugaree Swamp did not seem to him anywhere like it had in anticipation. He had made a joke at Papa'Budi's secret catfish pond about not coming back, but he had not actually meant it. While the Blacksnake and the Swamp were not a place where he would care to make his home, it was no longer a place that he would completely shun. It had begun to fascinate him.

He listened, while they played, for the sound of Budi Manigault coming through the brush, mouth-harp in hand, demanding to know why they had started the music without him. But Budi Manigault never came.

THEY WENT AT THE SEARCH for two more days up the Blacksnake, making camp each night on the riverbank, looking up into the Swamp at spots that Papa'Tee knew were his brother's favorite hunt or fish grounds, or at spots where it was just a guess, or a feeling, that he might have visited this time. The backriver continued to run just like its name, twisting around on itself over and again, backtracking, arcing, undulating, circling tree groves and mud islands, dipping into pools and bogs for a quick drink of clear water, running up into the Swamp and then back out again, taking meandering miles to travel only a few straight yards, so that it began to seem to Bo that they were wandering through a land that had no boundaries to it, up a river that had no emptying. He was in the heart of what his people back across had always called the hoodoo country, from where they believed the Shay'rees drew their strange ways. It felt as if they had come into a place of magic, in which all the normal law of things, in and out, up and down— dead and live, too—were suspended. What go in the Swamp must stay in the Swamp, indeed. He could see why Papa'Budi would say something like that. The world outside would never understand it. Bo knew that even though he had come to fashion a sort of peace with the Swamp, he could not possibly say that he himself understood it, even after having been inundated within its boundaries for so many days.

With nothing else to do between the rowing and the looking, he spent some of his time thinking about the woman named Timbi.

Even without confirmation, he was certain that it was her burying ground that Papa'Budi had intended visiting, since his father-in-law had not said anything about visiting her house or her peoples, but only visiting her. Once or twice Bo considered asking why they had not gone directly to the the gravesite to look for Budi Manigault, or for signs that he had been there, or even to wait there for him, but then thought better of it, and held his tongue. While that would have been the way he would have conducted the search, it was not his search, besides which, Papa'Tee and Ya and Bambo Saunders were men who knew both his father-in-law's ways and these river-and-swamp-woods as well, and were fully aware of what they were **doing**. And besides that, given all the bogland they had tramped over in the past few days, he could not be certain that they had not already gone to the Timbi woman's grave and had simply not bothered to tell him about it.

In the afternoon of the third day, the land began to close in again, with the beginnings of real woods and thickets here and there among the lagoons and palmetto groves and rushes. The air gradually developed a crisp sharpness to it, losing the dreamy intoxicance Bo had grown used to during their days since they had entered the Blacksnake. They were coming out of the Swamp. If he had his geography right, they'd soon be running into the great Randwoods briar-thickets that marked the northern boundary of Yelesaw Neck, a land that had the reputation of being even more impassible than the Swamp. He was not looking forward to the fact that this would probably be the most difficult part of their search, especially with the boat to haul overland along with them, and was wondering how they would manage it. He could just begin to see the beginnings of the dense brown tangle of briar-thickets lined up across their route up ahead when the river took a sharp turn around an outcrop of land, heading more east than north. Instead of turning with it, Ya, who was at the oars, banked back, turning the boat in a gentle half-circle in the middle of the river. When the prow was pointed directly downstream, he gave the boat a little nudge with a dip of the oars, and then let the slow current take it south.

It had all been done without conversation, as if it had already been discussed and decided upon sometime back, though Bo had certainly not been in on the discussion. He looked up at Papa'Tee, who was studying the water ahead with a blank expression. He felt the disappointment suddenly grow on him. The turn meant that they were bearing back the same way they had come, which also meant that their search would soon be ending, with no Budi Manigault to be found. Bo thought of Ula, and her look of deep disappointment when he walked though the door and she saw the defeat in his face, and a deep gloom sat on his shoulders and weighed him down.

"We heading home?" he asked Papa'Tee.

"'Pears like it," Papa'Tee answered. "We going back that way." He seemed either deep in disappointment or deep in thought or all both, himself.

They drifted with the river current all afternoon. Late in the day, with the sun just above the trees and already turning its back on the world, they banked the boat near the entrance to a narrow, rush-clotted creek. They had passed so many waterways on their search it was difficult to tell, but Bo did not think they had stopped at this one on their way up. His spirits were low as he got out of the boat. Without a word, Ya began gathering up the blankets and gear and setting up camp on cleared ground under a wideoak back from both the river and the creek. Bo went to help him but Papa'Tee did not, but instead walked over to the creekbank and stood there by himself, hands folded over his chest, puffing absently on his pipe, looking up the dark creekwaters. Bambo had pulled out a couple of canes from the bottom of the boat and was already at the edge of the river, putting out lines for their supper.

"Why we camping here?" Bo asked Ya as they worked. He lifted his head in the direction of the setting sun. "We still got a half-hour of good light left, seem like."

Ya had already gotten a fire going, and threw some dead branches on it to build it up. He gave a glance up at the sky himself, which was barely visible through dark clouds that banked across the narrow strip between the treetops, and gave the air an animal sniff. "Fixing to rain shortly," he said. "Pap ain't want for get caught in it out on the river. You best go out and fetch some more wood while it still dry."

Bo walked a little ways up the creekbank past where Papa'Tee was still standing, gathering sticks and branches as he did, putting them into small piles to be retrieved on his way back. After a moment he found that he had rounded a bend out of sight of the camp and the others, and he paused to take a long look up the creekbed, which ran for a ways beyond and then disappeared into a dark patch of palmettos and rushes and an overhanging canopy of vines and trees and hanging moss, almost as if the creek was running into a tunnel that burrowed down in the deeps of the earth. What was visible of the surface of the creek itself was smothered with cattails. Sunken, stagnant pools thick with yellowing lilypads jutted out on either side, passing over immediately into a jumble of underbrush that rose up shoulder-high. There was an oppressive stillness to the creekbed grounds that Bo had not noticed in the rest of the Swamp these past three days, not riding by on the river, not even in their search-hunts up into the interior. There was a dank scent of newlife-mixed-with-death that assaulted his nose and filled his head and senses, a scent that was like the rank coming out of the room after children were born and before the women had a chance to clean up, that smell of sweat and urine and excretement and blood-gorged placenta, of sweet amniotic water and swollen breasts full of mother's milk. This scent of growth and rot and discard came not from mother and child and their offal, however, but out of the very earth and water itself. It was as if the creek was an open vein thrusting deep into the innards of a bloated body, allowing its hidden nature to flow out. Bo was standing close to the creekbank and did not notice himself reeling until he felt a strong hand grip on his shoulder, pulling him a step back from the water. He turned to see Bambo Saunders standing there.

"You best be careful up in this-place here, boy," Bambo Saunders told him in his slow, sleepy drawl. "That a drawing water up there. It like for draw you in, you ain't watch you'self."

Bo gave a nervous laugh and took another step away from the creekbed. Hearing any words at all back in that menacing silence was startling in itself. Involuntarily, his hand went up to the little bulge under his shirt-front, and he put his fingers around the outline of Big Soo's toby.

"It got a name to it?" he asked.

Most of the innumerable waterways they had gone up or come across during the search had not been named, but for some reason, this one seemed important to be remembered.

"Sure do," Bambo Saunders said, blinking his big eyes. "That-there the Klá'soo Creek. You know what that mean?"

Bo shook his head.

"The buzzard roost. That-where them buzzard go in the night for do they dance. And they's more up there than buzzard. You keep a distance from that water, like I done said, or you be dancing the buzzard-lope you' own self."

He gave a quick smile that showed all of his teeth and then turned and walked back down the creekbank towards the campsite leaving Bo to come quickly behind him, gathering up his piles of wood as he did.

The rain did come, not long after they had finished setting up camp, and they ate a fish supper under a canvas canopy stretched between the oak limbs, talking generally as they watched the soft sheet of grey rain pattering in the rushes and water outside. They retired under their blankets early, weary from the day's work, Bo keeping the flat of his hand on the toby so that it pressed against his bare chest.

When he awoke in the cold dawn mist of the next morning, he discovered that both Papa'Tee, Bambo Saunders, and the boat were all gone.

THE RAIN HAD ENDED with only a soft mist in the air remaining, and Ya had made a fire over near the creekside, and was squatting beside it, boiling a pot of coffee. Bo went out and joined him taking a look around the campsite and the rush-thickets and water beyond as he did. All of it was still trying to hide itself in the soft gray of the morning light.

"Where you' pap and Bro'Bambo done gone'd?" Bo asked.

"Up the creek. Left out first light."

"What for?"

Ya turned from the fire to give Bo a questioning look, and then turned back.

"Look for Uncle Budi, what else you think they be going up there for? Don't nobodys go back into that Deepswamp for no pleasure."

"I thought we done finished with the searching."

"Who tell you that?"

Bo took the tin cup of coffee Ya offered him and blew on it as he considered. Actually, no-one had told him the search was over, he realized. He had just assumed.

"So we's still looking for Papa'Budi?"

Ya shrugged and said nothing, as if that sufficed as an answer.

Bo was not satisfied, however, and he pressed on.

"Why we ain't gone'd up there when we come by this way, the first? They seen something might show Papa'Budi been back there?"

Ya shook his head.

"I ain't think so," he said.

"Why they ain't take you and me?"

"I reckon 'cause they figure ain't need us."

Bo sucked his teeth. He was annoyed now, but did not want to show it, and so did not blurt out the anger and disappointment he was feeling at being left out of both the new search and the discussion that had obviously preceded it. Instead, he stood up abruptly and walked back over to the canvas covering to fetch some butts-meat and a couple of potatoes and a fry-pan and set out to cook breakfast. The two men sat on their haunches beside the fire not talking for a while, the smell of the fixings drifting over their faces.

Ya appeared to regret that he had been so abrupt.

"It ain't hardly room for more'n two back up in them narrows up in there," he said after a while as he tested the butts-meat in the pan with the point of his knife. "They going to be doing as much walking and carrying the boat as they is poling in the water, and us'a just be getting in the way."

"Why they take the boat with them then?" Bo asked.

"Them going back pretty deep up in there, and someplace, I reckon, it way too thick, and there ain't no place 'side the bank for walk."

From how he was describing it, Bo could not be certain how much Ya actually knew about the Buzzard Creek and therefore how much he might be hiding, or whether he had ever been up there himself or was just passing on a description given him by his father or someone else. For the first time ever, Ya appeared to Bo to be less self-assured and more unsure of what to say. In fact, he clearly seemed to feel the need to give further explanation.

"We been looking mostly up in the parts of the Swamp what let you pass through," he said, spearing a piece of the butts-meat and putting it onto his plate. "They going back in the Deepswamp, and it ain't so hospitable back there. The Klá'soo's 'bout one of the only creek you can ride far back up, and it ain't so friendly, itself."

"How long you figure they'll be up there?"

Ya shrugged. "Could be all day. Ain't no telling."

Ya said no more and Bo still felt a little put off and asked no more questions and so, with nothing else they cared to talk about, they ate their meal in silence.

After breakfast they pulled out the fishpoles, but before they could get down to the water, the rain came up again, this time in great rolls, and they retreated back under the canvas, stretching out and relaxing as country folk can always do when there is nothing else to be done. Ya, who did not seem to have had much sleep the night before, lay on his back with his hands clasped as a pillow under his head, his eyes closed. Bo lay close to the edge of tent and stared out at the sheets of rain, his mind turning over the entire several days of the search.

Having settled his mind down somewhat, he decided to try again to coax Ya into talkishness.

"You know," he said, "I don't think we seen sign of Papa'Budi back up in here, not one time. You reckon he ain't come back this way at all?"

Ya did not say anything in answer for a while, and Bo began to think that he had really gone to sleep. But then Ya grunted, turned on his side, and opened his eyes.

"That don't mean nothing," he said. "Uncle Budi ain't one for left sign. Him ever did took care folks couldn't follow him back here."

Bo let out a little laugh at that. "Who be trying for follow Old Budi Manigault back up in here but old dumb us?" he asked. "Whitefolk?"

Ya laughed in return, an unforced laugh, holding nothing back, and it seemed that whatever had come between them earlier in the day had been washed away in the drenching rain. "No, ain't no whitefolk coming back up in here, that for sure," he said, still chuckling. "Buckra don't hardly mess with Uncle Budi. Them more scared off'en him then they is for coming up in the Swamp."

"I heard about y'all and Old Man Jaeger and the pecan."

Ya rolled his eyes and sat up.

"Oh, I know that damn Ula done open she mouth on that. What that girl tell you?"

"Said Papa'Budi took her and you and which-one'a you' brother—?"

"Pakky."

"Yeah, Pakky. Said Papa'Budi took y'all over to Jaeger's Store one time when y'all been little chap—tell me if I ain't getting it right—and the old man 'cuse y'all of t'iefing pecan from out his barrel. And Pap'Budi say if y'all childrens done t'ief pecan, where they at? And Old Man Jaeger holler out 'them little nigger' DONE 'ET THEM UP!' And Papa'Budi tell y'all for drop you' drawers right there and shit on the storeporch, and if he find him a single piece of pecan meat 'midst the shit, he be done beat the black ouffen y'all and pay for the whole barrel, but if y'all shit come out empty, he be done turn'round and beat Old Man Jaeger up and down the Cashville Road for lying on y'all children. That what Ula told me. That the way it happen?"

Ya narrowed his eyes and looked up into the falling sheets of rain as if he were considering.

"Yup," he said, finally, with a grin. "I believe you' wife got it right, all what she tol'ded. Her ain't say all'a we been something glad her pap scare that whiteman off, and him ain't make we shit, is she?"

"I guess y'all been glad. Who want to show they ass to the world out in the big day like that, 'front'a whitefolk and all?"

"Oh, that weren't it," Ya said. "Hell, we'd done et so much'a Old Jaeger pecan, it'a come out growing branch and leaf iffen Uncle Budi had made we shit."

The two men roared with laughter, Bo laying back and holding his sides and shaking uncontrollably, tears running down his cheeks, as he thought of a little Ula stuffing pecans in her mouth, hiding it from both her father and the store owner.

"I ain't know iffen Uncle Budi'a beat Old Jaeger or not like he promise, but Old Jaeger sure-enough thought so," Ya said. "After that, whenever Uncle Budi go'cross that river, them oba'nigger used to turn to the whitefolk and say 'boss, ain't that that old Shayree nigger what don't take no shit and won't give none, neither?'" Through Bo's new explosion of laughing, Ya added, "but Uncle Budi had him a reputation with the whitefolk long time before that. You know how he got that bad eye, inn'a?"

Bo settled down his laughing and sat up again. "Not but what he told me," he said. "But it were two different things, so's I never could figure which one were truth. One time he told me it was a mule what kick him in the eye when he were a boy. Said his pap gave him a gun—said he weren't hardly big enough to tote it—and sent him out for shoot that mule. 'Shot for shoe, fair is fair.' That's what he said his pap told him."

"That one story. What were the other?"

"'Nother time, he say him mashed it up falling out a tree."

"That Uncle Budi." Ya began searching around in his pockets for his chewing tobacco. "He got all the story about everybody's else, but him like rabbit-in-the-briar when it come time for tell about he own self. You seen where I put my 'baca?"

Bo shook his head.

"Oh, I know. Pap run outten his, so I give'd him what I had. Let me have some'a yours."

Bo pulled his tobacco-packet out of his shirt pocket and tossed it, underhand, across to Ya, who turned it over in his hand several times and grimaced.

"You ain't got nothing but old Red Man?"

"That-what I chew." Bo held out his hand. "You can send it back over, if it don't suit you."

Ya sighed, cut off a thin slice, stuck it in his mouth, and tossed the rest of the pack back to Bo. "I'm a Beech Nut man, myself, but I'll chew this old rag paper of you'rn and spit it out, quick, since I have to." To demonstrate, he sent a stream out into the rain. "Anyways, weren't no mule had any part in Uncle Budi' bad eye. He were right about the tree, but it weren't no falling, it were a jumping. It happen the time the night-riders come over 'cross the river, and the old folk ran they ass back."

"The Klan been in Yelesaw? I ain't never heard nothing of that."

"No surprise you ain't. The buckra been shame' for what happen and them old folk, they wasn't the kind for brag. You ever knowed my Uncle Toot?"

"Not too good. He died right when me and Ula been first taking up time."

"He were the only one I ever knowed would talk about it. You know how the whitefolk come for left Yelesaw?"

"I heard that one back home, coming up. Wasn't it 'cause y'all burnt the Bethelia Big House down?"

Ya snorted. "Y'all? I ain't been back there in them time. And anyways, ain't nobody knows who burnt that old house down. Could'a been them slaverytime peoples, yep. Them been some rough-ass peoples. But it could'a been the Yankee. They been coming through the county at the time, from the story. Shit, prob'ly been that old buckra himself, the old man, Maw'se Grady, getting drunk and dropping a lamp and setting he own house afire. Grandma Effie used to say him been a drinking old cracker. Point be, ain't nobody knows who done it, but it don't matter, 'cause it spooked every buckra on Yelesaw, and they all broke camp and run'cross the river and ain't took box nor baggage, what I heard. And after that, them say it were the Yelesaw niggers what chased them off, and we was holding the land over here all ill-legalish and such, and them'a want it back. What Uncle Toot say, they talk-'til-they-talk-'til-they-talk, 'til they talk theyselves up to come'cross the river on horses one night for run we off. You know where Udi and Safa Brown and them stay, what they calls the Black Rock?"

Bo nodded.

"Well, that who they planned for hit first. Cu'n Udi grandpap were the one what supposed to have tooke'd Old Man Grady' rocking chair offen the Big House porch whiles the house been still burning, and when he built he own house down to Black Rock, he put it on he own porch and used to sit in it and rock and sing song about old maw'se.

> *Maw'se in the cold ground, dead*
> *But I ain't there*
> *I's in he rocking chair*
> *Just rocking and rocking*
> *Over he head*

"Udi still sing it, iffen he get'nuff corn in him. That where I heard it. And when I been little, I used to seen that big-ass rocking chair up on Cu'n Udi' porch with the tool-carve rockers and back and some'the old leather padding still on the arm and the seat. It were all tatter-up even then, and you couldn't sit in it no more, but they kept it out on that porch 'til the 'mites got to it and they burn it up for firewood, I believe. It still look'ded 'xpensive as hell, even back then, and you knowed good and well ain't no nigger had the money for go down to Charleston and buy something like that. Anyways, that-why everybodys calls that spot the Black Rock, 'cause'a that old black Kiz-Kiz—that were the old man name—what used to sit out on he porch and rock in old maw'se rocking chair and sing that song. Him been done dead before I been borned, so I never heard him sing it he own self, but I sure wish I had."

"What about the Klan coming over?" Bo asked him.

"Oh, yeah, that-what I been talking about," Ya said. He stuck his finger in his mouth and pulled out an extra bit of the tobacco that had stuck in his teeth, tossing it out in the rain. "It been a dry season, them times, and you could ford the river down near the junction, and them night-rider come across there on they horse with sheet and rope and torch and gun, and the plan—what Uncle Toot say—were to hit Tat'Kiz-Kiz house the first, which were the first house down by the ford, and then to ride up the River Road burning every cabin they come to and then go tearin'-up down through all the settlement', iffen they could find them, just like they been doing that same time all over the county. Hell, all over South Carolina, truth be told, and 'cross into Georgia and Tennessee, too."

"But that ain't how it happen on Yelesaw?"

"No, Cousin, that ain't how it happen on Yelesaw. Them old-time mens got word of the plan—who know how? One of them buckra talk too much in front of the wrong nigger, maybe, and them fetched it'cross. Anyways, the mens wait down in the woods around old Kiz-Kiz house, and when them whitefolk ride up, they set on them from all side."

"Set on them, how?"

"Set on them shooting, the few what had gun for shoot. Or with axe and pitchfork and rice-knife, what done brought those. Hell, some chunking rock. Anything they could get they hand on."

Bo could see the scene in his head, the torches waving wildly, making the great tree shadows appear to be leaping in dance, the horses rearing and screaming, nostrils steaming, the white men bucking their eyes on all sides as the dark figures leaped at them from out of the blackwoods, the glint of metal and the whirl of rock, the sharp bark of gunshots with the bright burst of yellow flame coming out of the barrels, men in both camps shouting in fear and anger, the thud of bodies colliding, men tumbling, falling onto the ground. Bo blinked the vision away.

"So what about Papa'Budi?" he asked. "How he figure into it."

"Well, that the thing. Uncle Budi were a chap back then, and none'a the chap were supposed to be out there. Hell, none'a the chap were even supposed to knowed about it. But Uncle Budi and Uncle Toot and some of the other boy, they sneaked on out to the Black Rock early in the afternoon, and hid up in the trees so's they could see. They wasn't far from some of the fighting when it been going on, but they would'a gotten by and nobodys would'a seen them, but Uncle Toot say when one'a them buckra ride right up under the tree he and Uncle Budi been in, Uncle Budi jump right down on top of him."

"*Jump* down?"

"Jump. Ain't fall. Ain't get push. Jump. Uncle Toot say Unce Budi must'a get all 'xcited over the fighting and wanted some for heself, and jump right in the mix. He say Uncle Budi land on that buckra back and most knock him offen he horse, and the buckra been'a scuffle for try and get him off whiles Uncle Budi boxing him all in the head and the side, and then that buckra got he pistol turn-round and fire at Uncle Budi. Ain't hit'im straight in the head, or it'd blowed a hole clean through, they been so close lock-up together, but it graze Uncle Budi 'cross the side'a he face, and knock him clean off that horse and into a berry bush. Must'a catch powder in he eye, too, 'cause he eye been cloudy-up, every since."

Bo sat for a moment unable to speak, astonished at the story. There were scarce few Negroes in Cantrell County or the counties surrounding who had the balls to fight a whiteman with fists, much less anything else. And of those few and widely-scattered instances, never before had Bo heard of colored folk fighting head-up with whitefolk, and staying around to talk about it. Either they had to leave the county, quick, or they ended up staying down in county ground, permanent.

"What happened to the buckra?" he finally asked. He already knew what had happened to the Yay'saws. Most of the ones that had been in the Black Rock fight were dead now, he figured, but not because of the fight.

"The buckra what shot Uncle Budi, or all'a them?" Ya asked, back.

"Either one."

Ya chewed thoughtfully a moment, trying to recall the end of his Uncle Toot's tale. "I ain't know what happened with the one what shot Uncle Budi, but the rest of them, they gone'd back down to the river faster than they come up, some on they horses, some on they two foots, and gone'd back through that water like duck taking off. One Yay'saw man got kill that night. Zimi Ravenel' daddy. I ain't think no buckra got theyselves kill, or there'd been some hell for pay, but I believe some of them got bust-up pretty bad, maybe shotted, too. And you know them nice horse what them Jackson boys be riding up and down the road on? Most of them come offen Bethelia, but some come from that same stock what them whitefolk left when them took off running from Black Rock that night. And that been the last time any buckra had a idea for come to Yelesaw for teach folk manners, or to run folk offen we land. And that why the whitefolk tend for leave a Yay'saw alone when we goes over into town."

He rocked back and forth on his backsides, simulating someone in a rocking chair, and began to sing again.

*Maw'se in the cold ground, dead*
*But I ain't there*
*I's in he rocking chair*
*Just'a rocking and'a rocking*
*Over that scoundrel head*

Bo sat and listened to Ya, watching the rain outside the canvas cover, which was coming down so steady now that it hid all view of anything of the clearing or the creek or river or the world beyond. He lay down on one side, propping his head up with his arm.

"You know, colored folk over in the county don't hardly mess with none'y'all, neither," Bo said.

Ya smiled and nodded. "Oh," he said. "That true, too. I reckon we got us a reputation over there."

Bo had started to say "none'a'we" instead of "none'y'all" but decided not to. He didn't feel like another argument with Ya over the issue. For his own part, he was not exactly sure what he was. Not a half-breed. That was his children. He was a 'tweener. In between oba and Yay'saw, no longer one, not likely to become the other, stuck somewhere in between. He laughed to himself at his predicament. "I got a song for you," he said to Ya.

"What song that be?"

"About y'all crazy Shay'ree folks. We had a song the childrens used to sing, back on the Creek End:

*Shay'ree 'uman throw the lye*
*Shay'ree 'uman scratch you' eye*
*Shay'ree nigger burn you' shed*
*Shay'ree nigger cut you dead*
*Shay'ree peoples likes to shoot*
*That don't do it*
*They works the root*"

Ya broke out in another laugh and sent his stream of tobacco-juice out into the rain past Bo. "I never heard that'un before," he said. "But I reckon they never sung'd it whiles any'a we been 'round."

"No, I reckon not."

"But you know you done ended up living with a Yay'saw 'uman right now, working root on you every night, inna'?"

Bo shook his head, unconsciously lifting his hand up and touching Big Soo's toby under his shirt as he did. Ya gave the gesture a quick look, but then his face relaxed, and if he thought anything of it, it didn't show.

"Ula don't allow no root in we house, or close-up to the yard, either. You know that," Bo said, quickly taking his hand away from his chest when he saw where Ya's glance had gone. He did not know why he was reluctant to reveal that he was carrying the toby...he just was. He raised up on his elbow. "My mama believe different, though. She thought sure that Ula been a rootdoctor or a woods-witch, one or all both, and you couldn't talk her out of it for nothing. She bust out and cry the night I tell her I been fixing to marry a Yay'saw girl. Fall down on her bed and holler, 'Benjamin, may God help me, I'll cast you outten my heart and scatter you' bones when you die iffen you take up with that Shay'ree girl. I done told you, don't eat from she plate. She done put powder in you' food 'for make you follow she around like a calf hunting teat.' She wail and wail and wail and slap my hand'way when I tried to comfort her. Mama thought everybody 'cross the Sugaree was a hoodoo and a conja'."

Ya chuckled. "That ain't stop the wedding, though."

"No, but she ain't come to it, neither, you notice. Ain't none'a my relative come 'xcepting for my cousin Peter, and he been dead drunk on stumphole." Bo got quiet for a moment, blinking his eyes. He had been telling the story in a light manner so far, as if none of the events mattered to him, but this one cut deep. He gave out a chuckle himself, to push the hurt away. "Onliest thing would'a held up we wedding were Papa'Budi," he went on. "Iffen he ain't been for it, ain't no way I'd'a marry Ula. No way under the sun. I tell'd you I been 'feared of him, something bad."

Ya's chuckling turned to a bemused smile.

"You thinking Uncle Budi been up for you marrying my cousin?"

"He *tol'ded* me he were for it. Soon as I let him know the plan, he sat me on the porch and tol'ded me for take care of he baby, else he'd come over to we house and bust my head in with a stave, iffen I ain't. And he been at the wedding and held one end of the broom when we jumped. Iffen Papa'Budi been against it, he sure showed it funny."

Ya snorted.

"You think that? Shit, Uncle Budi ain't want none'a he daughter for marry no *Yay'saw* nigger, much less no oba'dey. The night Ula tell him she were thinking 'bout taking up with a oba, him threatened for beat her blue with the mule harness. That been way before y'all court-up and think about marry. Y'all had just met."

Bo shook his head in disbelief. "For true? Ula ain't never told me nothing like that. How you know that?"

"I know 'cause I been there to the house when it happen. Ula been to Cashville that day, and she been telling me and Ree and Soo how she done meet this boy in town—*good*-looking boy, she said—and we'all been asking question 'bout how y'all meet and such, you could see her been all up and excited. And Uncle Budi come in the door right in the middle and ask what all the talking been 'bout, and Ula—that girl could'a lie, but she ever been bull-head, just like Uncle Budi—she told him she done meet a oba'dey boy in town, and she like'd'ed him something good, and had done told you that you could come to the house iffen you wanted. Ula ain't ask Uncle Budi. Her tell him. And Uncle Budi got hot, and him say ain't no goddamn oba'dey boy coming up on *he* porch for 'wisit with *he* child—him say even if her wait 'til him die and bury behind Papa'Leem and Mama'Effie for do some wrongful and scandalous thing like that, him would break open the graveyard ground and come up to the house in he burying clothes and slap that boy with a dead man's hands. And that old Ula, her ain't take a backward step. She say her been 19 year, and it were past time for courting, and it weren't fair for him to stop her, and she would run'way with you to Georgetown and marry-up in a jellyhouse iffen

Uncle Budi block the road. I think Uncle Budi'd done run-off or scare-off all the Yay'saw boy what had want for come-round and see her all along, and her been thinking she might end-up in the house with no man a'tall, like Orry and Soo. Anyways, when she sass back like that, that when Uncle Budi gone for the mule harness. I ain't never seen him mad as that. I thought he been fixing to kill her. I thought I been fixing to see my little cousin die in they house right in front of me."

"He beat her?"

Ya shook his head.

"What stop him? Ula run out the house?"

"Cu'n Ula? You must ain't know you' wife too good, Cousin. You thinking Ula ever done run from a licking? Her stay right there in the house and wait for Uncle Budi to come back with the mule harness, and ain't move, and would'a took the beating without the first flinch. It were Cu'n Ree what stop him."

"Orry?" It was Bo's turn to shake his head, but his was for incredulity's sake. He knew there was much about Yelesaw and the Yay'saws he did not understand, but he had thought, at least, that he knew the basic character of the people of the immediate family he had married into. Orry, especially, who by far had been his favorite among his new Manigault relatives. "All the days I known her," he said, "I don't believe I can ever remember her raising her voice, not even at the chickens or the goats when they got up in her garden."

"Neither me," Ya said. "Ree weren't much for shouting, and she ain't shout that evening. When Uncle come back in the house and raise them harness reins for bring them down on Ula, Ree got sheself in between them two. I ain't know how she did it, she did it so fast, big as she was. But them reins gone up and 'fore they come back down, there been Orry in the middle, and Uncle Budi turn'way the blow. And Orry look Uncle Budi dead in the eye, and she tell him, 'If you hit that girl this evening, you won't sleep easy in this house another night. And if you ain't give you' consent for that boy for come visit Ula from 'cross that river, it won't be just her what be done left. I'll pack my kit tonight and walk out this house, and won't ever set foot nor fat in it, never no more.' Said it dead cold, ain't raise she voice, and ain't stumble on she word. Whatever him been thinking 'bout it all, Uncle Budi ain't say nothing back, just look at Orry in the eye. Just look. And then him set them harness reins down on the table just as soft, and him walk out the house, and ain't come back for awhile, neither. And when he come back, he still ain't said a word to Ree, ain't even look at her now, but he told Ula that if a boy come over courting, he best be polite, 'cause '*there be too many goddamn sassy-ass folk up in this house, already.*' I had to bite my lip to keep from bust-out laugh when he said that. And then Uncle Budi tell Ula him ain't care one way t'other if she choose for court a oba or a blue-lip monkey, it had to be one boy or one monkey, and that been it. He wouldn't keep no house with one randy ass after t'other coming 'round howling in heat. And then he ask for he supper, and that been it. And that how you come for court Ula Manigault, and that how it work out for y'all to marry."

Bo lay on the ground and watched the rain and said nothing for a while, listening to the steady drumming on the canvas top, trying to sort all of it out.

"Why Papa'Budi care so much if Orry had left?" he asked, finally. "She been more than a marrying age. Ain't he had for expect, she might get marry herself and go off one day, anyways?"

Ya chuckled and spit out at the rain again. "I ain't remember much about Aunt Keecy. She pass on while I still been a little chap. But Cu'n Ree, she been the only 'uman I knowed what could put up with Uncle Budi ways and cook he food and keep he house. Onliest one I seen come close to what Ree done for Uncle Budi is that youngest girl of your'n, Yally, but, 'course, her ain't been in the picture, back then. Ula? Ula and Uncle Budi, them two been too much alike. If Ula had stay in the house with him after she'd got grown, the two'a them would'a beat each other to death one night, certain. All you'd'a find would be the bloody bones the next morning, and you probably couldn't tell which bone belong to which body, the scrap would'a been so tough. And Cu'n Soo. You see how long it took Soo for break camp after Ree cross'oba. Without Ree in that house, Uncle Budi would'a been lost. That why he wouldn't do nothing that would make her leave, and did plenty something what kept her staying."

It was left unsaid between the two men how lost Budi Manigault had become after Sister Orry's death, and how it had come, a little over a year after her funeral, for them to be sitting in the rain on the banks of the Blacksnake River that day, waiting for Budi Manigault's brother and Bambo Saunders to come back in the boat with Budi Manigault himself, or with news.

"You saying Papa'Budi run mens away from the house what come for courting Orry, like he run them'way from courting Ula?" Bo asked.

"Yes I is," Ya answered, nodding. "Been plenty what wanted to come. Plenty what asked me about her. But they ever been feared Uncle Budi would set the dog on them, if they tried. Or put pellet in'em. Or worse'n that."

"So all she life, Orry ain't never keep no company? I know I ain't seen nobodys come-round all the time I been over here."

"Nobody come, not that I know of or heard of."

"Damn." Bo scratched at the back of his head for a moment, and a memory caught up with him. "What about that man what come to she funeral?" he asked. "The one caused all that commotion."

"That mule-eye, cripple-up spooky son-of-a-bitch? What about him? You asking if I think he and Cu'n Ree been sweet?"

"You know that-what some folk ever said after that."

Ya paused in thought for a moment, spat out some tobacco-juice, thought some more.

"Sure, it possible," he said, at last. "Folk what thought they knowed my cousin good, ain't know the half about she. She been better at keeping secret than anybody I ever knowed, and she had a wild side to her most folks never see'd. But it would'a been a hard thing to pull off, iffen she did. They's deepwoods all-around Yelesaw, and things going on in them woods you wouldn't believe. But it would'a been something hard for hide if she been keeping company with *that* son-of-a-bitch, hide for long, anyways. Unless it were someone what knowed the Swamp and weren't afraid to lead her down in here. He'd have to know it, 'cause Orry never got closer to the Swamp than the ricefield, ever in her life. That I know of..." His voice trailed off as if another thought had struck him. He grunted and shifted his position against the tree, seeming like he had grown stiff sitting in one place, and if he had something else to say on the subject, he did not say it.

"Might'a been possible, them meeting up in the Swamp," Bo put in after seeing that Ya stopped talking. "I been a'feared of the Swamp, myself, up 'til I got up here in it. Now it don't seem so fearful as I thought it would be."

When they had made the turn at the Junction and started up into the Blacksnake, he had fully expected that they were entering a land of screams and terror at every bend and break of the river, and that along the way—and this he thought about now with a small smile—things would perhaps be reaching up out of the water to clutch at him with clawed fingers and try to snatch him and drag him down into the murked depths below. Instead he had discovered that the Blacksnake and the Swamp had no interest in devouring him. It was a countryside at ease with itself, stretched out behind its cover of oil-black surface and fog in a quiet peace. Here the whole world slowed and ceased its worry over the cares that ran along the busy Sugaree and the wagoned and motored roadways in the county across. What he had thought was rank and rot and repulsive only yesterday evening, standing on the banks of the Klá'Soo, now seemed to him to border on the sweet and seductive. Here was an ancient place, a land turned back upon the outside world, alive and breathing a dreamy incensed smell, a land moving backward in time at a slow and stately place, and carrying them along with it. Why had he ever feared it so? He began to understand what had drawn his father-in-law to the banks of the Blacksnake year after year, and to understand why, perhaps, the women of Millen Pond and Creek End had told such tales about it. Was it to keep their men away who might otherwise go down upon it and hear its siren song, fall in love with the river and the backland, and never come out again? It seemed entirely possible, now that Bo was here, deep within its boundaries.

Slipped into a reverie, Bo had not heard something Ya had just finished saying.

"What-say?" he asked.

"I were saying, don't let this old Swamp fool you, son," Ya said.

"Fool me, how?"

"Swamp ain't as peaceable as it been putting on. It a *ain't-seeming* kind of place. You know what I means by that?"

Bo shook his head, no.

"It ain't what it *seem* to be to folk what look at it from the outside, but it ain't what it *seem* to be once't you get in it, neither. It ever trying for fool you. It can sing you a song that will put you to sleep and then reach around and squeeze you' neck 'til you can't catch you' breath. What look like a solid patch of ground could be a bog for catch you' foots. Walk down a path a little ways, time you turn around for come back, it done grow'd up so much, you ain't recognize where you been and can't find you' way. You could walk just out of sight of this-here river and get so turn-around you could wander around back in there 'til the end of you' days, and you could holler and the rest'a we could be standing right here, and couldn't hear you for nothing. The Swamp a place what good for hiding things. Hide you. Hide me. Hide things what's up in it. And some'a them things, it good iffen them stay hidden. Anybodys ever told you 'bout the buzzard dance?"

"Only yesterday evening, when we done dock," Bo said. "Bambo told me. Said they go up that creek and do it."

Ya gave a grim nod.

"Bet Bambo ain't tell you who they suppose for do they dancing up there with."

Bo shook his head.

"That 'uman what you say Uncle Budi gone 'wisiting with."

It all suddenly fell in place. But before an astonished Bo could call out the name "Timbi," Ya halted him with a quick shush and a shake of his head and a fierce look. He glanced around on all sides before saying anything, as if worrying that someone might be listening, even though the beating of the rain outside must have made any of their words unintelligible a foot or two away from the canvas covering. Satisfied, seemingly, that no-one else was under the canvas with them, Ya leaned towards Bo and said in a lowered voice, "That ain't someone we ought for name out, not right here on the bank'a she creek."

Bo thought for a moment about what he might be allowed to say.

"But she done dead, right?" he asked, finally, lowering his voice as Ya had.

Ya seemed annoyed.

"Ain't I tol'ded you, her been a slaverytime 'uman? You think them peoples back there live-out to be two hundreds?"

Admonished, Bo shook his hand in the air. "I's just making certain," he said.

Ya made a gesture out in the direction of the creek. "Up in there, that-where her supposed to have gone'd for live when her left-out Bethelia. Might be true. Might be not. That-what them say. I ain't never been'd up there to see for my ownself, and I ain't going now. I know you done mad-up 'cause my pap left and gone'd without we, but I ain't."

"Oh." With the Yelesaw information tap flowing more than it had ever done over him, even if it was only coming in dribs and drabs, Bo tried one more time. "And they going up there for look for Papa'Budi?"

Ya frowned his face up. "Now you sounding just like a damn oba, Cousin," he said, sucking his teeth and spitting out a stream of tobacco all at the same time, a feat that had clearly taken hours of practice to perfect.

AFTER A WHILE, they went down on the riverbank to pole for

fish. Bo noticed that Ya did not put line in the water until he had
walked deliberately far down from the entrance to the Klá'soo, as
if, pointedly, he did not want anything that swam directly down out
of that tributary to get entangled on his hook. They caught several
good-sized fish, which they cleaned and fried and ate and then
went back down on the bank to fish for some more. There was
little else to do but mark time. They lounged around the campsite
all day, slipping back under the canvas covers for a bit when the
rain took up again. Night came with no sign of Papa'Tee and
Bambo Saunders, and so they lay down on their pallets and
chatted in the dark for a while. Ya did not seem worried that the
searchers were taking so long, and so Bo—who had begun to worry
a little, himself—did not make any inquiry.

They had just begun to settle down to sleep when the sound of
movement and talking came from the direction of the creek, and
they could see torchlight coming up from that way, and the figures
of Papa'Tee and Bambo Saunders walking up. Bo looked hopefully
for a third figure, but there was none, and he thought, after all,
that it had been a vain hope. If Papa'Tee had really thought his
brother had been down at the end of that creek, he supposed he
would have gone there, first off.

"See anything?" Ya asked.

Papa'Tee boxed his mouth and gave a slow shake of his head.
Whatever they had found up the creek that day, it had not been
Papa'Budi.

"Well, we save some fish for y'all," Ya said. "I know you
hungry."

Papa'Tee and Bambo wolfed down supper in silence before
dropping into their pallets and sleep, obviously exhausted,
offering no further explanation on the events of the day, and
neither Ya nor Bo asked for any.

Just before Papa'Tee laid down, Bo did ask him if they were
through with the search.

"I reckon so," Papa'Tee said, a touch of tiredness in his voice.
"I done gone'd 'round to all the place I know about he general'a
'wisit. Iffen him been up here, I ain't seen he track. We could run
the riverbank another week or so, I s'pose, but I guess it's best to
go-on back home and wait for my bubba to come back on he own.
He will or he won't. We done done the best we could."

In the morning they broke camp, and put their things into the
boat, and headed onto the Blacksnake on the long and solemn
trip back down the river towards home. Despite what Papa'Tee

had said, they continued to check a few more spots for Papa'Budi
along the way.`

IT WAS VERY LATE in the night when they docked the boat at the
cable-barge landing, and they met no-one on the walk along the
dark road back home. And yet, with a prescience that had long
since ceased to surprise him, Ula was up and waiting for Bo when
he walked up onto the front porch, supper warming in the pots on
top of the woodstove. They exchanged one long look at the door,
and he understood that there was nothing to tell her. Somehow,
she seemed to have known about the failure of their search up the
backriver, as well. He set himself down wearily, and heavily, at the
table and watched as she spooned the food onto his plate. Her
movements were methodical and mechanical. He had seen her
like this before, a dull, despondent deliberateness that was worse
than her explosions, because its length was unpredictable. She
could walk down in these sunken pathways for weeks at a time,
until something intervened to lift her mood, or else she simply
decided on her own to rise herself up again. There was little Bo
himself could do to mitigate. Ula was a flat, black pan-bottom on
which the easy grease of his wheedlings and humor would not
spread.

She set the plate of food down in front of him, but he reached
over and grasped her wrist before she could turn away.

She did not try to move, or even extract her arm, but only
looked down at him with no sign of interest or expectation,
waiting, as if time neither touch had any effect upon her.

"I'm sorry, Uly," he said.

"Sorry for what, husband?" her answer came back, her voice as
even and unemotional as the look in her eyes.

"I'm sorry we ain't find you' pap," he said, struggling to keep
his own voice from breaking. "I'm sorry I ain't stop him when he
first tell me he been going. I'm sorry I ain't get over to his house
faster to keep him from going, when you asked me. I wish I had."

She said nothing in reply, and the expression on her face did
not change.

He took her hand between both of his and gave it a small
squeeze. "Papa'Tee said ain't no reason to think he ain't still
coming back out," he said. "Weren't no sign of nothing bad
happening back up in there. Papa'Tee said back in the old time,
weren't nothing unusual for folks to go off back up in there and
stay for a while, when they got theyselves low in the spirit. And

when they spirit done rise'd, they just walked back out again. Papa'Tee said that kind of thing happen, more than once."

That stirred her, if only for a moment. Her eyes narrowed and storm-clouded over, and she gave the briefest of frowns before pulling her hand away from his and folding her arms over her breasts. She stood over him still, giving him a long look that slowly retreated back into itself.

"Papa'Tee, him say a lot of thing," she said, finally and quietly. "But him ain't'a tell all he know. Back in the old times, when people's gone out on the river or into the woods and ain't come back, the old folk used'ta say they must done gone'd for 'wisit with Timbi. I reckon that been they way of saying the Swamp, it done swallowed them up." Suddenly, Bo understood the concern both his wife and Papa'Tee had shown when he'd mentioned Papa'Budi's intentions. "That Old Swamp, it a people-t'ief, Ben Kinlaw," Ula went on. "It done t'ief more than one, down the year. More than one. And now it done take my papa." She said the last without any anger or despair, without a trace of feeling at all, and her eyes remained like dull, fireless black coals.

His heart broke at the sound of hollowness in her voice, but he could think of nothing to say that could relieve her sorrow. She turned away from him without another word, and went to work to clear the supper pots from the stove.

HE WONDERED, on and off for weeks afterward, at the reason he had been invited along with the searchers. There was no-one to ask, and no revelation came to him. It was only years later that he learned the why and wherefore from Ya. As soon as Ula heard that Papa'Tee was forming a search party, she had gone straight to his house and insisted Bo be among the number. She had known, even before he told her on the night they came back off the river, that he was blaming himself for not stopping her father from taking his trip up the Blacksnake. And though she knew her husband well enough to know that nothing could ever fully take away that stone of guilt that would ever weigh upon his heart, searching for Budi Manigault up in that back country with his own eyes and hands and feet would ease the weight and burden of it, some.

Hearing that explanation, Bo Kinlaw thought he had never loved his wife more.

TWO NIGHTS AFTER they came back from their search, he had

an unsettling dream.

> *He was walking through a gray and damping mist, pushing his way through wet things that clung and pulled at him, and all the time calling out for his father-in-law—"Papa'Budi. Papa'Budi. Papa'Budi."—until a voice as mournful as the opening of the earth came back in reply, "What you does want wit' down in this place? Why seek ye amongst the dead?" in words that were vaguely familiar but whose origins and context eluded him. Then he felt himself surrounded, with dark shapes rising up and looming over him, hollowed-out eyes staring, hair waving in the wind like tree-moss, or the bodies of living snakes...*

In the morning, he went out before breakfast to the shed, where he had hidden under a loose floorboard the toby that Big Soo had given him. He could not bring it into the house with Ula, of course, or even let her know that he had it, but he certainly would not throw it away, either. He sat, squat-legged, on the shed floor rubbing the outside of the pouch between his thumb and fingers, its scent slowly filling his nose, and after a while, it gave him a comfort. Ever after that, each night, he would make certain that he visited the shed and put his hand on Big Soo's toby before he went into the house and went to bed, and only on the nights that he forgot did he suffer any bad dreams.

IT WAS SEVERAL DAYS LATER that the High Sheriff and two of his deputies came over to Yelesaw at the cable-crossing and tacked up signs on several trees along the River Road near the Landing. They were followed by a gaggle of children who took it for a parade.

It was several hours before the Yay'saws could track down someone who could interpret them, because the writing was so legalistic, and few could understand their meaning.

They were notices from the County Courthouse at St. Paul.

> THE PEOPLE OF THE STATE OF SOUTH CAROLINA AND THE CANTRELL COUNTY ASSESSOR'S OFFICE HEREBY GIVE NOTIFICATION OF THE FILING OF COMPLAINTS IN THE CIRCUIT COURT OF THE STATE OF SOUTH CAROLINA AGAINST ALL REAL PROPERTY OWNERS IN THE ADAMS NECK COMMUNITY, SUCH LAND LOCATED BETWEEN THE SUGAREE AND THE BLACKSNAKE RIVERS IN

CANTRELL COUNTY, SOUTH CAROLINA. ALL SUCH REAL PROPERTY OWNERS ARE DIRECTED TO APPEAR BEFORE THE CIRCUIT COURT JUDGE AT THE COUNTY COURTHOUSE IN ST. PAUL, SOUTH CAROLINA AT 9:30 A.M. ON THE FIRST TUESDAY IN DECEMBER, NINETEEN HUNDRED AND THIRTY SIX, JUDGE HARRISON MANNING, PRESIDING, TO SHOW CAUSE WHY SUCH REAL PROPERTY SHOULD NOT BE SEIZED AND CONFISCATED BY THE STATE OF SOUTH CAROLINA UNDER THE EMINENT DOMAIN POWERS SUBSCRIBED TO THE LEGAL GOVERNMENT OF SAID STATE.
SIGNED,
ROBERT E. MUELLER
CLERK OF THE CANTRELL COUNTY COURT

Even after explanation of the meaning of all the words, no-one quite knew exactly what the notices themselves meant, except that it was about the Watercoming, and something was going to happen in Big Court in December, and after that, it was most likely that the Sheriff would be back across the river sometime soon, and with more deputies than just two.

A few said they wished Budi Manigault would hurry-on back from his hunting so they could plan a response. "Truth to tell," they explained, "Baba'Zambu and some'a the rest know how for deal with the spirit and when to put out crop and such, but it take Tat'Budi for handle the buckra."

Most who heard nodded in assent.

6

## The Place Of Tears

*(1852-53)*

Yally took her grandfather's disappearance almost as hard as Mama had, but while Mama shut her grievings up in a sorrow jar and closed the lid, tight, Yally put her feelings into work around her grandfather's house.

Although her brothers and sisters had ever claimed that as the youngest grand, she had been Grandpa Budi's favorite, she had never herself felt that to be the case. Instead, growing up, Papa'Budi had always been something of a distant and sometimes-frightening figure to her, ever present in her life but ever at arms' length, never raising his hand to her in discipline but, then, being so imposing a disciplinarian and powerful of will, he never had to. It would have never crossed her mind to oppose him or defy him in any way. Further, she did not think their joking times and play were any different in any way special from the way her grandfather treated the other Kinlaw children. And she always knew that no matter how much he teased and poked at her tender spots, there was an unseen and unspoken of but very real line over which she, herself, could never cross, else his wrath would spring up swift and sudden, and all laughing cease, and he would come down on her as hard as he did on any of the other children on the Bigyard.

But in the long months following Sister Orry's death, Yally found that she had not only become her grandfather's cook and housekeeper, but his companion as well. She had only come to this realization after his disappearance into the Swamp. She found herself missing her evenings with him terribly, and without being asked by anyone, took it upon herself to continue to go by his house to keep the place up. Some of the other family members dropped by to lend a hand from time to time, especially with the heavier work, but it soon became generally accepted that these were now Yally's chores, and no-one questioned it. She weeded the yard and raked the dead leaves out of the scuppernong arbor and swept the porch and floorboards inside and kept the cobwebs at bay, as well as cleaning out the pens and the barn and feeding the dogs and the stock. She lit a fire in the stove every day and sometimes she cooked a supper on it, as she had when Papa'Budi had been at home, and after chores she would eat her meal at his old table and lose herself in the memories of the stories he had told or the lessons he had given or the jokes they had shared or the conversations they'd had.

At the near-end of her mind she reasoned that she was doing these things in anticipation of his return home, knowing how much he would fuss and raise a storm of sand if he came back and found things amiss, but at the back-end, she struggled with the possibility that her grandfather might never come out of the Swamp.

It was never easy to get Papa to do more than make light over things he didn't have a mind to talk about, but it was clear to Yally that there was something about her grandfather's disappearance and the search in the Swamp that her father was especially not inclined to share. She dared not ask Mama anything about Grandpa for fear of stirring up the grief that was obviously there, and Big Soo was no better help. When Yally asked her aunt if she thought Papa'Budi would come back, Big Soo gave a pause long enough to make it uncertain whether she was answering the question or simply wandering around in her mind on a random thought, finally saying, "Iffen a skunk suck you' egg in the moonlight, he'll be back for breakfast, for-sure." This was both so scandalous and hopeful that Yally decided to leave it be without asking Big Soo to expound.

On a morning that seemed like any other morning in the bleak, early winter days since her grandfather's disappearance, she had intended to go to Papa'Budi's to open up the doors and shutters and air things out, but she was already past the house and on her way across the Bigyard without realizing what she was doing, or where she was bound. After a while, as if silently summoned, she found herself at Na'Risa's and Papa'Tee's. Walking around the back, she found her great-aunt heating up several tubs of water getting ready for a morning of clothes-washing. There were several white candles lit on the side of the back porch sending out an aromatic scent, their small length and the wide puddles of wax surrounding showing that they had been burning for some time.

Ná'Risa greeted her with a broad, birdish smile.

"Good morning, Ula Manigault' child," she said. "You here on errand, or you come all the way over this way just for 'wisiting with old peoples?"

Yally was not at all sure how to answer. At odd times during the past two or three days, she had been smelling a strange, sweet scent that she had not then been able to identify or place the source of, but which now seemed similar, very similar, to the scent coming out of the candles on Ná'Risa's back porch. But she could hardly answer, "I smelled you' candles and come." That seemed silly and irresponsible, and she had begun to feel herself, for the first time in her life, becoming a responsible person, what with her work taking over the operation of her grandfather's property. And so she merely said "Just 'wisiting is all, Mamarisa, seeing how y'all doing," with no other explanation.

"Well, iffen y'all ain't got work for do on y'all end, we got plenty on this'n. Give me a hand with that clothes-pile, there, sugar. That old man I'm living with can dirty-up clothes faster'n shoat-in-the-pen. I think he roll'round on the ground 'fore he get home every night, just for aggravate me. Look'it that. See what I means?"

She reached over to her dirty pile and held up a pair of dungaree overalls for Yally to see.

Yally nodded a "yes'm," but it seemed to her that the overalls were in a far more presentable condition than those which she was used to being handed by her brothers.

In a short while they were deep into the washing work, Yally stirring and mashing around the clothes with a pole in one tub, Ná'Risa squatted down and scrubbing over a washboard with a fat bar of lye soap in another. Watching her, Yally wondered—not for the first time—how old her great-aunt might be. Ná'Risa had nary a wrinkle on her, her shine-black skin stretched like stiff leather over her face and neck and arms, and she moved with a lean-muscled fluidity and grace that was both youthful and ancient. In fact, she seemed to have no age to her at all. Yally realized, again, how little she actually knew about Ná'Risa. She wanted deeply to be able to talk with someone today, someone older and with some sense and knowledge, and wished that she felt close enough to Ná'Risa to do so. She remembered well the day Ná'Risa had invited her over and they had talked about the Watercoming. That had been a special day, a golden day, and Yally had carried it around in her pocket ever since, pulling it out from time to time to examine its warm memory. She wondered for a moment why she had not thought to talk to Ná'Risa about her grandfather's disappearance after the search down in the Swamp, but almost immediately understood why she had not. Despite the conversation of that day, she still felt as distant from Ná'Risa as ever. That other day had all been at Ná'Risa's initiative and bidding and Ná'Risa had been the one who had done most of the talking, including the telling of the story about the Death-Rain. Yally found herself in the same position as she had been before with her great-aunt, unable to figure out a way to start a conversation about anything but polite and trivial things, childish things, unable to unburden herself about what was really pressing on her mind, and what she was feeling and needed to get out.

Ná'Risa suddenly looked up from her washboard, seeming to have felt that Yally was watching her, and causing the girl to look down in embarrassment at having been caught.

"How you' mama doing?" Ná'Risa asked her.

"Tolerable," Yally answered, without looking up.

"I know she worry about she papa," Ná'Risa went on. "It been a tough year for her, with Orry gone'd. Ula a lot like me. Her ain't no leaning-on kind'a 'uman. But such as she do, them been the two what she done ever rely on, all she life. You know you' mama ain't never knowed she own mama, inna?"

"Yes'm. She done told me that."

"That's good. Sometimes folk does overlook telling childrens thing like that. But it's good you know." Ná'Risa bent back down to her scrubbing, but more thoughtfully than before. "Orry been much as a mama to you' mama as she ever had, and you' mama took Orry passing harder than maybe you figure. And now, with she papa—" Her voice trailed off, and she did not finish the sentence.

"You reckon my grandpa coming back outten'that Swamp,

Nana'Risa?"

At last, the question to which she desperately wanted an answer was out.

Ná'Risa put her hands up, fingers spread, in a gesture of uncertainty.

"Some folk 'round these ways, they got a kind of sight for thing like that," she said. "My eye' done got so old, I can hardly see what going on right now. So that something I couldn't tell you."

Yally said nothing in reply, only waited.

Ná'Risa paused, considered, and then continued. "I don't go back in that Swamp myself, but I been living on the edge of it, all my days, and I know something about her," she said. "She got she a mind, just like peoples do. And got a feeling to she, too. Old Swamp, she get lonely back there sometime, she like for call some folks to she, for company. Some she keep. Some she turn-go, after'while. When I been a little girl, there been one man, Izo Simmons, gone'd in the Swamp and stay a year or better, and then him just come back out again and gone'd back and live in he old house, liken he'd never been'way. It just that way with that Old Swamp. Budi Manigault might come back out this afternoon. Him might come back out this time next winter. Or him might never come back out again, a'tall. I couldn't say. Like I done said, I got my share of gift, but seeing what coming up tomorr'y ain't one'a them."

They worked in silence after that, a flock of questions forming in Yally's mind, adding greater numbers all the time as it swirled around in there, now that she realized the way was open for asking things. She tried to settle on the most important question or, in the alternative, the one that had the best chance of not closing up the opportunity. She finally chose the question that had been most on her mind, next to finding out if anyone thought her grandfather was coming back.

"Who Nana'Timbi is?" she asked.

Ná'Risa did not stop rubbing against the bedsheet with the bar of lye soap, but its rhythm and intensity changed ever so slightly. She did not answer for a moment while Yally waited, the girl not taking a breath or daring, now, to look over at her great-aunt.

"Where you done hear a name like that?" Ná'Risa asked, after a time.

"I done hear folk talking, is all," Yally answered, trying to make it sound as if she had not been eavesdropping on grown folks' conversation, which, of course, she had.

Ná'Risa paused again, as if carefully picking out her words. Yally had never known her great-aunt to be so careful before. In conversations or gatherings where she had heard her speak, Ná'Risa had always seemed to just come out with whatever was on her mind, without weighing the consequences of her words. The subject of the woman named Timbi was clearly as serious as Yally had thought it might be.

"Folk be talking about Nana'Timbi?" Ná'Risa asked.

"Not really talking 'bout her, as such. Just saying that she be the one what my grandpa gone'd up in the Swamp for see. You think that is?"

Ná'Risa shrugged. "Mought be. Mought not," she said. "Folk used to say it been Timbi were one of them in the crew what call folk down into the Swamp."

Yally felt a shiver of quick fear pass through her.

"Her a gafa?" she asked.

Ná'Risa shook her head. "No. Her were a natural 'uman. She lived at Bethelia."

"You knowed her?"

Ná'Risa gave out a loud and honest laugh, a pleasant sound in the chill winter air that seemed to break down the tension that had risen since Yally had brought up the Timbi woman's name. She held her chest with the wide of her hand until she could get the laughter tamped back down again. When it did, finally she asked, "Child, you thinking I'm old as all that?"

"No, ma'am," Yally answered, embarrassed again.

"True, I were borned at Bethelia, but I don't remember none 'bout living back in there. I been too little when we walked out."

"Nana'Timbi come out of Bethelia with y'all?" Her tongue now loosened, Yally was surprising herself at how free she was feeling at asking all of these questions of Ná'Risa. But she did not pause, for fear she would stop completely, or Papa'Tee would come home or someone could come by to fetch her great-aunt for a healing, and she'd never get the opportunity again.

"No. You' great-grandmama Effie, her told me Sus'Timbi gone'd back into the Swamp longtime before we come out of Bethelia, and ain't come out again."

"Grandma Effie knowed her?"

Ná'Risa nodded. "Oh yes, knowed her good," she said. "You know," she went on, looking off into the distance over the trees back toward the woods-end as if she could see some old memory painted out on the vacant blue sky up there, "You' great-grandmama and me, the two'a we used to went round and round about the raising of my childrens. Tee were her youngest, and I were just a young thing when we marry, and her think I ain't know nothing about raising no childrens, even though I did. So didn't matter what I did and which-a-way I done did it, her had a criticize for me. I loved me some Sus'Effie. Her were a good mama-in-law with me, I couldn't ask for better. But it ever did raise welts on my back, her picking at me about raising my childrens, so I don't mess with folks and how they raise theirs. Now, why I say all that?"

Yally had no idea, but Ná'Risa went immediately on, so it was clear the question had not been put to her.

"Whatever reason you' mama done had for keeping some thing from you, they's some things you ought for have been told about, and weren't, or you wouldn't have all these troubles in you' mind, or questions, neither. So I'm'a tell you some, though it might make me and you' mama fall-out for it. You know who Sis'Yela been?"

"Yes'm. She were my—" Yally paused to figure "—my great-great grandmamma, inna? Weren't that Nana'Effi mama?"

Ná'Risa smiled. "Good for you," she said. "Yes it were. And she were the one what you been name for. Well, Sister Timbi and Sis'Yela, they been good friend back at Bethelia."

Yally felt a thrill go through her, as she saw that just for the asking, a treasure chest of Yelesaw and family secrets was suddenly being opened up before her eyes. Had it always been that easy, had she only bothered to ask the right questions, or the right person? And then, through the morning as they worked on the washing of the clothes, Yally listened with great attention as Ná'Risa took her back to the slavery-times, and Old Maw'se Grady, and the people who lived at Bethelia Plantation…

JIM GRADY ALLOWED a few of the favored hands at Bethelia to keep their own hog pens near the trees back behind their cabins. It was one of his theories of slave management, giving the niggers small ownership rights. The hogs were bartered back and forth between the darkies in some complicated trade system that Grady little understood, and were fed from the pickings of the personal gardens he also allowed his hands. It kept the niggers happy and busy in their off hours, and put some needed meat on their bones while costing Jim Grady nothing except for the first two or three of his own brood sows he contributed at the very start. A good deal all-around, he would think to himself, giving a small smile through a puff of good Carolina tobacco-smoke coming up from his pipe. A good deal, all-around, yes, indeed.

WHEN LITTLE YELA WAS OLD ENOUGH, she would go with her mother in the morning for the hog feeding. It was the highlight of her day. The hogs would raise themselves up from their cornhusk beds and set up a snorting and snuffling as soon as the mother and daughter started across the field. The hogs would race for the near side of the pen, slamming against the slats as they shouldered each other for the best spot, quick-grunting, squealing, their quivering snouts stretched out through the open spaces. The girl would stand on the bottom rung and fling the leavings over the top, just to watch the hogs scramble for it, or drop down on her knees and let them slop it out of her open palm.

One morning in the early fall, the father went with them down to the pen, along with the mother's brother. That morning the hogs hung back instead of pressing forward, huddling in the corner furthest away, and would not move any closer. The girl could not figure why. The father had the axe with him, but the father was always carrying something in his hand, axe or hammer or hoe or rice-knife, and neither his presence or the uncle's at the pen was anything unusual.

"What wrong with them pigs, Mama?" the girl asked her mother.

"It be the killing time," the mother replied. "Them ain't so dumb as you think. Them knows it."

The father and the uncle hopped the fence into the pen and coming from opposite sides, cut out one of the hogs from the pack and cornered it in the far end while the others scattered away. The trapped animal made a dash to break away but the father knew what was coming, and was the quicker. The father swung the axe in a swift, compact arc, striking the hog in the back of the head with the butt-end and dropping it to its knees. The hog struggled to raise up again on trembling legs but before it could, the uncle had dropped down into the mud beside it, and with a knife that seemed to come from nowhere, raked across the the hog's throat. A bright spurt of blood shot out across the uncle, drenching the father's arm and shoulder before he could pull back.

The girl had been peering through the fence slats, watching all of this with fascination, but when she saw the great bloody arc, she gave a sharp intake of breath, and turned her head away and tried to bury her face in the mother's skirts.

But the mother took a step back and said "Uh-uh, girl, you ain't hide from the supper table, you ain't hide from the fixings." She grabbed the girl by the back of her neck and turned her face to the slaughter. The girl had closed her eyes, tight, but when the mother said sharply, "Open them things," the girl, always obedient, opened them back up again. But she would not look at the hog, which was still jerking sharply on the ground as its blood soaked into the dirt. Instead, the girl looked imploringly at the mother and pleaded, "I ain't want for see that, Mama."

"Then look at the back of you' eyes," the mother told her.

The girl did not understand what the mother meant, and when she tried it, the mother put her fists on her long hips and shook with the laughing.

"I ain't tell you for look korry-eye," the mother said. "Look at the back, not outten the two-sides."

The girl was now completely confused.

"I ain't know how for do it, Mama," she said.

The mother stopped laughing. "Alright, child," she said. "Why you figure the catfish head don't fill with water through he eye whiles he be swimming in the creek?"

"I ain't know," the girl answered.

"'Cause he eyeball got a cover," the mother said. She leaned down and held the girl's eyelid between her finger and thumb. "I ain't talking 'bout he eyelid. The catfish ain't got no eyelid. Him only got him a cover. H'it ain't nothing you can see from the outside, but it there, sure-enough. You better'n old catfish. You got both, eyelid and cover. So's when you got for look at something you ain't want for see, and you can't close you' eyelid, you pull down them covers and look at the back of'em. Now go-on, girl. Try it again."

The girl tried it. She frowned up and squinted her eyes, first focusing and then unfocusing, trying to discover the location of this newly-identified portion of her anatomy. In a moment, her vision began to blur. She relaxed her brow and as she did, the cloud grew over her sight. Light and shadow merged, and colors blended, and figures danced in front of her, but faint and blurred and unidentifiable. The sound of the squealing pigs grew dim and distant. The mother put a hand on the top of her head and the girl blinked, and the mother's face was before her again, as sharp as ever.

"You ever do rememberate that, girl," the mother said. "It plenty a time on this old buckra' plantation, there be thing you need for ain't see."

The little girl, Effie, always remembered the incident at the hog-killing time, and told of it in a story, often, to her own children when she became a woman grown.

MAMA'EFFI COULD NEVER REMEMBER the exact age she was when the Death-Rain hit, the Ha'Woola, as the old ones called it.

*Folk didn't keep up with them kind of thing exactly like they does now (she would tell the younger ones who had not been born back in those times). I were just getting up old enough for have childrens of my own, but I were still living with my Mama and my Papa and my baby brother, Poso.*

*The storm come up one evening in the spring of the year. It were just after supper. Mama ain't been to the house. Me and Papa and Poso was sitting by the chimney waiting for some yam-potatoes to cook.*

*It ain't give no warning. It drop black-dark outside, of a sudden, and a howling wind took up. Papa look up and say, "What that is?" and then it hit 'fore him could say anything else, or anyone'a we could answer. It come busting through we house like the railroad train 'cross to Cashville, sent the house to kindling and knocked the chimney flat over on Papa and my baby brother. One of them stone gone flying and catch me in the cheekbone. You see that scar and where the bone done cave in right there? The Woola done that. And that chimney-falling, it crush little Poso dead up under it, and it come down right on Papa chest. I set up there with the rain coming down all over my head and hold Papa hand 'til the light gone'd out of he eye. I been, maybe, eleven year, or twelve, when the Death-Rain come. That night I come up into a 'uman-grown. It weren't long after that, I jump-broom with Leem, and we take up house together.*

*That old storm took many folk with it when it come and gone'd. We wasn't the only ones. It were much moaning and misery in the Quarters for day and day after that.*

*Now Maw'se Grady, him ain't like no niggers straight offen the block, and weren't much for trading niggers from close'by, neither. Used to say him done like he nigger like he like he horse; iffen him ain't see'd them in the foalin', him couldn't never trust how they might run in the mud. But after that bad rain hit that year, we was something short-handed in them fields, with so many gone, and so many too brok'ed'ed up to do much good out there. So when thing done settle down a bit, Maw'se Grady got in he wagon and gone'd 'cross to the auction house down to Charleston. And when him come back, he had him six or seven nigger in the wagon along with him. And one of them, it were the one what they call Panni.*

*I ain't seen much of that Panni, the first him been at Bethelia. They had a place down at the end of the Quarters them times where the men's lived what had moved out from they folks but ain't tak'ed up steady with a 'uman as yet—we called it Randytown—and wouldn't no respectable marry-up 'uman go down that way. And if I seen that Panni in the fields or walking roundabout someplace, I ain't paid him no attention. I been fresh marry, and the only man my mind been on in them days were my Leem.*

*But I run into him when I been coming back from the fish-creek one time, and I notice him that day, for sure, and I ain't disremember him not never after that.*

*That time, there still been plenty of tree what come down during the storm, and you had to climb through the limb of one what been block-over the fish-creek path. I were just coming out of them branches 'fore step down onto the path, when here been that one name Panni, coming up from the other side, blocking my way, and he ain't look like he had a mind to move aside. I been something of a sass-mouth girl back then— you wouldn't know it now, would you?—and I tell that man straight-out, "You ain't fixing to move, nigger?" But 'stead of him stepping back like a proper man would, or saying something chas'tizing like a low-class nigger, him just put out he hand for help me. And dumb old me, I ain't done nothing but pass over my cane-poles and fishbucket to that man and then give him my hand, and when he touch me, it been a shivering inside of me, right in my belly, like I done eat too much'a cabbage-and-rice.*

*When I got down out that tree, he ain't turn my hand go right-'way, he just hold onto it and look at me with them eye. That nigger had the gator-eye, you know what I'm talking about? Lazy-lid eye what look like him be sleeping and 'wake, all-two at once. And he look at me with them lazy gator-eye and tol'ded me, "You name him Papi." And when I ask him what the hang he been talking about, he tell me I done working on having me a baby boy, and I must name him Papi.*

*Oh, ya! I run straight to my Mama house with that—ain't I?— cane-pole and fishbucket just'a flying every whichaway, and tell her I fixing to have me and Leem' baby. And Mama tell me no, her ain't believe so, she been checking me all along. But I tell her for check me again and she did, and when her did, she tell me I been right, and how I know something like that before she did. And I tell her about meeting that nigger they call Panni on the way back from the fish-creek, and what him tol'ded me, and her say, "Well, that sound like a Hap'a'way man to me, sure-enough."*

*I ain't know if I see'd that Hap'a'way more after that than before, but I sure notice him more. After he called out my first boy on the path there, I ain't never stopped paying him attention, ever after. Every time I see'd him after that, I had my eye on him, and I notice something 'bout him, right-way. He had him a way of disappearing, like I ain't never see'd. You'd be looking at him and he'd be walking across the field or through the Quarters or something, and wouldn't be nothing unusual, and then you'd look away, and when you'd look back, he'd be flat-gone, like he never done ever been there, and you couldn't see what way him been gone that fast. Mama say, him been passing over to t'other side, when him do that, and that where him go for see the thing him be seeing.*

*NOW SISTER TIMBI, all'a time I know'd her, her been living by sheself out by what they used to call Yellowpond, a ways off from the Quarters. She were the only nigger at Bethelia what could live out' the Quarters. She had she a husband and childrens one time, but she husband and most of she childrens, they died in one'a the fever, and after that, she give up the rest of the childrens to she sister, and move out to the pond. All that happen before I been borned. What I known of her, she been a root'uman, and she been a midwife, and the whitefolk all been 'feared after her. Niggers, they wasn't too crazy about her, neitherways. Niggers would call her for medicine or root-work or for birthing baby, but up until the one call Panni come to Bethelia, my mama been the only one Sister Timbi would take up any time with. My mama were a 'dusi she own self, and Sister Timbi would come by sometime and they'd sit over the fire and talk they spirit-talk, lots'a evening.*

*Sister Timbi come to my mama house one evening when I been there—that were just after I told my mama I been pregnant—and she check my belly for me. Whiles she were checking me, she ask if it were true, a two-head man had touch my hand and mark the baby and name it. When I tells her yes, she tell me ain't my mama tell me nothing, must never let a two-head man touch me when I'm pregnant, else my baby come out with the feets turned back'a'ways. She spit the ground three time and make a sign 'round it with she toe and with she thumb, and get up right then and said she fixing to find that two-head man sheself and stop him from marking Bethelia baby, and gone. And afterward, I been something scared, and I ask Mama iffen it been for-true, my baby would come out with the feets turned back'a'ways, but she tell me she done already fix up a soup for me and been feeding me with it all along since I seen that man on the path, so not to worry over it none.*

*NOW OLD MAW'SE GRADY, him like for brag in front'the house-folk how he'd done gypsied that old Charleston trader when he gone and got that six or seven head that time, because he'd done got that Panni one on the cheap, for such a good rice-hand. But what some'a the hands at Bethelia said they done heard, that Hap'a'way come cheap because him been a run'way nigger. He'd done gone'd to the swamp twice't down to Savannah before they brunged him up to Charleston to the block. The Hap'a'way told some'a them niggers to Bethelia, the buckra wouldn't'a caughtten him either time, neither, but him had for come close-in for t'ief food and such. Him been'a study-up on running'way again, but this time, him'a plan for take a pack'a nigger with him, so's they could stay back in the woods and make they way on they own, and not have for come back in for nothing.*

*WELL, IF SUS'TIMBI went down to fix that old Hap'a'way, it might done been, he turn it 'round and charm her the first. If that the way it happen, he been the only nigger at Bethelia what ever been able to do that, that I knowed or heard of. Anyways, whoever done what to who, there been plenty in the Quarters what say Sister Timbi and that Hap'a'way nigger done j'ine-up with each other after that. I couldn't say. I ain't never seen the two'a them together, and I ain't know iffen she ever gone'd down to Randytown for 'wisit with him. But plenty others, they gone'd over there. The old oba'see had put the Hap'a'way in a cabin with two-three other hands, but right-off he built him he own place, a little ways away from everybodys else. And after'while, the niggers used to come in pack for set out on the ground outside he shack for sing and do the pigeon-hop and such as that. Old Maw'se, he like'ded he nigger' for dance and sing, so that didn't bother him the first. But other thing about the Hap'a'way, it done a torment to him.*

*It been some troubling thing gone on after that Hap'a'way come to Bethelia. Three months running after he come, there been a blood moon in the sky. And on the fourth month, a calf been done borned with no eye, and a shoat with no front feets, and they say the calf talk like a natural person 'til they took the axe to he neck and chop he head off. And after that, the Sugaree Lights done start-up. Maw'se used'ta let some of the niggers night-hunt out near the Old Swamp, and they come back talking about the lights they done seen out on the bog, and the chanting and the wailing they done hear, and when they come-up closer to it, the closer they come, the more chill that get to the air. You couldn't get them mens to go back down to the Swamp in the night after that, not for beans or cornbread or a bowlegg'ded woman or nothing. And folk done started saying it been Sister Timbi and the Hap'a'way nigger out there, working they spell. And everybody say it been something fixing to happen. It happen, but ain't the way nobodys figure, and it weren't until after my Papi been done borned.*

COOMBS WAS BETHELIA'S HUNT NIGGER. He kept Maw'se Grady's hunt dogs and for that, he had a privileged place at Bethelia, with his own shack close to the Big House. Coombs always told the other Bethelia hands that Maw'se Grady had put Coombs up in that shack so that Coombs could be close to Maw'se, but Maw'se had really put him there so that he could watch over the dog pens at night.

Coombs had one other thing at Bethelia that he kept watch over, a redboned Quarters woman named Titi, of whom he was wildly jealous. He suspected her of entertaining other men in her cabin and so sometimes, when he was not watching the dogs, he would walk down to the Quarters late in the night and lay out in the woods near her cabin, knife at the ready, to see if he could catch her in the act.

He crouched down just behind a sand-ridge on the woods-edge an hour or so after midnight one night in mid March, silent and unmoving like the hunter he was, darker than the black earth around him, chewing on a bit of sassafras bark to keep himself awake. A misting fog had crept up from the pond, spreading out over fields and woods and covering the bottoms of the Quarters cabins.

On this night, his vigil was rewarded. Without any noise or other warning, a single figure—visible in the dark only to keen hunting-eyes like Coombs' own—came out between the jumble of cabins from the far end of the Quarters, moving in the direction of Titi's, crouched down like the fellow was trying to keep from being detected.

In his hiding place along the ridge, Coombs tensed and then gathered his legs under him, his fingers tightening around his gutting knife. He intended to wait only until the interloper got to Titi's door, whereon it was his intention to slip up and catch the boy both in the act and somewhere in the back of his shoulder. But before Coombs could do that, something made him pause.

A second figure came from in between the cabins where the first had emerged, following in the first one's footsteps, creeping along only a few feet behind. That caused Coombs to ease himself back down behind the sand-ridge, only his eyes peeping over, and

making him re-evaluate his plan. He could sneak up and surprise
and throttle one nigger, easy, but never two. Still, his anger fought
in the dark with his caution, thinking that Titi was such a whorish
woman, she was keeping company with two men at a time. He felt
in his pocket to see if he'd brought some matches with him. He'd
just have to burn-up the whole lot of them, shack, niggers, and
Titi, too. He'd just have to wait until they both got inside and got
settled.

They never did. Instead, in quick succession, another figure
emerged from the far cabins, then another and another, until
there was a whole line of them moving along the edge of the
cabins, ten or twelve, from what Coombs could make out, all of
them bent low like the first two. Then, before they reached Titi's
cabin, they turned into the field, making their way across it almost
straight at him.

His heart thumping, he spread himself down as flat as he
could get, his palms and the balls of his feet bracing against the
ground, so that he could stay hidden and undetected or either
bolt up and run, whatever was needed. The figures moved so
silent—they seemed to float across the field through the fog rather
than walk through it like normal people, their legs hidden in the
mist—that he was convinced now that they must be ha'nts.
Coombs was not afraid of ha'nts, but he preferred them at a
distance, not floating over him, and the thought that they might
be aware of his presence and, in fact, might actually be coming for
*him*, made him feel an uncomfortable looseness in his privates.

They only came within several yards of him, however, before
they turned at an angle, crossed the sand-ridge a little ways up, and
headed towards the woods in the direction of Yellowpond, never
seeming to notice Coombs where he lay hidden. They were mere
shadows moving through deeper shadows as they reached the
woods-edge, but Coombs had night-eyes, and he could still make
them out against the black backdrop. As the last of them was
moving into the trees, one of the figures stumbled, maybe over a
root, and the one behind moved quickly forward and caught its
companion by the arm. They both steadied and then, just like that,
the procession was all gone into the trees, the fields and woods
and Quarters dark and quiet again in the bank of fog, as if nothing
had passed that way.

Silent as he could, Coombs raised up on his palms and peered
down into the woods where the procession had disappeared. He
could see nothing that way now except a darker mass of trees

against the dark, open space of the night sky. He let himself back down and lay there on the ground for a moment, considering.

"I ain't never made no study'a ha'ants," he said to himself, "but I knows me two things. Ha'nts ain't trip, but niggers do. And what business niggers got in the woods, this time'a night?"

He jumped up and took off running towards the Big House, and within a half an hour, the hallooing of hounds woke up the people in the Quarters.

ALL NIGHT a troop of armed overseers tracked the runaways on horseback, and all the next day, too, through the fens and marshes and bramble-patches and cypress forests that ran down into the Swamp from the Bethelia Plantation grounds. Along towards dusk they thought they had cornered some of the group at the end of a finger of land that jutted out into a shallow half-bay, but the runaways took a chance, leaping out into the slimy black waters, half-swimming, half-running, crossing in a storm of flailing arms and legs, and then passed over into a deep palmetto thicket just ahead of the bounding dogs. The horsemen followed hot behind, coming to a halt only when the thickets closed in too close for the horses to pass. There they sat for a moment on their quivering mounts, their rifles at ready across their laps, the steam from the horse's hot withers rising up in their faces, listening to the baying of the hounds. The baying turned to a frantic barking, a signal that the dogs had brought something to corner, but then the barking rose in pitch, ending in high screams, and then, dead silence.

It took more than an hour for the overseers to find out why. Making their way around the thicket they came to a weed-choked, brackish pool, where three of the niggerdogs were found lying in a jumbled pile, eyes open, tongues out, gutted, their blood seeping in widening circles out across the black-green surface of the water. Beyond that, the swamp-pools with their cypress sentinels stretched out in dark silence. Nothing moved, and from that eerie sanctuary, no sound came back, only a feeling of a heavy coldness that ran a quick chill over the trackers' bodies. It was growing dark by then, too late to travel into the heart of the Swamp, and so they turned back, the dead dogs tied down and laid across the backs of their mounts, behind their saddles.

The dogs were Jim Grady's heart. Coombs was the dog-nigger at Bethelia, but it was Maw'se Grady who had handled each one as they came out of the mother bitches' bellies, stroked them, fed them himself, raised them in a kennel close to the house, strutted them proud in front of visitors, hunted them in the surrounding woods, ran them in competitions with his neighbors, studded them out around the Lowcountry. When the overseers came back to the Big House yard with three of his beloved great dogs laid out dead and butchered like so much supper meat, they thought the master of Bethelia was going to go insane right there in front of them. He jumped off the porch and ran to the horses, pulling off each dog in turn and embracing it like a woman, the blood and mud-stink splotching his face and arms and the white front of his shirt, and then, finally, sank to his knees in the yard between them, crying inconsolably. One of the overseers later told his wife that the sound of Jim Grady's wailing "was like a Donegal banshee, I'll tell you, and then that black nigger, Coombs, come up and took it up like a whooping Cherokee, and the two of them given me the Sweet Jesus shakes to hear it. Coombs was broke up over them dogs, but I couldn't say which one Maw'se Jim took the worst: coming back without them runaways, or coming back with them dead dogs." By then, one of Jim Grady's sons had sent two of the drivers into the Quarters to wake the niggers up and take a count. Eleven head were gone, one of them the new nigger, Panni.

As soon as it was light, a new party went out to hunt the runaways down in the Swamp.

*IT BEEN TO THE EVENING, mought been two night later, maybe three, I heer'd the calling bell ringing through the Quarters, and the oba'see's riding through on they horses, banging on the cabin' with fist and stick, hollering for we for come out, Maw'se want all he nigger on the ground. Leem try for take me out with him, but I wouldn't go. I ain't afeared for my own self, but I had Papi at my ninny, then, and I ain't know what bad thing I might be seeing out there that night, for give my child vision the rest of he days through my milk. But Mama come up and make a sign over the baby, and tell me when we get out there for look out the back'a my eyes, so I give'd in, and let the two of them take me and my baby outside.*

*They been herding all the niggers down towards Yellowpond, and the Quarters 'most been empty by the time we get out on the path. Maw'se Jo'sup—that been one'a Maw'se Grady son—him been rounding up the stray. Him been a holler and a holler—I can't recollect now what him been'a saying, I been all confuse up in my head, so much thing been'a happen—but when Maw'se Jo'sup come up on us on he horse, he lean down to say something low in Leem' ear, and I heer'ed that good. Him tell Leem that he pap done got the high fever that night, and when we get down to the water, we must get so he's between us and Maw'se, him ain't want Maw'se for hurt my baby. I won't never forget that. And when Leem ask Maw'se Jo'sup where they been taking we, him say down to the pond, they done cotched some of the run'ways. So we follow Maw'se Jo'sup and the crowd down to the water.*

YELLOWPOND WAS ABLAZE with light. A full moon hung in the black sky at the edge of the trees, big and yellow and bloated, and the torchflames held aloft by several plantation hands chased its reflection over the restless brackish pondwaters like a hundred dancing hags. The oba'see's sat on their horses, shotguns like sentinels pointing in the air, the horses skittish, nostrils wide, stamping and turning like children's tops in their spots, so that the men riding them had to hold tight to the reins with their free hands, jerking, shouting, to keep their mounts from trampling the hands and servants, or running away.

The long string of black folk—field and house intermixed—stood in a dark semicircle along the bank of the pond, swaying back and forth in rhythm as one, some folding and unfolding their arms across their chests, shuffling their feet in the sandy ground, not a one's thoughts wandering, not even the little children taking their eyes off the four captives kneeled down in the mud at the ponds-edge, all trussed together at the neck and the ankles, like the dozen-heads at the nigger-blocks in Charleston.

They had already tied the crocus-sacks over their heads and set them facing the pond, so close to the edge that the cold waters lapped at their knees. Even without seeing their faces, Effi recognized them by their bent-over forms.

Big lazy-eyed Wanadzi, strong as two mules, who had courted Effi in the time before she'd taken up with Leem.

Leega, the little pretty boy, who had often kept them up late-nights with his dancing antics 'round and 'round the fire.

The old man, Lanty, who did carpentry-work.

The one woman of the caught group, Nina, who had often washed clothes with Effi by the creekwaters running into that same pond, and who sang whenever she worked and wherever she went, no matter the occasion, good or sorrowful. She was not singing now. Her head under the crocus-sack hood was bent down low over her breasts and she was not moving.

All of them had been regulars at the gatherings at Panni's cabin.

Effi had looked immediate for Panni among the captives but

he was not there, and she felt a stab of guilt and shame pierce her because her first feeling—instead of sadness for the ones caught—had been relief for one who was not. She looked around quickly and wondered if anyone in the crowd could read her thoughts, and then squeezed Papi against her breast, and Leem's shirtsleeve tighter with her other hand. She searched in the crowd for her mother, who had gotten separated in the jostling and confusion when they got to the pondbank, but could not see her anywhere.

Maw'se Isaac, Maw'se Grady's oldest son, was standing over the run'aways, leaning down and saying something to them in a low voice that most in the crowd could not hear. The Big Maw'se himself was standing next to him, not speaking, his face ashen-white and clammy-sweated, his chest heaving, his eyes wide and darting back and forth over the whole scene, his yellow hair wild over his head, like as if he had run all the way from the Big House out to the pond on foot.

Effi began to tremble, and could not stop, and she wrapped Papi tighter in her arms so that she would not drop him. It was going to be a dunking, she knew—everybody knew, that's why they were down at the pond—and a dunking weren't no good, not at all. It was the Big Maw'se' worst punishment and she had seen it before, more than once. Maw'se had done it first, in earlier years, in the horse trough, but had found that taking the most disobedient and rebellious of his niggers out upon the swaying waters of the pond was infinitely more frightening to them, and therefore more effective. They ran them out into the deepwater in the flatboat and laid them down on the edge and dunked the chastised's heads in and held it down, and the punished ones talking about it afterwards said they were kept under the water 'til the blood seemed to explode in their nostrils and eyes and the place where their skulls met the top of their necks, and bright, bursting lights arced across their vision. The crocus-sacks made it worse, holding the water against their nose and mouth, blackening out the light so that they lost all knowledge of whether they were in or out of the pond. Those who'd been dunked said it was like the passage over into death. Afterwards, if they were up for punishment again, they begged Maw'se for the whip or the strop or anything else. Nobody needed a dunking twice.

Yes, Effi had seen dunkings before. And with the memory of her dead brother and her dying father still fresh in her mind, and her newborn firstborn in her arms, she did not want to see any again.

Just as they were bringing the flatboat around the little boy, Leega, suddenly let out a wailing cry from under his crocus-sack that raced across the night air, splitting it in two.

"Please, don't, Maw'se. *Please*, don't! I's sorry I run'd. I 'clare I's sorry!" he called out.

Maw'se Grady did not seem to even notice, and Leega did not say anything more. An oba'see's hand was raised and a whip-end went down, striking the boy on the side of the head and knocking him sprawling into the water's shallows as the oba'see snatched him back up to his knees. His legs crumpled and could not support him, and so the oba'see, looking greatly irritated, had to hold little Leega up by the fabric of his shirt-back, Leega now trembling all over, head to foot, low sobs coming out from underneath his crocus-sack.

Look at the back of you' eyes, Effi felt her mother telling her from somewhere across the crowd. You won't see nothing. You don't need for see nothing.

The oba'sees were milling in between the servants and field-workers, eyes darting from dark face to dark face, watching intent, making sure they watched, that nobody closed their eyes, or looked away. That was the purpose for bringing the niggers down to the pond for the punishing, so they could all see.

They can make you watch, Effi's mother was telling her. They got that power. But they can't make you see.

Effi took a deep breath and shifted Papi in her arms, pulling herself closer to Leem so that the back of his arm settled into the hollow of her shoulder.

Some of the oba'sees had drawn the flatboat up to the bank, and were pulling the run'ways up to their feet because their hands were trussed behind their backs, and they could not get up on their own, even if they would have. Now there was a restless murmuring and movement among the black crowd, and the oba'sees drew their horses closer in and were looking quick, left and right, shotguns and rifles held away from their bodies, fingers nervous around the trigger guards. Effi let out her breath, and lifted her head up, her features motionless. By practice, it was long since she even had to squint-up. Only the pupils of her eyes narrowed. A grey film rose up over her eyes, and before it she saw dark, dancing figures, and the sound of singing was in her ears. Without moving, she felt herself stepping into another world, closing a veil behind her. Her breath grew slow—and low—and steady—and a calmness overtook her and lifted her up with it. She felt herself alternately dancing and then drifting, as if she were floating along the broad current of a calm river in a peaceful and mist-gray land.

And so she did not see the hooded run'ways led out onto the flatboat and set down squat-leg on the boards, or the boat poled out to the deep, yellow waters at the middle of the pond, or see one of the oba'sees take one of the run'ways by the back of the neck and push him suddenly down and out, so that his back bent and the hooded head was thrust under water for a long count— one—two—three—all the way to ten—and then pulled back up again, gurgling and straining for a brief beat, repeating the dunking a second time before going to the next captive. Head thrust down into the water—one—two—to ten again, and then up, and then down again, the two dunked captives now laid out, prone and splayed, on the floor of the flatboat, and the gasping for their breath could be heard across the thrashing waters. None of this Effi either saw or experienced.

Then to the third captive. Only later did Effi learn that it was the old man, Lanty. But before his head could be pushed into the water, he stiffened and braced against the boatboards, managing to reach with his shackled hands and just grab the cuff of the oba'see's coatsleeve, holding on with death's tight grip, so that when the oba'see pushed down on the back of his neck with all of his weight, he pulled the oba'see off balance. Both went tumbling over the side of the flatboat and into the water.

The oba'see reached back and grabbed the edge of the flatboat, but deep underwater now, Lanty still held onto his other arm. The weight of the two of them made the flatboat lurch and tip on its edge, and with shouts and cries, all that were on it, bound and hooded captives and oba'sees alike, slid over into the water. The flatboat rose up in the air like a great whale breeching and then turned over and slammed down, flat, on top of them.

Now fully away in another world and time, Effi did not even hear the great splashes, or the gasps and shrieks from the watching crowd.

She did not see the mad dash of men from the beach into the water, Quartersmen and house-hands and oba'sees, all, or the frantic swimming race to the pond's center, where death had dragged the figures down, or the dives into that cold, unfathomable dark where sinking hands clutched at them and threatened to pull the would-be rescuers down with the drowning.

Effi looked at the back of her eyes and did not see any of that, and did not learn until later that the four run'ways never came back out of the water that night, neither two of the oba'sees who had taken them out in the flatboat.

And she was glad, for the rest of her life, that she had not seen all these things, nor carried the visual memory of it with her, nor passed it on to her suckling child. All she knew of that part of the story, she heard from the others who were there on the pondbank that night.

THE WATERS WERE still again. The only sound coming from the pond was a quiet lapping against the bank, as if the events of the night had spent all of its energy, and it wanted only to be left in peace.

More than an hour had passed since the flatboat had tipped over, and the frantic search for survivors had long since ebbed, faltered, and died.

No-one was keeping the Quartersfolk or the house-hands by the pond now, but none of them had left to go back home. They were still milling around the bank in agitated confusion, some stamping their feet on the sand and pounding on their breasts or pulling at their hair in their grief. A dirge-song had been taken up and many had begun to spread mourning mud over their faces. The men who had returned from the water—both the two oba'sees who had been on the flatboat and come out and those who had gone in as rescuers—were laying about on the bank exhausted and discouraged, in no particular order, white men intermingled with black, chests heaving, staring into each other's eyes with looks of defeat and the shared vision of what they had seen down in the depths of those murk-black waters. The Big Maw'se had stood on the bank and watched until long after the last of the would-be rescuers had come back out of the water, standing apart from everyone else, looking with dead-vacant expressions out over the pond. Finally, his eyes still on the water, he backed against a sycamore tree and slid down to a seat on the ground. What was in his secret thoughts, if he shared the horror that everyone else felt in that night, he did not show to anyone around him.

Intent on the waters, he did not see her, at first.

She came down from the opposite end of the bank, walking with slow, purposeful strides along the pathway from the direction of her cabin, and with an uneasy murmur, the crowd pulled back, and allowed Nana'Timbi to pass.

Her hair was scarfless and wild over her head, and she had thrown off her dress and was naked, her old body sweat-drenched and glistening and ringed from her neck to her ankles with gray-white ash-markings. In the hush of the crowd that came with her entrance, the only sound that could be heard was the clanking of the copper bangles at her wrists and ankles. An oba'see's horse reared up in fear as she passed. It could not be calmed and raced madly away from the pondbank, the oba'see pulling fiercely at the reins to try to control its flight.

Nana'Timbi did not look to either side—not at the Quartersfolk, nor the house-hands nor the oba'sees—but kept her eyes direct on the Big Maw'se as she walked through the crowd toward him in his seat under the sycamore. He became aware of her, finally, as she was almost up on him, and scrambled quickly to his feet, his back against the tree, his eyes growing wide as it seemed she might come all the way to him and, maybe, put her hands upon his body. It was the first emotion he had shown since he had come out to the pond that night.

Nana'Timbi stopped a few feet in front of him and stood there for a moment, her fingers resting on her withered hips, looking her master up and down. She gave a quick laugh, head back and mouth full open, showing the uneven blackened knobs of her teeth.

"You does like my pond-water, Big Maw'se?" she asked him.

He did not answer, but only stared back at her, his expression deadening again, as if she were speaking in a language of which he had no knowledge and did not care to know.

Without warning she squatted down diretly in front of him, and as he watched, urinated deliberately on the ground in a hard patter through her naked, spread legs, the steam from her yellow piss rising up from the puddle she made in the sand. She stood up again, gave a long look at the business she had made on the ground and then shook herself from the shoulders down, animal-like.

"I done asks is you like my pond-water, Big Maw'se?" she said again.

He did not move and still did not answer.

All eyes in the hushed crowd were riveted on the two of them.

Nana'Timbi put her head back again and gave out another cackling laugh that echoed against the trees out on the other side of the pond, sounding as if the woods were laughing with her.

"Oh, it be *you* what be 'fraid now, inna', old Maw'se?" And when he still did not answer and showed no other reaction, hands held loose at his sides, she went on. "You is like for put fear on you' niggers, but you ain't so like the fear, you'self. And you ought for be 'feared, you old buckra. You done put the tutu in the water, yes you is. You done kill them niggers for nothing. You done put the death in the water, and can't nothing but the death can come back out again. Not no nothing else."

She squatted back down on her haunches and dipped her cupped hands into the puddle of urine she had made on the ground, which the ground did not seem to want to accept, and so it had not yet been absorbed. She closed her eyes and blew on the pisswater in her hand, and then, in one motion, swifter than an old woman should have been able to make, she stood up again and flung it out over the air towards Maw'se Grady, clapping her hands together, hard, as soon as she did. He jumped to get away from it, stumbling over a root and falling over backwards as he did, and with a cry of terror put his open hand over his face to keep the water from touching it.

But no water came down. With Timbi's clap, something in the dark night had snatched it away.

Nana'Timbi stretched her skinny arms wide on either side and worked the thick, toil-bent fingers of both hands in and out, rapid, in his direction.

"Mind, Maw'se," she said. "You done run-way from the water, tonight. But one day you fixing to need this-here water, and the water, it gon' run-way from *you*. You hear me, old Maw'se?"

The tone of her talk—like nothing a plantation nigger had any right to throw at her master—suddenly got his blood up, and realizing how he must look to his niggers and his men, his embarrassment made him lose his fear of her. Bracing himself against the tree, he got up from where he had fallen on the ground, his face now red and furious with anger. He took three quick steps towards the naked old root woman, raising his fist above his head as if to strike her a terrible blow. She did not flinch, but put one hand up in front of her and made a sign at him, pointing with three spread fingers, the ring finger held down with her thumb. It was a hoodoo sign to throw bad things out, not to ward them off. Along the bank behind her, many of the Quartersfolk and house servants gasped and covered their faces. Her gesture made Big Maw'se stop dead, holding his hand above her head, frozen, as if he were a statue, and then, saying something low and harsh under his breath, he turned abruptly on his boot-heel and walked away from her. One of the oba'sees was standing close by with his horse. The Big Maw'se brought the flat of his palm against the side of the man's head, who staggered back and let go of his horse. In one quick motion, Jim Grady was up and in the saddle. With a jerk of the reins and a quick kick with his boots, he sent the animal galloping up the path toward the Quarters and the Big House. Along the pondback, the only sounds now were the steadily diminishing thump of the horse's hooves on the sandy road, and Sister Timbi's long and shrieking laughter following him into the dark night.

"You hears me, Maw'se," she called after him. "You does hear me, yes you is."

LATER, after all had gone back to their cabins and doused their lights and settled into an uneasy, sleepless vigil on their pallets, they heard Nana'Timbi coming through the Quarters from her house out by the Yellowpond, singing her saltwater songs. No-one dared look out to see what she was about, or where she was going. She passed over in the direction of the Big House, and gradually, her singing died away into the night.

AT BREAKFAST-TIME, they heard the news. A couple of the house-hands came down to the Quarters to tell them that Timbi had gone up to the Big House that night, now clothed in a white dress, and had sat cross-legged on the lawn out in the front, singing and chanting so they could hear it in every room, and how she stayed out there like that, they didn't know, because a cold, talking wind blew across the grounds the whole of the night, rattling the panes and the shutters all around the Big House.

And Big Maw'se? Oh, Lordy. When the house-hands got back from the pond themselves, they had found that he had shut himself in his room, and would not come out or utter a word, except to send for his jug, and they had not seen him since. And then, when Miz Grady had looked out the window and seen the old black woman sitting out there on the lawn where she never would have expected a nigger to be, keeping a vigil on the house, the missus had let out a shriek, and took the two youngest boys with her to *her* room and locked *herself* in. Hearing that shriek and Timbi's chanting and singing, and peering through the windowpanes and seeing old Timbi for themselves, the servants had all scattered to hide, some of them fleeing to one of the servants' rooms in the back of the kitchen, which was the furthest part of the house from the front door and the lawn, and there they had spent much of the night with candles blazing, praying and singing themselves to drown out the sounds of Timbi from outside.

The two oldest sons, Isaac and Joseph, stayed out in the parlor, drinking, and if they went outside to confront the nigger woman out on the lawn, and if they slept on the parlor divans or went back up to their rooms, finally, to go to bed, none of the house servants ever knew, as the servants kept away from that part of the house all night.

Somewhere between three and four in the morning, they said—no-one dared to look in the face of a clock, for the bad luck it would bring—the singing from out on the lawn abruptly stopped. None of the servants would venture out there, not while it was dark. They stayed in the back, not a wink of sleep among the lot of them.

Some who were at the Big House that night later claimed they had heard a single gunshot, and then a scream, from out on the lawn before Nana'Timbi's singing had stopped. There was fierce disagreement, from those who said they'd heard it, over whether the shot had come from the upper floor of the Big House or from somewhere outside. And there were others in the house who said there had been no gunshot at all, but only a high-wailing from old Timbi that broke off short, ending in a sudden silence. In any event, all agreed that Timbi's singing had stopped sometime deep in the night, and when Coombs came up from his shack out by the dog pens at first light, he declared to all who would listen that he had found her stretched out, dead, on the front lawn. At least, Coombs surmised that she was dead, after going only close enough to be able to chunk two or three pebbles in her direction. Noting no movement from her body, he rushed into the Big House and slammed the door behind him. And the events of the last day had so shook them that nobody even took notice that a nigger had come into the Big House without summons, or had dared to slam Big Maw'se front door.

A BROODING, RESTLESS SILENCE hung over Bethelia all that day following the Yellowpond drownings. The work-bell did not ring that morning, and so most of the Quartersfolk did not go far from their homes. Some of the men went down to the pond in the morning to fetch the drowned ones from out of the water, hoping they would have better luck by daylight than they had the night before. They were there most of the day, crisscrossing the pond in boats, dragging the water for hours, and then afterwards squatting on their hams on the banks and watching for anything to rise to the surface. When they returned home after dusk they carried no bodies back with them, only puzzlement and more than a little fear on their faces, because no bodies were to be found.

The Quarters hands never went to the Big House unless on a special errand or if they were summoned, and there were no errands or summons strong enough to take them up that way on this day. But the house-hands continued to slip down to the Quarters all through the day to fetch more news.

Maw'se Grady stayed up in his room, alone, all that day, and for all the house servants knew, he might have been dead as well, as no sound at all came from behind his door. The missus sent for dinner for herself and the two youngest boys, and then supper, only opening the door a crack to take the trays, and not coming out. Both Maw'se Joseph and Maw'se Isaac had disappeared from the house by the time the house servants began stirring in the morning, and they were absent all day. The oba'sees, either by direct order or by inclination, kept away from the Big House that day, as well as from the Quarters and the fields. Except for the servants scurrying about their chores as fast and as quietly as they could manage, nothing stirred in the dim hallways of the Big House. And all that day, the old nigger woman, Timbi, lay prone on the front lawn, and not even the birds out of the sky flew near her. When the next night fell, a chill fog came up out of the Swamp and enveloped her body, and it disappeared from all sight.

Early the next morning, one of the house servants rushed back down to the Quarters with more word. The servants had awakened with a determination that they could not leave the woman out on the lawn any more. Whether she was dead or alive, they believed that her spirit would surely haunt them harder if they ignored her. But when they dressed in their clothes and dressed up their courage and went out on the front porch to attend to her, they found the front lawn was empty, and Timbi gone.

No-one ever admitted to observing how Timbi departed, whether she had actually been dead on that lawn for that day and two nights and had been removed by someone's—or something's—hand, or had only lay there trancing and got up on her own power when she was finished. But one thing was indisputable. Nana'Timbi was never seen at Bethelia again after that day. And many who felt that she had not been dead on the Big House lawn believed she made her way down into the Swamp to join the runaways who had fled there.

ON THAT DAY, the folk of the Quarters changed the name of Yellowpond where the four runaways and the two oba'sees had died, referring to it from then on as the Gaya, the place of tears, and all the people of Bethelia, black and white, went out of their way to avoid it if they could, and made signs in the sand along the way, both coming and going, if any errand or work ever forced them to go within its sight.

And Maw'se Grady himself, he never again went down to that pond, not for any reason, whatsoever.

"WHAT HAPPEN with them other folk?" the girl asked.

"Which other folk?"

"The other ones what gone down into the Swamp. The ones what ain't get theyself caughted. They been more than them four what got theyselves caught, inna'? What happen with them?"

Ná'Risa gave a small smile to herself. The girl, who had always been so shy with her, was now bold enough to sit at her table and ask questions, and insightful enough to know which ones should be asked. The day had turned into afternoon and they had transferred the talk to the kitchen table, where the elder woman had fixed coffee for the both of them.

"Them stay back there in the Swamp, I reckon," she answered.

"And they ain't never come'd back out?"

"Well, they was folk what would say that back in the old days, before we come outten Bethelia, they seen'em passing deep down through the woods sometime, just a glimpse, or hear'em singing late in the night, faroff. And the Sugaree Light, what the mens see's off the swampwater sometime, they say that be them swamp-people' torchlight down in there. And folk say they would come all'away out the Swamp and t'ief girl out the yard or in the field, iffen they catch'em by theyself."

Yally's eyes widened and she gave a sharp intake of breath.

"What them do that for?"

"Ain't for no harm, not that I reckon. It were mostly all men what make it all the way back there in the Swamp when they first run'way. And mens can't make it long without no womens being around, don't matter how tough they think they be. But that been longtime back, and ain't nobody hear nothing from them folk back up in that Swamp for year upon year. So maybe they's still back there, the childrens and grands of the ones what run'd, or maybe them all took off and left for other parts. I couldn't say, for sure."

"And what'bout what Nana'Timbi say about the water?" the girl asked.

"What about the water?" Ná'Risa asked back. She knew well what the girl was referring to, but she threw the question back at her because she didn't want the girl to know that this one had taken her by surprise. It had shown far more perception than even Ná'Risa had expected. The day was going far further, far better, than she had hoped.

"You said her had told the old Maw'se, he fixing to need the water but he run-way from it, but it gonna' run-way from him, someday. What her meant by that? Did the water run-way?"

The delay had given Ná'Risa time to frame her answer.

"You done hee'rd how the old Big House burn-up 'fore us walk outten Bethelia, inna'?" she asked.

"Yes'm."

"Well, what the old folks said, all the water at Bethelia dry-up all to dust the night of the fire. The well, the creek what run-down near the Quarters. The Yellowpond. Them say the water been dropping in them for day-and-day before that, but when that old house catch a'fire that night, they couldn't get more'n a bucket or so outten any of them. Said when them mens went out to the Yellowpond 'fore fetch water, it weren't nothing but a mudflat what you could walk all'a way 'crost. And two day after the fire been a hard-rain, and all the water come'd back, and fill the pond and ever'thing."

"Oh," the girl said, deep in thought now, as her mind turned the information over and over.

"Anyways, talking about mens—" and here Ná'Risa took a last sip of her coffee, then set the cup down and pushed it away from her "—I got one coming back from the field what stay here sometime, and iffen he can't sniff he supper when he hit that door, he get him a ornerishness on him to beat Gana's goat, and then I got for box it out of him." She balled up both her fist and her mouth in a way that made Yally break out in laughter. "And I reckon you got chore for do at you own house, so you better get," Ná'Risa continued.

She had thought about telling the girl not to reveal to her mother any of the stories that she had been told that day, but decided against it. The girl was smart enough to know that already. As smart as Ná'Risa had thought she would be.

For Yally's part, she left Ná'Risa and Papa'Tee's house feeling better than when she had come, as if it had been she who had been telling the stories all day, and not Ná'Risa. She still did not have the answer she wanted about her grandfather's return. But somehow, now, that seemed a somewhat easier burden for her to tote.

7

The Trouble At Jaeger's Cross

*(Winter, 1937)*

T he new year turned, bringing with it a long stretching-out of cold weather. One January morning of swollen gray clouds looking like the forerunner of a winter storm, Papa sent Dinky across to Cashville to sell one of the hogs at the stock auction. Dink would not think of making the trip without Cu'n Boo, of course, and they asked Papa's permission to bring Mookie along, as well. Yally had wanted Mookie's help in patching up several pieces of tin that had begun to loosen on Grandpa Budi's roof, but even though the three had left early in the morning, she knew that while Mookie would come right-back after the auction if he was by himself, Dink and Boo would take advantage of the winter slack season to stop in at one of the júk joints over in Jumptown. She did not expect them back until late, and so put off plans for the roof repairs for the day.

Late in the afternoon the rain finally began to fall, not quite the storm yet, but a dreary, drizzling rain that drove Mama and Big Soo and Yally inside to work on quilts. Yally had no special dislike for quilting, but she wished that she were riding in the wagon across the river, instead. While she had been to Cashville many

times, she had never been to Jumptown, but she had heard all the
tales, especially from Eshy. It was an ill-repute settlement on the
back-edge of town where the low-class niggers lived and
congregated. According to Eshy, the 'umens in Jumptown wore
the hems of their red dresses high up their thighs and danced 'til
the sweat ran down the hollow between their ninnies, while the
mens drank corn liquor and cold beer and gambled all day, and in
the joints they played blues music and danced themselves sweaty
and often cut each other up bloody afterwards, the mens and the
womens alike.

> *Down in the Jumptown*
> *It ain't no fun*
> *They be done shot you if you stand still*
> *Turn the dog out if you run*

She was not certain if she had sung the song out loud instead
of silent and to herself—she had the habit of doing that,
sometimes, without realizing—but when she looked up sharp at
Mama and Big Soo across the table, both of them were absorbed in
their work, and apparently hadn't heard anything. The only sound
in the kitchen was from a pot of black-eyes and sidemeat, which
had been simmering on the stove all afternoon and was making
the pot top rattle up and down with puffs of sweaty, aromatic
steam. There were yam-potatoes banked in the coals, as well, and
the smell of it all had begun to announce that suppertime had
come, and Yally was just thinking of asking Mama if it was time to
go out and fetch Papa from out by the pens when they heard the
sound of feet on the back steps and then a sharp banging on the
back door.

"Someone sure-enough in a terrible hurry," Big Soo said, to
no-one in particular, "and ain't got the manners for come to the
front."

"Don't bust the door down, whomsoever you is!" Mama
hollered out. "It ain't latch!"

The door jutted open slightly and a head thrust in. It was one
of the Manigault cousins, Wawa, his eyes wide and his mouth open
and panting, as if he had run a long ways. He looked quick around
the room.

"Where Uncle Bo at?" he asked.

"Out to the barn," Mama said. Before she could say anything
else the door had slammed, and they could hear the sound of
Wawa running around the side of the house and then out through
the back yard.

They all stopped what they were doing. Mama and Big Soo exchanged quick glances and frowns, and then Mama was up on her feet and to the side window without Yally ever remembering how she got there, and had opened the shutter and was looking hard out into the rain. No-one said a word. Yally felt a great pit of fear gather in her stomach, the worst kind of fear, because it had nothing to latch itself onto.

In a moment, Mama closed the shutter and they heard the sound of footsteps coming up the back steps again. Papa came in the back door, water dripping off of his hat, which he did not bother to take off.

"What it be, Benjamin Kinlaw?" Mama asked him, her voice not reflecting the tension and worriation she was obviously feeling.

Papa did not break his stride towards the big bedroom. "Been some trouble cross'oba-the-river," he said over his shoulder.

Yally's body suddenly lost all knowledge of how to breathe, and she felt the air that was already in her lungs hold there, and begin to expand and burn. She saw Mama mouth the name "Mookie," but no sound came out, and she rushed into the bedroom behind Papa. Big Soo's hand paused in mid-stitch, and then she sat stone still at the table, watching the swaying of the bedroom curtain-door behind which both Papa and Mama had disappeared, the forgotten quilt settling back down on the table on its own. The sound of excited talking came from the bedroom, but the patter of the rain on the tin roof—steadily growing heavier now—drowned out any words.

They were back out of the bedroom in a moment, Papa resting his rifle in the crook of his arm. They walked past the table together without saying anything. At the back door they exchanged looks, and Mama put her hand on his shoulder, just for a second, and then he was out the door and gone. Mama kept the door open, and Yally could see Wawa walking away with her father towards the pens and sheds. Mama stayed at the door and watched out into the rain.

"What'a happen, Uly?" Big Soo asked her.

Mama gave a last look, closed the door, and came back to the table. "Them boys, them been in a fight with some whitefolk over at Jaeger's," she said.

All the air went out of Yally now in a great rush. But before a panic could take hold of her, Mama put her hand up and shook her head.

"Them all right, them all right," she said, and Yally knew it to be true, or otherwise Mama, while clearly concerned, could never have acted so calm. "Ain't none'a them getted hurt, and they all back'cross. They out to Lusi's. You' pap ain't know no more than that."

Big Soo started to rise up from the table.

"Us going out there?" she asked, but Mama shook her head.

"No," she said. "Best for we for stay inside. Bo going out there now. He say he'll fetch back word or come back heself and let we know what going on."

Yally wanted to ask more, but dared not. Mama's eyes had narrowed, and a thick veil had been drawn over them, discouraging any further questions. Mama sat down at the table and went back to her quilting, her fingers working automatically as she continued to watch the back doorway, not saying a word. Without realizing she was mimicking her mother, Yally did the same, watching the door as she stitched on her portion of the quilt, though what she was looking for, she was not quite sure. She looked back to Mama every now and again, to see if she could glean anything from her expression. She could not. She felt the rapid beating of her heart in her chest, like a hummingbird hitting its wings against a bone cage, trying desperately to get out.

Big Soo kept her eyes down and went on with her own quilting, and began to take up a humming, rocking back and forth in the chair as she did, pushing off with the balls of her bare feet.

They waited like that for what seemed like several hours but might only have been a few minutes, time having lost all sense for them. The sound of the beating rain picked up as it pounded on the roof. A wailing wind crossed the yard and played with the shutters at the windows as if trying to get inside.

Then came a low knock at the back door that was not the wind.

Yally jumped and held her palm over her chest. Big Soo looked up from her quilting at Mama, and some kind of understanding passed between them, without a single word being said.

The quilting dropped to the table and then slipped beneath it with a hushed, muffled sound and Big Soo stood up and glided across the floor on silent feet to the front door—quicker and quieter than Yally thought she could possibly move—and reached up and got the old shotgun down from its rack above the door. She reached up again and got a shell from its place on the shelf, broke the barrel open and slipped the shell in, snapping the gun shut again, all in one fluid, unbroken motion. Yally watched the movements in a growing fear. The shotgun had been Papa's boyhood gun that he had brought with him when he had first married and come across to Yelesaw, and had not been used for many years, since he'd gotten his rifle. Yally wondered if it would even shoot.

Mama watched Big Soo without saying a word or moving and then, when her sister stood balancing the shotgun on her big forearm, the barrel pointed down towards the floor but in the direction of the back door, Mama called out, without a tremble in her voice or a trace of emotion, "Who?"

"Ya," the answer came back, through the door.

Yally closed her eyes in relief and took a long breath.

"Come on in, then, if that who you is," Mama said, quietly.

The door opened and Uncle Ya walked in, his pants and work-coat soaked, his own shotgun held loose in one hand. He looked quick around the room, his eyes lingering for a moment on Big Soo at the front door, still with the gun over her arm. He nodded at her, ever so slightly, and then looked across at Mama, who had remained in her seat at the table.

"Just checking on y'all," Ya said. "Just stay inside, and don't worry, none. We watching."

"Us ain't going nowheres," Mama said, and then Uncle Ya was out the back door again, calling over his shoulder "I'll be back directly" as he left and the door shut behind him. Big Soo walked back to the table and laid the shotgun on the floor next to her chair, sat down, and took up her quilting again as if nothing happened, but she was keeping her eyes, now, on both doors.

Yally could not stand it any more. She reached over and put a hand on her mother's forearm and drew her chair closer to where her mother was sitting.

"Is the whitefolk coming here, Mama?" she asked in a low voice that sounded nothing like anything of her own.

Mama looked across at her, and her eyes softened, for just a moment. She put her hand on top of Yally's where it held her forearm, and the warm, steadying touch was more comfort to Yally than anything her mother could possibly say. She noticed that her own hand had begun to tremble, and Mama pressed down on it, slightly, to still its movement.

"Go take them 'tatoes out the stove and move that pot," Mama said, evenly and quietly. "Wouldn't do for burn-up supper, would it?"

The girl was glad for something to do.

In her nervousness, she could not seem to figure out where things were supposed to go or even how they were supposed to be lifted, and she burned her hand on the hot pot rim and had to fetch some butter to ease the sting. She took so long at such a simple task that she had not finished moving the food when Uncle Ya came back in the back door, the shotgun still held in one hand, the rain running off his shoulders and pattering onto the floorboards. Keeping his hat and coat on, he sat down heavily at the table, as if glad to get a weary load off his feet, laying the shotgun on the floor next to his chair. Yally could see the strain set into his face. It came to her, guiltily, that his boy, Boo, had been one the three cousins gone across the river, guiltily because until just now she had not been considering the effects of all of this on anyone but her two brothers and Boo, themselves, and her own immediate family.

"What-all Bo did tell you?" he asked Mama.

"Said there been some trouble over to Jaeger's Store with the boys and them and some buckra, is all, and that they back'cross and up to Lusi's," Mama said, and now Yally could hear the emotion began to break, just a little, in her mother's voice. "Him say them alright."

"They alright," Uncle Ya said, nodding assurance. "Kess got them down to he hunt-shack. Ain't no buckra going down there, even if they knowed where to go. Anyways, we ain't taking no chances. We's watching everywhere."

Yally felt her head turning like a whirl-a-gig in the air.

"Anyways, I reckon some'a them might get hungry waiting out there. Had to pull 'em from they supper, and they ain't had time for fetch nothing with'em. They'd appreciate some of them yam-potatoes y'all got there, iffen you got enough."

When the potatoes were wrapped in a paper—all of them—Ya stood up and put them in one of his coat pockets.

"Cu'n Toot, he out by the chinaberry tree," he told Mama. "Iffen you wants him, just go out on the porch and whistle. Don't y'all go out in the yard, though, unless you really has to. Don't put no light out on the porch, and might be best, y'all dim the light inside here, a bit."

"Where you gon' be?" Mama asked him.

"I'm going back to Lusi's right now. Ain't know where, exactly, after that."

"I'm going, too," Mama said, standing up. She walked all the way across the room to the curtain-door in front of her bedroom, her steps as firm and purposeful as ever, but stopped there and turned back to the table as a thought struck her. "Why y'all think the buckra might be coming here?" she asked. "How buckra supposed to know where them boys does stay?"

"It been some oba'niggers in the mix-up, too," Ya said. "You' boy supposed to know one of them."

"Know him enough for them for know where we does live at?"

Ya put his hands up. "I couldn't say," he said. "They's a few nigger 'cross the river what know some of the lay over here. Might not know which house, but might know the road down into the Hill."

Mama snorted air out of her nose and disappeared behind the curtain-door. Ya watched her go and then turned to Big Soo. "How you doing, Sus'Sudi?' he asked her.

Big Soo grunted back at him.

He turned to Yally now for the first time and smiled at her.

"And what about you, babygirl?"

She raised her shoulders and cocked her head to the side and gave him back a weak smile of her own.

"It be alright," he said. "We ain't fixing to let nothing happen." He reached across and put his hand into her hair and rubbed it with his big fingers. She smiled back at him, but weakly. Something had *already* happened. She had a sudden, sharp aching for Grandpa Budi. If anyone would know how to handle problems with the buckra, it was her grandfather. But Grandpa was still off in the Swamp somewhere, mourning for Sister Orry. She wished hard, with all her thoughts, that he would come back, and come back tonight.

AS SOON AS Mama and Uncle Ya had gone out the back door, Big Soo got up, and leaving the shotgun where it lay under the table, walked to the back window and peeked out the crack in the shutter. She watched for a while and then, satisfied with whatever it was she had seen or not seen, she came back to the table, dimmed down the kerosene lamp a turn, and then walked into the girls bedroom and disappeared behind the curtain-door. Yally heard her rummaging around back there for a moment, and when her aunt came back out again, she had a thick, yellow candle in one hand, the wick already lit. Walking over to the front door Big Soo opened it, and the damp wind came into the house with a blast, flickering the candle-flame. Shielding the flame with one big forearm, Big Soo got down on her knees, turned the candle on its side, and let three dops of tallow-wax fall on the porch just outside the door in the shape of a triangle, the circles of wax as big as bo-dollars. When she was finished, she examined her work carefully, then shuffled backwards a little on her knees and repeated the procedure on the house floor, just inside the door. The points of the two wax-drop triangles now faced each other over the threshold of the house.

From her seat at the table, Yally watched in astonishment, her mouth half-open, her mind suddenly taken off the problems with her brothers and Cu'n Boo. She'd seen hoodoo marks before, of course, but she would not have thought anyone would dare to make them at Mama's doorstep, not even Big Soo. Whenever Mama got back, there was going to be pola-to-pay, she knew it. She wondered if any of them would be able to spend the night in the house.

Meanwhile, while she desperately wanted to ask Big Soo the meaning of what she was doing and the marks she was making, she dared not. She believed that the very asking would make her somehow complicit in Big Soo's act, and further, that Mama would, by some fashion, know. Mama always seemed to know what was going on in her house, even when she wasn't there.

Although she must have felt Yally's full attention on her, it had to be crossing the room so hard and loud, Big Soo did not acknowledge it or respond, but continued to go about her work with a methodical grimness about herself. She set the candle down on the floor, fished in her dress pocket, and pulled out a piece of charcoal. Bending back down again, she sketched out a rough black circle around the three wax dollops, first the ones on the porch, then the ones on the floor inside, then drew lines connecting the dollops and, after that, marked some symbols in charcoal on the floorboard below and above both circles, x's and other such marks that Yally could not quite make out from her seat at the table.

When Big Soo was finished with marking the symbols, she put the charcoal back in her dress pocket, took out a knife, scraped off the candle-drops with the flat of the blade and deposited them in her pocket with the charcoal. Then she lifted up the hem of the dress, hawked and spit on it, turned the hem over, and wiped away all traces of what she had just marked in charcoal on the porch and the floor. Then she stood up from the floor with a grunt, fetched the broom from beside the back door, opened the front door, and with quick strokes, swept the floorboards clear and all the remaining residue out on the porch and, from there, out into the yard and the rain.

Still not saying a word to Yally, not even looking at her as she went by, Big Soo walked to the back door with the candle and repeated the procedure she had done at the front, wax triangle dropping, charcoal marking, and then cleaning it all up again.

Her task completed, Big Soo blew out the candle, set the broom back in its place by the door, and walked into the girls bedroom. She was back out again shortly, a bundle of fabric scraps and two more unfinished quilts under her arm. She set them all in a pile next to her chair, sat down, put her bare feet on top of the shotgun stock under the table, pulled one of the quilts onto her lap, and took back to her sewing.

Yally sat across from her, not saying a word herself, staring at the spot before the back door where the symbols still must lay, but now invisible to the eye.

Big Soo suddenly stopped with her mending and looked up into her niece's eyes.

"You ain't got nothing for do?" she asked, sharply.

"Yes'm," Yally answered quickly, looking away from the back door.

"Then get to doing it. Just 'cause you' brother' and that Boo taking off, having they fun over'cross the river, ain't no need for you doing the same up in here."

There was no possible way to answer that without getting herself in trouble. Yally took one last look at the cleanswept spot in front of the back door, reached over for one of the quilts, and got to work herself.

THEY WORKED THROUGH THE NIGHT in the lowered lamplight with scarcely a word between them, listening to the woosh of the wind outside and the rain washing intermittently over the tin roof, Big Soo rocking back and forth on the back legs of her chair, humming softly to herself. Every once in a while a tap or a scratch would come at the back door and Big Soo would get up and walk over and open it a crack, hold a conversation too low for Yally to hear with someone outside that Yally could not see. These conversations never lasted for very long and did not seem to concern anything that needed doing something about, as each time Big Soo immediately afterwards returned to her seat at the table and her quilting. After a while Yally put on a pot of coffee, but she found after she took the first couple of sips that she hardly needed it. She couldn't have closed her eyes for a minute, even if she had tried.

They worked until the roosters began to give their morning calls out in the yard, about the time the far corners of the house began to grow more visible, signalling the coming dawn. Yally had just started on breakfast when they heard a set of footsteps on the front porch and a knocking at the front door this time.

Big Soo leaned forward and took her feet off the shotgun under the table.

"Who that is?" she called out.

"Bonk Jackson son, Sus'Manigault," came the answer. "Can I come in?"

"Come in if you coming, stay out there iffen you ain't," Big Soo called back.

It was Dokie Jackson, Lam's younger brother, who came in the door. His high-boots and pants were splotched with mud and, like everyone else who had been out that night, he was drenched wet from the rain. Giving his good mornings, he came up to the cookstove and turned around it slowly, first warming his frontside, then his back, then his front again, like a pig on a spit, the water coming off his clothes and falling onto the stovetop with loud hisses, or rising up towards the ceiling in transparent clouds of steam. He gave Yally and Big Soo a weary look through eyes that, like Lam's, were as large as their mother's. Sus'Oona Jackson was one of the few people at Yelesaw of whom Yally was genuinely and truly frightened. When angered, which was often, Sus'Jackson's eyes pushed out so much, she looked as if she were about to propel them at you like shells coming out of a shotgun barrel, as if the eyeballs themselves would burst in the air and spread out into pellets. But there was nothing frightening about Dokie, who usually had about himself a sort of boisterous, infectious goofiness. But this morning his large eyes were squinched-up and red, and he looked like he'd been up all night his own self, and done much traveling, as well. He gave Yally and Big Soo a smile showing the dark gap between his front two teeth, the smile not as wide and cheerfullish as his usual.

"Cu'n Kinlaw sent me for see iffen y'all alright," Dokie Jackson said, leaving the cookstove a little reluctantly and sitting down at the table. "Y'all alright?"

"We here," Big Soo said. "Him send word 'bout them boys?"

"Yes'm. They doing alright."

"How you does know?" Big Soo asked him, a little sharply. "You just fetching word, or you done see'd them?"

"I done see'd them, Sus'Manigault, and they's doing better than me," Dokie Jackson said. "I done been running back-and-forth down in them woods all the evening, and I ain't even had time for get more'n that much my stomach." He held up two fingers with just a small space between them. "Cu'n Kess got Dinky and Boo and Mookie shut up tight down in that shack. Them boy' ain't got nothing for do but eat supper and snack and supper again and push checks and slap dominos."

He glanced around the kitchen hopefully, and especially at Yally and her breakfast fixings, which had advanced to butts-meat frying in the pan and grits beginning to bubble in the pot. But intent upon the first direct news about her brothers and her cousin, Yally did not get the hint.

"They tell you what happen over to Jaeger's?" she asked him, breathless, from the countertop where she was slicing potatoes. "Nobody ain't done tell we nothing."

"Ain't nobody had for tell me," he said. "I been'ded there."

"Been'd where?"

"To Jaeger's. I been'd 'cross there when it all happen. And I'll trade you what I seen for some'a that sidemeat in that fry-pan."

Big Soo continued to stare across the table at him. If it had been anybody else but Dokie Jackson, they would have certainly long ago wilted under her penetrating look, but Dokie was generally unfazed at things like that.

"You been there with the fighting?" Big Soo asked him, as if she doubted what he had just said.

"Yes'm."

Big Soo turned to Yally. "Get that boy some't'eat, girl," she said. "You ain't see him'a hungry? Where you' upbringing done flow'ed to?"

"I'm sorry," Yally said, both to Big Soo and to Dokie Jackson. She was embarrassed that she had not offered him anything, but her mind had been far too frazzled to think of so many things at one time. "I'll get you a plate, Dokie. You want you some coffee whiles I'm fixing?" She put her hand around the pot. "It done cooled down. I'll put it back on the stove."

He smiled at her more generously, shaking his head and reached his hand out, beckoning with his fingers. "Cooled down is good-enough. Just gi'me here, please."

He gulped down the coffee as Yally scraped the sidemeat onto a plate and put the plate on the table in front of him. The sidemeat was gone before the grits were ready to be ladled out, and those soon followed the sidemeat, the plate scraped completely clean. Dokie Jackson took another cup of coffee while he was waiting for the potatoes to fry, and then pushed the chair back to give his stomach some room.

Big Soo had been watching him carefully from the other side of the table, and now she reached over and pulled the plate away from in front of him.

"That girl done fed you and you done et," she told him. "Now tell us what you seen over to Jaeger's."

"Thanky, ma'am," Dokie Jackson said to her, flashing his broadest smile. "Dink and Boo ever does say the Manigault womens burn the best on Yelesaw Neck, but I never believed it, not 'til right now. I sure hope y'all does invite me back for a real supper, when all this confusionment settle over." To Yally he pointed at the fry-pan and wided his eyes and mouthed the word "potatoes?" She smiled and nodded and mouthed back, "when they's ready" and dropped a stray scrap of butts-meat onto his plate, which Big Soo had pulled into the middle of the table.

"A h'ongry dog wag he tail at any back step what toss-out scrap," Big Soo said, still glaring at him. "Get on with you' story."

"Yes'm," Dokie Jackson said, still grinning and ignoring her glare. He leaned forward in his seat, picked up a last bit of meat from the plate, held it up in front of his face between his thumb and his forefinger, and said, "What happen over there were, me and my brother, Lam, us been coming back in the wagon from buy some supply for Papa over to Cashville, when we come up on a house 'crost the road across from Jaeger's Store."

Big Soo's glare at Dokie Jackson turned to a frown.

"What you talking 'bout, boy?" she said. "Ain't no house 'cross no road from Jaeger's."

"I ain't means 'cross the road, Sis'Manigault," Dokie answered, earnestly. "I means—" he paused to try to find the right word "— 'crost the road." He set his palms down on the table. "Flat-out 'crost it. Right in the middle of the road, blocking the way."

"A house?" Big Soo asked, as if she still did not believe him.

"Yes'm. You ain't been 'cross the river of late, I reckon, Sister Manigault, but they be done moving house up and down the road right and left over there, every day, getting ready for the flooding. They jacks them up on wheels and latches them to a truck, and there they goes, the house riding down the road like they been toting horse or rice sack or cotton. Anyways, this one was coming from out to Sandy Station, and I believe they been trying to make the turn onto the Cashville Road, and it been raining so, and one'a the wheel, it'a bog down in the ditch mud. So there it sat. Right-out 'crost the road. You does see, now?"

He looked hopefully at Big Soo, who only grunted. Yally nodded, however, to help him out, and so he went on, something of his infectious enthusiasm coming back.

"Ain't nobody never seen no house sitting in the middle of the road before, so's everybody's come out from Jaeger's Store to take a look, even old Mr. Jaeger, and all the truck and car and wagon what been going up and down the Cashville Road, or out from Sandy Station, them stop, and the folk been'a get out and look, too. It been some old Cottontown buckra been driving the truck, with a whole load of oba'nigger 'long with them, and they had them boys out there trying to jack up the wheel out of the mud with plank and pole and stuff, but you ever try for lift up the side of a house?"

He looked to Yally exclusively for his answer this time, and she shook her head no.

"Well, Dink and Boo and Mookie, they done already been out there when me and Lam get out there, and them been standing with the crowd watching them nigger try for jack-up that house. And you know folk, they been talking betwixt theyselves over whether them boys could lift up that house or no and most'a them been saying weren't no way. Some were even laying down bet.

"So one time, when they got the house most all-the-way jack-up, them planks slip and jump up, and flip all them nigger over into the mud. And you know old Boo, him a'laugh most the loudest, and then him say some thing I ain't think I should repeat in here—" he paused, gave a glance at Big Soo, and went on— "and one'a them oba'nigger ain't so like'ded what Boo had done say, 'cause him come right out the ditch and up in Boo face, and the two'a them went to it. They start out just talking. But iffen they went on talking them bad thing in each other face like that too long, one'a them were fixing to box the other one, sure. And Boo big, but that oba'nigger had him, heightways and weightways.

"That when one'a them Cottontown buckra walk up betwixt them and tell Boo him best not mess with that big oba'boy, 'cause he done seen that boy take on three nigger to-the-once't over to the mill at Sandy Station one time and whip'em good, but if Boo think he could take him, fist-to-fist, they'd make it a fair fight, and the buckra say he'd put up five dollar and a RC Cola if Boo could prove him wrong.

"Well Boo, him'a look that big oba'nigger up and down. Then him start to rubbing he shoulder, and stretching out he arm, and whirling it 'round and 'round, all'a time paining-up whiles he's doing the doing, like it hurting him so. And then Boo say he'd'a fight that big boy iffen he could, but he done strain up he arm that morning and ain't feel right-up for no fight. But him say him had him a little cousin 'long with him might step in for him and take that nigger on for the five dollar and the RC Cola, iffen that been all right. And Dinky step up out the crowd.

"Well, all'a we Yay'saw boy what been out there, we take to snickering at that, 'cause we all done seen enough'a Dinky tussling, some'a them oba'nigger, too, what he done wrestle at the stockyard or to the fair. But that big oba'nigger and that buckra, them ain't had no clue. Them look Dink up-and-down, and you could see them figuring in they heads, this fixing to be nothing but grandma-pluck-the-hen, and so them 'gree to the fight. And the whole crowd, we walks over to the yard at Jaeger's Store, and Dinky and that big oba'nigger they 'trow-off they shirt and square off, and get to getting.

"Well, y'all know Dinky. Him don't box worth a cussing at, but you can't let him get them big hands on you. That big oba'nigger swing at him two-three time, like to knock a tree down with the wind of it, but ain't come close to Dinky, and then Dink jump in and got that oba'nigger by the leg some kind'a'way, and there go that nigger, toes over nose, and Dink got him on the ground with he face in the sand, got one arm and one leg lock together like a arm and leg ain't supposed to go, 'til that oba'nigger slap the ground and holler 'Over. Over. Turn me go.' And that been it.

"Then Boo gone'd up to that Cottontown buckra for get he five dollar and he RC Cola—he been laughing all'a time him asking, 'cause he knowed they done put one over—but the buckra tell him he wouldn't t'row him a Indian nickel if it was heated in the fire and burning-up in he hand. He said the deal were for a fighting, fist-to-fist, but he ain't say nothing about no wrestling, called Dink *and* Boo a packle'a cheating, stealing bluegum, liverlip, tarhead, swamp-running neckerniggers and said him be goddamned iffen—"

Here Dokie Jackson stopped abruptly, putting his hand over his mouth in embarrassment and looking across the table at Big Soo. When Big Soo only stared back at him, saying nothing, he

looked quickly over at Yally, who could give him no advice, only
widened eyes, and so he decided to pretend he hadn't cursed and
continue on.

"Now Dink done dust heself off and him step up in it. And the
buckra cuss at Boo and Dink, and Dink—well—Dink don't hold
back, so Dink cuss him back. But Dink—" Dokie Jackson hesitated
again, fumbled with his words, and finally decided to keep
plowing—"well, y'all know Dink can't hardly talk when him get
excited, and he sure-enough was getting excited, so Boo jumped
back in and helped him, and now it been Boo and Dink and that
Cottontown buckra, all going at it."

"And ain't you neither you' brother think to help them out?"
Big Soo butted in. "Y'all just left them by theyselves?"

Dokie Jackson looked over at her helplessly. "Ain't seem like
the two of them needed no help, Sus'Manigault," he said, his voice
taking on a pleading tone. "After what Dink did to that big old
oba'nigger, weren't none of the rest of the nigger' in that crew
fixing to jump in, 'specially when they seen Dink been the littlest
one beween him and Boo. And wouldn't'a been no help needed at
all iffen that other cracker hadn't'a gone for he shotgun."

Yally had been somewhat enjoying the excitement over the
story of the confrontation, now that she knew the ultimate ending,
and her brothers and cousin were safe back across the river. But
this new twist made her take a quick intake of breath, and her
heart jumped. Meanwhile, Big Soo's dark brows met together in a
deep furrow, and she frowned across at Dokie Jackson with a look
that would have melted butter in a cold pan.

"What happen with the cracker and the shotgun?" she asked.
"Ain't nobody said nothing 'bout no cracker and a shotgun."

"That what 'cause all the confusionation, Sus'Manigault,"
Dokie Jackson said. "Weren't for that, nothing probably would'a
come to it. But that second buckra what been with them come out
the truck with the shotgun, and that when Mookie come up
behin'ded him and cold-cock him."

Big Soo stiffened at the mention of her favorite of the Kinlaw
boys, who she had forgotten while she had been following Dokie's
story, and Yally suddenly found her voice. "*Mookie?!*" she almost
shouted, her eyes wided up. "*Mookie* hit a whiteman?"

Dokie Jackson gave her a quick nod. "Yeah, Mookie. You
wouldn't'a known it, would you? Old quiet Mookie, ain't never
heered him raise he voice to a mule or a row of rice. We been
paying so much 'tention to Dink and Boo and that first buckra, we

ain't seen when the second one gone'd over to the truck. Mookie
must'a been watching him, though. I ain't never seen where
Mookie come from. There been the buckra walking from the truck
with he shotgun point to the ground, but in them boy' direction,
and I been thinking 'O! O! Him fixing to shoot them!', but then
Mookie been behind him, and BAM!—Mookie clock that buckra
side the head—" Dokie Jackson slammed his fist into the palm of
his other hand "—and there go the buckra one way, and the
shotgun t'other, and there go all'a'we to we wagon, and down the
road we go."

"*Mookie?*" Yally said again, still unbelieving.

Big Soo was still tensed up across the table from Dokie
Jackson. "That cracker shoot at them boy?" she asked.

Dokie nodded his head, yes, to Yally's question and then
turned and shook it, no, to Big Soo's.

"No, ma'am," he said. "Ain't had no chance for shoot. Mookie
hit him too quick. I ain't know iffen he been fixing to shoot,
nohow. Maybe just had it out for scare them boy'. But that weren't
nothing you could count on. You know how buckra is. 'Special
them one outten Cottontown."

Big Soo had settled back in her chair again with what looked
like a brief smile along her lips. She murmured something that
might have been "good for little Mookie" or something like that,
but Yally could not be sure, and anyway, her attention was all on
Dokie Jackson and his story.

While he had been talking, Yally had put the coffeepot back
on the stove, and when it had steamed out its readiness, poured
him another cupful. He stopped to take a long gulp of it now, and
then went on.

"It been me and Lam in one wagon and Boo and Dink and
Mookie in t'other, and it been like the Camptown Races, doohdah-
day. We gone down the cable-barge road, but we ain't know'ed
iffen them been coming after we or not, so's we turn off on a side
road after we get down a'ways. We hide the two wagon way down in
the woods back there, and tie down the two mule, and walk on out
to the river up'a'ways from the crossing, and got we a boat, and
come on'cross."

He stopped, coffee cup in hand, and looked from one to the
other of them, Big Soo to Yally, as if he expected some comment.

"So, y'all done lost all two the mule and the wagon," was all Big
Soo would say.

Dokie Jackson shook his head. "No, ma'am" he said, with a

grin. "Ain't lost'ded neither. After late-dark, Lam gone'd back 'cross in a boat with some'the other boys, and them fetch them all and take them up to we cousin' place, way up to Abraham, 'cross the county line. Them got them a nice-size farm up there. Ain't nobody fixing to notice. Them say them'a keep'em up there 'til all this done die down."

For a while, neither Big Soo nor Yally spoke.

Yally had sat back down and was rocking nervously in her chair, taking the whole story in. Finally, not caring that the question had already been asked and already answered, she asked Dokie Jackson, "But them all alright, ain't they, you said? Dink and Cu'n Boo? And Mookie?" She could think of nothing else to say.

"And eating much as you' sister can fix them," Dokie said. "Her fixing to spoil them boys like bad meat."

They both looked to Big Soo for comment.

"Fix that boy another plate," she said to Yally, with a grumble. "You ain't want him for sit at we table and starve, is you, after all that riding and walking? Or did they hide you' manners down in them woods with the wagon and the mule?"

While Dokie Jackson dove in greedily to his second helping of breakfast, Big Soo leaned back in her chair, closing her eyes and began to hum again. Although neither Yally nor Dokie Jackson could see it, under the table she set her bare feet down on the barrel and stock of the shotgun on the floor, pulled it closer to her, and began playing on the wood and metal with her toes, continuing to hum as she did, ignoring the other two in the room.

TWO DAYS LATER, the High Sheriff came across the river on the cable-barge and spent a day looking for the boys, making a great show of it, as only the Sheriff could. He had a deputy drive him around in his big black Ford car, and everywhere they stopped, the Sheriff—a tall, straw-haired man with wash-blue eyes over a narrow nose—would get out of the car and ask in a quiet but compelling voice if anyone knew the three colored boys who were being sought in connection with the assault on the white men in the yard at Jaeger's Store, calling them by their courthouse names, Michael and Daniel Kinlaw and Joseph Manigault. Though everyone he asked tried to be helpful, there was considerable confusion and argument over whose boys they were and, therefore, where they actually stayed. Almost every parent on Yelesaw was mentioned— except, of course, the real ones—and so the Sheriff's big Ford car took several trips up and down the River Road and then back along winding sand-roads into many settlements and yards, and, once, down a long, narrow stretch towards the ricefields that left them bog-stuck for several hours. A colored boy accompanied the Sheriff on the day's search, sitting timid and big-eyed in the back seat alongside a whiteman in work clothes. Everyone assumed the colored boy had been one of the oba'niggers in the back of the truck out at Jaeger's on the day of the fight. He never moved from the back seat of the car, leaning back in the shadows as deep as he could to keep from being seen. No-one recognized the whiteman in the work clothes, though some thought he might have been the Cottontown buckra who had been the driver of the truck that was pulling the house. Every time the High Sheriff got back into his car after talking with folks about the fugitive boys, they noted that he shared a word or two with the whiteman in the work clothes in the back as they were driving off.They spent most of the day on Yelesaw Neck and, when the sun began to drop behind the trees, drove back to the cable-barge and rode over to the other side. They did not find the three cousins, and they did not return.

YALLY WAS IN THE KITCHEN seasoning the supper pinto beans when she heard the roar of the Sheriff's big Ford car coming across the yard at Goat Hill. She had heard engine motors many times before, of course, but never on this side of the river, and the noise of it startled her so, she jumped and knocked the bowl from her lap, sending the beans rolling across the floor. There was a howling of dogs outside and the chickens took up a frantic cackling. Ignoring the beans, Yally went to the side window to join Mama, who had been at the counter cleaning fish with a knife. They watched the Sheriff's car roll past their house without pausing, neither the Sheriff nor the deputy driving even glancing their way, and continuing on towards the other end of the Hill, past Grandpa Budi's, and then pulling to a stop at one of the houses beyond.

As soon as the car motor turned off, Yally could hear a small knocking sound next to her. She turned and saw that Mama was tapping the point of the knife on the countertop as she watched the Sheriff's car across the way—tapping slowly, methodical, and pointed—until the Sheriff's car had taken off again and pulled to the far end of Goat Hill and out of their view. As soon as that happened, Mama murmured "damn-ass buckra" under her breath, then stopped her tapping and went back to her fish-cleaning. She sliced the belly of a fish with one swift, deliberate stroke, twisting the guts on the knifepoint and cutting them out, and then, without ever touching the leavings with her hand, flinging them away from her almost with distaste into the bucket next to her on the floor. The guts made a soft, splattering sound as they hit the other residue in the bucket. Mama herself, as she worked, continued to look out the open window at the far side of the yard where the Sheriff's car had disappeared. For the rest of the day, she made no more comment on the Sheriff's visit, and Yally made no effort to press her on it.

Until last year when the Old Socky had come over to try to talk folks into giving up their houses and moving, Yally had never seen a whiteman on Yelesaw Neck before. Now they were coming over in droves, and in cars. She felt as if the whole foundation of her world was slipping out from under her, leaving her with noplace solid on which to stand.

TENSION WAS HIGH among the whitefolks across the river after the Jaeger's Cross fight and it was not prudent for any Yay'saws to be seen over there, so they kept on their side of the river for many days. Somehow, Papa'Tee got word to the High Sheriff to set up a secret talk, and they met at a farmhouse over the county line in Berkeley County, where the Sheriff had family. The High Sheriff, Papa'Tee later reported back, had more things on his mind than a one punch roadside fistfight between niggers and poor whites that ended with nothing more than hurt feelings and a bruised head, and if it were up to him, he'd be willing to turn his back on the whole thing. It wasn't up to him, however, and he was feeling much pressure from Cantrell County's white citizens to get something done. But because the Sheriff could not figure whether finding and arresting the boys would cool things down amongst the whitefolk in the county or simply put more fat in the fire, he had not yet decided what to do. For now, the Sheriff told Papa'Tee, he was not going to go out of his way to find the boys, but he would not promise he wouldn't be back across the river for another run at them. It all depended on how hot the seat of his pants got from folks jabbing at him with their hot pokers.

For the time being, therefore, Papa'Tee thought it best that the boys stayed out of sight at Kess Butler's hunt-shack, and do nothing else.

AS ALWAYS, the tension slipped across the boundaries of Yally's mind and into her dreams.

Tonight she dreamed about fighting again, as she had been dreaming of fighting every night since Dokie Jackson had told them the story about the events at Jaeger's Cross. This time she was not in the store yard, however, but in the middle of a field, a familiar field which she had dreamed about several times before and which she seemed to remember vaguely from her days of early childhood but which she could never locate in waking times, and now could only visit in her dreams...

*...She was in the middle of the fight, and for a while there were shifting sides. Or, maybe, it was just the other side that was shifting. At first they were fighting against a crowd of white peoples, mens and womens, people from town who she could almost recognize, but not quite place. They were trading blow for blow. But then it devolved into a children's fight like they often had on the Hill, cousins against cousins, mostly wrestling, and her face was being pressed down into the grass so that she could not breathe, and she was struggling and trying to holler out that she needed air, but she could not get the words out because her throat was thick with grassclods and clotted earth, and there were many on top of her, and now they were white peoples again, no longer cousins, too many, and she thought if she could only shrug her shoulders she would throw them all off, but she could not even move her shoulders. She wanted to scream from the press of them upon her. And on the ground she saw a figure striding across the field, she could see the shiny boots and now a uniform and now it was the Sheriff—she recognized his beak of a nose—and in his hands was a shotgun, which he deliberately raised as he walked. He took a shot at Mookie, who was suddenly there, and whose face grew large and large and larger until it dominated her view and blotted out everything else, and then Mookie's face exploded with the shot, now less a face than a rotten pumpkin hit with a rock, the slime-orange chunks all shooting outward into all directions, the pieces breaking up as they flew. A great orange mist-liquid flew out from the center where the buckshots had hit, another face forming where Mookie's face had been, and it was Grandpa Budi's face, his bad eye black and ragged and bloody and dripping, the whole face dripping, dissolving like a candle might do in a fire, his mouth open and trying to say something, something important, but the words diffusing before they could reach her, and Grandpa's hand coming out of the waxmelt and grabbing her shoulder, hard, and shaking, and shaking, and shaking...*

...and her eyes were open and she was laying on her pallet on the floor in her room and it was Big Soo's big hand gripping her shoulder and shaking, and Big Soo's face looming in the dark above her, eyes glaring, Big Soo telling her something which, in the bewilderment of her sudden waking, she could not understand.

She sat up in her pallet, abruptly, moving backward to break her aunt's hard hold. Her aunt continued to loom over her, however.

"What you say?" Yally asked in confusion, rubbing the place where Big Soo's fingers had been.

"Him been here, inna'?" Big Soo said, a look on her face so intent that it hurt almost as much as her grip had. "What him a'tell you?"

"Who been here?" Yally asked in a growing panic.

"What him a'tell you?" Big Soo demanded.

"*Which* him? Which him you talking about? Tell me what?" Her voice now rose in a shrillness that threatened screaming and she thought, for a terrifying moment, that she had lost track of the line between sleep and awake and she was back in her dream again. Only the hard pain in her shoulder, and the biting cold of the room where the quilts had fallen off her body, let her know that this was not still her dreamworld. She shook her head at her aunt, vigorously, fighting against both Big Soo's aggression and her own disorientation, and put her palms out in front of her as if that would keep Big Soo off of her. Big Soo sucked her teeth in disgust, gave Yally a last hard look, and then turned away. She did not ask again about the who she thought had been there in the room with them or what he might have asked, nor explain her question in any fashion, neither what Yally might have done or said in her sleep to prompt it.

She could not go back to sleep again that night for the longest, and the next night, and for several nights afterwards, she faced the approaching bedtime with an uneasiness around her stomach, worrying over what she might have to face either in her sleeping or her waking.

SHE VISITED THE BOYS down at her brother-in-law's hunt-shack as often as she could. As Dokie Jackson had said, they were having a good time down there, not much work of any kind to do, plenty of cousins coming by, checkers and dominos to play all day, and, Yally learned, Bro' Kess' corn liquor stash to sneak into. During one of her visits, Yally also learned that Dokie Jackson had left out an important part of the story of the aftermath of the fight at Jaeger's. She had assumed that when Dokie had mentioned

getting a boat and coming back across the river after hiding the
mules and wagons in the woods, they had found a stray boat
somewhere on the bank. They hadn't, though they had looked for
one as far as they had dared along the exposed riverside. When
they came across no stray boat, they had resolved to wait until dark
and then all of them would make the swim across, but according to
Boo, Dokie Jackson had butted in to say that didn't make any
sense. Dokie had insisted that he was the best swimmer of them
all—which was true—and that it was better that he go alone and
fetch back a boat. The rest had argued against it—saying either all
should go or none—until Dokie made the argument that while
Boo and Mookie were like fish, themselves, Dink and Lam were
only adequate in the water, and there was a good chance that one
or both of them would run into trouble on the long way across the
wide Sugaree, and maybe take one or all of the others down with
them. And so they made a compromise. Dokie and Boo had made
the swim, braving the freeze-cold river-water in only their pants,
coming back in a couple of hours, shivering, in a boat they had
borrowed at the cable-barge dock. The nighttime swim, and Dokie
Jackson's logic, had made him rise considerably in Dink and Cu'n
Boo's eyes.

"The boy still ain't got much more sense than the rest of them
Jackson," Boo had said, "but him got heart. You can give him that."

"He play him a good harmonichord, too," Dink had added.

IT WAS A BLEAK and bad-luck winter.

Just after the fight at Jaeger's, a rolling series of driving
rainstorms hit the county, one behind the other, some lasting two
days or more at a time, swelling the Neck's two boundary rivers
with boiling, gray-black water and spilling many of the ponds and
lakes and creekways over their banks. In the second week in
January the earth along the rice-dikes gave into the pressure and
the water overflowed, flooding acres of ricefields two months
before their time and washing away much of the diking system.
Every available worker at Yelesaw went out to the fields—men,
women, and all but the smallest children—working in the freezing
water to bail out the flood and rebuild the system. The work went
on for three weeks, all day and deep into the torchlit nights, in
some of the bitterest frigid-cold even the oldest amongst them
could remember. Many went down with sickness and before the
dikes were put back in order in mid-February, four Yay'saws—
Lundy Cooper, the elder cousins Kit Prioleau and Zuna Brown

and, most tragically, the little twelve year old, DeeDee Jackson—all succumbed to pneumonia.

The hard-rain did other damage as well. It played havoc with the winter crop, washing out many of the I'sh-potato and yam-potato banks completely, and leaving others to be discovered fouled with mildew when they were dug up after the water had receded. Deep in one weekend night, the big creek running behind the Dingle and Simmons settlements rose up and out, drowning several pens of chickens and piglets before sandbars could be laid and the rest of the stock saved. Two days after the stock-flooding came a worse accident, on the river, when Sala Saunders tried to take his family over on the cable-barge to go to Jaeger's Store. Folks had warned him that there was still too much unsettlement among the county whitefolks to trust a trip across the river, and Lem Washington was reluctant to go out on the water with the weather and the river still so skittish. But Sala Saunders insisted, and so they went. Midway across the river a sudden flood-swell came roaring from upriver and upset the cable-barge. Sala's little daughter O'nusi was tossed into the water and drowned, and Lem Washington lost part of his arm when it got tangled in the cable. Lem's son, Dibi, who had luckily come along because of the danger of the passage, had to cut his father's forearm off with his knife to keep Lem from being pulled under himself. Lem Washington's bloody forearm went into the roiling waters as a sacrifice, and the others only just barely escaped with their lives.

For many weeks afterwards, people on the Neck spoke about the omens that had been revealed in the tragedies of the winter's rains and wondered, in many conversations over hissing woodstoves, what might be the message. There had been rumors abounding all winter that some compromise might be able to be worked out about the whitefolks' Watercoming, a plan in which Yelesaw might be diked up all around and built into an island, which it already was for all practical purposes, and where they could remain even if all the surrounding lands were turned into a lake. Where this idea came from and whether it had any validity, no-one knew. But some now began to speak, in hushed tones, that perhaps the breaking of the rice-dikes was a sign, a bad sign, a sign that argued against the island solution, and that in defying the buckras' orders to leave Yelesaw because of the coming flood, the Yay'saws had not avoided the flooding at all, but had only hastened it upon themselves.

# 8

# The Return Of The Wanderer

## (Spring, 1937)

Within a few weeks following the fight at Jaeger's Store, Dink and Cu'n Boo were able to leave Kess Butler's hunt-shack. They might have returned sooner but they professed that they were worried about bringing danger to their families and the others on Goat Hill, and only came back home upon their wives' insistence, the wives figuring—correctly—that the two of them were having far too much fun down there in the woods, drinking Kess's corn liquor and playing checkers and cards every night away from any scrutiny.

For Mookie it was different. There had been a story in *The Southern Call* newspaper giving some details of the fight and identifying Mookie by his courthouse name and not even mentioning the two others, and so Mookie had become the focus of the whitefolks' anger over the incident. While Mookie could work out in the ricefields every day—no-one thought the High Sheriff would come out there—Papa'Tee felt there was still the chance that the Sheriff might show up in the evening on Goat Hill and so, until the excitement wore down, he believed it best that Mookie stay put. It was Yally's misfortune that it became her job to bring a plate of Mama's cooked Sunday supper down to Mookie every week, the misfortune being that she had to pass the Yelesaw Crossroads to do so. Even worse, on the first of the warm spring days after the bad winter had finally worn away, all of the wagons and mules readily available were being otherwise used in the planting-time rush, and so this day she had to go on foot.

Amidst the myriad maze of wagonpaths and walkways passing around and through Yelesaw Neck, there were several places where the roads intersected, but only one true crossroad. It sat on a lonely stretch up on the northern half of the River Road just before the turnout that led to Sosoville, where the Butlers lived, and where Yally was going. A hundred years before it had been a proper crossing, wide and well-traveled, where the wagonroad from the old river dock landing passed over the River Road and became the wide carriage lane that ran down into the grounds at Bethelia Plantation, ending in a circle around the trimmed lawn in front of the Big House, where the finest satin-black buggies and horse carriages would park. It was a landscape that existed now only in the memories of the eldest living. Only a handful of people went out to Old Landing these days, which was now exclusively a spot for fishing, and not especially popular, even for that. The landing itself had long ago been abandoned as a river-crossing, folks choosing now to use the cable-barge crossing further south. As for Bethelia Plantation itself, that was a place the Yelesaw folk had no use for and no need to visit for any purpose, even the Butlers and the Jacksons and their close-kin, who lived on its boundaries. It was a bad-spirit place, gloomy, eerie, of sudden shrieks and howls, where dark things came wandering out on moonless nights from the oak-lined lane to meet at the Crossroads, things with clawed hands and hunchover backs, black hollows where their eyes should be, singing old chants and banging on kettles and drums made of stretched human skin. The lesser crossings around Yelesaw could be passed with the use of minor signs and sayings and other small precautions. Getting through the Crossroads in front of Bethelia was a more serious matter. Few Yay'saws ever tarried there, even in the broad day, and most did not dare to go through the Cross without making elaborate signs in the road-sand, invoking the most serious of charms, and calling for protection from the spirits in the surrounding trees or creeks or ponds or fields.

Because Yally's sister Lusi had been so inconsiderate and thoughtless as to marry Kess Butler, whose family lived on the other side of the old Bethelia Lane from the Manigaults, there was no way to get to her house but by going through the Crossroads. Yally had never liked to pass it, even in the wagon with her family members surrounding. On visits to Lusi's house, if Mama was not riding with them, she would throw the quilt up over her head and lay flat on the wagon-bed after they had passed the big turn in the River Road just beyond the Jacksontown turnoff, and would not emerge again until the mule had stopped and she could hear the cackling of the chickens, and Eshy and her brothers were laughing and climbing down, and poking at her under the blanket with sticks or the points of their fingers, and she knew she was safe in the heart of Sosoville, in sister Lusi's yard. Of course, that would only work if her mother was not with them. Mama did not allow what she called gafagaggling of any kind, under any circumstances. With Mama in the wagon, Yally would have to close her eyes as tight as she could without seeming that she was doing anything more than drowsing in her place, crossing her ankles and all of her fingers, and sitting as close as possible to her mother until the bad section was behind them. The ankle- and finger-crossing was for added benefit, because being next to Mama was protection in itself. Something about Mama, stern and stiff and frowning, kept bad spirits at bay, even though Mama never, ever acknowledged them. Or, perhaps, *because* Mama never acknowledged them. Yally could never be sure.

But today there was no Mama for Yally to cling next to, nor quilt to cover her, nor mule and wagon to speed her along and keep her high off the ground, and her uneasiness and worriation about it—which she was able to ignore while she was still in hollering distance of home—grew as she drew nearer to that comfortless spot.

She had been walking for a while at her usual easy pace, eating up the road with her long, effortless strides, the small tie-sack containing Mookie's supper balanced on her head. The day had started out in an early spring cool but now it was late in the morning, and the sun was high and drawing sweat down her neck and making the cotton fabric of her dress press damp against her chest and grab at her legs. Along the way she met several other walkers, and folks driving wagons or on muleback, and the ones who were going her way, she chatted with for a while, until they made their turnoff to their various destinations. But as she got nearer to the dreaded spot, she came across fewer and fewer people, until, on the final long stretch before Jacksontown, the last settlement before the Crossroads, the way emptied out completely, and save for an earlyseason blacksnake that rustled along beside her in the tall-grasses at the edge of the road for a while, she found herself alone.

At the Jacksontown turnoff she stopped and peered down the rutted wagonpath, thinking that maybe her luck might be good that morning, and one of the Jackson boys would be coming out just then in their father's wagon or on horseback and not only take her the rest of the way, but if she could entice them with the smell of Mama's supper fixings, back out again to Goat Hill. But she saw no sign of any of the Jackson brothers, no sign of anyone at all, just a crow she could not see calling dark and raucously to her from a treetop, and so, with a sinking feeling, she walked on.

Past the Jacksontown turnoff the River Road bent around to the left in a deep curve in the direction of the river and then straightened back out again, widening and flattening out on its way to the Crossroads. The road was lonely and completely vacant now of anything in either human or creature form, and even the sky was suddenly abandoned of the long trails of north-flying birds that she had been seeing all morning. She began to walk faster. On either side of the road, the hidey-hummers began taking up their buzzings, as if announcing her coming to things waiting up ahead. She knew they would grow still and quiet if she walked into the tall-grass from where they clattered, so that she would never be able to find them, only taking up their call again when she stepped back out. It was an old game that she had often enjoyed playing with them, but she had no mind to step into the tall-grass, not here, in sight of the Crossroads, and so the hidey-hummers did not hush down, but instead their clack-and-rattle grew higher and more shrill as she passed.

"*Brrrrr-kkkkkkk, brrrrrr-kkkkkk, brrreakkkkk, brrreakkkkk,*" they seemed to be saying.

Break what? Break her bones? Break her head?

Holding the supper-sack tighter against her headscarf, she began to walk faster.

The sun in her eyes was making her squint. It was hovering down right above the line of the trees, for some reason, so that she was looking almost directly into the glare. It seemed odd that the sun was still so low so late in the morning. In fact, it seemed that it had been higher-up earlier on. For a moment she had a thought that the day must have been running backward, turning back towards its dawning rather than forward into the afternoon. But that, of course, could not be true, and she shook her head to clear it of those confusing thoughts, as well as of the growing smell of moist rankness in her nose, which she was not certain of from where it was coming. She was much too far away from the Swamp for its stench to reach her, and the river, which ran parallel to the road somewhere just through the trees to her left, was too clean and swift to have such a stink. Probably something had died in the bushes nearby that the buzzards had not yet found.

She held up the flat of her hand over her brow to ward off the brightness in her eyes and saw that she was approaching the break in the line of trees ahead that marked the Crossroads.

Tightening her grip on the supper-sack with one hand and gathering the loose parts of her lower dress with the other, she broke into a loping trot. Several hundred yards from the entrance to Bethelia Lane, the trot turned into a full run as she felt— without bothering to go through the motions of thinking it through—that it would be best for her to pass over the Crossroads so fast that anything jumping out at her from its hole in the ground would have no chance to get a good grasp.

She could run fast and for the longest, effortless, with long, easy strides like a deer, so that few of the children on the yard at Goat Hill could keep up with her, and even fewer could catch her. But that was for fun. This was from fear. She ran just on the verge of panic, with a sudden burst across the ground as if a flood-storm was blowing behind her, lifting her in great, bounding blasts, so that it seemed as if she were fairly flying over the River Road, her heart booming against the walls of her chest, her bare feet barely touching the sand beneath her, aiming to blow past the Crossroads like a summer tornado.

Leaping, straining, bursting against her last breath, she had come within a hundred yards of the Crossroads when she saw it, a figure in the middle of the road, that she had somehow not seen before. It was squatting on its haunches, bent down and making signs with its finger in the dirt, and she could not see how she could possibly have missed it before, it was sitting out there in the big broad day, in plain sight. Even as she watched, the figure stood up, turned on its heel, and began walking down into Bethelia Lane.

For a moment, she did not realize that she had pulled up to a dead stop, her toes digging into the sand of the road.

She could not see the figure clearly with the sun in her eyes, only that it was a man walking, and she had to squint to try to

make him out. It was a tall figure, lanky, wide-shouldered, with a
long and purposeful walk, a familiar walk, a walk she had seen so
many times going across the yard at Goat Hill or through the pens
behind the houses or along the ricefield bottoms ...

...her heart jumped...

..."Grandpa!" she shouted.

Her grandfather did not slow his walk. He turned his head and
gave her a brief-enough glance and then turned back in the
direction he was going, as if her arrival had not startled him, as if
there was nothing in the world unusual about the fact that he had
been squatting out there in the middle of the road just at the same
exact time as she was passing through, the person in all the world
she had so much wanted to see, but had stopped even daring to
hope.

"It *me*, Grandpa!" she called at him. "It Yally-Bay!"

But he paid her no attention now, only kept on walking. Just as
he reached the line of trees that marked the entranceway into the
Old Lane, however, he paused and turned to look over at her
again, raising his arm and making a beckoning gesture to her.

The sun dazzled bright colors in her eyes, and the smell of the
road dust in the back of her nose was heavy and overwhelming.
She bent over and sneezed the dust out, several times, and when
she was finally able to look up again, the road ahead was empty
again, not a single thing stirring, and he was gone.

"Grandpa!" she shouted. "Grandpa! Wait up!"

She took off after him at a quick trot, not realizing that in her
excitement, she had dropped Mama's supper-sack in the road
during her sneezing fit. There was no thought of supper now, or of
Mookie down at Sister Lusi's, or of the day's errand. Fear was not
driving her any more. All thoughts of the dangers of the
Crossroads had left her, crowded out by a burst of joy. She had
known her grandfather was alright and would turn up—she had
just *known* it, despite the gloom that had settled over the house
and yard since his disappearance and the sense that he was gone
forever. How happy and surprised Mama and the others would be
when the two of them came back together, walking up the path,
and everybody shouting and crowding and gathering 'round! She
picked up her speed, running long and loose, feeling her bare feet
kicking up the road-sand behind her. In her hurry she barely had
time to make a circle in the air with her fingertip and spit through
it as she made an angled turn through the Crossroads, and only
slowed down to a walk when she had entered the Old Bethelia

Lane.

It was dim, and quiet in the Lane, the only sound of her feet a hushed crunching on the old crushed shellcover of the road. Once wide and swept clean by an army of dark hands bearing hoes and brooms, but now narrowed by running vines and bushes over seventy years of unuse and disrepair, the Old Lane was bordered on either side by two long rows of moss-bearded liveoak trees, their branches spread so close together that they met across the top, leaf and moss intertwining, like a canopy covering a great hallway. The tangle of branch and leaves and moss was thick and dark and heavy, holding off the better part of the sunlight from reaching the ground below. Here, in the space between the trees, no wind stirred. The air was thick and heavy, bearing on her shoulders, pressing down on top of her, and from all sides. She took in a gulp of air, realizing only then that she had been holding her breath since she had left the familiar River Road.

Far down at the end of the hallway of trees she could see an opening where light played, but she could make out nothing distinct, only an arched opening into what seemed to be a sunlit field of bushes and thick grass. Except for herself, all around the Lane was empty. There was no sign of her grandfather.

Walking slowly now, her head turning back and forth both to look for him as well as for anything that might be lurking there, she wondered where he might have gotten to. She didn't see how he could have disappeared so fast. She gave a quick glance behind her. For a quick moment, she entertained the thought of turning and going back, walking on to Lusi's to get more help to find her grandfather. But just as quickly she abandoned the thought after figuring the fussing she would get if they came back down here and no Grandpa was to be found, either that she had seen no Grandpa at all or, worse yet, that she had seen him and let him get away again. "Why you ain't keep him when you had him, ass?" Lusi would say. She braced herself and walked on.

The uneasiness continued to gather about her, however, like the fog at dusk coming up out of the fields, rising slowly with a feeling of growing darkness.

"Grandpa," she called out again as she walked, although not as loud as she had before. The sound was like a child trying to chunk a rock too big for her. In the heavy stillness of the Lane, it lobbed only a short distance and then fell, dead, in a smothering pile of leaves and grasses. She called out once more, "Grandpa!", this time a little louder, and was instantly sorry she had done so.

The answer came back at her, but not from her grandfather.

It came from the road behind her, and from the trees on either side, voices calling back her name.

*Yally.*

Low voices.

Hushed voices.

Rattly voices.

*Yally.*

Voices without form, voices that were thin smoke wafting out from hidden holes and hideaways.

*Yally.*

*Yally.*

*Ya'lleeeeeee.*

Kneading her name like old fingers over bread dough, breaking it open, turning it over, calling it not as if they were calling *to* her, but calling *about* her.

*Ya'lleeeeeeeeeeeeeeeeeee.*

With a quick, quiet cackle, at the end.

Children's voices. Old folks' voices. Voices calling singly, but in chorus, first from behind her, then to each side, but when she looked, one way or the other, she could see nothing, only the empty Lane, and the canopy of trees above, and the broken, abandoned fields beyond.

Her chest heaved. She could not catch her breath. She felt a drumming at her temples, a thousand hands beating from inside her head, struggling to burst their way out. There was no thought of turning around and going back out the way she had come. That's where the voices were the strongest, where they seemed to be gathering. She took off at a trot again toward the opening at the end of the Lane, not looking back, trying to leave the voices grasping behind her.

They were pushing her forward, driving her.

*Ya'lleeeeeee,* they called after her, the voices dissipating, breaking apart, as she put a distance between them, their spell broken, dandelion thistles separating, dispersing, blowing away in the warm spring wind.

By the time she reached the end of the Lane she was at a dead run again as she had been out on the main road, panicked, running as fast as she had ever run in her life, and as she came out from under the hallway canopy of trees and broke into the bright sunlight, a flock of crows rose up from the ground before her, chattering ferociously, their wide, black wings beating at their flanks as they scattered into the air above. She plunged straight ahead into a sawgrass field, plowing out a pathway as she ran, the long, notched leaves grabbing at her clothes, razor-edges slicing the skin on her forearms and legs, her feet stumbling over the roots as they clutched at her. Deep into the field the sawgrass finally tripped her up, and she found herself sprawling through the air, tumbling head first into a tangle of plants and earth. A circle of stars spun around her head, and then it was night...

IT WAS ALL OF A PEACE around her. She heard the piping of birds from somewhere above, and the buzz of insects close by. She opened her eyes. It was broad day, the sun burning and high in the sky above her. Sundaysuppertime, for sure. But she was not at her sister Lusi's with the fixings for Mookie, as she should have been. She was sprawled out in the middle of a sawgrass field, and the midday sun was drawing sweat out from all over her body.

She lay there for a moment, not moving, blinking back the bright light that blurred her vision, hoping that the tall-grass would hide her, from what, she was not sure. She only knew that she dearly did not want to be seen. She curled up on her side amidst the tall sawgrass and pricklebushes, pulling her knees up far into the folds of her dress and wrapping her arms around herself and gripping her back.

Gradually the colors separated and grew less fuzzy, the dim outlines took shape, and she began to see again. The gray-green sawgrass close to her face, dotted here and there with the red-brown eruptions of old fire-ant mounds, the soft outline of tree-limbs raising up beyond, the bright, blank spring-blue sky above.

The chirping of the birds gave way to the calls of two or three crows, who were giving out the kind of loud and scandalous bird-curses that only crows can manage.

*Caw-caw-caw-caw-cawwwww...*

*Caw-caw-caw-caw-cawwwww...*

*Caw-caw-caw-cawleeeeeeeeeee....*

...sounding suspiciously like they were calling out her name.

She began to remember what had brought her into the sawgrass field, her frantic run down the Old Lane and then her great, tumbling fall, all precipitated by things in the woods that had been calling out her name...

Sitting up, it suddenly came to her, what must have happened, and she sat up and a fit of giggles took her, and then her shoulders began to shake with laughter, and the tears streamed down her cheeks, and all she could think of was what Eshy would say, later on, when she told her sister the tale.

"You big, dumb, goat-head, ass-backward ninny! You done thought'ed you hear somebody's calling you' name, and you ain't hear'd nothing but old cawing crow. Look at you, girl. You done scare you'self all pissy-up."

She reached around in the grass for something suitable to chunk at the crows, but could find nothing suitable. It was good she couldn't, she finally realized, since crows were thought by some to be returned spirits, and she might have hit an auntie or a cousin in her haste. The crows did not know that, however, and they did not wait for her to look further. With a last, scandalous comment thrown back over black-winged shoulders, they took off for other parts, leaving her in the sawgrass field by herself.

It now began coming back to her why she had come down the Old Plantation Lane in the first place. She had been following her grandfather. Both the joy of seeing him and the anguish and confusement at losing him again, so quickly, hit her simultaneously.

While she was trying to sort her feelings out, she examined herself all over to see how she had suffered in her fall. Both knees and one of her elbows were bloody where they had scraped against the ground. There was a rent in the side of her dress, and a run of welps and deep scratches up her thigh and side where the skin showed through and the sawgrass and burr-bushes had snatched her. She felt over her forehead and, sure enough, there was a small, wet lump where her head had struck the ground, painful to the touch. She pulled her fingers away and looked at them, and the tips were slightly blooded. Wiping them on her dress she stood up, much too quickly, and a dizziness came over her, fueled in part by the sun burning down on her head. She dropped back down to one knee and braced a palm against the ground to steady herself.

As she knelt there, waiting for the shakes to wear off, she began to wonder if it hadn't all been a day-vision, even the seeing of her grandfather in the middle of the River Road and then disappearing down into the Lane. Thinking that the crows had been calling out her name certainly had been. She'd often had such day-visions as a little girl, vivid wake-time trances that had seemed as real as these at the time. But it had been a very long time since she'd had any like that, and she thought that she had grown out of them. But maybe it was all the fear and anxiety she had generated within herself going through the Crossroads by herself that had triggered it.

Her heart sank at the conclusion, but she knew now that it had to be true. She had not seen Grandpa Budi, not at all. She had only conjured him up out of her own mind, so vividly that he had seemed real.

What actually was real was that she still had to get to Lusi's.

She stood up, slower this time, and brushing herself off as best she could, she tried to get her bearings.

Where was she?

Now that she had time to settle herself and think, she realized the full implication of the answer. She was in a field at the end of the Old Bethelia Plantation Lane. But how far the plantation itself was from the River Road and, therefore, how close she was to the plantation grounds themselves, she had no idea. She didn't even know what they looked like. She might be in them right now.

She stood up on her toe-tips and looked around.

The sawgrass in the field was too tall to see over, except for the tops of the trees spreading out on all sides. Only in one direction was anything visible. Through the pathway she had flattened down when she had run into the sawgrass field, she could see the near entrance to the Old Lane and the first two or three of the canopy liveoak trees at its beginning. Back that way was the River Road.

She thought about what was best to do.

She could simply walk back up the Lane, easy-enough, and be back on her way down the River Road to the Sosoville turnoff, and then to Lusi's. That was certainly the most direct route, to go back the way she had come. But something troubled her about that, and at first she could not put her finger on it. "Come on, Yally'Bay," she said to herself, "why that vex you?" She walked herself through the way back. The voices in the Lane did not bother her any more, now that she knew their source, and that it was crow-calling, and not spirits calling out her name. But as soon as she reached the end of the Lane in her mind, she understood immediately what was bothering her. To go back that way meant she had to go back through the Crossroads. That was no crow-talk. That was real. And even without the unsettling experiences that she had gone through already that morning, going through the Crossroads was not something she wanted to repeat.

What, then, was an alternate way to get to her sister's house from where she was? There had to be one.

She thought about it, hard.

The Old Lane had come up straight-shot from the River Road,

without a turn, and she had continued on, straight, for several yards into the sawgrass field. What did that mean? Facing the Lane, Lusi's house was to her right. If she cut across the field that way she would come into the woods, the top of whose trees she could see. If she were lucky she would find a path through the woods, but that really didn't matter. So long as she bore to the left, taking her out of the woods instead of deeper into it, she would either come to the Sosoville turnoff itself, eventually, or come out on the River Road somewhere below the turnoff, but well away from the Crossroads. And that might keep her out of the plantation grounds, which were probably somewhere straight ahead.

That was the way to do it.

She took her headscarf off and spit on a piece of it and dabbed at the knot on her forehead to wipe away the blood and make herself more presentable. She repeated the action on her side and legs and her elbows, until the headscarf was damp and pink. She smoothed out her dress as best she could. There was nothing she could do about the rents, and so she tried not to think about that.

While she was straightening up, she looked around her for the supper-sack. It was nowhere to be found where she had landed in the sawgrass field, and she could not see any trace of it down the path she had trampled coming out of the Lane. She could not think of where she might have lost it, only that it had to be somewhere between where she was and the River Road, where she last remembered holding it to her head. She let out a long breath. After she got to Lusi's, she would have to come back out in the wagon with Cu'n Kess or one of the boys down there and search for it. She didn't look forward to that, but at least she'd have someone with her this time.

Turning to her right, she took a deep breath and pushed ahead through the sawgrass, taking a sighting on the top of one of the tallest trees ahead of her at the far edge of the field so she would not lose her bearings.

The day had grown very warm. The effort of her running, and now walking with some difficulty through the heavy grass, made the sweat begin to pour all over her, running down into the open scratches, and making them itch. She took off her headscarf again as she walked and dabbed at the wet spots over the scratches as she pushed on through the grass, but that provided little help. The more she walked, the more she scratched herself on the sawgrass and the harder she sweated, and so the more the scratches itched, unbearably. She closed her mind to it and quickened her pace so that she could get out of the field as fast as she could. After some hard walking the sawgrass suddenly fell away, and she came upon a patch of bare sandy dirt that ended, after a few feet, at the edge of a thick stand of pine trees that marked the beginning of the woods, one of them the tall tree she had been marking on.

Standing and looking up and down it, she could see that the sandy patch was actually a small wagonway that ran between the sawgrass field and the pinewoods. A good portion of the way was covered with grass patches and pine needles and dotted now and then with low bushes and looked sadly untended, but there was no doubt that wagons must have once run here, a long time ago.

Walking a road was better than pushing through a sawgrass field or the woods, of course, but only if it took you where you wanted to go.

So where was this road going?

Though she could only see a little ways down it, the left-hand way certainly seemed to be curving back around towards the entrance to the Old Lane, where she had already decided she did not want to go. That left either the right-hand way or going straight into the woods to try to catch the Sosoville turnoff somewhere up in there, as she had originally intended. She voted against the woods for now, at least, and turned up the wagonway to the right to see where that way would take her, since it was heading in the general direction of Sosoville, though somewhat south of where she eventually needed to be to run into her sister's house. She knew that if worse came to worst and the wagonway went too deep into the eastern portion of the woods or began to turn back to the south, she could easily return to this spot where she had entered and rethink the other two choices. That was one of the good things about roads, and why you tried to get on one of them instead of wandering around in the woods. Papa had taught her that.

She had not walked far when the old wagonway came to an abrupt dead end at the intersection of another road and then the extension of the sawgrass field beyond. She stepped out onto this new road, which was only new to her, and just as unkempt and overgrown as the wagonway. To the left the road led straight into the woods, the way that led to the Sosoville turnoff, and exactly the direction she wanted to go. Smiling at how her woods-sense—and Papa's teaching, of course—had gotten her out of her dilemma, she turned on the road and started into the pinewoods without giving a thought or a glance back the opposite way. The sun was still high overhead, and judging the distance that might be left, she hoped to be at Lusi's within an hour or less, and so not too terribly late.

Before she had taken two or three steps she stopped apruptly and looked back over her shoulder, drawn as if to a flame, as if something had called to her from back that way, though she had heard no sound at all.

The road behind her ran directly into the sawgrass field.

With a clear pathway to look down through, no tall sawgrass intervening, she could see it clearly in the middle of the field. It was the remains of an old two story house. For a moment she wondered why she had not been able to see it from the spot where she had first come into the sawgrass field and fallen, until she noticed the copse of tall trees that screened any view of the house from the front. Those were the trees she must have seen from the field and not the woods behind, as she had thought. They did not appear to have been planted but were set out irregularly though not randomly, as if they had grown up wild, and only in that one spot in front of the house, as if their purpose was to screen the house from spying eyes.

From what she could see of it from the side, it must have once been a great and magnificent house, but now was only the cindered hollow of one, a broken, crumbled ruin. She could see what looked like the beginnings of a brick stairway at its front, but most of the bannister on the side closest to her had long since fallen away, and the steps themselves were overgrown with weeds and bushes. The house had clearly been in a devastating fire sometime long back. Most of the second story was gone, with no roof at all, and only foundation beams and three once-great chimneys rising into the sky above the first floor, the beams charred and blackened, the chimneys cracked down their middles and with many bricks missing from their tops. The first floor was gutted but some of it still remained, a collection of burnt and weatherstripped boards attached to their columns showing where the outside and inner walls had once been, some of the boards with great fire-holes rent in them or hanging off at odd angles, interlaced with a lush collection of blackberry bushes, a handful of scraggly trees rising up here and there in the middle of the structure. The jagged timbers and chimney tops stood like mute sentinels, themselves all overgrown thick with plaited ivy, still and quiet in the spring air, like a great animal that had fallen alone and then died, limbs stiff and pointed upward, all that were left of it because the buzzards had already come and gorged out the innards. No sign of life emanated from the carcass, not even the stirring of birds or other creatures who might be making of it a home. It sat mournful and forlorn, empty, a dead thing, long abandoned and forgotten, falling slowly in on itself.

With a slow dawning of recognition, she realized that she was looking at the remains of the old Big House at Bethelia Plantation.

A brooding, menacing silence hung about the spot, and so as her consciousness slipped away from her, she held onto just enough of it to know that the rising sound of buzzing in her ears was coming from inside of her. She felt her body swaying. Her private parts felt loose and watery and her head began a slow spin. Her eyes misted over, and it was only then that she could see it clearly in the noon day...

*... a Great House, swallowed up in flame, its fires roaring, consuming, reaching into the sky above, a night sky, not a noon sky, the pyre so intense that the trees set near the house seemed to lean back in fear, trembling violently, even though the fiery licking tongues had not yet breached the outer walls. She could hear the timbers inside splintering, splitting, breaking, collapsing—smell the metallic sting of smoke up the passages of her nose—feel the hot breath of the fire's fierce wind on her face. The house stank as if it was burning, living flesh, and its foundation-columns writhed like maggots in a pile of roasting dung, and she gagged on it. The whole building seemed to swell and rise on its toes, unable to contain the billowing conflagration within. The board-seams strained and groaned and cried out their agony, and then all the doors and windows burst asunder, all at once, and the flames roared outward, sounding like the cracking of a thousand whips. From out of the burning building a man strode onto the front porch— an old man, white-bloused and black-booted—an old buckra man— gray hair all awry and lit in a fiery halo. As she watched, horrified, she saw that the old buckra had caught a'fire himself, the flames now racing up the front and back of his body to his face, and his eyes wided, swoll-up, and ruptured, the eyeballs melting into the wrinkles of his cheeks and down his neck, coagulating like rancid cream as he stood there on the blazing porch, legs wide, clawing hands wildly raking at his hair, which was flaring out like a bright matchhead, his toothless mouth open and working wildly, from which no sound came, only a silent screaming, screaming, screaming...*

The old buckra man could not scream, and so she screamed for him, a piercing scream, splitting the afternoon air, breaking the blue sky into two halves that fell away from each other and smothered the world.

She felt herself losing control of her water, her bladder voided itself, and just in time, she half-squatted and pulled her drawers out of the way, and a long stream of hot urine ran down from inside of her and onto the sandy ground.

SHE DID NOT EVER REMEMBER how she came away from that spot. She did not recall how she broke off her contact with the vision of the burning house and man, or of standing up, or of walking away. She only knew that when she came to herself she was walking along the the roadway in the opposite direction of the house, and had come out of the sawgrass field and into a stretch of pinewoods. A little creek ran beside the road, and she stopped there to pull off her drawers and wash them, wring them out, and put them back on again. It was cooler here under the trees than out in the field in the sun, but she welcomed the added coolness of the water-damp drawers around her middle. Her body felt hot and draining-weary, as if she had not slept in several days. She took off her headscarf and dipped it in the creekwater and mopped her face and the back of her neck and her chest, then dipped it again and wiped down the insides of her legs where the urine had run down. "Poor headscarf," she said to herself as she washed it back out again. "You doing washrag duty today." She left it sopping wet and tied it around her head, letting the water run down her forehead and face.

In all the time she was there beside the creek, not once did she look back up the road into the sawgrass field. She knew what was back there. She could feel it stretching out its burnt limbs towards her, angered that she was out of its reach. She could see it in her mind if she wanted to, every detail, without ever having to look at it again.

It was not hard, this time, to make her decision as to what to do next. Returning to the sawgrass field to get back to the River Road that way was no longer an option. She would take her chances taking the roadway into the woods in the hopes that it would eventually hit the Sosoville turnoff or, at the worst, connect back down to the River Road.

Still a little shaky from her experience back in the sawgrass field, she took up walking again.

It was not deep a woods at this point, only a short expanse of pines that she went through quickly, the ground opening up again as the roadway passed into another field that was mostly thick brush and palmettoes and tangles of vines and blackberry bushes that ran along for yards and yards like deep mazes. She found that she was suddenly hungry, and realized that she had not eaten since breakfast early that morning back home. She stopped and picked a bunch of blackberries, popping a few in her mouth as she picked, but mostly filling up the bottom of a tote-pouch she made out of her headscarf so she could eat them as she walked.

"Poor headscarf," she told it, once more. "I'm just using you and using you and using you for everything today, ain't I?" She promised the scarf she would sew a pretty fringe on it, or something, when she got back home, payment for all the trouble she had caused it.

She passed two or three wood buildings in between the berry patches, storage sheds or old barns, maybe. They were rotted, decaying, leaning to the side, planks split and pulled away from their foundation posts, the posts and roofs in a suspended collapse, slowly sucking inward, and it looked as if you could just puff on them and they'd fall into dust. Flocks of birds had made their nests among the hollows between the boards, and they made a riotous racket as she walked by. On one of the buildings, a door hung from its top hinge at an odd angle, catching the gusts of the warm spring breeze, swinging back and forth, banging itself against the side of the building and then falling back again, creaking, groaning, at each swing, like an exhausted old man, in pain and hoping to sling hard enough to yank itself off and drop down on the ground to sleep.

The road passed through another small bit of woods and then a second field of weeds and wild bushes and several copses of trees. She continued to hear the sound of the creaking hinge coming back from the farm building long after it should have died away. She thought at first it was a trick of the landscape, like a riverbottom or a hollow through the trees making it seem that someone was talking right next to you when actually they were half an acre away, but as she walked, she realized that the sound was now coming from in front of her rather than from behind. After running on for a bit across the second field, the road made a slow leftward turn—good, she thought, as that took her closer towards the River Road rather than farther into the woods—then straightened and broadened out to a wide, flat avenue, and now she found herself passing through a settlement that had been blocked from her view by one of the stands of trees. The settlement had long been abandoned. On each side of the road was a long row of cabins, boards cracked and rain-warped, tin-tops rusted and sunken or bent up at the edges, foundation blocks choked with weeds. On three or four, the roofs were missing altogether, blown away in some long-ago storm. Few of the structures stood upright any more. Most leaned to one side or the other, some of them close to the ground, and some had collapsed entirely from the weight of their own roofs, spreading the wood in a circle out from the tin tops in odd-looking piles. Vines grew wild between the cracks and up the shafts of all of the cabins, and grass had long since invaded the undersides of the foundations. Years before, a lightning-struck pine must have fallen on one of the cabins, bursting it like a strike from a great axe. The pine had long since rotted and blown most away, leaving only a long mound of black and brown powder in the cleft it had formed in the middle of the cabin. Brown squirrels played among the ruins and near one of the cabins she passed a raccoon, which stood up on its back legs to watch her as she passed. In another place, she just caught the glimpse of the end of a long tail—a snake, maybe— disappearing into the dark hollow between a pile of boards.

The creaking-hinge sound grew louder as she walked between the cabin rows, with a sort of a rhythmic cadence to it that seemed to become more melodic the closer she got to whatever its source was. She could almost pick out a tune to it, if she tried hard enough, reminding her of something vaguely familiar that she struggled to recall, something she had often heard, on a porch...

She stopped dead in her tracks.

Just up ahead, an old man was sitting on the top step of one of the last of the cabins, head down, work hat pulled deep over his eyes, playing methodically on a mouth-harp, tapping one bare foot on the sandy ground in rhythm. She could not see his face, but she did not have to. Her heart rose in her chest, she gave a quick jump, and ran the rest of the way, stopping only a few feet from where the old man was sitting.

Thinking it had all been a vision back out at the Crossroads, she had put him out of her mind, but he was not a vision, he was real, and she had found him, without even looking. Or had he drawn her to him? In her joy, she didn't care which.

"Grandpa!" she shouted.

The music stopped, mid-note. He tipped the brim of his hat up from his eyes and looked up at her.

He seemed more refreshed and rested than when she had

seen him last back on the Hill—almost younger—the lines less deep along his forehead and cheeks, and the old play of a smile around the corners of his mouth, as if his time away had done him much good. He cocked his head to one side and looked at her like a bird would, quizzically, raising his eyebrows and widening his eyes. She wanted to leap across the few feet between them and hug his neck, but something held her back, and she stood in place. "Grandpa!" was all she could manage, so she said it again.

He leaned his head towards her and examined her closely. The mouth turned down again, the lips pursing in and out.

"Grandpa?" he asked her, as if he had never heard the term before. And then, "How I come for be you' grandpa? Who child you-is?"

After all the disquieting events of the day, his words were comforting and familiar to her, so much like being back on the yard at Goat Hill again, and her grandfather starting in with his regular question-games. Her whole pot was bubbling. She suppressed a grin.

"Benjamin Kinlaw," she answered, standing first on one foot and then on the other in her excitement.

He gave a low *humph* in his throat. "Must *be* a oba'dey Kinlaw," he said. "Ain't no Manigault child ever walk'round all bumdraggly-ass like you is. Look like the niggerdogs been running you, girl."

She had not really looked at herself closely when she tried to clean up at the creek after she'd left the sawgrass field, but now she did. Her legs were lined and crisscrossed with long marks— welled-up with dried blood—from more thorn scratches than she could count. Her arms and elbows were scraped from where she had fallen, and the rip in her dress exposed an ugly welt along her thigh. The dress itself, which she had not even bothered to try to clean, looked like something Mama kept to put on the crow-scares in her garden. She felt at the wildness of her uncombed bare head with one hand and remembered her headscarf, which was still clutched in the other hand, the last of the blackberry pickings still in it. Wincing, she tried to smooth the front of her dress with her palms, closing up the rent between two fingers as she did.

"You' peoples ain't check you 'fore you come-out the house like that?" he asked her.

She started to answer him but the question seemed so ridiculous, and there was no possible way she could explain all that had happened to her since she had left home that morning. And suddenly, the troubles of the day combined with the all the troubles and worries of the last few months after his disappearance, up to the fight across the river, and the High Sheriff coming over to search for the boys, and Mookie's exile out at Cu'n Kess' hunt-shack. It all boiled over, and the words came bursting out of her, unchecked and unbidden, tumbling over each other in their anxiousness for her own questions to be answered. "Grandpa. Oh, where you done *been'd*, Grandpa? Everybodys been so worry—Mama, she most having she a *fit*! Even Aunt Soo. And Papa. Papa and Papa'Tee and Uncle Ya, alla'them, they been out a'hunting and a'hunting and a'hunting for you in the Swamp—" She stopped talking and let out a big breath and took another long one in. "Where you *been*, Grandpa? I done'd miss you, and worry-up over you so much..." She stopped again, leaving the sentence unfinished, tears beginning to fill her eyes.

He gave a slight hitch to his shoulders.

"I been 'wisiting," he said, in reply to her question. He seemed to think about that a moment, taking a long look up and down the long, ruined row of deteriorating cabins as he did, then back at her.

"You know where we is, girl?" he asked.

She shook her head. She'd gotten herself so turned around, she really had no idea, except for how she planned to get herself home.

"This be the Quarters," he said. "This-here the Old-Home." He caught the growing look of realization that rose over her face. Of *course*. This was Bethelia Plantation that the Yay'saws had come out of. For the first time since she'd entered the Old Lane, the full impact of that hit her.

"Yeah, child, *we* home," he told her, nodding in agreement with her unstated conclusion. "*My* home. Where the Manigault' come from, after we come-'crost. Where all'we used for live. Nina and Iso and Sister Yela and Tat'Kumbi, my Pap and Mama. Boot. Tee. I come up right here, right in this-here shack—" He broke off, lapsing into memory and old thoughts again as Yally stared in something of an awe at the fallen-down cabin behind him. Then he went on again, pointing a long finger at the place where the next cabin had once stood, now little more than a mass of tin scraps and termite dust—"and over'cross there been Zambu and Lumbi and O'kra and little Wa"—he gestured across the road, and further up—"and Pambi and Risa and they mama 'cross there. Would'a been more in they family. Five head more. Six, maybe. Baby' ain't last long back then, like they does now. Caught the collar', mostly. Many thousan' done gone'd, girl. Many thousan'..."

She was not certain which babies he was talking about, or which families now, but it did not matter, because she was hardly listening any more. She looked again at the cabin on whose steps he was standing, only a few rotted boards and some rusted tin, its foundation bricks showing only a few steps in length from front door to back and hardly more than that from side to side, not much larger than Papa's chickencoop. But as he had said, this was the spot from where their family had sprung, where her own seed had lay waiting, a hundred years before she'd been born.

She could see them, as clearly as she could see him. A tall woman, heavy-breasted and clean-limbed sitting on the porch step next to him, so dark the sun sparkled off of her skin and made the sweat look like translucent diamonds on black velvet, a rough-seam cotton dress draping her body, shelling sugarpeas and tossing them into a tub between her legs, humming to two naked babies who were playing with a fat puppy on the cleansand ground beneath her feet. At the sound of singing coming from down the road, the woman looked up with a face that was just like Yally's, the features dead-on identical, flat-nosed, the eyes just as large as hers, and just as full of questions, as if Yally was looking into her own face, though she knew she was not, because the woman had a knowledge in her eyes that Yally, herself, did not possess. She looked along with the woman on the steps—her double—her predecessor—her ancestor—at where the song was coming from, and here was a long line of people approaching, men and women, hoes slung over their shoulders, rice-knives hung from their rope-belts, swinging along with long strides towards the cabins, singing their way home from out of the fields.

The song drifted into the sound of the wind passing through the rotting eaves of the cabin remains, the vision faded, and they were alone again in the abandoned Bethelia Quarters.

Her attention turned back to him, reluctantly, because she had not wanted the people—especially the woman on the steps—to leave them. Their people. Her people. She wanted to find a way to bring them back. She'd had the feeling that even as they had disappeared from her view, they had been walking around her in a circle of gone'way elders, the gauzy ends of their now-transparent garments just barely touching her arms and shoulders, kissing her cheeks, beckoning her, welcoming her, welcoming her back, summoning her to come and join with them. But just as the mist in her head was clearing and she was seeing the beginnings of a path to follow, the old man shifted on the porch step and it groaned beneath him. Her body gave a quick shiver at the sound, and the spell was broken, and though she closed her eyes and sought them out, she could not recall the look of them to her mind, not at all. The harder she tried, the farther they receded into a place she could neither reach nor see, until she gave up in a deep sadness, and opened her eyes again. It was suddenly darker—and colder— where she was standing, and another shiver went up her spineparts. She looked up to see where the sun had gone, and found that a large patch of cloud had passed in front it and was hovering there, as if it meant to stay, with others of its kin rising behind it on the wind. She could smell the iron-heaviness of moisture in the air that she hadn't noticed before, when the day had been clear and warm.

He was looking up at the gathering clouds with her.

"Water done coming," he said, more to himself than to her.

"Yessir," she agreed, coming fully back, at last, to his presence and their conversation. "Look like it fixing to rain."

His gaze snapped back down to her, and he fixed his eyes on her in disapproval. "That ain't the water what I'm talking about," he barked at her.

She shrunk back a little under his glare and the sharpness of his words. But his look softened, and he gave her a small smile that seemed strangely sad.

"You's a good girl, Ula-child," he said, quietly. "You's ever been that way. You does listens, not like them other childrens. So this be something you must listen at, and you listen good. The time done come for left-here."

She was glad of that. As elated as she had been only a moment ago to have come to the old family home, the thought of Goat Hill made her suddenly impatient to return there. "Yessir," she said, beginning to feel a rising eagerness about it. "Mama and the rest, they gon' be so *happy* for see you! I were going out to Lusi's. You want for go that way? We can fetch a wagon and ride back. Or we can walk. Whichever you wants, Grandpa." She was so happy, she felt herself babbling. She stopped abruptly, because he was continuing to stare at her in a way that threw her off balance again.

He shook his head.

"No," he said, his voice quiet and serious, smothering her enthusiasm. "No." He said the word again and shook his head to it, to make sure she understood. "That ain't the lefting what I's talking about."

Feeling the chill of the afternoon growing, she wrapped her arms around her chest and shoulders, grabbing the back of her dress. She now felt completely confused.

"What you does mean, Grandpa?" she asked. "Left for where?"

He did not answer her directly.

"You know, it ain't the buckra what bringing the water," he said.

She opened her mouth to ask another question, but no question would form itself.

"Folk be thinking it the buckra bringing that water," he went on. "Buckra thinking they bringing it, too. But it ain't."

The wind took up again now, a cool wind, and brisk, making a low rustle in the trees across the field from the Quarters cabins on both sides. The old buildings that had any standing left to them bent before it, and straightened back. Somewhere she thought she heard a pair of birds calling to each other, stop, call again, and then grow quiet. There seemed to be signs of something giving out all around her, but she could not make a meaning of any of them.

She was shivering all over now.

"It cold, Grandpa," she said, almost in a whimper. And then, "Why-fore you talking about the water?"

"'Cause it got for cleanse, that-why," he answered, his voice a little harsher. "It got for wash it all 'way. It done rot, and it stinking. And it got for cleanse. I done'd talk with all the peoples, and that-what they done say." He pointed up the road, away from the direction that she had come out of the sawgrass field. "You must go back and tell them. You hear me? You must tell Baba'Zambu and the rest. Tell'em y'all got for left here. Y'all got for left Yelesaw and go over on t'other side. Now get!"

She stood there in the road in front of him, swaying back and forth, feeling thoroughly miserable and bewildered.

His tone did not invite a challenge, but she felt she had no choice.

"You want me for left you, Grandpa?" she asked him. "You ain't coming back with me?"

He continued to fix his eyes on her. "What I done'd just tol'ded you for tell Baba'Zambu?" he asked.

She tried to recall, exactly. She had been so struck by his telling her to leave, she had not paid much attention to his message.

He sucked his teeth in anger and said it again, this time more emphatically, then made her repeat it, to make certain she'd gotten it right. The water was needed for a cleansing. The "people" had told him. What "people?" He did not explain, and so she could only guess. The water was coming, and they needed to leave the Neck and go across the river. The meaning of his words began to sink in.

"We must left Yelesaw?" she asked him. She was now trembling almost uncontrollably.

"Y'all is. And *you*, girl, must left here, *now*, and fetch that news to Baba'Zambu and the others," he answered, jabbing his finger in the direction up the road. "Now *get*, girl, like I done'd say!"

The final "get" was said with such vehemence that she jumped and took a step backward. The movement grew upon itself and she began to back away from him, slowly, one foot behind the other, still looking at him, still holding her arms wrapped around herself. Tears clouded her eyes and began to spill over. She half-turned and took a step in the direction she'd been going when she'd first seen him, down towards the woods. But he stopped her with another question before she could go any further.

"You know where you's going?" he asked her.

She nodded, miserably, rubbing her running nose with the back of her hand as she did. "Over to Lusi's. I'm fetching supper for Mookie." That errand—which had been so important when she left out from home—now seemed like something out of another era of her life. And, of course, she now didn't even have any supper to fetch.

"That way go down past the Gaya," he told her. "You know what the Gaya be?"

"Yessir," she said. Her mind was clear enough to remember that. "Mamarisa done tell'ded me."

He gave a grim nod of approval. "Good thing *somebody's* telling these ignorant-ass childrens something," he said. His voice got firmer, again. "You skirt that Gaya, girl, you hear? Don't you tarry down there. Walk'round it, and don't you 'sturb'em, none. 'Round the far side, you be done pick up the path over to the Butlers. It ain't hard for find, iffen you ain't let them confuse you."

Disturb *them*? Let *them*? Let *who*?

She did not get the chance to ask him for any clarification, because he was ordering her off again. "What'wrong with you' feets?" he asked her. "How many time I must told you for get? *Damn*, you'se a dis'bedient heifer!"

She turned and started walking away, slowly, forcing each step over a road that held to the bottoms of her feet like sticky cane-syrup, step upon step, trying to fight off the feeling of devastation of his dismissal of her and of him calling her out of her name.

He had taken up his playing on the mouth-harp again, and she turned her head as she walked to see that he was sitting there on the top step of the cabin as she had first seen him, head down, work hat pulled over his eyes, concentrating on the mouth-harp, seemingly having put her out of his mind altogether. She wished that she had hugged his neck, just one time, to show him how much she loved him, and how happy she was to have found him again, after he had lost himself up in the Swamp. But it was too late now. There was no way she could go back.

She looked away from him and continued up the road, and as she crossed over into the field beyond the cabins, the music of the mouth-harp began to turn—gradual—back into the sound of the creaking hinge. She turned her head back again to get a last look at him, but the road had begun to bend, and a stand of trees blocked her way, and he was gone from her sight.

SHE WALKED FOR A WHILE as if she were coming out of a foggy haze. She had wrapped up all that had happened with her grandfather and put it down deep in the pocket of her dress, blocking it from her mind. She was determined to only think about it again when the day was over, and she was back in the yard at Goat Hill, and able to see things clearly and sort them out.

She noticed that the day had grown even cooler as soon as she had left out of the vicinity of the Quarters. The rising clouds had coalesced to form a great battlement over to her right, in the direction of the swamp-side, all tall, gray-black towers and massive walls mounted one upon the other, with billowed gates that opened for a view deep into the fade-blue insides of the sky. Small, wispy vapor scouts had already been sent up to form a screen over the sun, making it a weak, pale-yellow circle in the midst of a rising dark tide. Rain was definite coming, sometime before evening, for sure. She began to walk faster.

The road took another turn, this time back to the right, came out of a tangle of shrub bushes and palmettos, and then ended abruptly, giving way entirely to a field of yellow-green marshgrass.

She stopped at the edge of the field.

Straight ahead, in between the grass patches, which rose as high as her lower hips, she could see a glint of pale water spread out in the middle of the field. There could be no doubt. That was where the Gaya Pond lay.

She paused to pull the one thing out of her pocket about her grandfather's conversation that she needed to remember right now. She must not tarry at the pond. She did not wonder or worry about the "them" he had told her not to disturb. She did not have to know who the "them" were. It could be snakes or even gators out sunning themselves at the water's edge, or nothing more than wasps or hidden hornets' nests. It didn't matter. She had no intention of going near enough to the pond to find out. She had only to follow his instructions to skirt the water and pick up the road to the Sosoville turnoff somewhere on the other side, beyond it, and she would be alright.

But now that she no longer had the road to be her boundary guide, she had enough woods-sense to figure out her path before she took it. From the rank and brackish smell coming out from it, she figured the field must be the beginnings of a wetlands. That meant bogs and sinks, which the thick marshgrass would hide until you had already fallen into them. Even without her grandfather's warning to keep her away, she knew that the closer she came to the pond, the more likely she was to run into such waterholes.

She thought, therefore, for the briefest of moments, that she might circle the marshfield around its edge and pick up the path she was looking for as it entered the woods somewhere opposite where she was standing. She decided against that, almost immediately. Her grandfather had said that the path out to the Butlers was somewhere on the "far side" of the pond. Though he hadn't been specific, she'd taken that to mean that the path was an extension of the one on which she'd been walking. If she went around the edge of the field, there was no telling what paths she would encounter, or whether they would be the right one, or where they might lead, perhaps even down into the Swamp. No, she would have to stick as close the pond as she dared, and trust that the right path would somehow show itself to her after she got around the waters.

With a squaring of her shoulders she started off, straight ahead across the marshfield towards the Gaya.

The pond was ringed by cattails that began amidst the marshgrass, the grass gradually thinning out until it began to be all cats, which continued on into the pondshallows and ranged out some ways into the water. Several yards back from the edge of of the cattail ring seemed a convenient boundary for her make her way around the pond, not too close to the water, but close enough to keep it in her sight. She marked a spot in the grass to make for. Long before she got to her marker, however, she stepped into a patch of soft mud, invisible under the marshgrass. Careful to keep her other foot on solid ground, holding one arm out for balance and grabbing a fistful of the thick marshgrass for support with her other hand, she lifted her foot and pulled it free. It was thick with black muck, and stank. Now that she was close to it she found, in fact, that the whole edge of the pond stank, a pungent, brooding smell of plant-rot and slimed earth that rose up her nose and gave her shoulders an involuntary shudder.

She wasn't as close to the cattails as she had planned, but this was close enough. She turned to the left and resumed walking, parallel to the cattails and the edge of the pondwaters, stepping more carefully now for fear of bogging herself again. But even though she had been watching out for it, she had only gone a few feet when she stepped into another patch of soft mud, her foot sinking up above her ankle before she could pull it back out again.

Before she made another move, she considered the best move to make.

She looked to her right across the waters of the pond. Now that she was close enough, she could see a great flotilla of dragonflies were hovering just above its surface, stretching far out into the center until she could no longer detect their individual bodies, but only a sort of transparent sheen. Beneath them, the water itself was no longer pale and reflective, but dull and dark-amber under the graying sky. She could see why the old folks had once called it Yellowpond. It wasn't a very big pond—you could swim it if you were fool enough to have a mind to—and she could easily see across to the far ring of cattails and the other side of the marshfield beyond that. Somewhere over there was the way to Lusi's and then home. She just had to get around the water. That *damned* water. That's what her grandfather would have said.

Thinking of him made her give a small smile, and raised her spirits out of a seriousness that had begun to oppress at her.

You just got for walk slow, girl, she said to herself, and reckon before you take every step, and you won't get yourself in no trouble. That was Papa talking, now. Papa, who had given her and her brothers long lessons in how to conduct themselves in the woods. Or, rather, Papa had given the lessons to her brothers and Boo on fish-trips and such, and she had been close enough by to be able to get the benefit. The worst trouble you could get you'self *into* in the woods, Papa would always say, was trying to get you'self away too fast *outten* trouble. She repeated his axiom to remind herself, and to make sure she followed it. You just got for walk slow, and reckon before you take every step.

Now that she had stopped, she could hear that a sort of light rattling had taken up in the field somewhere directly in front of her, somewhere beyond the muddy patch, a rattling so low that it had probably been going on for some time, maybe as soon as she had entered the field, but she either had not heard it before or hadn't paid it any attention. It didn't seem to be anything loud enough to be dangerous, not a rattlesnake, certainly. And it wasn't the dragonflies out on the water. They never made any sound at all, except for a soft whirring of their wings that you could only hear if you lay still in the grass and waited until they came close by. Maybe it was only a swarm of small bugs. Hoping they weren't the stinging kind, she decided she had more pressing things to figure out and manage, and gave the rattling no further thought.

She turned slightly to the left again, keeping the pond in sight, now somewhat back behind her and on her right, and took off through the grass, hoping that a few feet would take her to where she could turn and skirt around the edge of the mudsink. She hadn't walked far, though, before she ran into it again, or another one, it really didn't matter which, both feet sinking in dangerously deep before she could stop herself.

You *ass*, she thought, now angry with herself for what was obviously her continuing carelessness, even though she had believed that she was being especially careful after bogging the first two times.

It took a while, this time, to get herself back out.

The bug-rattling—if indeed it was a bug-rattling—was coming from behind her now, and it had risen a little in volume and intensity, as if in reaction to her predicament. The confused sound of it didn't help her any, and was beginning to annoy her. She shook her head to rid herself of the sound, and concentrated on what she needed to do.

There was no way that she could turn around in the mud to reach the edge from where she'd come in, she was stuck down so deep with all two feet. The left-hand edge of the mudsink, thick with marshgrass, was easily within reach, however. She bent at the knee until she could get a good enough grip on a big patch of the grass with her left hand, close-down to its roots, and pulled. Her left foot sank deeper in the mud but her right foot slipped free, and she was able to swivel her body and get a grip on a second grasspatch with her right hand. That gave her leverage enough, and with an effort, she was able to pull her whole body free of the mud. She turned on her hands and knees and crawled a couple of feet ahead to make sure she was entirely clear, and then turned and sat down in the grass to to get a look at the mudpatch she had just freed herself from.

But something about the view was immediately confusing.

The mudpatch was just ahead of where she was sitting, where she had left it, and she could see the long depression—slowly filling up with its own ooze—where she had laid herself over and pulled herself out.

It was the pond which was not at all where she thought it should be.

It should have been over to her right, unless she had gotten herself thoroughly turned around, but when she looked that way, all was unbroken field of marshgrass, with the far line of the woods-tops rising above and beyond it.

She looked to her left and there it was, the yellow waters of the pond just behind the cattail ring.

She reconstructed her pathway from when she had been walking within sight of the pond on her right, to her bogging into the last mudpatch and getting back out, to where she was now sitting in something of a confusement in the grass. Everything told her that the pond should have still been on her right.

She was not at all certain how she could have gotten herself that thoroughly turned around, and the thought momentarily shook her, given that she still had to navigate the marshfield and get through a long stretch of woods she had never been in, before she found the familiar Sosoville road. She felt herself as ignorant as a town girl, who needed the names written on signs at each intersection of a street or road, so she wouldn't forget which one of them she was on.

Behind her, as she sat, she noticed that the bug-rattling paused for a second, held its breath, and then resumed.

She took a long breath herself, blinking slowly.

The rattling sound had begun to interfere with her thinking—and maybe that was the problem—and she wished that it would stop for more than just a brief moment so that she could get her bearings. What she needed was a landmark to sight off of other than the pond, which, she was beginning to suspect, seemed determined to trick her and make her lose her way. She stood up and tried to find a distinguishing tree in the circle of woods that surrounded the marshfield, but could find none that remained long enough for her to be able to rely upon. It seemed that every time she thought she had found a landmark branch among them, taller than the rest and in an odd shape that could be easily remembered, after she looked away and then looked back again, she could no longer pick out what it was she had just thought she had seen.

This is flat-out mule-stupid, Yally'Bay Kinlaw, she said to herself, and sucked her teeth. You mough't-well be a ninny-baby wandering you' way back'a the woods.

She took another quick look to her left to make sure that the pond, at least, was still there. It was.

The way around the pond showed no obvious barriers—what was hidden she'd have to deal with when she came up on it, of course—and so she could see no other choice but to continue walking around it as she had been. She found an old tree branch not far from where she had been standing, broke it off at the right length, and using the branch as a probe, took off again through the marshgrass even slower and more carefully than before, one tentative step, then another, testing the ground with first the tip of the branch and then the balls of her feet before she put her full weight down.

Around her as she resumed her walk, the buzz-whisper rose, and then fell, and then rose again. With it also rose the wind, swirling around the marshgrass and the cattails and sending wave-ripples across the pondwaters, blowing the mud-stench scent up into her nose. She sneezed, several times, but the smell did not blow back out. She reasoned, ruefully, that it was probably because she was so covered with bog-mud that she was carrying the smell of it along with her. She stopped and broke off a handful of marshgrass and tried to wipe the mud from the side of her and her legs, but though some of it came off, a good deal only smeared and spread, and she gave up the effort. She decided that even if she had time to take a long bath in the tub at Lusi's, she would most certainly jump into one of ponds near the Hill as soon as she got back there—a *clean* pond, she said to herself, with emphasis— clothes and all. She began to look forward to her anticipated swim, and it gave her a renewed determination to get herself home.

The marshgrass grew somewhat taller here, at points rising to her waist, thicker, and more difficult to pass through. Poking at the ground in front of her with the branch, she pushed the grass stalks aside with sweeps of her free arm as she took careful, tentative steps forward, looking alternately ahead—to watch for mud and bogs—and to her right—to make sure that the pond continued to stay in the same place she thought it should be.

She had gone only a little ways before she felt something coming up through the air behind her, as if something had been thrown at the back of her head.

Her heart jumped and she dropped down, instinctively. Something large passed over her head, very large, so low that she could feel the wind from it in its wake, and then it rose at a low but steady angle as it made a wide bank to the right and flew out over the pond. She could see now what it was, a great blue heron, a magnificient bird, the largest she had ever seen, long body straight as an arrow from pointed beak to curled feet, massive wings spread out wider than Yally was tall, its feathers a soft-blue gray reflected in the waning sun, calling a "yak-yak-yaaaaaakkkkk" as it passed over the water.

She squatted amidst the marshgrass and watched the heron disappear beyond the far side of the pond, envying it. By now the big bird was probably over the Sosoville turnoff, which its sharp eyes could easily see from flight, and in a few more moments it would be over Sosoville itself, avoiding all the tangle and trees and undergrowth below. She wished she could transform herself into a bird for that few moments so that she could be walking up Lusi's front steps right now, or, at the very least, grow herself some wings. She was not looking forward to the walk that was left to her, most especially the getting of herself around the pond and out of the marshfield, which had become far more difficult and taking much longer than she had ever thought it would.

"Hope you find what you hunting for, quicker'n me, old bird," she thought.

She stood up and began her careful walk again, the pond remaining to her right. She realized that she had not bothered to count her steps to measure her distance when she first sighted the pond, as she had often seen her mother and her aunts do when they were figuring out their gardens, or the men out in the fields. She sucked her teeth at her thoughtlessness. When she got around the other side of the pond, that would be the way she would calculate how far to walk to find the right path on that end. Now she began to count. One, two, three, poking at the ground with her tree-branch. Before she had gotten to ten, however, she was distracted from her counting by a small, dark spot dropping down from high in the air on the other side of the marshfield, growing larger and larger as it approached. She stopped to try to figure out what it might be, until it let out a call of "yak-yak-yaaaaaalll111," and she realized it was the big blue heron returning.

She watched as the bird continued to drop down towards the water, beating its wings once or twice to gain speed as it approached, and it was clear that it was coming straight towards her.

She knew that she should move to get out of the bird's path but could not, could only watch, fascinated, like a squirrel in a shaft of growing light, as it converged its mass upon the spot where she was standing, growing, spreading, mighty wings extending, blocking off all possible escape to both left and right, until, just at the last possible moment, she came out of her trance, and dropped down again into the grass, stone-quick, as the heron swooshed over, its claws almost brushing the top of her headscarf as it passed, giving out another angry "yak-yak-yaaaaaaallllllleeeee"as it did.

She stayed hunched down in the marshgrass to catch her breath and slow her heartbeat.

When she stood up again, finally, there was no sign of the bird anywhere.

She was beginning to become frightened now, unsettled, anxious to be out of the marshfield as quickly as she could. The bird seemed to be deliberately hunting her, which made no sense, but there it was. Abandoning her plan to go around the edge of the pond, she decided it was best to go straight to the closest patch of the woods, which she could easily see above the marshgrass ahead of her, and take her chances finding the path that way. Still mindful of the hidden bogs and mudpatches, she walked forward at a slightly quicker pace, furiously poking at the ground ahead with her branch, her head now swiveling back to front and side to side, watching all around her to see where the heron had gone.

Even though she thought she was being especially attentive to its whereabouts, she heard it before she saw it, a call of "yak-yak-yaaaaaaalllllleeeee, yak-yak-yaaaaaaalllllllleeeee!" coming up rapidly from her right, away from the direction of the water.

She turned her head sharp and saw it coming, low over the marshgrass, skimming the very grasstops, ruffling them with its breastfeathers. Before she could even move again, she realized, in a flash, what was happening. The heron wasn't hunting her. It was driving her. That was the only explanation. It's nest must be somewhere close by, and she was threatening it. The longer she stayed in the vicinity, the more furious would be the heron's attacks, until it tried to throw itself through the air upon her and into her with its sword-pointed beak. Why hadn't she realized that before?

Forgetting all about bogs or anything but getting away from the bird and its nest as fast as she could, she took off through the marshgrass at the dead run, getting a tighter grip on her branch in case she needed it to fend the heron off if it got too close again.

Turning her head to her right as she ran, she saw that it had taken notice of her flight and was banking in her direction, in a pathway to intercept. It was rapidly closing the distance between them, and even though she was now leaping forward in great bounds, straddling the marshgrass like a hurdler, the woods were still too far away. Just as the heron was almost upon her and she was tensing herself for a dive to the ground, the ground itself suddenly dropped beneath her feet, transforming from firm into fluid, and she realized that she was already several splashing steps out into the waters of the pond, and the muddy bottom had caught her legs and ankles and were slowing her to an abrupt stop.

She winced and ducked to her left and threw up her hands to cover her head and braced for an impact, but the heron must have begun to ascend even before it reached her, because as it passed over her it was already several feet above and rising with a few swift beats of its stately wings, making a sweeping turn to the left and continuing to rise as it crossed the water again, mounting, lifting higher and higher in the sky, until it passed into a great bank of gathering clouds and disappeared from her sight and it was gone, leaving its final, fading call of "yak-yak-yaaaaaaalllllleeeee, yak-yak-yaaaaaaalllllleeeee!" as the only sign that it had ever been there.

And leaving her trapped calf-deep in the bottom-mud of the pond.

Standing there with the cold, straw-colored waters just hitting her lower thighs, her grandfather's warning came back to her.

"You skirt that Gaya, girl. Walk'round it. Don't you tarry down there. Don't you 'sturb'em, none."

She decided it was best not to think about that, because she could not undo what she'd already done. She could only get herself back out of the pond.

AT FIRST SHE DID NOTHING to try to extract herself while she looked around to take an assessment of her situation.

At first she thought that she must have lost sight of the pond as she was running and stupidly stumbled into it. She found that she had not. Instead, the main body of the water was still to her left, but a spur of it, hidden by the marshgrass ahead of her all the way down to its edge, was extended out to the right, directly crossing her path. Of course, whether it was by carelessness or not hardly mattered, as she had still gotten herself stuck in the muddy bottom of the pond, regardless.

Even just standing there, not moving, she could feel herself sinking into the mud in the smallest of increments, the line of water slowly creeping up her thighs. The pondwater stank, and she did not relish getting any more of it on her than already was. She was only a few yards out from the bank behind her, fortunately, so there would be no need to swim herself out and so immerse herself in it entirely.

She tried to lift first one leg, and then the other, but the motion did not free either one, and, in fact, made her sinking accelerate, just a bit.

She stopped trying to free herself that way and waited to see if she would reach a more solid bottom below the mud-line. There had to be a bottom down there, somewhere. While she was waiting and feeling with her toes in the soft mud below her, she turned her head around and took a more precise calculation of the distance to the bank. She was more than a body's-and-arm's length away from solid ground, and so she knew it was no good to try to lay out and grasp something on the dry land to pull herself out, even if she could somehow manage to twist her body around to manage the attempt.

But that gave her another idea.

There was a patch of cattails growing out of the water to her right, just within her reach. She leaned in that direction, trying to ignore the fact that it made her right leg sink even deeper, caught the cattails as far down in the water as she could manage so that she could grasp them nearest their anchor point, and pulled on them, hard, bracing down on her right leg and trying to get enough leverage to lift her left. She could feel the pressure around her left ankle and foot give just a little as the mudbottom began to loosen its grip. But then the cattail bunch stretched, strained, and snapped off completely in her fist, the brown tips flying up into the air and settling back down in the water, bobbing up and down in it like little canoes. The recoil sent her back to her left, digging her left leg down deeper in the mud, and she wobbled back and forth for a moment as if she were about to lose her balance, thrusting her arms up and out to keep from doing so. But she was anchored in the pond-bottom and so she could not be tipped over, and in a moment she had settled herself. The rank, yellow pondwaters had now risen above her privates and were lapping at her waist in the backlash of her effort, and the mud had tightened its hold around her legs, its dark, slick fingers now up around her mid-calf, and holding firm.

She looked across the pond in front and to the left of her, empty of all life except the for the flocks of dragonflies skimming its surface. She looked up at the acres of marshland grass surrounding on all sides, and the circle of silent woods beyond that. There was no need to cry out for help. There was no-one to hear. She was by herself.

And then the clouds split, broke themselves open, and fat drops of rain, scattered at first, but quickening, began to fall first upon the waters and then upon her.

She continued to sink, the water now just above her waistline, and rising.

The thought that she could die—right here, and right now—rose up in her in a panic.

She was not quite ready for that, and her mind rushed ahead of her, grasping at ways of escape, tossing them away as their uselessness became quickly apparent.

She let out a low, despairing wail, expelling the fear from her as she did.

The horror of the rising yellow waters was rising within her, but she that there was no other other choice but to get down in them.

Steeling herself against the shock, she took a deep breath amidst the rising rainfall and bent her knees and let herself drop down into the water until it covered her head, her behind now floating just above the mudbottom. The cold, murky waters were as frightening as she thought they would be. They pressed inward against her body from all sides, especially around her head, the water so thick and silted that she could see little of nothing in it, not even the cattail stems that she could feel only inches away from her, only the few bubbles rising involuntarily towards the surface from out of her nose. She thrust her open hands like two spades deep into the mud on either side of her legs, dug them in, and pulled outward and upward through the resistance of the water, trying to pull enough of the mud away so that she could get her legs out.

The water pressed and pounded on her eardrums, but as she dug at the entrapping mud, she thought she heard something else drifting up through the dim water from the mudbottom below her.

The swirling from her disturbement of the waters around her was confusing her, and so she stopped her digging, just for a moment, to try make out what it was that she was hearing.

She'd thought the sound was coming from the water itself, but now she could see that it was not.

Instead, it seemed to be rising up from the mud beneath her, at first dim and indistinct, but gradually losing its ambiguity as she concentrated her mind on it. Her long-held breath was beginning to burn her chest and lungs, and a band was tightening around her forehead, but she ignored it and focused on the sound coming up from below, at first a muffled whisper, but beginning to grow in both volume and intensity.

There could be no doubt about it now. It sounded like a moaning.

At first it seemed like one voice only down there under the waters, but as it became louder and more clamorous and intreating, joined by another, and then another.

Now it was rising, and swelling, and filling the waters all around her, and it became a chorus.

A great chorus.

A chorus of watery human voices moaning their pain from out of the mud below the pondwater, hollowed and echoing, as if coming up from out of the depths of some great pit, crying out, as if they had waited for many years for just this moment for someone to step out into the water and hear their sorrow-song, voices drawing her down into the earth itself down deep below the pondwaters. The voices wailed, and the mud tightened its grip upon her calves and ankles and pulled, as if hands were pulling her downwards deeper into the water, into the mud, into the pit beneath the mud. She tried but she could not hold them back, and felt herself being dragged into the ink-dark blackness below. Down there she could see their faces, the eyes rolled up white in their sockets, and around their heads was the streaming of tears, and the flowing of blood, that formed the deep and unseen rivers that were the dark source of all the waters of all the world.

They had been waiting.

They had been waiting.

They had been waiting for her.

The moaning turned into a single, water-hoarse word—*Yalleeeee*—and with that word, she knew them for who they were.

The people at the bottom of the Gaya Pond.

They knew her name, and they knew her, but she was not yet ready for them to have her.

Compacting herself down deep in the water, coiling, tensing, bracing, she suddenly sprung toward the pond's surface with all of the strength she had gathered to herself in all of her young life, trying to launch herself out of the trap of mud, as if she could fly.

FAR DOWN on the other end of Yelesaw, at just that time, the Eldest stirred in his bed. The great-granddaughter looked up from the table across the room, first at the chimney to make sure the fire had not gone too low—the elder one loved a high fire no matter what the season—and then at the Eldest himself, who was lying on his back now, his eyes open, staring up at the ceiling. The great-granddaughter had been singing to herself as she was cleaning the snapbeans, and she hoped she hadn't sung too loud and awakened him. She was worried that the Eldest did not get nearly enough sleep, these days. He was generally up most of the night, every night, and only rested fitfully by day.

"You all right, Tat'Zambu?" the great-granddaughter called across to him. "You' foots done paining you again?"

Baba'Zambu grunted no, and then turned on his side to see her better, wiping at the phlegm caked in the corners of his eyes, which would not focus at that distance, and could only show her as a soft blur.

"Who been by'yere just now?" he asked her.

"By here? Ain't nobody been by here, Tat'Zambu. Me and you the onliest ones been in this house all day. That door ain't even done been'a open since this morning. I done tol'ded them childrens, don't be coming all in and out like coon in the chickenshack and disturbing you' rest. They out in the yard out them, playing. Maybe them's what you heard."

He shook his head.

"Who done left a message for me, then?" he asked her.

"Not no message with me. I ain't been outside all day, 'xcept to holler at them childrens from the porch, and ain't nobody been in, like I done say, Grandpapa." She walked over to his bed and sat down in the chair next to it, putting her hand down on the covers beside him as a gesture of comfort. "You hungry? You want some soup, or something?"

Baba'Zambu shook his head again. He was not annoyed by her trying to get his mind on another subject, as if he were so old that something like that would work on him. She was a good girl, one of the several of his grands and great-grands who traded shifts to look after him, and she meant no harm. He coughed to clear the mucous out of his throat. "Him come up in the house, here," he said, patiently insistent as one who was used to possessing knowledge others around him did not have but needed to hear. "I hear him when he come in and say what him had for say, and I hear him when he done said it, but now I can't hardly recollect what it been him done say—" He paused. "You ain't hear what Budi Manigault say?" he asked her.

"Tat'Budi?" The great-granddaughter gave the Eldest a look of puzzlement. "Tat'Budi, him ain't been by here. Him gone'd up to the Swamp and ain't come out, yet, you ain't remember? Nobodys ain't seen Tat'Budi since winter gone."

The Eldest started to say something more but his voice drifted off without a word coming out, and he turned on his back again, adjusting himself, painfully, under the covers, not saying anything more. The great-granddaughter sat and watched him for a while, and at first she thought that he had gone back to sleep again, and was glad. But after she got up and went back to her snapbeans, she noticed that every now and again, the Eldest's eyes eased open again, and he would stare up at the ceiling for a while, as if in deep thought. He went on like that for the longest, all the rest of the afternoon.

Outside, it had taken up a raining.

IN THE WOODS just on the other side of the Gaya Pond marshfield, near the far boundary of old Bethelia Plantation, it was just letting up raining, and Yally was walking.

She was not certain exactly how she came to be walking there. She remembered, with great clarity, all of the events of the day leading up to her getting out from the Gaya Pond. She also remembered a little of lying in the grass on the edge of the pond afterwards, sobbing in both sorrow and relief as the rain pelted her body and drenched her even more than the pondwaters had, washing away its mud and stench. But how long she lay there, she was not at all sure, nor did she recall gathering the strength to get up, at last, and come down through the marshgrass to the woods, or of circling the woods-edge until she found what seemed like the right way. She only knew that she must have done these things because when she came to herself again, she was walking down this pathway deep into the trees, and everything in her told her that she was walking away from Bethelia, and not deeper back into it.

She was as weary of mind and spirit and body as she had ever been in her life, and, nursing an ankle that had gotten itself twisted coming out of the pond, she limped along in the growing dusk over bushes and roots and the dead remains of fallen trees along a clearly long-abandoned pathway whose course she could only just barely make out, it was so overgrown. She did not know if this was the right pathway, and she did not care. Anything to get her far away from the marshfield and the Gaya and Bethelia would do.

She had walked for what seemed like quite a distance through the woods when the path wore itself out at the beginning of a bramble-thicket. Not wanting to veer away from her straight retreat she pushed forward, unmindful of the bramble-thorns that tore at what remained of her dress and flesh. She was through it in a moment, out into a well-traveled wagonway that both seemed and looked familiar. She turned to the right on it, and walked down into Sosoville.

THE SETTLEMENT WAS STRANGELY SILENT and empty of all human life for any hour of the day before bedtime. She passed several houses, all mute and unlit, with no movement at all around them except for the packs of dogs which wandered out to greet her. Though it was not unusual during the planting time for the field-workers to be out after dark, there was no sign of any of the women who would have stayed home with the house chores, or the little children they would have been minding, or of the cooksmoke or the smell of supper fixings which should have been rising from every chimney. It was an unsettling ending to an unsettling day.

Her sister's and Bubba'Kess's house, which was set off in its own grove a little bit aways from the main Sosoville settlement, was no different, still and dark as all the others. She stepped up on the porch and, without knocking, pushed the front door open and walked inside. She found a box of matches on the window sill where Lusi always kept them, and lit the kerosene lamp hanging on its hook next to the door. Raising the lamp high to take a look around, she did not have to go further than the main room to see that Lusi had not been there for many hours and must, indeed, have left in something of a hurry. While the house was not in what anyone would call disarray, it had an untidiness about it that her oldest sister would never have allowed to remain, if she'd had the time or thought to correct it.

There was no need to call out but she did, saying her sister's name loud, twice, and then waiting. Nothing stirred inside the house, and no-one answered.

She blew out the lamp and replaced it on its hook, then walked back outside and slumped down on the top steps of the porch, elbows propped up on her knees, her face buried in her hands, fighting off exhaustion, trying to figure out what to do next. She could go down to the hunt-shack to see if Mookie was there, but it seemed unlikely that the whole of Sosoville would have suddenly evacuated while leaving her brother behind by himself, and anyways, it was such a long, long walk down through the woods to the shack, and she was so very tired and spent of spirit. Too tired, in fact, to try to figure out what might have happened to make everyone in the settlement just up and leave. She figured she would find out, soon enough. All she wanted to do now was to get herself home.

She got up and limped around back to the barn, trying to ignore the paining in her ankle. As she had expected, the wagon was gone, as well as Bubba'Kess's good mule from the pen. His old mule was there, however, and after some coaxing, she got it to stay still by the pen fence long enough for her to mount it, and she started off across the Sosoville bigyard and then down the wagonpath back out to the River Road, glad to be able to ride and so put everything more rapidly behind her.

IT WAS FULL-ON DARK by the time she got out on the main road but she had no trouble seeing, as a three-quarter moon had risen and was flooding the way with its pale-yellow light. There were no more decisions to make about which way to go, nothing for her to do but keep the mule pushing forward, and so she rode without paying much attention to her surroundings, her mind slipping in and out of awareness. She had already gone through the Crossroads and had turned the bend beyond its sight before she realized it, but she no longer had the energy to worry-up over that, and she made a few half-hearted signs behind her without thinking too much about them. The Crossroads had surely had its way with her that day already, she figured, and needed to bother with her no more.

The River Road was long and lonely and as empty as Sosoville

had been, and she met not a single wagon or walker or rider upon
it. Now her mind refocused, and she began to put it to work on the
mystery of everyone's disappearance.

She did not think that there had been some great disaster, like
the cable-barge collapsing with many wagons on it, or a major fire
in one of the settlements. Lusi's house had been untidy, but not in
the kind of chaos that might have been expected if everyone was in
a rush to get out somewhere to save folks' lives. Perhaps some news
had come, maybe about the whitefolks and their Watercoming,
something that required immediate response, and they had all
been called out to the Goma. That seemed more likely. She hoped
that there would be at least one person left on Goat Hill to provide
an explanation, but even if there wasn't, she was not of a mind to
go hunting anyone any more. As she made the turn into the
wagonpath down into Goat Hill at last, she realized that she was
too tired to even go for the swim she had anticipated before, but
now only looked forward to filling the tub out behind the house
and washing all of the day off of her, and whenever all of them got
back home from wherever they had been, they would find her
under the covers in her pallet in her bedroom, deep in sleep, and
wake her up if there was anything that needed telling. Right now,
she cared about nothing else but bed.

But something was happening down in Goat Hill that would
not allow her troubled day to end, just yet.

As she came through the last stretch of the wagonpath, she
began to see a glow filtering through the trees coming from the
direction of the Bigyard, growing in intensity as she rode forward,
too bright and reaching too far into the woods and up the path to
be coming from the normal settlement lights. Slowly, too slowly—
her mind was still not functioning right—the conclusion dawned
upon her that it could only be from somebody's house on fire,
maybe more than one house. Her heart now thumping hard in her
chest and seeming about to burst, she spurred the mule forward
and around the last turn and out onto the beginning of the Yard,
where she reined it in to a dead-still stop as she came into view of
something completely unexpected.

Across the way, it was Grandpa Budi's house that was ablaze
with lights, but not from any house fire. A multitude of lanterns
had been hung at every free point along the rafters of the front
porch, and there were several more lanterns set along the porch
railings as well, at the front and on both sides. Two great burning
torches had been put in the ground on each side of the walkway

leading up to the front porch steps, and a little bit to the side of them, an enormous log fire was alight, the flames rising as high as the bottom eaves of the roof and sending cinders far up and out into the sky. Grandpa Budi's house itself was all lamplit up inside in a way that it had not been for more than a year, maybe not ever, certainly not since before Sister Orry's passing, when it had been a house of many and frequent visitors.

And far from being deserted, Goat Hill—or, more particularly, Grandpa Budi's house—was where everyone on Yelesaw Neck seemed to have come.

A great crowd was milling around out on the front porch, spilling over into the yard and then around both sides towards the back, and the hum of their conversations could be heard all the way out to where Yally was sitting on the mule. From what she could see through the open door and shutters, the house itself was also filled to overcapacity. A great fleet of wagons and mules, ox carts and even goat carts were parked a little ways off from the house, leaving no doubt that if all of Yelesaw was not there, it was not missing by much. She had never seen such a crowd assembled before except at the Goma gatherings or at the Sambu.

It did not take her long to figure out what must have happened.

Half a day had passed since she had seen her grandfather down in Bethelia, and it was clear that he had either afterwards met up with someone else who was more persuasive than she, or had decided on his own to come back home, beating her there by enough time so that the word had gotten all around Yelesaw, and so this great crowd had come to welcome him back. That was not surprising. Budi Manigault's return out of the back eddies of the Blacksnake and the deeps of the Swamp would have been the most important news they had heard since—well, since the announcement that the whitefolks were planning to flood Yelesaw—and no-one would have wanted to miss such an event.

She watched the gathering for a moment from across the Bigyard under the shadow of the trees as she sorted out her feelings.

She was glad, so glad, that Grandpa Budi had come back home, and his house was opened back up again, and this terrible time in the life of the family was ended. But for her part, she had no need to join in the celebration. She had already seen her grandfather, and talked with him, and that was enough for her. Conscious of how bedraggled she must look, and beyond fatigued, and overwhelmed by the thought of seeing or talking with anyone else that night, she turned the mule's head from her grandfather's, and over towards her own house.

She crossed the Yard listening to the indistinct buzz of their talk, feeling a sudden pleasure at hearing people again—after being by herself for most of the day—without actually having to engage with them. Nobody at her grandfather's noticed the lanky, slumping figure of the girl riding through the moonlit sand on muleback. She headed the mule towards the back of the house and the pens, where she intended to put it down for the night. Bubba'Kess was certainly over at Grandpa Budi's, but tomorrow would be soon enough for him to get his mule back. She had already decided that she no longer had strength or interest enough in the act of filling the tub and stripping and washing, and her mind was already on the feel of her own familiar pallet and the quilt pulled over her body when she was startled by a shriek from the the front porch as she was passing, and a shout of "Yally!" that made her jump and almost lose her balance on the mule.

It was Eshy.

"Oh, Yally! Oh!" her sister cried out again. Eshy leaped up from the back of the porch where she had been sitting unnoticed in the dark, bounded across to the mule, somehow getting Yally off onto the ground without Yally taking any part in the effort, then grabbing her little sister around the shoulders and shaking her, embracing her in a squeezing hug, then stepping back and shaking her again. Yally was too weak to ward Eshy off, and so all she could do was let herself be jerked back and forth like an old raggy doll, only managing to lift her sprained foot up on her toes with as little weight as possible on it so as not to let it hurt it any more than it already was. It did not help. Then, just as suddenly, Eshy stepped back and balled up her fists against the sides of her hips, glaring at Yally and saying, "Where the *hang* you been-at all day, girl? Mama most had she a *fit*! We-all thought something done happen to you!"

It was the final prick of her spirit, and Yally felt everything draining out of her. She was deflating, growing smaller and more tired as she absorbed Eshy's fussing, holding onto the mule's withers for balance as she did.

"I gone'd down to Lusi's," she answered. "Mama knowed that."

"You done gone'd down to Lusi's all'a'way back this morning, and Lusi say she ain't seen you' ass all day," Eshy shot back, fiercely. She took a step backwards and eyed her little sister critically, seeing her more clearly now for the first time by the half-light of the moon. Her voice softened a bit. "Where you done got you'self to, girl? You done look like you been'd crawling around through the woods. You'se alright?"

Yally nodded. "I'se alright. But I like for sit down, though, iffen you let me."

She turned the mule loose and balancing one hand on Eshy's shoulder and wincing at the pain in her ankle, she took a long step to the side of the porch, turning on her good foot and setting herself down on the edge of the boards.

"What-wrong with you' foot?" Eshy asked her, all of the scolding now gone from her voice.

"Done twist it, is all. I just need for get offen it, for a minute. I guess I should soak it, 'fore I go to bed." She looked up at Eshy with pleading eyes. She was beginning to feel weak as water, and close to collapsing, now that she was in contact with the house. "I'm just tired, is all. What you doing over here?"

Eshy waved her hand in the direction of Grandpa Budi's and made a slight grimace, a gesture Yally took to mean that she was taking a break from all of those people, many of whom Eshy had a decidedly low opinion. Yally closed her eyes against the pain in her foot, and when she opened them again, she saw that Eshy was standing over her, looking her up and down, taking a long inventory of her baby sister. Drawing some sort of conclusion she did not offer to share, in a voice far more subdued than the information within the question deserved, Eshy asked, "You done heered about Grandpa, inna?"

Yally nodded. "I know," she said. "Could you tie the mule up, for me, Esh? I'm going on in the house."

"Sure, child," Eshy said. "Get on in and get you'self clean-up and change, so's we can go over to Grandpa's. You want for put a wrap on that foot?"

Too weary yet to move from where she was sitting, Yally shook her head.

"I'm'a just soak it, is all," she said. She stood up on her good foot, tested a little of her weight on the sprained one, winced, and grabbed onto one of the porch column boards to keep from falling. "I ain't think I'm going over there. I ain't feel like seeing nobody's, just now. And anyways, I done'd already see'd Grandpa today."

Eshy had taken a step or two towards the mule, but now she turned back to Yally, eyes widened, mouth dropped open.

"You done *see'd* Grandpa?" she asked.

Yally gave a spent nod, hoping that Eshy would have enough compassion not to make her recount the day's events, not tonight, before she had gotten some sleep. Tomorrow she'd be both willing and happy to tell the whole story.

Eshy did not seem interested in a recounting. Instead her face turned into a look of both pain and sympathy, as if she had understood completely what Yally had been through, and said, "Oh, Yally! No wonder you is looking like that. Why you ain't tell me? You see'd him down by the water?"

Thinking that Grandpa must have told everybody something about being out near the Gaya Pond, Yally was at the beginning of wondering why her grandfather had not included seeing her in his story. She had no time to complete her thinking on it, however, because Eshy had grabbed her around the shoulders again, and pulled her little sister to her in a hug, squeezing her, hard. Eshy's body was shaking, almost uncontrollably, and sobs began to break from her. "Ain't it *awful*," she said, pressing her trembling cheek against Yally's, her voice cracking.

The bad day, which had slowly appeared to be sorting itself out, now seemed to be breaking all out in a confusement again. Yally could not understand what could possibly be awful about their grandfather's return, and a flash of anger—at what, she was not sure, maybe at the day itself—brought some of her strength back. She braced herself back against the porch column and got her hands in between Eshy's and pushed her sister away to arm's length, where she could see her face.

"Ain't *what* awful?" she asked, frowning.

Eshy stood before her, hands dropping to her sides, staring back with a look that seemed almost stupid, and now it was her sister that Yally's anger turned on. She wanted this dumb conversation to stop, and stop now, so that she could go into the house and get into her bed, and put this day behind her. There was no way, no way at all, that tomorrow could be ever as difficult, and so she wanted to hurry on to tomorrow as quickly as she could.

Eshy continued to stare at her, with the oddest of looks that Yally was having no success in interpreting.

"I thought you said you done see'd them bringing him in," Eshy said.

"Bringing him in? I ain't said nothing like that. Bringing *who* in? Damn it, Eshy, what the hang you talking about?" Yally's voice rose, and she felt herself beginning to break apart, with the strain.

She wanted to hit her sister, hit her hard, hard enough to hurt her Eshy and make her leave her alone.

But against all the signals she was sending out, Eshy would not leave her alone.

"Bringing Grandpa in," she said, quietly, her body slack and dispirited as her voice, but keeping her eyes focused and penetrating on Yally's, either to make sure her point was understood or to judge the reaction, Yally could not figure which.

"Bringing Grandpa in from where?" Yally shot back, and now it was her turn to grab her sister by the shoulders. "*I just see'd him*. IS SOMETHING HAPPEN TO GRANDPA?"

Eshy put her hand up and touched the side of Yally's face, lightly, with her palm.

"Oh, girl, you ain't know, inna'? You sure ain't know. Me and Mama and everybody, we done said you must not know, else you'd'a been the first one back here."

"KNOW *WHAT?!!*" Yally was shouting now, her voice rising almost into a scream.

She made a half-effort to push Eshy's hand away from her face but Eshy would not let it be moved, pressing a little harder, rubbing the skin with her thumb.

"Just listen at me, Yally, and don't go to no pieces, and don't say nothing or ask nothing 'til I done finish," Eshy said, her voice now dropped almost to a whisper. At that Yally's heart stopped, and all about herself went still, and she stopped trying to fight Eshy off, or hurry her on, but could do nothing but listen, and hear. "Guba Simmons and Tunk Prioleau, they founded Grandpa in a creek, over off the Blacksnake," Eshy continued. "Them been back there hunting, and they found him in the water. Him done drown'ded, them say. They brought him down to the house in the wagon. Him up there now."

"Drown'ded?" Yally's voice now dropped to a hush, as well. The word seemed foreign to her, alien. She could find no meaning to it. "Drown'ded on the Blacksnake?" she said again. "Drown'ded, how?" That made absolutely no sense, so she asked, "Drownded, when?" An awful, terrible awareness was beginning to grow in her.

"I ain't know," Eshy answered, shaking her head. "Last fall maybe, when him gone'd back there, hunting. They ain't want for let none'a we look at he body, it gone down so, but Mama, she look. I ain't look. I couldn't. They say him been in the water for the longest. He been laying there in the water—all by heself..."

She stopped, choking off the sentence. She took a breath and went on. "Grandpa dead, Yally. We Grandpa, him done dead…"

Eshy stopped, and could say no more, but stood there in the yard in front of Yally with the tears now flowing down her cheeks and onto her dress, and as the recognition came full-force into Yally, a great sob was rising in her own chest, and the sob seemed like it was held back by a great dam inside her, which was about to burst, and bursting, would let out a river of grief that would flood-up all the world.

# 9

# The Caul-Child Speaks

*(Spring-Summer 1937)*

They buried Budi Manigault by torchlight on a warm spring night behind the old house at Goat Hill, next to the gravesites of all the Manigault kin who had passed on before him. Of the family members who had come out of the plantation grounds at Bethelia on the night the Big House burned, only Budi's younger brother, Tibo, now still walked among the living.

At the funeral, Mama had been all but unconsolable. She had lost her older sister and then her father in a little over a year, and because she had never known her actual mother, it was as if she had seen the death of both of her parents in that small space of time. Her youngest son, Mookie—her heart—was hiding out in the Yelesaw woods. And though he had come out to his grandfather's house the night they had brought Budi Manigault's body back from out of the Swamp, and had attended the funeral, Mookie could not tarry on Goat Hill for long for fear that the Sheriff could still show up any time and take him away. At the funeral, all of the grief of the past year poured forth from Ula Manigault as if the pipes of her life had cracked and then burst. Her three daughters, Yally and Eshy and Lusi, sat on either side of her at the Sambuhouse services, leaning against her as props both for her and for themselves, alternately trading places so each of them could be close to their mother, feeling their own earth move with the rhythm of her sobs and shaken frame. At the cemetery it had taken Big Soo and Lusi and several of the other strongest women in the family, all holding her together, to keep Mama from throwing herself into the grave on top of Papa'Budi's casket.

For her part, if Big Soo felt any special grief over her father's death, she did not show it, but only kept a stoic calm during all the time from the finding of his body, through the funeral, and in the days beyond.

On the walk back from the gravesite, holding Papa's hand, Mama seemed to steady herself, all on her own, gradually lifting her head and setting back her shoulders until she was walking like a Red Indian again, as her aunts used to describe her, straight-backed and proud and with her head in the air, and by the time they got back to the house she seemed almost Mama once more, though more indrawn and subdued than anyone in the family had ever known her to be before. She raised her voice less and less frequently, and it took more to set her off. Family members were undecided whether it was best to leave her be and let her grow out of her low mood on her own, as they had always done in the past, or to do something to stir her up and force her out of it. There was no ready answer and so, by default, they waited, and did nothing. Sometimes in the weeks just after the funeral, Yally caught her mother paused in her work, her fingers poised over cloth or cooking, her eyes open but staring off into other worlds. It would only last for a moment or two, however, and Mama would go back to work without looking around, as if it had never happened. But it was part of the many signs that she was slowly closing in upon herself.

WHILE ULA MANIGAULT BROODED over her father's death, talk continued to travel around Yelesaw Neck over how he had died, the finding of his body raising as many questions as it had answered.

Guba Simmons and Tunk Prioleau had said that they had found Budi Manigault lodged up under some exposed and overhanging tree roots in a shallow, narrow creek coming out of the Swamp and emptying into the Blacksnake River, not far from the junction between the Blacksnake and the Sugaree down at the bottom of Yelesaw. The body had been too badly decomposed for any definitive determination of a cause of death, so decomposed, in fact, that they could only identify him by his clothes and the single boot left on him. There was no sign of his shotgun or any of his other gear nor, for that matter, of the dog, Du, who had accompanied him on the trip. It did not seem to Guba and Tunk possible that Tat'Budi could have drowned in so little water, barely enough to cover his stretched out body, and the current in the creek did not appear strong enough to carry a dead man very far. But that was where they had found him and so, both being practical men and not given to rumor-spreading or overspeculation, that was where they left the matter. Meanwhile, for all Guba and Tunk knew, Budi could have drowned, or fallen out of his boat somewhere and hit his head, or stroked or heart-attacked out and then dropped into the water. Since it hardly mattered which to them, they opted to bring back the body with the word that Budi Manigault had drowned.

Many others on Yelesaw Neck did not agree with that conclusion, however.

They noted the absence of any of Budi Manigault's gear near his body, which they reasoned would have dropped in place if he had drowned where he had been found, or at least some of which would have made its way along with him if the body had been carried by the creekwaters from somewhere upstream. More particularly noted was the absence of Du from the death scene. It seemed hardly likely that the dog would have died at the same time as Tat'Budi, and since Du knew the Blacksnake and the Swamp almost as well as his master, it seemed odd that he had never made his way back out. Many therefore believed if some harm had come to Budi Manigault, it had come to Du, too. But if Du was not at the death site, where was he?

It was a conundrum, the most obvious answer to which—to those who followed this line of speculation—was that Tat'Budi had come to harm by somebody's hand—*somebodys' hands*, more likely, stressing the plural, as no-one on Yelesaw thought that Budi could be brought down by one man alone—his body then brought down to the creek and stuffed under the bank, Du disposed of, and the shotgun and hunt and fish gear t'iefed away.

The theory that Tat'Budi had been murdered somewhere on the Blacksnake was fueled by a rumor—never confirmed by Guba or Tunk but never specifically denied—that the body had been found with a hole at the back of his head, of larger or smaller caliber, depending on who was doing the telling.

None who advanced this theory bothered to specify what type of folks it was who they believed might have been the perpetrators of Budi Manigault's death. They didn't have to. Though few whitemen were known to travel the Swamp itself, many fished and trapped in the Sugaree-Blacksnake Junction waters near where the body was found, whitemen who certainly had no love for Budi Manigault and his biggity ways, whitemen, even, who might have thought he was a main leader in the opposition to evacuation of Yelesaw, and so might have concluded that getting rid of Budi might help break that opposition's back. And then there was the rumor that a black-skinned man had been seen wandering the evening Yelesaw backwoods in the weeks before Budi went on his last hunt-fish trip, a wool-headed Black man, who folks only saw at a distance, and when a twilight fog was rising, making his tortured way between the trees and through the underbrush, a man who'd seemed to have an old grudge against Budi, a wool-headed, raggedy Black man with a limp...

And so one of Yelesaw Neck's great mysteries was born.

IT WAS NOT LONG AFTER things had begun to settle down following the finding of Budi Manigault's body that his youngest daughter, Ula, suffered another blow.

Confined to his brother-in-law's hunt-shack down in the woods below Sosoville since the fight with the white man over across at Jaeger's store, Budi's grandson, Mookie, had grown restless under the restrictions of his confinement, and had begun to ask his parents, more and more insistently, for a reprieve. He understood why both his brother, Dinky, and his cousin, Boo were free to wander all over Yelesaw, while he was not. Even though they had been the ones who had provoked the fight out at Jaeger's, it was he who had hit the white man in the head and knocked him cold, and it was his courthouse name that had gotten out to the buckra and the High Sheriff as the culprit and fugitive. But Mookie, raised all of his life under the belief that whitefolks would never dare come over to persecute Yay'saws on Yelesaw ground as they regularly did to the niggers back cross'oba, pointed out to his mother and father with increasing frequency that an imprisonment of indeterminate sentence in the woods was worse punishment than it was likely the buckra would ever be able to mete out. Had it been Dinky who'd been lodging the complaint, it would have been

quickly dismissed, because even married, Dink was wild as
fieldgrass. But Mookie rarely complained about much of anything
and normally enjoyed all the time to himself that he could secure.
The fact that it was he who was now petitioning to be released
from confinement showed how much the walls of the shack were
closing in on him. His father therefore was both sympathetic and
amenable to the request for parole, but his mother—now even
more protective of her youngest son than ever since her father's
death—was adamant that he remain in hiding until it was assured
that all of the whitefolks' turmoil over the fight had completely
settled down. It was the only issue, these days, that Ula Kinlaw
seemed to be able to get roused up about.

There it should have stayed. But Bo Kinlaw soon learned from
Dink and Cu'n Boo—who had their own way of knowing such
things—that Mookie had taken matters into his own hands and
had begun to leave the hunt-shack on his own in the evenings,
visiting two or three of his young women friends in secret in the
woods behind their houses, either walking or riding on muleback
on the Yelesaw roads and wagonpaths by himself.

Bo was inclined to overlook that as, like his son, he did not
believe it possible that the whitefolks from out to Cottontown
would ever work up enough nerve to stage a Klu Kluxer raid across
the river in Yelesaw, and even if the High Sheriff returned for
another search, he could be expected to conduct it with enough
noise and bluster that there was plenty of advance warning and
only during daylight hours.

A few weeks later, however, Bo learned of a transgression far
more serious. From Eshy's husband, Nu, he got word that Mookie
had also been sneaking over the river on the cable-barge some
Saturday nights, hidden by a couple of his cousins in the back of
their wagon, going up to the júk joints in St. Paul and beyond.

That did it. Over his wife's fierce objections, and not telling
her the real reasons why because of fear that it would have sent her
already-strained nerves over the edge, Bo arranged with his New
Jersey relatives to have Mookie go and live with them up the road.
Ula and Bo had such fierce arguments over the plan in the
evenings behind the curtain-door in their bedroom that Yally
feared they might come to blows, but this time, at least, her father
put his foot down and kept it there, and on the night Papa took
Mookie down to Georgetown to catch the train, she heard Mama
sobbing and wailing in her room until Yally thought the sound of
it would break her own heart. For weeks after that, Ula had little to

say to her husband about anything at all, and there was a winter chill in the Kinlaw house in the late spring that stretched down into the hot days of the young summer.

THE DEPARTURE OF MOOKIE—the first person in the immediate family to leave Yelesaw—tore a hole in Yally that refused to fill, but that was far from the only—or even the worst—thing pulling at her that spring.

She had refused to take place in the closing down of Grandpa Budi's house. While Big Soo and Lusi and Eshy and even Mama went over and did a final cleaning and straightening and a sorting and passing out of Grandpa's things, Yally remained in the Kinlaw house and around the yard with her own chores, not even able to look through the scuppernong arbor at the work being done across the way.

She struggled to reconcile herself with her grandfather's death. There was some comfort in the finality of the return of his body from out of the Swamp. In all the long months after his disappearance, she had kept his house with a slowly declining hope that one day he would come back down the river on his boat and step up on his front porch again and play his mouthharp and tell his stories and play his games with her, and all would be as it ever was. But that hope itself had long been an ache as well as a comfort, which the finding of his body had eased and then ended. What replaced it, after the shock and pain of the reality of her grandfather's death, had been an emptiness and a longing that was far worse than what she had felt when Aunt Orry had died. As much as Eshy, she realized, Papa'Budi had become her friend in his last days, and looking around her with hollow eyes, she could see nothing in her world or outside of it which could possibly replace that.

But bad as those feelings were, it was not that which bothered her in the warming spring months following her grandfather's funeral. It was the fact that she could not bring herself to tell anyone of the encounter with whoever it was, or whatever it had been, that she had met in the old Quarters back out on Bethelia Plantation that terrible day.

At first, with Grandpa Budi's wake and then the funeral taking up all emotion and attention, there had clearly been no appropriate time to tell her story. Afterwards, she told herself that she was only waiting for the right moment and circumstance to bring it up. But as the days passed, and rolled over into weeks, and she had shared nothing with anyone in the family, she began to understand that it was reluctance, and not timing, that was holding her back. Every time she told herself, I got to tell it, I got to tell it, today, she would, without thinking about it, busy herself up for long periods with some work project far away from everyone else, and when she finally got back amongst company again, her mood had shifted, and she remained silent. Why she acted so, or, rather, failed to act, she did not explore, only that something within her was holding her back.

From time to time, she began to believe it possible that she had only dreamed what had happened that day out at Bethelia. Her dreams had become more active and more vivid since her grandfather's funeral. She was chased, she was drowning, she was lost within labyrinths, in endless, ever repeating cycles that spilled over from her nighttime sleep into her waking hours. The scabs and deep scratches eventually faded and disappeared from her legs and arms and elbows and her sprained ankle healed, leaving no physical evidence of the events of that day, save for one. Several odd marks had appeared just above her shins, faint, elongated discolorations that wrapped around that part of both her lower legs, appearing as if something had grabbed her there and held, hard enough and long enough to leave a permanent impression. The first time she saw them, she went out behind the barn and stared at the marks for an hour or more, running her finger over them, pushing slightly in, noting that they had no pain or feel to them, enveloped in the memory of how they must have gotten there in the mud, in the pond, in the middle of the marshfield. It was not a memory she cared to carry around with her, and so she closed it off from herself, and if she happened to look over the gripping marks on her legs again, it was with eyes that did not see them.

But she could not put out of her mind her encounter and conversation that day in the old Quarters. She brooded upon it daily, and it weighed on her as a great burden she carried with her, always, growing heavier and heavier as time went on, and which she did not know how to put down.

She had questions that needed answering, but her dilemma was she could not go to someone who would probe for the reasons she was asking them, since whether or not she should reveal those reasons was what she needed information for to decide. That left out Eshy, who could wheedle anything she wanted out of her in half a minute, or Ná'Risa, who had such powers, Yally believed, that she would not even have to wheedle. She had no desire to put more burdens on her mother, who was worn down too much already by Grandpa Budi's death and Mookie's departure. Papa was out of the question, as he would only put her off with a joke, as was Lusi, who would simply put her off. She dearly missed Mookie more than ever, quiet, reliable Mookie, who would have listened patiently and answered thoughtfully and respected her need to keep her secrets until she was convinced they should be told. But Mookie was up in New Jersey now, doing railroad work, from the news that had come back down, and so no longer within her circle of reach.

After thinking on it for several days, she settled on Big Soo as both the best and the most logical one to approach.

"Do the spirit ever talk?" she asked her aunt one morning as they were feeding the hogs in the pen back behind the shed.

"Sure, they does talk," Big Soo answered, not looking up from the mess of pigs that were scrambling for the leavings just on the other side of the fence. "When them got something for say. When them ain't, they keeps close. If the childrens was more like that, it'a be a quieter yard. Grown folk, too."

"Talk with peoples, I means," Yally said.

"I done tol'ded you 'sure.'"

"How does they talk?"

Big Soo stopped her pig-feeding to give a slow look around the yard and back towards the house. Yally wondered if she were checking to see if Mama was anywhere near, and in hearing distance. Satisfied with whatever she saw or didn't see, her aunt turned back to the pigs and, not looking over at Yally, answered, "Depend on what them got for say."

Encouraged that Big Soo had not immediately put her off, Yally pushed on.

"I mean, iffen they just want for talk with you, and make sure you ain't miss they point. Does they talk like natural folk, in a natural voice?"

Big Soo now turned and regarded Yally thoughtfully before answering.

"Sometime them talks with a natural voice, sometime not," she said, with a shrug. "Sometime they holler like them pig does, sometime cackle like the crow. Sometime it be a noise like the wind blowing. Them talk like them figure you can understand. They been one I recamember what would whistle like a train in the night when her wanted to get you' attention. I knowed another what would rattle the pot on the stove."

"You knowed it?"

Big Soo kicked at one of the hogs that had taken her boot for something to eat, and was nibbling on it. "Weren't a 'it,'" she said, throwing out more leavings. "That one were a 'him,' and sure, I knowed him. Knowed him good. It were Pusa Davis. Sis'Nina little boy. Died of the 'sumption, same winter you been borned. After that, him used to come around and rattle they pot at night, after all he peoples done gone'd to bed. Rattle them pot, rattle them pot, 'til sometime he knock 'em on the floor. Wake'ded everybodys up in the house, and them had for get up and light up all the candle them had and walk'round for see what done done it. Thought it been a raccoon got in the house, but it weren't. It were that little boy, Pusa."

"What-for him rattle the pot?"

"Them couldn't figure, not for a while. But Sis'Nina, her sit up and study, and after-while it come to her. Them pot ain't rattle none but when her cook the okra soup, and that ever been that boy favorite. Him couldn't never get him enough'a he mama okra soup. That how they knowed it been him. After that, every time she cook that soup, her leave a little bit for him in a bowl on the table after they done gone'd to bed, and that done satisfy him. Not a pot rattle on the post, and them all sleeped through the night, and the soup been gone in the morning."

The leavings were exhausted, the pigs swirling around in a furious crowd in the pen below, hoping for more. Still, Big Soo did not move on to the next chore, but stood up on the bottom rung of the pen, her big arms draped over the top rung, continuing with the conversation as if it were something she thought important to talk about.

"But what iffen it wasn't Sis'Nina' boy at all?" Yally asked her. She was getting to the heart of her concerns now and thought carefully on her questions, pausing before she asked. "What iffen it been something else, something pretending it were Sis'Nina' boy, just so's it could t'ief they soup?"

Big Soo gave out a snort and tapped Yally two or three times on her temple with the point of her index finger.

"You figure like Bobo's nigger, you figure 'til you fool," she said. "You ain't reckon a mama know she own child?"

"But what iffen it weren't? Or what if it left message telling them something they was supposed to do, and so they done it, but what were lefting the message really wasn't they kin at'all, but just pretending it been kin, but they ended up following and doing something bad?" It was a long speech that blurted its own self out. Her caution was evaporating as they came closer to the heart of her concerns. Even before Big Soo could answer she pressed forward, anxious to be able to explain the thing that had been vexing her most these past days, without really naming it. "I mean, ain't they spirit what try for fool you, make you think they's somebody's else, so's they can spread gossip and rumor and get you on the wrong track?"

Big Soo turned her head and gave her an intent look, one eye half closing in a way that made her look disturbingly like Grandpa Budi. Yally had not realized until just then how much the two of them looked alike when they held themselves a certain way. She fidgeted on the pigpen rail, overly anxious for the reply now that she felt she had gotten it all out.

But Big Soo did not answer directly. Instead she blew a hard breath out through her nose, like a mule might do, and said, "I ain't never known you to study on the spirit, so. Something 'sturbing you?"

"No, ain't nothing," Yally answered in a small voice. "I were just wondering."

Big Soo continued to stare at her, as if she could bore right down into her thoughts and ferret out the whole lie. It wasn't a big lie, not a lie that hurt anyone, but a lie, nonetheless. "Just wondering" had nothing to do with it.

But if Big Soo came to that conclusion, she did not let on. She suddenly and abruptly ended her stare-down, turning away to look over the pen out at the line of trees in the direction of the woods and the Swamp.

"You gots to watch for the tricksy ones, yes you is," she said, but she was talking over the fencepost now, almost as if she were in a conversation with herself, and Yally now forgotten. "Them got they tricksy ways. Them can put someone else face on theyselves and try for lead you 'stray."

Yally felt able to breathe again, now that Big Soo was not trying to probe her. "But how can you tell iffen it one what being tricksy, or iffen it one for-true?" she asked.

Big Soo looked back at her, suddenly and sharply.

"You talkin' 'bout that thing at Orry'sendin'-home, inna'?"

Her mind focused on the conversation in the Quarters, she had not expected that. It had been months and months since she had thought about the man at Sister Orry's funeral, but she had no trouble deciphering what her aunt was talking about. It was a twist in the conversation that she had to stop and think about it before answering.

"You think that man at Aunt Orry's funeral were trying for trick we?" she asked, finally.

"Weren't he?"

Yally tried, in vain, to recollect exactly what it was the man had said. All she could now recall was his declaration that they must not put Sister Orry down into the ground, and the confusion that his words had caused, especially with Mama.

"Him been'a trick we about what?"

"'Bout that water. You ain't hear him?"

Yally started to answer, but Big Soo cut her off.

"Don't fret, I got that old thing in my sight," she said. "Iffen it come near-to again, I be done grab it and won't turn go."

Her mood had soured, and she brought the conversation to an abrupt end. She swung the empty leavings bucket over to Yally, hitting her in the chest with it before the girl could grab it, and then dropped down from the pen fence and walked away towards the barn, muttering to herself as she did, feeling at the moca sack hidden somewhere beneath the folds of her dress, back to her old familiar Big Soo ways.

For a long time, Yally stayed at the pen with the bucket held loose in her arm, thinking. Since Yally had long ago stopped thinking about the man at Sister Orry's funeral herself, she'd had no idea that he was still hard and heavy on Big Soo's mind. But Big Soo's revelation that she had it in her sight—the "it" obviously meaning the stranger—explained so much about her aunt's behavior in the past year. But that was only a passing thought, and Yally turned, almost immediately, to her own pressing concerns. Big Soo had ever thought the stranger to be a bad-spirit gafa. And if a gafa could change its appearance, as Soo had said, it could come in the guise of a broke-leg, mule-eyed wandering man one time, and then return as her grandfather. And now that Big Soo had reminded her about the stranger's words, Yally realized that both of them, indeed, had fetched message about the whitefolks' water.

She went over the whole conversation with her aunt in her mind. She was not certain if Big Soo had set her on the right path, or, for that matter, if she had set her on any path at all. It was a problem that self-canceled its own solutions. Because she could not ask straight-out what she needed to know, she could only expect ambiguous replies. With a sinking feeling, she felt like the dog that had walked around in a circle in the yard several times, round and round, only to find that it was still in exactly the same place where it had started.

She put her hand across her forehead and closed her eyes and for the first time said it clearly to herself, undisguised, so that she would admit the magnitude of the decision she was facing.

She had been given a message out in the old Quarters to fetch to Baba'Zambu, that they must all leave Yelesaw for the coming of the flood.

If it had been a bad spirit that had been pretending to be her grandfather, and she fetched that message, and the Yelesaw elders heeded it, she would be the cause and conduit of all of her people abandoning the land of their birth for no reason but a gafa's trick.

But if it had really been her grandfather who had talked with her, and she did not fetch it, she had no idea what things would result, only that they would be equally bad.

She was afraid to tell her story because she might not be believed.

She was afraid to tell her story because she might be believed.

The dilemma pressed down on her, bore into her, and there was no way for her to resolve it.

NOT UNEXPECTEDLY, as her tensions intensified, her visions escalated.

One night, a few days after her conversation with Big Soo at the hog pen, she lay back on her quilts, staring at the blank blackness of the ceiling. The crickets had stopped chirping in the hollow up under the porch, and the lone owl had ceased its hooting in the chinaberry tree near the house. Big Soo's breathing had grown deep and regular in the pallet next to her and all the rest of the world had stilled. But Yally could not sleep.

She spread her arms and let her hands rest flat against the bare floorboards.

Her palms felt damp, as if dark, silent waters were already rising up underneath the house, pressing up against the bottom of the planks.

The wetness lapped against her nightclothes, washing over her thighs and chest, the weight rolling over her, pushing her head down under the darkling water, and it was almost as if she were back at the Gaya Pond and she heard the whispering, raspy voices calling *Yalleee* again, and felt the pulling hands on her legs from down in the mud-pit below...

She raised up with a great lurch, taking in air in one great gulp.

Her body shook with chill, and though she wrapped her quilts around her and tucked the ends under her feet, she could not get warm again, even in the late-spring night. She lifted one hand and rubbed it across her forehead and then down her face and neck. She was dripping sweat and shivering at the same time, the water running in streams down the front of her night-dress.

She could not find her breath. The air seemed to be drawing out of the room, as if her aunt was using it all up in the deepness of her sleep. Yally stood up and taking the quilts with her, pushed aside the curtain-door, stepping out into the bigroom. There was no moon out, and so the window-shutters were only formless portals through which nothing passed in either direction, the table and chairs and woodstove and couch only hinted at in memory, black shrouds blending seamlessly into deeper shadows. The whole house slept. Yally walked across the bigroom, a floating nay-nay in the dark of the night, her bare feet sliding without sound over the smooth floorboards. Careful not to make the front door creak and call attention to herself, she opened it and slipped outside.

The light breath of wind out on the porch was warm on her damp body, taking the away the chill. She sat down on the edge of the steps, leaning against the railpost with the side of her face, encircling the wood with her long arms. She looked beyond the steps out into the yard. Not a light was visible from any house and so, in the moonless night, she could not tell how far she was looking, maybe not even past the treeline on one side, the scuppernong arbor on the other. It did not matter. She closed her eyes, to see it all better. She knew every inch of Goat Hill. She could run it eyes-closed, full-out, from her house all the way down to the far end, to Uncle Osi's and Aunt Mooby's—around water-wells and chickenpens and tethered mules, under clotheslines and fruit trees, past barns and sheds and flower gardens and around berry bushes and back porches steaming with the smells of simmering suppers, even through the cemetery behind Papa'Leem's and Mama'Effi's, where the spirits of all the gone'way Manigaults were resting. She could do this all without running into a post or stumbling over a bench or scraping her leg against a single bush. She held the map of the Bigyard within her head and heart. There had never been a morning of her life that she had not awakened to its sights, nor a nighttime she had not looked on it last before closing the door and going to bed. Everyone she loved lived within this boundary of bush and tree. She had no other existence but here, in this low patch of land between the two rivers. She could not imagine what it would be to have it all gone.

If she fetched the message, and it was wrong, she could be the cause of it all going.

But if it was really her grandfather who had given her the message...

She tried to vision up Grandpa Budi to ask him what she ought to do—to think of what he might say to her at such a time, a story he might tell, a piece of wisdom he might pass on—but he hid from her, refusing to come.

When the big brown-and-yellow rooster looked up and saw that it could just begin to make out the black outline of the trees against the lightening of the morning sky, its first crow of the day met Yally Kinlaw sitting up on the front porch of her parents' house at the end of Goat Hill in the Yelesaw Neck community of Cantrell County, South Carolina, the quilts pulled up around her shoulders, her eyes wide open, either unable or unwilling to go to sleep.

ESHY CAME OVER ONE EARLY AFTERNOON in the first hot spell of the new summer. There had been sickness that spring in Kimbitown, and several deaths, and it was the first time in many weeks that she had been able to get away and visit back home. She found her little sister sitting in a chair in the shade of the chinaberry tree in the side yard, shelling butterbeans. Eshy was shocked at what she saw. She had always thought Yally far prettier than Yally herself believed she was, but that prettiness was no longer in evidence. All the youth seemed to have gone out of Yally's face and body. Her cheeks were sallow and sunken as old folks, dark blotches under eyes that seemed without spirit and had sunken down into deep hollows in her face. Ever too skinny, she had lost more of her weight than she ought to have. And Yally, who had the quickest hands of all the Kinlaw children, was picking at the butterbeans listlessly, aimlessly, with fingers that had a tremble about them, and every now and then she absently reached up to scratch at her at her scalp up under her headscarf, as if she were plagued with sores or worse. Squinting into the sun, Yally gave out only a wan smile and a dispirited greeting as Eshy walked up.

"Hey, country," Eshy said, as cheerfully as she could. "How you be?"

Yally gave a small shrug of her shoulders and continued with her shelling, not saying anything in return.

Arms akimbo, fists pressed against her hips, Eshy gave her sister a long look. Yally did not flinch under her gaze or bother to look back and holler "*What?!* What you want?" and that told Eshy more than anything. She had no idea what the cause of Yally's afflictions might be, but she knew from long experience that her little sister brooded over troubles and took them deep to heart, and that it always had a physical effect upon her. Never this bad, though, because Eshy would have never allowed it to go on until it reached anywhere near this point. If Eshy had been there, she would have found a way, as soon as she saw the first bouts of excessive quietness or too-much introspection, to do something, say something, to have Yally screaming and giggling and running'round the house and yard in circles, and get everything off of her mind for a time so she could get a fresh start at whatever was tantalizing her. She could see, however, that her sister was too far gone down for any tickle or quick-fix to put her back right. She wondered how long Yally had been going down this way, and whether anyone at the house had noticed, and if not, why not. Probably still mooning over Mookie's going up the road, she figured. Mookie could more than take care of himself. She knew that Yally—the one who caused the least trouble of all the family— was ever being overlooked and taken for granted. She was furious, but tried not to show it, for care of not disturbing Yally further.

Instead she asked, "Where Mama at?"

"Down in she garden hoeing, I expect. She been fussing about the weeds, this morning."

"Okay. I'm going for see her. I be back." Eshy patted her sister on the side of the head. Yally winced and drew her head away, as if something about it pained her, and that small gesture made Eshy angrier and more anguished all at the same time. She turned on her heel and walked back towards the garden. Yally barely watched her go.

It seemed to her that Eshy was gone for barely more than a minute or two. When she realized it, her sister was back in front of her, and saying, "Okay, you can put them beans down, girl."

Yally gave a slight frown. She had managed for the first time that day to clear all thoughts from her head and had been enjoying her respite under the shade of the chinaberry, and she did not feel at all up to tussling with Eshy.

"No I can't," she said. "I ain't got time for play."

"Yes you can, and does I look like I's playing?" Eshy's tone was indignant. "I'se a 'uman-married. I don't play no more. Childrens play. And you can put them beans down 'cause you's coming for visit with me for the day. We ain't talk for the longest, and I'm missing you. You can sit on the porch and drink lemonade 'til you piss yellow and pass seed, and me'n Nu'll bring you back this evening. I got a peach pie cooling, too. And a big supper."

Yally pursed her lips in a look of weary annoyance.

"I can't go nowheres, Eshy," she said. "I got supper for fix myself, and chores—"

"Hell with you' chores," Eshy shot back. "They can stand sand on they porch for one evening and anyways, I got leave from Mama. So put that pan up in the kitchen, and let's get."

Yally stared helplessly at the pan of butterbeans in her lap. Having been struggling with the biggest decision of her life for days upon days now, she could not face even the smallest one. Go or stay? She could not figure out what to do. "I can't leave this for Mama," she said, finally, looking back up at Eshy. Tears welled in her eyes. A pleading "tell me what to do" was left unsaid.

Eshy blew air out of her nose—a gesture that could mean anything—and plopped down on the sand next to her little sister's chair. "Okay, then, don't leave it." She reached for a handful of beans. "Faster we finish, quicker we can go. Them damn greedy-ass Kimby childrens ain't going to let no pie cool out on the sill by itself for long."

A small smile came at the corners of Yally's mouth and reached up towards her eyes, the first time anything like that had appeared on her face in some time.

THE SUN WAS WARM out on the River Road, passing in and out between the trees as they rode in Eshy's wagon, running warm fingers over Yally's face and bare arms and legs. She sat back in the wagon-seat feeling the wind playing up under the folds of her dress and over her body, cooling and comforting her, the contrast between warm and cool the pleasantest of feelings, and she was glad to be in her sister's care, and that this was all she needed to think about, at least for a little while.

The visions had been coming more frequently, more frightening, and more intense, waiting for her, always, now, just at the edge of sleep, indescribable visions whose details and patterns she could not remember—or did not want to remember—as soon as she had torn herself away, only that there was a terrible imperative to them, an overwhelming pattern and feeling of something that needed doing but that had been left undone. She knew the thing that needed doing, of course, knew it well, only in all of her long agonizings it still remained split between two choices, with no conclusion as to which was the proper one to do.

She was paralyzed. She could not make a decision and there was no way for her to fight off the visions that came in her sleep, so long as she had not made a decision. And so she fought off sleep, getting up from her bed each night as soon as Big Soo had dropped off, coming back out to the bigroom table to work on sewing chores or other busy tasks. She had put together and pulled apart an entire quilt during the past few weeks in those nighttime vigils, pulled it apart because the stitching was horribly butchered, like a child might have done seeing someone doing quilting from a distance, and trying it out for the first time, herself, without any guidance or help. She did not mind having to take the quilt back apart again, as the only result she was looking for was to keep her mind awake and busy. It had not worked. There was no way you could keep sleep at bay forever. And so, night and day, whenever she relaxed her grip on her mind for the briefest of moments, her eyes closed, her head nodded, and the monstrous things lying in wait inside of her pounced.

Eshy had been quiet all the way out from the house. Feeling herself begin to drift, Yally turned and put her hand on her sister's arm.

"Talk to me, Esh," she said. "I want for stay awake."

"You can go-head and sleep," Eshy answered. "I ain't mind. You done slept on me before."

Yally raised her head up, and both her eyes and voice focused. "No!" she said, shaking her head. "Just keep talking."

Eshy nodded without fully understanding. "Okay, li'l bit," she said. "I ain't never had no trouble with talking."

"No, you ain't." Yally settled her head back again and managed another small smile.

A crane took off from the bushes beside the road as they passed by, its white feathers and yellow beak and legs brilliant in the early afternoon sun, and she watched it as it followed the line of road in front of them for a time and then turned and rose and disappeared far out over the trees. She realized that Eshy had been chattering away for a while, and she had not been paying attention.

"What you say?" she asked.

"I been saying you taking too much of a burden up on you'self, Yally'Bay."

"Why you says that?" Yally did not really care about the answer. She only wanted to stir herself up with a small dispute with her sister.

"I says it 'cause it be true," Eshy snapped the reins over the mule's back, which had slowed its walk and turned its head towards an interesting patch of sweetgrass at the side of the road. "They's three 'uman's grown in y'all house, you know."

She watched as Yally furrowed her brows, counting.

"I gots you in that crew, silly-ass," she went on, when it was clear Yally could not figure it out on her own. "Don't look at me like that. You ain't no baby-child no more."

Yally was having trouble figuring out what point her sister was trying to make, but it was the best possible therapy she could get, squabbling with Eshy. She sat up straighter in the wagon-seat, focusing on the line of Eshy's assertion.

"What that got for do with taking up burden?"

"They's working you like Grady's field-hands, that's what it got for do." Eshy's ire was up, and she gestured at Yally with her hand. "Look at you. You done wasting away most to nothing. I know Mama got thing on she mind, but one'a them thing ought for be she youngest. That ain't right, letting you go down like you is. I tol'ded her that, too."

Yally frowned and shook her head.

"Don't fuss with Mama, Esh. Really. Her doing worse than you think."

"Ain't worse than you," Eshy snapped, fully aroused now. "And that old big-ass Soo can pull more'she weight than she do, too. She done eat she enough." She interrupted Yally's weak protest. "I got you a break for the day, but that ain't enough. We fixing to do this regular, one day out'the week. Even mule does get theyselves *one* day off. And one Saturday, I'm'a get Mama to let you go 'cross to Cashville with me and Nu to the júk-joint dance. You need for meet some boys, and let them meet you. After we done fill you back up with some food and get you' hair right again. That okay with you?"

"Going 'cross to Cashville?" It was too much to think about, too difficult to see past her current troubles. She could only see as far as the ride out to Kimbitown. "But really, Esh, I don't got too much burden. Don't put that on Mama. Or Aunt Soo."

"Yes you is, so don't argue. I been thinking 'bout one'a Grandpa' stories 'bout that, just this morning." She let the mule slow itself so she could tell it, proper, the way Grandpa Budi told it.

*Rice-dike bust-up and flood one time in the hard-rain, and here come the mens down for fix it. Water been'a coming through the breaches every whichaway and them ain't had nothing for stop it. So half them niggers got down in the ditch in a long line and brace the dike-wall with they back, all'a way up and down the row, whiles the others runs for fetch board-lumber for the bracing. Them niggers work that dike all the afternoon and into the night, and when they got it all brace-up with wood, them set out in the field the rest'the night for make sure it done hold. Morning come and they been on they way home, when they come up on one'a them nigger they'd done set in the ditch way down to the end, and done'd forgot about him all night, 'cause that the end what ain't breach. And that dumb-ass nigger. He done stay he black ass out there all the night, ain't holler out neitherways say 'here I is' or nothing, and he cotched the 'monia and die two week later. And that-what come from nigger taking on too much'a burden on they own self, ain't got sense for call for help when help been right'round—*

Eshy stopped in mid-story, because Yally had reached over and taken the reins from her hands, and had pulled the mule to a stop. She was looking at Eshy intently, with the oddest of expressions, her eyes red and inflamed, but wide-opened.

"Esh," Yally said, "Grandpa tell you that story?"

Yally was sitting up fully erect, her voice clear and direct, and Eshy couldn't figure what it was she had said to cause such a sudden change in her sister's demeanor.

"'Course, Grandpa tell it," Eshy said.

"*Grandpa* tell it?"

"You ain't hear'd me? Yes, Grandpa tell it. Why that so important?"

"And you thought 'bout that story—when, you say?—this morning? How it come at you? What you been doing when it come at you?"

Eshy frowned and considered. For whatever reason it was important to Yally, it was clearly important, so to indulge her baby sister, Eshy tried to recall the exact circumstances, something she ordinarily would have never bothered doing. "It come to me at breakfast, I think. Yeah. Me and Nu been eating breakfast, and I just bust out laughing, and him ask'ded me what I been laughing for, and I tol'ded him I just thought about Grandpa, and one of he funny story. And that were right when I think'ed about you. I think'ed about how you and me, we used for sit on Grandpa' porch and listen to he story. And I think'ed about how you keep he house after he'd done gone'd, 'case him been coming back. And I told Nu I ain't seen my sister in the longest, and I got a mind for come over this side for visit. And so I come."

Abruptly, Yally pulled the mule's head to the left with one of the rein ropes and flicked it on the haunches with the other. Reluctantly, because he had thought they were actually going to take a real break, the mule turned in the road and straightened, and Yally set it to a trot back up in the direction from where they'd come.

Now Eshy was thoroughly confused.

"Us going back to the Hill?" she asked.

Yally nodded, but said nothing.

A deep concentration had taken over her, eyes narrowed and focused on the road in front, but clearly she was deep in thought at the same time. It was unusual for Yally to just up and take the lead on something, but it was also hopeful, considering the circumstance of her so recent depression, so Eshy decided to let her be and ask no more questions. Whatever was up, Eshy figured she'd find out soon-enough. Besides that, Yally now had a look of determination on her face that Eshy knew well, and knew not to mess with unless she wanted a pitched fight.

They rode in silence down the River Road and back onto the wagonpath into Goat Hill. But when they got to the Bigyard, instead of turning to the right towards the Kinlaw house, Yally turned the mule's head towards the left, in the direction of the main body of the settlement.

"We ain't going back home?" Eshy asked her.

"Nope."

They continued on to Ná'Risa's and Papa'Tee's, where Yally finally pulled the wagon to a stop.

"Okay, child," Eshy said. "What we fixing to doing here?"

Yally tapped the reins on her open palm while she considered something, and then turned to Eshy once more. "And you'se certain-sure you heard that story from Grandpa."

Eshy sucked her teeth and did not answer. She was beginning to become mildly annoyed, but out of sympathy for Yally, tried to hold it back.

"You know when that story done happen?"

Eshy shook her head.

"That happen this winter past. It were Kit Prioleau what got left out on the line all night, and died of the 'monia. You ain't 'member? That-when the rice-dike broke and the mens all had to go out there."

Eshy frowned and shook her head vigorously, though the similarities between Grandpa Budi's story and Kit Prioleau's death last winter were already beginning to grow on her. "Uh-uh," she said. "That can't be. How Grandpa could'a tell that story, then, and Grandpa been already gone, last winter—"

She stopped talking, her mouth left open, and she felt a tremble rise up from within herself and her breathing begin to quicken.

Yally had not bothered to wait for the revelation to blossom, but was already getting down out of the wagon. She was thinking that some spirits were tricksy, yes they were, but this one knew way too much, and which folks to turn to, and was going to far too much trouble to get her attention. She had decided, finally, that she had folks of her own to which to turn, and actually, yes, there *was* no need for her to take the burden on all by herself. She walked up on the porch with more purposeful a step than she'd had in many weeks.

IT WAS GETTING ALONG towards dusk-dark, with a warming breeze blowing in through the open shutters, when the old woman came back out from the bedroom to join the old man at the supper table. They had listened for the better part of an hour while the girl had told her story—the old man, the old woman, and the sister—none of them stopping her with questions, but letting her talk uninterrupted, and when the girl was finished and seemed about to fall out from exhaustion and the strain of a long ordeal, the old woman had put her to bed while the old man sent the sister home to tell her folks that they were keeping her for the night, with no further explanation. The old man knew that the girl's mother would not like that—not necessarily the staying overnight part, but the not knowing why—and he figured before she came across to find out, he would walk over to their house himself and explain what the girl had told them, and that Baba'Zambu had already been informed and wanted the girl's story repeated before all the Yelesaw elders in the morning. His niece would be furious at her daughter having been brought into spirit things, he knew, but furious or not, the old man figured she would not contest a call from Baba'Zambu. And besides, he would explain to his niece that it was the girl who had come to them.

Under those circumstances, what else could the old man and the old woman do?

"How her doing back there?" the old man asked the old woman as she came out from the bedroom.

"Poor thing done talked she'self into a sleep," the old woman answered. A lazily-pleasant, calming aroma had followed her out from the bedroom, where she had lit an array of mind-clearing candles. "Look like she done been up night and day for week-and-week. A wonder she ain't fell'd out no sooner. She done been making sheself serious sick."

"Her got strong blood in she," the old man said, to which the old woman nodded agreement.

They sat there for a moment in silence, sparring with each other without saying anything, the old man patching up a hole that had burnt itself in his pipe-bottom—thinking with some regret that the time might have come, finally, to toss the old thing out and start on breaking in a fresh one—the old woman humming a little as she set out her herb fixing things on the tabletop in front of her.

"Well, you mought-well to tell it out loud and be done with," the old man said, finally, not looking up from his pipe. "You thinking it so loud, I done hearing it anyways."

The old woman cocked one eye up at him. "If you hearing it already, ain't no need for say it." she said. When the old man said nothing in reply, only pursed his lips and kept on with his pipe-patching, she grumbled something under her breath and went on. "Alright. I'll be done said it, iffen it'll give you some peace. *Ain't I been telling you about that girl in there since she been done borned? Ain't I? Ain't I been telling you we must do something about she? And is you listened? No. Is you done'd something'bout it? No. So now that girl in there most tear sheself up with the confusement over what she hearing and seeing, and now here we be.*" She stared over the table at him for a bit, then turned back to her things, with emphasis. "There, old man. I done said it, and that ain't the first time I done said it. You got-you you' peace now?"

"Alright, I knows you done said it, old lady," the old man answered with a sigh. "More than once't."

The old woman was not finished, not by far. "I knowed it when I pull she out she mama and seen the caul on she face," she went on, putting down her fixings again. "I knowed it when she been sucking at she mama' ninny. Sometime I can feel that girl so hard all'a way 'cross to Budi' daughter' house, I most have to bite my lip keep from hollering out. That girl got the sight in she, and more'n that. If her say she seen something down on the Old Ground, her done *seen* it, and ain't no two ways to it. That girl be Sis'Yela come straight back, sure-enough. Yela ain't even pause for take a cool drink'the water on the other side, just come right back in that child. I knowed that. I been knowed that. And *you* knows that, too, old man, even iffen you ain't admits."

The old man shifted uncomfortably in his chair under her glare. "I knowed all that. I ain't never said I ain't. Ain't I'm the one what give she my grandmamma name?"

"And that all you done done," the old woman said. "You ain't said nothing to that girl and you ain't said nothing to she mama, not the first day, not the last day. Not a mumbling word." She tightened her mouth into a scowl, for emphasis. "It ain't right what Ula done did with that child, and I told'ded you, and you knows it. Should'a *been* brung'd her over for she learning. It ain't right, keeping that girl ignorant, so."

"I knows. I knows," the old man said. "You tol'ded me, and I knows. So put it on me, but don't put it on she mama. All Ula done-done were to walk-down the row what done been already plow. It ain't she fault."

"I ain't placing no fault nowheres on nobodys, old man," the old woman said, "'xcept on Budi Manigault, and I hope him listening." She gave a defiant look around for her late brother-in-law's benefit, if he was. "All I'm placing on you is, what you be fixing to do 'bout it right now? That girl done gone'd to working, ain't got idea the first what she working with or working on."

The old man sighed again, stretched out one leg from under the table, and rubbed at the old ache-spot around his knee.

"You can't tell her nothing, not yet," he said.

"Then when?" the old woman asked. "You reckon she ain't'a figure thing out she own self by now? And what you figure she gon' think after she face all y'all terrible old mens over to Zambu' tomorrow?"

The old man shrugged. "She'll figure what she figure," he said. He leaned forward towards the old woman, his eyes fixed upon her and his voice now taking on a more authoritative tone. "I can't say nothing more, and you can't, neither. You does hear me? You'se bound with the same cord what done bound me, and that done seal my lips and your'n." The old man closed his mouth and drew a line over it with his fingertip for emphasis.

The old woman snorted. "Old man, I's bound with what you

bound you'self to, only so long as you walking the earth on man's feet. Once you pass over, I ain't bound by nothing but what I done tie-up my ownself, and I ain't said nothing to nobodys for keep my mouth shut to that girl."

"Fair enough," the old man answered, leaning back in his chair. "I won't come back tormenting you over that."

The old woman put her palm up to him. "Now," she said, "keep you' voice down. She fixing to need all'a sleep she can get, for-true, for what her got coming at her tomorrow."

THEY KEPT IT DIM in the spirit room in the back of the Eldest's house because that was how he always wanted it in these latter times. Brightness burned at the rims of his eyes, which were always rheumy and running now, and besides that, he had lost almost all of his ability to see things on this side of the veil, and so lighting was unimportant to him. One small candle—not even a lamp—was set on the table at the far end of the back room; the only other light was from the low fire in the stone chimney, which was always kept going, summer and winter, because the Eldest ever had a chill about him. The girl sat on an old woven chair with her back to the flames and facing the Elder men, who themselves sat in a semi-circle on the floor in front of her, expressionless, like the carved wooden Dogo'men outside in the Eldest's garden. The Eldest himself lay in a curled position in his bed at the end of the elder line, close to the chimney, eyes half-closed and fluttering, now and then, as if in a dreaming, but in fact the Eldest was very alert, and aware of everything going on around him.

For her part, the girl knew all of the Elder men well, had seen them and been around them all her life, singly or in small groups or even all together, at work or at games or eatings or celebrations or at Sambuhouse gatherings. Today was different, however. She had never been the center of attention of the Elders of Yelesaw before, and the seriousness of what she had done—or, more exactly, had not done—hung all the heavier on her. Papa'Tee was there, but it was a different Papa'Tee even than had been at the breakfast table that morning, a quieter Papa'Tee, grave and somber as the rest, no trace of his usual smile or normal bemused look of understanding sympathy which always came to her mind whenever she thought of him. And though he had told her on the wagon ride over not to worry, just to tell her story and to tell the truth, repeating what she had said at the table the evening before, that was all that mattered, she found the words no comfort at all, now that she was inside Baba'Zambu's house and facing this imposing row of old men.

She had thought that they would ask her many questions, and that was what she had dreaded the most, but just like Papa'Tee and Ná'Risa the night before, they had not. They had mostly let her talk, without interruption. After a while she lost all sense of their presence and only followed the trail of the story of that day, the sighting of the figure at the Crossroads, the voices in the Old Lane, the vision at the ruins of the Bighouse, her conversation with her grandfather at the Old Quarters, and, finally, what she had seen and felt when she fell into the Gaya Pond. She talked low and quiet and steady and without hesitation, except when she came to the voices at the pond, which she had purposely avoided thinking about from that day to this. At that point in her story her knees began to tremble with the memory of it, just as they had trembled the night before at Papa'Tee's and Ná'Risa's. The source of those voices had never gone away, but was hovering somewhere near and could come again. Had come again. Came again every time she could fight off sleep no more. As she talked, without realizing it, she rubbed at the grip marks on her lower legs.

Her head kept up a low ache to it and she felt the pressure at her temples, her stomach unsettled, and at points it seemed to her during her story that she might even reel over and pass out, but every time that happened, she balled her fists up and dug her fingernails into her palms, hard, and that helped to focus her thoughts and keep her from spinning out and away.

They only questioned her about one part, and that was Grandpa Budi's message.

*Say what him tell you, again, girl. Say it 'xact.*

*The time done come for left-here. ... It ain't the buckra what bringing the water. Folks thinking it be, but it ain't.*

And then—

*It got for cleanse. It got for wash it all 'way. It done rot, and it stinking.*

And, finally—

*Y'all got for left Yelesaw and go over on t'other side. You go back and tell them. Zambu and the rest.*

The last, the command that she fetch the message, burned at her in shame and she dropped her head as they made her say it again, humiliated because she had not come to them with the message at once, as she had been told to do. But if they took note of that fact, they did not mention it.

*You certain that what him say? It ain't the buckra what bringing the water. You certain-sure of that, girl?*

She raised her head and looked around at the half-circle of eyes staring back at her, intent, in the dim light.

*I's certain-sure of that, yessir. I's certain-sure of all of it. That what my grandpa tell'ed me.*

As she waited for their next question, she was thinking that always before the Yelesaw Elders must have seen her only as the skinny, ash-leg half-oba girl running around on the Manigault yard, if they noticed her at all, no different than one of a hundred Yay'saw children on the Neck, and so easily dismissed as interchangeable and, therefore, inconsequential. And why would they not? But now, as the collection of old men fixed their eyes upon her, she felt them actually looking at her, looking into her, searching her, studying her, the collected gaze merging as one as they sought to figure who this child really was who had been chosen to fetch to them so important a message. She felt as if she were being pulled into a fold and that a circle of protection— invisible but real—was being quietly and deliberately drawn around her, at least for the moment. She hoped she would be able to carry it away with her, out of Baba'Zambu's back room. But at the same time she found that she could not give them an answer to their questions of who she really was because she realized— perhaps for the first time in her life—that she really did not know.

ESHY WAS WAITING FOR HER in the front room of Baba'Zambu's house, along with Ná'Risa and a group of the older women who were working on different parts of a great quilt that was spread out over the table.

"You alright?" Eshy asked her as she came out through the door from the back.

Yally said nothing, but only leaned heavy on her sister's arm as Eshy stood up, and the two of them walked out onto the porch, her legs suddenly wobbly and most unable to support her. Once outside she felt her head grow hot and twirl itself in a slow circle, and all her control over herself was lost, and she broke free of Eshy and stumbled across to the porch railing, just making it in time to throw up out into the bushes. She leaned over the rail for the longest, holding onto the board to keep from collapsing, heaving until her insides felt empty and scraped raw and clear of all contents.

When she was finished, finally, she straightened up and wiped at her mouth with her fingers and gave Eshy a wan smile.

"You figure you can walk 'cross to my house?" Eshy asked her.

Yally closed her eyes and shook her head.

"Sit down on the steps then, and I'll fetch the wagon. You sure you be alright? You want me for fetch Mamarisa?"

Yally put her palm up and shook her head, no, to the request to get their great-aunt from out of the house. With Eshy's help, she eased herself down on the top step of the porch and draped her arms around the stairpost, leaning her head against it for support. She felt, rather than saw, her sister leave. She opened her eyes a bit and noticed for the first time that there were folks sitting or standing on the porch behind her, and more people had gathered out on Baba'Zambu's yard. They were saying nothing, only staring silently at her. No-one came any nearer. Unable to connect any of this to herself, she wondered, absently, why they were all there.

She did not know how long it was, only that in a while, she heard the clop of hooves and the creaking of wagon-wheels coming up to the porch, and then Eshy was back, throwing a quilt over her shoulders and leading her to the wagon, where Nu was waiting. They both helped her up and sandwiched her between them on the driving seat. She had been feeling a chill come over her as she had sat by herself on the porch, and the collected warmth of her sister and brother-in-law and the quilt was something of a comfort to her. As Nu turned the mule and the wagon began to pull away back across the yard, some of the people in the crowd put up their hands in hails, and she heard her name called out from two or three of them. She gave back a single weak wave and then sank down in the quilts, lowering her head until it rested on her knees.

Nu reached over and squeezed her shoulder.

"How you doing, little sister?" he asked her. "You ain't let them old mens spook you none, is you?"

She squinted up at him, shading her eyes with her hand from the glare of the sun, smiled, and shook her head, no.

Yally closed her eyes again and let herself be rocked by the rhythmic bounce of the mule-wagon. "Where we going?" she asked.

"I done told you—over to we house," Eshy said. "I done fixed-up oxtails for you, iffen you want, and then you can go to bed, and ain't nobody else fixing to bother you 'til tomorrow, if then. I ain't care iffen they beats the door down."

Keeping her eyes closed, Yally shook her head, which was still resting on her knees. "Take me home, please," she said.

"What-for? I done sent word you was staying over another night with we. Them don't need you back there for nothing. Big Soo can take up you' chore'."

"No," Yally answered, without opening her eyes. "I need for see Mama."

She hoped that Eshy would require no more explanation, that her sister would know, intuitively, that her story must be told one more time so that she would never have to tell it or even think about it again, if she did not want to, but that she could not go to sleep again before she had recounted to their mother the last meeting and conversation with her grandfather. And after that? She was something like an old plow mule that had reached the end of the last row of the day, like the yoke and collar had been slipped off her shoulders, and she could feel the relief of it, and the release into weariness that could not be allowed before, and she only wanted her head turned towards her own barn, and have the smell and feel of familiar things around her. From behind her closed eyelids, she watched the sunlight play in and out of shadows of the tree branches, feeling herself pleasantly drifting, feeling no fear or any more need to hold herself awake. There was no-one and nothing waiting for her at the bottom of that pit. She had done what had been asked of her, and they needed her services no more. It was in someone else's hands now.

Nu gave his sister-in-law a long look as her body settled and stilled in the quilt next to him, her face softening and relaxing, her chest beginning to rise and fall in a deeper rhythm, and then, seeing his wife give him a nod, he clucked his tongue at the mule and turned it to the path that led back to the River Road and to Goat Hill.

THE ELDERS HAD DISPERSED from Baba'Zambu's house, all but Buka Brown, who was Baba'Zambu's favorite, and who he had asked to stay, so he could see what was in the mojo-bones. Baba'Zambu already knew what was in the bones but still, he wanted to see Buka toss them and interpret them for himself, to make sure.

The great-granddaughter—one of the ones who stayed at the house and looked after him—sat by herself at the table across the back room, quietly humming a soothing song as she fixed some ingredients for her medicine pot.

The house was still, except for the great-granddaughter's

humming, and the sizzle and popping coming now and then from
the fireplace, and the hushed rattle of Buka Brown's bones as they
walked the floor and hit, gently, against the fireplace stones.
Something about the reading was disturbing Buka, and he made
several tosses, bending over the bones each time after they came to
a settle, studying their configuration by the dim firelight, and then
frowning, picking them up, and throwing them again. Not far
away, Baba'Zambu lay in his cot almost completely wrapped up in
two quilts, like a wrinkled worm inside its chrysalis, only the dull,
yellowbrown glint of his sunken eyes showing out from inside the
quilt-folds as he watched the throwing and re-throwing of the
bones without comment. He could not see the configurations that
were coming out, could not see much of anything at all, of course,
but he was patient, and for a while he did not comment or ask or
interfere, but waited until Buka had fully completed his reading.
But when the tossing went on overly long, as if Buka might be
trying to change the outcome rather than unable to get the right
meaning, he finally coughed, raised up a little in his cot, asked,
"What them say, Cu'n Book?"

Buka Brown tossed the polished bones again, watched them
settle, and hovered over them as he read. He leaned back into his
squat and gave a shake of his head.

"Them ain't acting right," he said.

"How so?"

"Them telling what done been, but them ain't say what got for
be," Buka Brown answered.

Baba'Zambu rubbed at the inflame around the edges of his
eyes with the side of his index finger and then moved back deeper
into the cocoon of his quilts.

"It ain't matter," he said. "I done seen it myself, what must be
done."

Buka Brown's head came up from the bones, and he gave the
Eldest a searching look.

"In that child?"

Baba'Zambu coughed and nodded.

Buka Brown widened his nostrils and blew a quick, dismissive
blast of air out through them, folding his arms across his chest.

"I goes by what these tells me, nothing else," he said, gesturing
towards the bones spread out in front of him. "Not on what no
fresh split-tail done hee'rd, or think her done hee'rd. Could be all
her'a hearing be some boy out under she window, howling for her
for meet him out under the tree'."

Baba'Zambu's head was no longer visible from down in the quilts, but his voice came out, low and hollow.

"Iffen we can't trust what the split-tail say for do, tell-me what the bones say, Cu'n Buka, and we'a do it."

Chastened, Buka Brown settled back on his haunches and said nothing in reply.

Baba'Zambu's head emerged, slowly, from the quilts. He coughed to clear the phlegm from his throat.

"I does believe that girl," he said.

"Why you is?" It was not a challenge. Buka Brown had given as much of a challenge as he was going to on the issue. He'd passed on all the message out of the bones that he could, and had let the Eldest know where he stood. Now it was time to listen, and follow, if following was what the Eldest required, and not more deliberation.

"I believes her because I done seen her coming before she even done get here. I know who she be."

"Who she be?"

Baba'Zambu started to answer but now the coughing came, and he could not stop it. It was a rough, raking coughing that went on and on, sending sharp pains from inside his chest and up his throat as if someone were drawing knifepoints along the raw flesh. He held his palm open and coughed into it. The great-granddaughter had stood up at once and hurried over, asking, "You want you some water, Grandpa?" She did not wait for an answer, but told Buka Brown, "They's some water in that bucket, Tat'Buka. Fetch it for him, will you?" while she went to the shelf for a medicine jar. His coughing fit stopped for a moment, and while their attention was elsewhere, he opened his palm and held it up close to his face and looked to see what he had coughed up. Even his dimming eyes could make out that the thick, heavy liquid was a dull black color against the pale brown of his palm. He knew exactly what that meant. He'd seen his own father cough up the same, the night he had died. He closed his palm over the mess and drew his hand down into his quilt before the others could see.

The great-granddaughter returned to his bedside, and Buka Brown, with the water, and they gave him a spoonful of tart medicine—speedwell, he could tell from the taste—and then a ladle of water.

The great-granddaughter hovered over him.

"You must stop with the talking, now, and rest you'self, Grandpa," she said, her voice firm with the commanding tone of the healer in charge.

"I can go," Buka Brown said. "Us can talk in the morning."

Baba'Zambu summoned his strength and rose up on one elbow, grabbing Buka Brown's forearm with his free hand, not the one with the cough residue still in it.

"No," he said, his voice hoarse now, but filled with an urgency they had not heard before. "I must tell you who that girl is." Buka Brown sat down on the edge of the cot, putting his own free hand over Baba'Zambu's, patting it and then holding it firm. The great-granddaughter stayed standing at the cotside, trying no more to make a pretense that she was not listening.

Strengthened a little by the medicine or his own will, or a combination of the two, Baba'Zambu went on, talking longer than he had for many days. "That same day them fish Leem Manigault' boy out the river," he said, "I been laying right here, right in this bed, and the door to the front, it open up and a man walk in. That were before the news done got on this end 'bout the finding. The man, him been so tall, him had for stoop he head down for clear the doorway, and when him did so, I seen him had leg what ain't bend forwards, like no natural man, but they done bend-back backward, like a bird, and I knowed him been a taya-man what done come for tell that someone done dead, and I ask'ded him, who it been. And him tell me it were Leem Manigault' boy what done been losted and been foun'ded in the water, and the boy had word for me, which him would be sending by messenger. And I been waiting and waiting on that messenger every day since that taya-man come up in this house, and this morning, it been her what come in the door, and I knowed who she were even before her come in."

Baba'Zambu's throat began to fill again, and he half-rose in his cot and tried to cough, but either because the speedwell was doing its job or because there was nothing left in his lungs to cough up, the fit passed quickly. He lay with his head near the side of the cot for a while, feeling a great, cold weariness walk over him, a thin trail of spittle marking a line out of his open mouth and down into a puddle on the floor below. The great-granddaughter reached over with her kerchief and wiped his mouth dry.

Buka Brown sat quietly on the cot beside him, watching him.

"What must we do, then, Baba?" he finally asked.

Zambu Dingle summoned his strength again, but there was little strength left in him to summon. It was all beginning to drain out along with the inside of his lungs. "That message what Leem

Manigault' boy done fetch were the message what were give him for carry—it ain't come from him, and like him say, it ain't come from no buckra." The words were spoken so low that Buka Brown had to lean down close to the Eldest's face to make out what he was saying. "In the morning, iffen I ain't be here, you must gather the others and tell them. I done study-up on it. It ain't no way'round. Us must left here."

The gravity, and finality, of what Baba'Zambu was saying was setting in on Buka Brown. He searched for an argument strong enough to turn the Eldest's will.

"What it mean, Baba, 'it got for cleanse?' Us got for all up and left, for a cleansing? Ain't we pap' blood and we ma'm' blood—ain't all the saltwater in the ocean us carry-cross with we—ain't all the bucket'a the sweat us done dropped down in this-here ground all'round for water all them crop'a rice—ain't all'a that enough for wash it clean?"

"Blood can't wash-way blood," Baba'Zambu said in reply, a deep sadness about his eyes. "The land, it done done'd enough for we. It done'd carry we alla'way down to the next passage, and it tired from the hauling, and sick'ed at what it done see'd. It done tired, and can't give no more, and want for rest. You must let t'ing rest when they must rest, Cu'n Book. Let'em rest. They's other land for we. Fresh land. Young land, just like this land been young, one time. Let the old land pass'oba like we old peoples must pass'oba, and let the young land have it' turn. Us done cross the Big Saltwater. Us done walk'outten Bethelia. Crossing that little river out there, it ain't nothing. Us can walk'outten Yelesaw."

The long speech seemed to take all of what was left of Baba'Zambu's strength, and it looked to Buka Brown and the great-granddaughter that the elder man was beginning to slip away from them.

His voice faltering, Buka Brown tried one last time.

"You done told we iffen we left this place, the old spirits would be lost, and must wander and wander, with no-one for show them where they peoples done take up they new home," he said. "That-what you done say out at the Tree, Baba."

"I ain't done said, everybody's, they must go," Zambu Dingle said. He let out a long, rattling breath, and his voice was now only a thin, reedy piping that it took great effort for him to force up his throat and out. He closed his eyes for a bit and then opened them again, and for a moment they seemed a little brighter in the firelight, or else lit from an inner glow. "Somebody's fixing to stay on this side of the water what know where y'all be going, and that one, him will be a guide, and ain't a one will be lost." He patted Buka Brown's forearm, and gave a him a small smile. "Nary one."

He started to cough again, and when they moved closer to him, he put up his hand and waved them away.

"Now, go, now. Go!" He said. "Let a old man rest. I'm something weary."

He settled into his quilts, his head disappearing from their view. Buka Brown and the great-granddaughter did not move away from him right away, not until they could see, from the slow rise and fall of the quilts, that breath was still working through his body. There was nothing else to be done. They exchanged a long look of understanding between themselves. In the soft brown eyes of the great-granddaughter, a pool of tears began to form, and she did not try to hide them.

HE SLEPT, but only for a short time. As was his habit, he woke after a while to a darkened and quiet house. The great-granddaughter had banked the fire so that it would keep for the rest of the night. She was on the other side of the backroom, retired to her bed. He did not know how much she herself slept, only that if he groaned in the night, or ringed and twisted inside his quilt too much, she was up and at his bedside, as if all she did in her bed was lay and listen for his sounds. He found a position on the cot that gave him the least pain, pulled the quilt back up higher, tucking it under his chin, and lay with his face to the fire and thought. The pains had begun to bother him as they never had before. It pained him now no matter what he did, no matter what side he lay on, or on his back, however he moved or if he did not move at all. He was looking forward to the end of his pain. But he had thinking to do tonight, so he put away his pain, and stared into the red glow of the fire and concentrated.

After the girl had told her story to the gathering of Elders, and they had withdrawn a little to talk among themselves, he had called her over to sit in front of him with the intention of fixing her with his eyes. He had wanted her to understand the gravity of the message she had carried, and the responsibility she must take up, to know what it was to be a messenger. And so he had told her to come close to him, to put her face down near his. But instead of fixing her, he was taken by surprise—complete surprise—when it was she who had fixed *him*, striking him with what he saw in *her* eyes. The warm, inviting eyes looking back at him were too familiar to be those of a young girl who he could not remember ever having been in his presence. Then where had he seen those eyes before? He had looked deeper—straining his own olding eyes to aid him at least one more time in this world—and then almost pulled back, with a shock, when he of-a-sudden recognized who it was in front of him. It was Sis'Yela there, standing in the yard in front of her cabin, stirring her bubbling black clotheswash pot with a clean-peeled oak-stick and suddenly, in a rush, he had been in the Old Home again, among the spiced smells and the busy hum of voices, among the stories and conversations and the children playing in the sand-road, among the line of the women, washing their clothes up and down the row, lifting and bending and scrubbing again all in unison, though each at their own individual houses, singing their a'luba' songs across the quarters, Sis'Yela, as ever, taking the lead. "Where you been all this time, Sis'Yela?" he had asked those eyes, wordlessly, into the eyes of the young girl in front of him. "I been missing you, so." Sis'Yela did not answer, but only put her fists on her hips and her head back and gave out that big, quick laugh so that her braids shook from underneath her headscarf, her great breasts shaking, too, and, oh, that had sounded so familiar, and so much like back Home, and he had missed the old people so, and the companions of his youth, all of them long gone, now, passed through the veil.

The young girl, Leem Manigault' great-grand, she was Sis'Yela, come back. He saw her, and he knew it, and more than anything else, that was why he had believed her.

WHEN HE SLIPPED BACK INTO SLEEP, the Eldest dreamed that he was hearing music in the clearing behind the Old Quarters. They had gone back there to dance, as they did, so many times, on sweat-warm nights. He had not danced in many years, but that did not matter tonight, because he had cast off his old body, and he was in a young man's clothes again. The sound of the singing and the shouting, and the stick-beat on the jars and the playing of the wood-flutes, all called him. He pulled the quilts from around himself, and turned to get out of his cot so that he might join them, and dance the old dances again, and leap into the air, and feel young man's breath drawn deep into his lungs.

That is where the great-granddaughter found him when she got up from her own bed in the middle of the night, as she always did, to stir the fire and check on the Eldest. He was laying in the bed crossways, his bare feet on the floor as if he were about to get up. She leaned over quickly and held the back of her hand to his nose for a breath, then felt his neck for a pulse. There was neither, only a great and awful stillness about him. Through the beginning of her tears, she saw that his face was clear and without pain for the first time she had ever seen it, a calmness and contended joy in it that she would never forget, down to the end of her days. Whatever the Eldest had seen in his last moments, or was seeing now with unblinking eyes into a vastness opening beyond her reach, she was certain that he was happy with it.

"Good-bye, Grandpa," she said. "I be done seeing you again, forever." And giving him a kiss on his withered cheek, she pulled the quilt up closer around his neck, out of habit, and then gently closed his eyes with the tips of her fingers before she went out into the morning to carry the news.

Bán
(It Is Done)

# Author's Note

*Sugaree Rising* is a work of fiction that combines two historical events that never actually came together in real life.

The first was the Santee Cooper Project, the building of the Pinopolis Dam in Berkeley County, South Carolina, in the late 1930's that created the two connected lakes—Moultrie and Marion—that split the Carolina Lowcountry landscape up the middle. Eventually Santee Cooper brought electrical power to close to two million South Carolinians, but in its birth agonies, it also destroyed scores of communities located in the path of the new lakes, and dislocated close to one thousand families, almost all of them African-American.

The second historical event around which *Sugaree* revolves was the gradual breaking down—from the 1930's to the present day—of the geographic and cultural isolation that had originally created one of the most unique peoples in the United States: the Gullah of the Southeastern sea islands.

I first learned about the Santee Cooper relocation in the 1970's from an older African-American gentleman then living in the rural Berkeley County community of Cross. In answer to a question of where he was originally from, he gestured out across the Lake Moultrie waters, which cover the center of the county. I thought that he meant one of the communities on the other side of the lake but he shook his head, no, to each one I named, and finally gave the name of a community I had never heard of before. It was only after several moments of questioning that I discovered that the home in which he was born actually now lay under the waters of the lake, in an area—now lost to the world—known as St. John's Parish.

From that older gentleman and several other people who lived in the communities surrounding Lake Moultrie, I gradually learned the story of how hundreds of families were forced to move homes, farms, livestock, churches, and even graveyards in the late

Depression years to make way for the coming lake.

They also told me stories of resistance to the dam-building and forced relocation in a county—Berkeley—that was still heavily-Black deep into the 1960's. Like the communities covered by the lakewaters after the Pinopolis Dam was built, these are stories that are now virtually lost to history. While several works of fiction were written and movies produced about resistance in Alabama and Tennessee to the Tennessee Valley Authority (TVA), the far more famous rural electrification project on the Tennessee River that preceded Santee Cooper, I have never been able to find similar accounts concerning the South Carolina project.

An excellent 2008 book by Douglas W. Bostick (*Sunken Plantations; The Santee Cooper Project*, The History Press) concentrates almost exclusively on the historic plantations flooded out by the lake rather than on the small-farm landowners and farmworkers who lost their homes. And while the 1984 fifty-year anniversary official *History Of Santee Cooper 1934-1984* by Walter B. Edgar (R.L. Bryan Company, publishers) gives some tantalizing information on the human dislocation that resulted from the building of the dam and lakes, the descriptions are all too brief, and most of the book concerns the building of the dam and the resulting changes to landscape and electrical power. If there are any other books, fiction or nonfiction, which speak to the human cost of the flooding of the Moultrie and Marion basins, I have not yet found them.

The record of resistance to the Santee Cooper Project as taken down during the time when the project was being built appears to be virtually non-existent as well. In April of 1939, the Charleston News & Courier newspaper printed a quarter-page essay—possibly a paid advertisement—written by an organization called the Land Owners' Association of the Santee Cooper Basin, giving reasons why landowners in the area were refusing to sell their property to the Santee Cooper Authority. I have found no other information about the Land Owners' Association or the manner in which their challenge was resolved, and there is no indication in the published essay of the race of the association members.

But it is indisputable that it was African-Americans who were most affected by the mass dislocation of the Santee Cooper Project. Close to two-thirds of Berkeley County's population in 1940 was African-American, and Edgar's *History Of Santee Cooper* notes that "almost all" of the 901 families relocated from the Santee Cooper basin were black.

Fortunately, the historical record of the Santee Cooper relocation is not entirely bare. Portions of it were documented by photographers working with the Farm Security Administration of the United States Department of Agriculture and have been preserved by the American Memory project of the Library of Congress. The faces of the Santee Cooper evacuees—most of them certainly now passed away—call out in the black-and-white photographs from across the long, intervening years, asking for their stories to be finally told. The face of the young woman represented on the cover of *Sugaree Rising* is one of those Santee Cooper evacuees. It is my hope that I have been able to call her spirit, and the spirit of all her kin and companions and neighbors, into my novel, and perhaps to put them, finally, at rest.

From these stories and photographs and small and scattered bits of information, the determination slowly grew in me over four decades to tell the Santee Cooper resistance and evacuation stories. But that was not the only South Carolina story that beckoned to me.

Like almost every other African-American writer who has lived in or visited that state, I have also long wanted to write a novel based among the Gullah people of the South Carolina sea islands. In particular, I wanted to write about the slow loss of the distinct African culture that has been retained among the Gullah, a loss that has come about because of the gradual ending of their isolation from the dominant white culture and the more-assimilated African-American culture.

The Gullah also seemed a perfect vehicle to write about another area of my interest: the conflict between Christianity and the elder African religions that African-Americans brought with us to America during the slave trade. That conflict—which took place in fierce cultural battles during the first years of slavery—is not much talked-about in literature about African-Americans. Instead, the concentration is almost always on the later conflict between Christianity and blues culture. Although the Gullah today primarily identify themselves as a Christian people, the elder African spirit-elements in practices identified by such names as "hoodoo" and "root" are still very much present in their culture, and so I had another reason for creating a book about the Gullah.

But while I lived for many years in the South Carolina Lowcountry and counted many Gullah Folk among my friends, I never lived on the sea islands or in a Gullah community. I did not and do not, therefore, feel myself competent to write a Gullah-based novel.

Still, the longing to write something that satisfied my interest in writing about Gullah culture and the Gullah situation remained.

Eventually, during the long period of the writing of *Sugaree Rising*, a solution emerged. If the Gullah culture was created based upon isolation and a high Black-to-white population ratio on the sea island slavery-time plantations, why couldn't those same conditions have been duplicated in selected areas in other parts of South Carolina? And if that were so, then such a people could have existed in an area, unlike the sea islands, where a dam-building project could have threatened to relocate them. And so the Yay'saw of Yelesaw Neck were born, a people who retained their African culture in some ways that are very similar to the Gullah, and in some ways that are distinctly different and their own.

For a long time while this book was being written, I did not associate the term Gullah with the Yay'saw in any way, even to identify the Yay'saw as being inspired by the Gullah. That changed in recent years, however, after I learned about the organization known as the Gullah-Geechee Nation. Based on the sea islands and dedicated to the preservation and advancement of the Gullah culture, this group of Gullah Folk has expanded their reach to include any African-American communities in the country that have retained and passed down African cultural ways and traditions from the slavery-time days. The Yay'saw of *Sugaree Rising* certainly qualify under that umbrella and so, while I do not identify them as Gullah, I feel free now to describe the people of my creation as Gullah-like, or of Gullah kin, who came down through the same woods from the same origins as the Gullah did, but by following a similar but somewhat different path.

*Sugaree Rising*, therefore, is not a Gullah book, and anyone looking for information on the Gullah of the southeastern sea islands should search out another source.

As the Yay'saw are a created people, so Cantrell is a created county, which does not conform in geography or location to any actual existing South Carolina county. If Cantrell did exist, it would lie in the South Carolina Lowcountry with its southeastern portion somewhere near or on the coast in between the present Charleston and Georgetown county line, with its northwestern portion running up and through Williamsburg County.

Finally, to acknowledgments.

The creation of *Sugaree Rising* owes a deep debt to those

Berkeley County Black Folk who first told me the stories of the Santee Cooper relocation out of St. John's Parish. Their names are now lost to me, unfortunately, but not the world they opened me up to.

I also give thanks to the many elder Black women of Berkeley County—T.C. Brown, Beauty Banks, and Cessie Jaeger especially, but there were many more—who kept a young stranger going with many breakfasts and cups of hot coffee and salted his imagination with their rich stories and beautiful accents and colorful phrases, so many of which have ended up in this book. Each time as I was leaving her house, Miss Cessie would walk me to the door and send me off with one word of advice: "Do the best that you can." I hope that with *Sugaree Rising* that I have, and that she would be satisfied with it.

Much thanks, too, go to my good friend Barbara Ginsberg, who served for many years as sounding-board and unofficial editor during the writing of *Sugaree*. She was and is the midwife to this baby.

A special acknowledgement goes to Dr. Lorenzo D. Turner, the African-American linguist who first traced and documented the connection between language spoken on the African continent and the language of the sea island Gullah in America. All of the proper names of the Yay'saw in *Sugaree Rising,* as well as most of the African-based terms, were taken from Dr. Turner's pioneering book "Africanisms In The Gullah Dialect," originally published by the University of Michigan Press and later republished by the University of South Carolina Press.

And thanks to the folks of the Freedom Voices collective, who chose my novel for publication and worked in many ways to make it a better book.

Finally, in deepest respect for those who came before me:

To the Ibo People, who did not want to stay;

To the Black Folk of St. John's, who did not want to go;

And to my parents, Ernest and Maybelle Allen, who kept a house of books, and so began my love of the written word.

J. Douglas Allen-Taylor
Oakland, California
Summer, 2012

CPSIA information can be obtained at www.ICGtesting.com
Printed in the USA
LVOW081331141212

311682LV00004B/115/P